After The Fires Went Out:
Coyote

Book One

Regan Wolfrom

DEDICATION

To the various women in my life, starting with my wife, and moving backward and forward from there.

ACKNOWLEDGEMENTS

This book would have gone nowhere without the support of quite a few people, including a good portion of my family, some very helpful friends, and, of course, many hours of reading and watching stories where things go so nicely and completely to shit. Thank you everyone for working so hard to keep my own life from going to shit, at least long enough for me to pass this thing out of my system.

PROLOGUE

THERE WAS a moment right after The Fires went out when I thought Fiona and I were the only people left for a thousand miles around. It looked as though the whole world had burned, the air surrounding us so hot that it felt like even the water of Lillabelle Lake was close to boiling. I had trouble imagining that anyone else could have survived.

She was lying beside me on the beach, where the rocky sand was still hot like a stovetop from the fire. Her eyes were open but she didn't really seem to see me; I think she was still in shock.

I didn't know her name then. I barely remembered Fiona and her parents from the sea of faces at the last town meeting, back when the dirt blocked out the sky and it felt like we might never see the sun again, back when I was the big man around here for some reason. I didn't know how sweet and smart and funny she is; she was just some pretty fourteen-year-old girl who reminded me of the daughter I'd lost, and who was now just as alone as I was.

That was the moment when I promised the universe and Cassy that I'd take care of Fiona, no matter what. I thought I might be the only person left in the world to take care of her.

But it didn't take long for us to realize that we weren't the only ones left out here; we weren't even the only people who climbed out of Lillabelle Lake that day.

That didn't make my promise any less important.

1

TODAY IS TUESDAY, DECEMBER 4TH.

I THINK it's time for me to keep some kind of record of our life up here at McCartney Lake. I'm sure we're not the only place that got slammed with shards from the comet, that when the kicked-up debris came back down in other places it set the air on fire just as much, that the skies went dark all over the planet.

But those places aren't here, and I'm sure most of the world has forgotten we exist.

I used to write a journal when I was in my twenties and even into my thirties. I wrote an entry almost every day up until my daughter Cassy was born, long-winded and self-absorbed stories scrawled in little notebooks and probably uninteresting and illegible to anyone else. I guess it always helped me wind up the day, like some kind of buffer between real life and falling asleep.

I wonder if any of those notebooks survived when they tore my house down.

This time the journal will be on my tablet, lifestreamed and written: the life and times of Robert Jeanbaptiste, village idiot. I guess this one is even less likely to last, unless I print it out or share it or something, but I'm not sure I'd want people reading everything I feel like putting in. What's the point of a journal if you're not putting it all in, right?

I wonder if Ant had ever expected us to read what he'd written.

To be honest, I was pretty surprised to find out that he kept a journal, and a handwritten one at that. Maybe I can imagine him writing out his sexual fantasies in nauseating detail, but a diary... that just didn't fit.

That isn't the Ant I knew.

He wrote it in French for the most part, with patches of English here and there for slang and swear-words, and for lines that maybe didn't work so well in a gentler language. His English always sounded

5

so natural that I would forget that he was born and bred speaking French, just like Sara and almost half the district. Living in Toronto makes a man forget what's going on north of the 407.

And Ant's French isn't anything like the French my father used to use when he called back home to Port-au-Prince, or even the French they taught us in school. Sometimes I can read a whole sentence of his and not understand a word of it.

But let's face it: I barely understood Ant.

He was kind and funny and completely shameless, and there was something about his baby-faced grin that let him get away with pretty much anything. And he'd fiddle around with the world's most dangerous shit, like blow torches and blasting caps, but I'd always had a feeling he was too smart to screw up.

It's hard to believe he was shot to death yesterday.

I remember once Sara caught him in her bedroom; he'd snuck in while she and Lisa were both downstairs and she came up to find him lying on her bed, with her photo album open right beside him. And Ant being Ant, he was completely naked with his hand on his dick, and when he realized she'd found him, he made absolutely no attempt to cover anything up.

I don't know what that little perv was hoping for, that Sara would see him fapping to old pictures of her and her sisters and she'd decide she wanted to join in on the fun, or maybe that she'd simply take a good long look at his naked body and let the other girls know that not every part of Little Ant Lagace was smaller than average.

Whatever his plan, Sara just started to laugh, so loudly that all of us came running upstairs and saw a little too much of Ant that day.

It was only funny because Ant was the one who'd done it. There's no way it would have been funny to see me lying there, my middle-aged cock in hand, rubbing one off using Sara and her dead sisters as inspiration.

I don't really give off a funny vibe.

Today was pretty warm for December.

It felt like being back home, like those days when Cassy and I would take the streetcar over to Eaton Centre for the painful tradition of finding Christmas presents for her mother. The crowds would crush against us so hard that I'd usually grab onto the sleeve of her sweater as well as her hand, just for the extra grip.

On days like today I can feel that same little nub of anxiety balling up in my stomach, even though streetcars and shopping and my daughter seem so far away now.

Seven hundred klicks and a whole world away.

We've decided to take things easy; we're all still pretty messed up about losing Ant, and it just feels like we need a break.

Sara came up with the idea of a hayride and drafted me into helping her; she figured we ought to do something fun, and that we ought to do it *together*.

Together means the whole cottage when Sara says it. To her we're a family, even if our family is made up of eight random people who are only here because they don't have anywhere else to go.

Actually… there's only seven of us now.

I managed to convince myself that it was okay for all of us to go; we'd lock up the cottage and we'd be back soon enough. After what happened on Sunday, I'd prefer to keep everyone together today; I doubt anyone would show up at just the right moment in time to rob us blind. I was also looking forward to the idea of making some good memories with that cart, something better than the one of carrying Ant's body north to the stand of sugar maples along the creek.

We'd gotten the two horses and their cart by way of a good-hearted family, a couple klicks east of Cochrane. They listened to me at first, and they hadn't left on the advice of that sack-of-shit Fisher Livingston. And they waited it out for a couple months, after The Fires, after close to half of the summer without a sun, but eventually they decided to pack it in. And since they'd known that Graham and Fiona and I would pretty much be the last ones to give up, and I guess because they took pity on a couple of outsiders like Graham and me, so they gave us a quick lesson on hitching and driving before they hopped into their truck and hit the highway, never to be heard from again.

The horses make a good team, a mare and a gelding, both saddlebreds. The cart is built completely of wood, even the wheels, with railings and a bench; it's a little clunky at times, but the horses are used to it and now we are, too.

We threw some bales onto the cart and then I hitched up the

horses, the mare first as always. She backs into place on her own, always on the right, and all that's left for me to do is connect the harness traces and the centre shaft. The gelding goes second, and he's just as quick. I can do it all now in less than ten minutes; Graham can do it in under five.

I stood and watched Sara as she spread a little loose hay around the box. She was dressed light for the weather, but that's how women are up here.

There's something different about beauty in Cochrane District, in the landscape and in women like Sara... they're more *striking*. You notice the flow of the lines, soft and hard, angled and rounded, gentle mixed with tough. For Sara, it's pale blue eyes and coffee-coloured curls, and her sexy clenched-lip smile that makes me forget pretty much everything else.

She noticed me watching her.

I could see her blush a little.

"Oh, and make sure you let Graham drive," she said, as if we were right in the middle of the discussion. It might have been something we talked about twenty minutes ago; Sara just picks up where she left off, and I'm left without any clue of what she's saying.

"You have a problem with how I drive?" I asked, not really sure if I should act playful or offended.

"I want you on the cart so I can throw you off. Isn't that the whole point of a hayride?" There was a cheery sound to her voice that I'd longed for over the past few days.

"There's no way you'll be able to lift me over the railing. You have weak little girl arms."

"They're not that weak. Besides, I'll have plenty of help. I'm not the only person around here who fantasizes about seeing you face-down in the dirt."

"I think most people want to see me face-down in the Abitibi River," I said.

She chuckled. "Yeah... that or a toilet bowl. Maybe when we get back I'll see if my little girl arms can hold your head under the yellow water long enough to make all of our dreams come true."

I laughed at that.

The hay in place and the horses hitched, I started to load up the waggon with everything we'd need for the trip. I threw in a couple thermoses of water, my binoculars and headlamp, and of course my constant companion, the defibrillator, charged from our battery bank and ready to go. I'd recommend it for any geezer over fifty, but obviously for me it's pretty much required; the only two reasons I'm still here at all are my trusty defib and the six months of heart pills I still have left.

There's nothing like heart disease to remind you every goddamn day that you're not invincible anymore. And there's nothing like slowly running out of pills to make sure you never forget what's coming.

I grabbed the shotgun too, checking to make sure it was loaded, but that the chamber was still empty. I know this twelve gauge Mossberg pretty well, but I'm not always the last one to have carried it and I really don't like the idea of an accidental discharge taking a chunk out of someone's ass.

I have my service pistol too; at least it's mine now, a SIG Sauer issued by the Ontario Provincial Police and definitely not issued to me. I have it holstered as always, along with my handheld transmitter, in the belt that I only take off for sleeping, showering and screwing.

I may also want to take it off when I'm being unceremoniously thrown from a hayride... I'm not sure on the procedure for something like that.

I placed the shotgun in the cart, up by the horses where the spotter sits. Where they "ride shotgun", I guess you'd say.

"You're not on lookout, either," Sara said.

I sighed and nodded. She knew all my tricks by now.

Sara gave a loud shout and people started to wander outside. Graham and Lisa came out first, and together, which was usually a sign that they'd agreed to another ceasefire. Lisa was dressed lightly, like Sara, with a knit hat hiding most of her short and nearly spiky dark hair, and wearing what I'd term a spring jacket. But Graham had his parka on, and while it looked like Lisa had talked him out of a scarf for plus five, he had his black toque pulled down as far as it could go, right down to the upper fringe of his close-cropped hipster beard.

"You guys don't match," Sara said. "And you're going to die of heat, Graham."

"I'm not used to this," Graham said. "I don't think I'll ever get used to this."

"He's a pussy," Lisa said.

Sara scowled at the word.

Lisa laughed. "But he's my pussy."

Matt and Kayla came out next. Together they looked almost too perfect, Matt with his dark hair and broad smile, wearing a navy blue peacoat, and Kayla dressed about the same style but in a colour closer to robin's egg blue, with a pink scarf and a matching pink toque, with tufts of her pretty blond hair spilling out.

I tried not to stare at her for too long.

"Who's driving?" she asked.

"Why does it matter?" I said.

Kayla gave me a mischievous grin. "Your presence is required in the rear."

We all waited for the joke to come, probably something about Kayla's rear and just how many invites it sent out per Annum. But Ant wasn't there to make it.

It took a good ten seconds for us to recover.

"Sara's already made it clear that you all hate me," I said.

"She's sort of our spokesperson," Kayla said, still grinning.

Graham took his place on the front bench and Lisa found a spot beside him, gripping the shotgun as it rested on her leg like she was itching to use it.

Our two inside dogs hopped up front with them, little Juju nestling at Lisa's feet while Des stood up on the bench, his thick tongue hanging out as he stared at the back of the horses.

I always wonder if big old Carcassonne is jealous when we leave him behind with the chickens and goats. Somehow I doubt it. Some dogs were bred to live with the livestock. Some dogs would never be willing to give that up.

Everyone else took a place near the back of the cart, leaving a nice big hole in the middle, open just for me; it's great to feel wanted, even as a primary target.

"Just waiting for Fiona," I said, still standing beside the cart. I rapped a fist against the railing, trying to appear impatient.

The truth is, I kind of like it when Fiona takes a little longer... I'm not sure why.

"Fiona makes us wait again," Lisa said, tapping her left hand on the forestock of the shotgun. "Big surprise."

"I don't think she's coming," Matt said.

"She can't stay here alone," I said.

"Well *you're* not staying behind," Sara said to me. "We have plans for you, Baptiste. Evil plans." She hopped down from the cart. "I'll go grab her."

"She went out for a walk," Matt said.

"By herself?" I asked, already feeling my control slipping.

"Yeah... so?"

I glared at him. "What the fuck are you thinking?"

"Hey... I told her not to."

"You told her not to? What the hell good is that?"

He rolled his eyes at me and gave me one of his little smirks. "She doesn't listen to me," he said, like none of it was his problem, that it didn't really matter that Fiona was out there alone.

That was the same goddamn attitude he'd had about Ant, like he wasn't the least bit responsible for what happened, that he shouldn't feel the least bit guilty that he'd made it back alive and Ant hadn't.

I wanted to grab him by the throat, grab him and start twisting until something popped.

"Seriously," I said, trying to slow my breathing. "You need to grow up and take some goddamn responsibility."

He scowled at me. "If you don't want me around I've got plenty of places to go."

"Bullshit."

I felt Sara's hand gripping mine; she didn't say anything, but I got the message. Losing my shit wasn't going to help.

"Which way did she go?" I asked.

"South," Matt said. "Along the lake."

I called him an asshole under my breath.

I ran around the cottage to where the path that traces around the lake begins, Des running in front of me like he knew just where we were headed.

I saw one set of fresh footprints in a patch of wet muck I ran along the trail as it cut through the leafless trees, holding my right hand close to the handle of my pistol. I didn't expect that I'd need to use it but I had to be prepared; you never know what's hiding just beyond the bend out here.

"Fiona!" I called. I tried to conceal my panic, but I knew it was deep in my voice. "Fiona!"

I saw a red wool mitten floating on top of a pile of brown leaves. Fiona's. I bent down and picked it up. I couldn't see any tracks aside from hers, no signs of anything. She must've had it shoved in her pocket or something, not noticing when it fell out.

She had to be okay...

I kept running, all the way to where the creek drains into the lake, and up across the two logs that were lashed together to bridge the marshy stream. There were new tracks here, three sets of paws in the mud.

They were narrower and sharper than what Des would make: coyote tracks. And they were fresh, in places landing on top of Fiona's footprints.

Des was sniffing madly at the tracks and shuffling his feet; he could smell them, and I wondered if he could also smell Fiona through her boots.

She should have brought the dogs with her.

I called her name again, and picked up my pace even at the risk of tripping on loose rock or an upturned root. I was pretty sure she had no idea the coyotes were out there, stalking her.

I drew my SIG and without giving it a thought I asked God to help me.

I came to a low spot where I noticed the coyote tracks veering off into the woods; Fiona's footsteps kept to the trail, steady and straight. There was no sign of violence, no change in her gait. The coyotes may have heard me and Des coming. They may have run off, or else they were watching us from just behind the trees.

It didn't matter as long as they weren't after Fiona anymore.

I caught a glimpse of her just beyond a bend, her scarlet red jacket poking through a small stand of birch trees. She was walking back toward me, her red-brown hair bouncing in a tight ponytail.

I'd already warned her about wearing her hair like that.

Des met her halfway, jumping at her hips, his tail wagging.

"Fiona," I said. My voice was hoarse, not from yelling but from trying to catch my breath; I'd pushed myself a little too hard to reach her.

She flashed me a quick little smile, but I could see that she'd been crying once again.

I tried to give Fiona a smile of my own, one just as fake, but I couldn't make it stick; all I wanted to do was scream at her.

As much as I love her — and maybe I love her almost as much as Cassy — for that first few seconds, after I thought I might've lost her forever... it's the rage that came first.

I managed to hold it in.

"What's wrong?" she asked as she knelt down to scratch behind Desmond's ears.

"It's not safe. You know that you shouldn't be out here alone."

"More double standards," she said in classic sixteen-year-old, chock full of outrage and disgust. "Is it because I'm a woman, or because I'm the youngest?"

"It's because it's not safe." I wrapped my right arm around her and used my left hand to brush a few stray strands of hair aside from her face. I gave her a kiss right next to the little mole on her left cheek, at that spot where her skin first starts to blush.

"Matt goes out by himself all the time."

"Matt's an idiot. Always travel in pairs... that's the rule. Matt doesn't listen but I expect more from you."

"I know you do," she said, her eyes meeting mine.

I think she understood what I was trying to say. Fiona understands me pretty well.

"Why were you out here by yourself?" I asked. "You didn't even bring the dogs."

I didn't mention the coyotes.

"I'm always by myself. I just decided to be by myself out here for a change."

I sighed; Fiona's helped me remember just how melodramatic teenagers can be. But I know that she's not putting on a show for me; there's hurt in there, more than enough for someone that young.

I shot her a smile. "You'll always have me, Fiona. I was put on this Earth simply to annoy you."

"I know..."

"You know... but..."

She shook her head. "I just wish I fit in a little better... you know, with Kayla and Matt and everyone. Now that... now that Ant's gone, I'm kinda on the outside of everything."

"It'll take some time," I said. "But soon the day will come when you'll have transformed into a godless alcoholic and you'll fit in perfectly."

I saw the start of another smile creeping onto her face. It looked real this time.

"Now there's this hayride..." I said. "We're going to go down to

New Post and back."

"I'm not really in the mood."

"None of us are in the mood, Fiona. That's why we need to do it. We need something good to happen."

"Why bother? There's no point." She shook her head. "There's no point to any of this... stuff." Her smile was gone again.

"It'll get better," I said. "Today will be better than yesterday... and yesterday was a hell of a lot better than Sunday. And tomorrow —"

"Just don't... nothing's getting better for me. Tomorrow's going to be just as bad."

"Today, then... think about today, okay? Today I'm going to strut around like a rooster on the back of that cart, and that's when your cue to throw my cocky ass into the mud. Multiple times. Until I cry like a small child. Have you ever seen me cry like a small child, Fiona?"

She gave a little smirk.

"You know you want to see that," I said, hoping she'd give me a chance.

Her face softened a little. "Well obviously I can't pass that up."

"I know what you young people like."

She nodded her head and smiled, but there were still tears in her eyes. I knew they wouldn't just dry up and disappear in an instant.

We headed back toward the cottage where the cart was waiting, our feet crunching through the dried leaves along the path.

Des continued to sniff the air, keeping his gaze on the trees. I didn't expect the coyotes to show themselves to the three of us; they only seem to attack when the numbers are on their side.

As we walked I kept my left hand on the small of Fiona's back, and a couple of times on the way we'd glance at each other, and she'd smile gently, and I'd nod, and that would be it.

We didn't need to talk.

Fiona was still hurting; I think Fiona will always be hurting. Our past gets carved into us, like markers in our genes.

Whoever Fiona was before The Fires... I never got a chance to know that girl.

TODAY IS WEDNESDAY, DECEMBER 5TH.

I MET Justin Porter at the junction with Nelson Road this morning, a lot closer to my cottage than his. It was cold, but not too bad; the overcast sky probably brought the temp up a couple of degrees. Last winter had been the coldest I'd ever known, the dust clouds choking out what little heat you'd get from the hidden sun; we'd all take shifts cutting wood from morning 'til midnight, worried to death that we'd run out of heat.

That was what we had to do. And that was all we did.

The skies have cleared now.

The weather's back to normal.

That's about the only thing that's back to normal.

"No sun," Justin said, his first words to me when we met. He didn't wait long before he started running again.

"I don't miss it," I said as I struggled to keep up. "My eyes aren't used to the bright anymore."

"Bah," he said. "I hate waking up without the sun. I like to keep tabs on it, make sure it's still around. We'd be royally hooped if we lost it again."

I almost said something, that I was sure the dust clouds wouldn't be coming back.

But what the hell do I know?

"I couldn't get enough of it when it first broke through," I said. "I remember Kayla spent hours in the sun, burning herself on purpose."

Justin grinned. "Sexiest lobster I've ever seen."

"Man was she red."

"She still looked real good. Really, really good. Seeing Kayla in a bikini was like getting a rimjob from Jesus."

"What?"

"You know what I mean."

I know how I feel when I see her. But I'm not about to talk about

15

it. Kayla's only twenty two; that makes Justin at least a decade too old for her. And I'm a lot older than he is.

I was feeling out of breath. We were running at full pace now. Justin runs with a full load, humping a pack and a rifle like he's in basic. And I'm pissy because I don't have a proper jog holster for my gun.

I wanted to ask him to slow down. My defib was back at home, and I hadn't even stretched yet. But the last thing I need is to look old and weak in front of Justin Porter. I wouldn't say we're competing against each other, but I'm sure some people wonder why I'm calling the shots around here and he's sitting back and letting me.

"I'll slow it down," he said. "I forget that you don't do this every day."

"Go fuck yourself," I said. "I'll bet you won't be doing five klicks on gravel when you're my age."

"I'm not sure I'll be upright when I'm your age. Tell me, what was Napoleon like? Did you know him personally?"

I huffed. "He wasn't as short as people think."

I heard a squirrel chattering in the trees, laughing at the old man pretending he could keep up.

Justin slowed down a little. Probably not enough.

"I'm sure if you really wanted to you could get back into it, Baptiste," he said. "You just need to make it a habit again."

"Tell that to my antique heart."

I took a shallow breath.

"The coyotes are back," I said.

"I heard. Matt told me."

Of course. I assume Matt also reports to Justin every time he takes a big boy shit.

"We should bait 'em," Justin said. "One plump little chicken should do the trick."

"I don't think so. I can try the rabbit call again."

"Don't worry, Baptiste. I'll make sure the chicken doesn't get hurt. I know how close you are to each and every one of them."

"We shouldn't start drawing the pack over to us. The last thing we ought to be doing is screaming out 'hey, guys, free meal over here'."

Justin laughed. "You're kidding, right? They already know there's a meal here."

"I doubt even a starving pack of coyotes would be dumb enough to take Carcass on." I wouldn't be dumb enough to mess with our Great Pyrenees, and I'm the one who feeds him.

"I'm not talking about the chicken coop. I'm talking about Fiona. Or whoever else is dumb enough to wander off by themselves the next time. That trail around the lake might as well be a buffet line."

"That's a little overstated."

"You should close that trail off completely. That's what I'd do."

"Yeah," I said, "if you were in charge, eh?"

"It's just a suggestion."

"Yeah... noted."

He grinned. "Don't worry... I'll take care of these damned coyotes."

"Just don't bait them," I said.

He gave a nod that I knew meant nothing.

We reached the steel gate on Nelson Road. I was tired and I'd had about enough of Justin. I was tempted to pretend I'd forgotten my key.

"I've got it," Justin said as he ran up to the lock.

"Since when do you have a key?"

"Matt and I cut some last time we were in Cochrane. They have one of those coin-operated jobs at the Home Hardware."

There was a reason I'd only wanted two copies of each key. Now I wouldn't be able to keep track of who had what.

Justin knows why I had it that way. He knows but he doesn't care. He was making a statement, taking another shot at me.

"You'll still set off the alarm," I said. "Unless those key-cutters can magically copy a dongle."

"I already have a dongle."

"What?"

"Matt gave me Ant's."

"That's completely unacceptable."

And it was a fuck-up on my end. I should have kept better track of it.

He sighed. "Look... if you don't trust me, just say it. But don't expect me to hand it back."

"Whatever."

It wasn't like I had a way to take it from him, short of shooting him in the face.

We crossed through the gate and kept on our way. I knew the

route; he'd drag my ass all the way to the Linden homestead at the end of Nelson Road. The Lindens had left town with Fisher Livingston. So naturally, they're good and dead.

"There's no electricity at the Home Hardware," I said.

"Don't worry... we brought our own. I do know how to run an extension cable from my dashboard." He grinned. "The beauty of owning an electric car is that you don't worry so much about using up a little extra juice. Don't you wish you had one, Baptiste?"

Another shot.

I tried to speed up, but I could feel that all I'd get for that was a cramp. I didn't have any extra in me.

I'd just have to maintain.

"So I got into another classic discussion with Marc Tremblay," Justin said.

This was going to be interesting. For friends, those two weren't particularly friendly with each other.

"Let me take a shot," I said. "Transgendered priests?"

"Burma."

"You didn't kill him... did you?"

Justin shook his head. "He said that the only Right-To-Protect in Burma was the right to protect the Mottama oil fields."

"He has a hard-on about oil."

"Yeah. Fucking French... they hate oil but they'll gladly spend the proceeds." He looked embarrassed for a moment. "You know what I mean... French Canadians... pea soup and shit."

"I get it. Don't worry... I'm the good kind of French. Chocolate covered and dipped in Scotch."

Justin laughed. "I like that."

"He must've forgot you served in Burma," I said.

"No... he mentioned it. Told me it wasn't even a real war."

I'm not sure Marc was that far off about Burma. But then again, people used to say that about Afghanistan, too, so I'm probably just being a dick.

"He's trolling you," I said. "He wants to stir the shit."

"I know. But I couldn't help it. I just kept arguing with him."

"That's a stupid thing to do."

"Well, since I was only in Burma because I'd volunteered for rotation, it's clear I'm not that bright."

I chuckled at that.

We crossed New Post Road and kept on toward the Lindens. I was able to keep up at Justin's pity pace, but only just.

"Okay," Justin said. "I've gotta ask. I mean, you haven't even mentioned it."

I knew he'd bring it up eventually.

"I don't want to get into it right now."

"We know who killed him," he said. "They weren't trying to keep it a secret. What did they call themselves?"

"The Mushkegowuk Spirit Animals."

I thought back to Matt sputtering out the words. Three men in a grey Toyota, wearing visored combat helmets painted to look like a coyote, a tiger, a bear. They'd stopped our truck and they'd made Matt climb out. The man in the coyote helmet had walked around the back, to Ant. Three shots, no warning.

Then the man in the tiger stripes had started to laugh, as Matt had pleaded for his life.

"One of them is Ryan Stems," Justin said. "I know it."

"Maybe... we don't know for sure."

"Who else would come after us? Who else would be that god-damn stupid?"

"Our guys weren't protected. Ant wasn't wearing his vest or his helmet." Another deep breath. "And he was out riding in the back of an open grain truck with a fucking target on his back. Any idiot could have taken a shot at him. And given us some bullshit name so we'd put it all on Stems."

Justin slowed right down to a walk. "Ant wasn't shot by some hunting rifle."

He didn't have to tell me. I was the one who had to clean him up before we buried him. I was the one who had to tell Kayla and Fiona just how he'd died.

I slowed his walk down to a breather. I'd barely be able to get through the argument standing still.

"You know it was Stems," Justin said. "You must be thinking the same thing I am."

"I'm not."

He almost laughed. "You're not serious, Baptiste. We know what we need to do. We throw on our gear and we find him. We don't make the same mistake again."

"Not right now," I said. "We're not ready."

"Not ready? What the hell are we waiting for?"

I could tell that he honestly didn't know. He was so wrapped up in getting Stems that he wasn't thinking of what really counts. Sure... Justin has a family, but you'd swear he forgets that most of the time.

And I'm always the one who has to remind him.

"So you want to get him," I said. "You and I up against Ryan Stems and who knows how many men. So maybe we'll bring Lisa along, since she's probably a better shot than either of us. And then you know what will happen? We end up driving halfway to Kapuskasing looking for him, we probably get ourselves killed, and then we're down three people, the same three people who are the best chance for keeping the rest of us alive. That'll make everyone who's left a lazy fucking Sunday for Ryan Stems."

"Maybe ask your precious Supply Partnership for help." He kicked his head back with a fake laugh. "Oh, what's that? They don't care if we live or die? Really?"

"No one wants to throw their lives away."

"I can get a pile of guys down here from Detour Lake. We pay 'em with something and they'll fight."

"That's no better than baiting coyotes," I said. "Let's go get those crazies sniffing around here."

"We do this now or we'll regret it, Baptiste. Just like I'm sure you regret the last time you let him go."

He was going to keep on it. I'd let Ryan Stems go.

That meant that Ant's death was on me.

Justin kept on talking. "If he's taking shots at us on the road, it won't be long before he decides to come at us where we live. We need to kill him. We should have killed him a long time ago."

I was starting to feel my heart beating too fast. I didn't want to have this conversation. I *couldn't* have this conversation.

"You need to take charge here, Baptiste," Justin said. "You're the guy, aren't you? We're starting to look weak."

"You mean I'm looking weak."

"If we don't hit back he'll think we're a bunch of pussies. I don't know about you, but I'm not a pussy. Are you a pussy, Baptiste?"

I wanted to punch Justin Porter in the face.

"I don't want to talk about this right now," I said, trying my best to hold in the rage. "It's been a rough few days. I'm really fucking tired."

"We're all fucking tired. But we need to retaliate."

He didn't get how far he was pushing me.

"Just drop it," I said. "It's a stupid idea, alright? Revenge is something idiots do."

"So I'm an idiot."

"You're definitely sounding like one right now."

"You sound like a coward, Baptiste. I thought you were better than this. If you're too chickenshit to handle it, I'll just grab Matt and the Tremblays and we'll take care of it for you."

"Go ahead, Justin. Go find Stems and get yourself killed."

"Fuck you."

"Well, that's your plan, isn't it? Team up with Captain Useless and the guys with dirt-clogged starter rifles? That's your backup against a man who's seen more action than the two of us combined? Brilliant fucking plan. Oh... I guess you'll have a handful of those prepper assholes from Detour Lake with you, too, eh? You'll still get yourself killed. By Stems or by the guys you just hired to watch your back."

"Well I'd rather die on my feet than on my knees. You know, sucking Ryan Stems' dirty cock."

"That's because you're an idiot, remember?" I said, feeling the adrenaline and wishing I could turn off the tap. "Dying isn't as much fun as you seem to think it is. Especially when you drag your family down with you."

"You're making a mistake, Baptiste. You stand there and you call me an idiot, and meanwhile you're risking all of our lives because you're not willing to make something happen. That's just fucking stupid. We need to kill him before he kills us. It's that simple."

"It's never that simple."

"Stems can't argue self defense this time. There aren't any excuses left. You can't just let a murderer run wild. "

"We'll get him," I said, holding up my hands almost like I was expecting that to shut him up. "But when we're ready... when we know we can win."

"So come up with a timeline, then. Some kind of plan, for Christsakes."

"I'm not going to waste my time convincing you that I know what I'm doing. I don't care what you think, Justin. I'm still in charge around here, no matter what kind of shit you've been pulling behind my back."

"What the hell does that mean?"

"Secret trips to Cochrane... cutting keys... taking Matt down to the river and teaching him how to shoot..."

"It's a deep-rooted conspiracy," Justin said. "We're all in on it. We're going to replace your morning tea with goat jizz."

"If you have a problem with the work I do you'd better start talking to me about it."

"What do you think I'm doing right now? I'm talking to you, Baptiste. I'm telling you right here, right now. You're being stupid... you're making bad decisions... and yes, we're losing faith in you."

"So you're losing faith in me. Big fucking deal."

"It isn't just me, buddy. The only people still on your side are the ones you're fucking and sucking."

That was the line. I felt like I was twenty again, inching toward the first punch. And probably about to get my ass kicked, assuming I didn't just pull out my gun and shoot him.

I started with the clenched jaw, then the glare...

"Shit," Justin said. "I shouldn't be bitching at you, Baptiste."

"Too late for that."

"Look, I'm sorry. I'm just... I'm pissed off, alright? With Marc and his crap, with what happened to Ant..."

"Yeah..."

"But I'm serious. You know... about Stems. We need to kill him. He's going to come for us. It's just a matter of time. I'd rather we chose the time and place, Baptiste. Preferably before you run out of pills for that fucked-up heart of yours."

"When I'm gone you can do whatever the hell you want."

"God, Baptiste. Let's just get it over with. It's him or us."

My chest was tightening. I couldn't keep talking about it.

"I'm heading back," I said.

"Too much?"

"You're pissing me off. I've got better things to do."

"I'm not going to drop this," Justin said. "We need to retaliate."

"I'll see you later." I turned and started walking back towards McCartney Lake.

Justin didn't follow. "Whatever, Baptiste," he said. "Just run away."

I didn't bother answering. He'd be pissed at me either way.

And I certainly wasn't going to go along with his revenge fantasies.

It didn't make sense for Ryan Stems to be coming after us. For one thing, he's not a marauder — sneaking around, murdering and raping and taking supplies — despite what everyone seems to think around here. He works to keep his people safe, just like Justin and I try to do. It's not like we're running around shooting people for a few extra cans of Alphagettis.

Killing Ant didn't make any sense.

They killed Ant and they made Matt piss his pants, and then they let him go. What was the point?

Hell if I know.

I made my way home to the cottage, relieved to be alone but still rolling into the anxiety. I looked up at the grey-and-purple sky, trying to find some birds to distract my thoughts and settling for another chatty squirrel scrambling along the tops of the full-figured white pines.

I got back just as a cold rain started to fall. I found Fiona making breakfast in the kitchen and I gave her a quick hug, barely brushing against her. I didn't want her to notice that my hands were still shaking.

"Want help?" I asked.

"Always," she said with a smile. "We'll put you in charge of setting the table."

"That about matches my skill set."

She laughed. "I think you're ready for it, Baptiste."

That made me smile. I was starting to feel a little better.

Not really calm... but better.

I grabbed the plates and the cutlery and got to work, Fiona telling me a story about her latest attempt to get Sara to admit she's been sneaking off and reading some of the smutty romance novels from the bookcase in the upstairs hallway. One of these days she'll nail that confession.

Cassy was the one who used to calm me down before, more so than any SSRIs or beta blockers ever could. When I had to go off my anxiety meds so I could take the Laneradine for my heart, it was Cassy who kept me grounded, kept me smiling, kept me going.

That's Fiona's job now. She does it really well.

I hope it's enough.

23

❦

We spent the rest of today getting the yard ready for winter, Fiona, Sara and I in the garden, Lisa and Kayla by the chicken coop, and Graham and Matt with the goats. I don't mind days like this, but that might just be because I don't have to do this kind of work all the time. I'm not chained to the homestead like they are.

Graham grew up on a hobby farm in Illinois; as he likes to say, it's the part of Illinois that has nothing to do with Chicago. He seems pretty happy being back to it, tending the goats and planning the big planting for the spring. It makes me wonder why he chose a career where he was always on the move, upgrading equipment for railroads that ran through places he'd never wanted to visit.

But I guess that's what we do when we're young... we do the opposite of what we want, just to find out what that is.

After dinner was cooked and eaten and the dishes were cleaned, we all gathered in the living room. Graham and Lisa were curled up together on a recliner, snarled together in a way that makes you sick even when you're not the least bit jealous, while Sara sat in the rocking chair, Ant's journal in her hands, sitting but not really rocking. Kayla and Fiona took the striped brown and white couch and Matt sat between them, either to keep them from fighting or to live out his fantasy of a sexy Matt sandwich. I sat on the floor, my head against Fiona's couch cushion, my bald brown scalp occasionally brushing against her thigh.

For a while we all just sat quietly. I looked out the window, staring into the night.

Through that window and out past the side veranda there are mostly trees, but if you look a little left of centre you can see through those trees to the lake, the water cold and calm, glistening in the moonlight. On the far side of the lake it's still mostly forest, with a few patches of grass and some wood-frame cottages painted in unnatural colours.

It's been five months since the dust cleared. The view outside that window is December grey and full of the oncoming winter, but it's still more beautiful than the best days from our first summer at McCartney Lake, when we wore sweaters in May and worried that there wouldn't be a single blade of grass left alive by the time we saw the sun again.

Looking out there now you'd think we're surrounded by never-ending forest, trees and more trees from here to Quebec. From here you'd have no concept of just how much of that forest is gone now, the black spruce and tamaracks burnt away, young stands of birch poking up through the leafy new undergrowth. I think we've lost more forest than we've kept.

Places like McCartney Lake are little islands of the old world; a new and emptier place surrounds it, not just countless new clearings of saplings and low brush, but rubble-strewn villages and farmhouses and the ruined town of Cochrane itself, where there are still charred bodies that have never been buried.

No matter how peaceful it seems out that window, I never manage to forget the dead emptiness gathered just a little further out.

Everyone else seemed to be in a pissy mood like mine, so Sara decided to read us a passage from Ant's diary, dated last February, about tapping two of the maple trees up north along the creek.

It was time to prove myself, Ant wrote. *Graham le bigshot knows everything about tractors and battery connectors and goat semen, but he's never made maple syrup. The last time my grandfather and I had sapped a tree was when I was still in elementary, but I knew enough to show off.*

It was warm enough today that I figured I'd get as much as two hours before my nuts froze off.

I packed up the cordless drill, an 11mm leader bit and six large buckets and then I took one of the ATVs and the utility trailer up to the creek. I'd scavenged four spiles, so I figured on drilling two holes each into the two biggest trunks I could find.

Kayla and Fiona went with me, which was terrific. They would surely be turned on by my manly work with the mighty maple trees. They both ran along beside me as I drove, and I felt like an American President flanked by my secret service bitches. That's the taste of power, my friends. Everyone should suckle that teet at least once in their lives.

I drilled the holes into the trees and attached the spiles, and the sap drained into the buckets. We had all six buckets filled long before I could convince either of the girls to conserve body heat with me through upright and pants-free spooning.

Kayla and I loaded the buckets onto the trailer.

"How much will this make?" Fiona asked as she watched us do all of

the work.

It takes serious guts to be that unhelpful.

"Tons," I said. "We must have over a hundred litres of sap here."

We took it back to the cottage and we boiled the sap on the stove. I lost interest after twenty minutes or so.

I came back after a couple of hours and found that the syrup was ready to sample. The girls had poured it into a rinsed-out milk jug. It didn't fill up the full four litres but it was more syrup than Graham would have been able to get. He probably would have tapped a squirrel in the nutsack and wondered why the sap was thick and white and tasted so goddamn gamey.

The girls know how to make more of it now, so my work was done. I rewarded myself with a joint, a fap, and a nice, long nap.

"I loved that," Kayla said once Sara had finished reading. "I honestly felt like he was right here with us."

"It reminded me that we still have Ant's collection of fine herbs curing in our basement," Matt said.

Kayla grinned. "One of us is going to have to go full-pothead to get through all of it," she said.

"I nominate Baptiste," Sara said. "If anyone needs to mellow out..."

"I'm perfectly mellow," I said. "When I'm not surrounded by idiots, that is."

"You love these idiots," Kayla said. "I know I do."

Matt then suggested a toast to the idiots. Kayla brought out a bottle of rye and six hiball glasses; I guess she'd given up on offering any to Fiona.

We had the toast, a drink, and a good laugh. And Sara read the next entry, about the time Ant drew a twelve-panel comic strip depicting Graham and Lisa as nymphomaniac zombies. Lisa still had it, and once she'd retrieved it from her bedroom we passed it around and talked about the sequel Ant had always promised to do.

Tomorrow morning Matt's going to find a frame so he can hang the "Chronicles of the Erect Undead" in the middle of the living room. Hopefully it'll help us feel like part of Ant never left.

SARA

FROM ANT'S "Cast of Characters", scrawled over several pages at the back of his diary:

Sara, Lisa, Kayla and Fiona. I love every single one of those ladies. And yes, by love I mean I squeezed one off for each of them, and often in sets of two or three...

Let's start with Sara, since she's the oldest and according to science doesn't have that much time left before she goes from delicious to dietary supplement. I think she's into Baptiste, actually, so she must think she's already too old and saggy to do any better.

But she's probably the prettiest one, with white, white and white skin, creamy brown hair and light blue eyes, and just the right amount of late twenties plump. She's also the kindest and I'll bet the smartest, not just because she sees through most of my bullshit.

Legend has it she was married once. It wasn't that the guy died in The Fires, he just left her because he found some chick with bigger boobs. That's the kind of stunt you pull when you're dating maybe, but you ought to have your act together by the time you sign up to be someone's husband. I'd never pull that kind of crap on anyone.

Ant's secret is: never get married.

But Sara, as smart as she is, she's still hoping to get married again someday. I can smell it on her, that commitment stench.

She might settle for Baptiste if his gimpy heart doesn't explode like a fucking briefcase nuke. Or maybe one day she'll realize that she could steal Graham and his douchey yellow beard away from Lisa if she would just put a little effort in.

You see, I happen to know that 'Muricans love French girls. All the things that piss me off about the crazy bitches I used to date are somehow alluring to hipster idiots from Illinois.

Sara's not that bad, really, for a French girl. I wouldn't say she's not a little high-strung and a little bit self-absorbed, but she's better than most of the women I've known. And I'll bet she treats a man right. And unlike Lisa I doubt she's the type to shoot you in the face for checking out another girl's assets.

I'm not sure who Sara will end up with in the end. But for now I'd be more than willing to give her a slice of my boudin blanc*.

* According to Sara, *boudin blanc* means "white sausage". It's a rather unfortunate visual, but then again it wasn't something we hadn't already seen from him time and time again.

Ant never believed in bathing suits, bath towels, or the proper use of that little button on the front of his boxer shorts. It makes me laugh now to realize that out of all his many flavours, I might miss "naked Ant" most of all.

TODAY IS THURSDAY, DECEMBER 6TH.

JUSTIN SHOWED up at breakfast time; I'm sure he'd planned it that way for dramatic effect.

Just as he chose to wrap the dead coyote over his shoulders like it was a forty-pound gold medal.

Fiona and Matt were downstairs with me; Sara was upstairs taking a shower, and I had no idea where anyone else was.

Fiona stared at the creature like she expected it to jump onto its feet and attack; they don't see a lot of fur stoles down in the GTA.

"One down," Justin said with a wide grin.

"And two to go," I said as I held open the door. "At the very least."

He tossed the coyote off onto the floor, barely missing the rug. I'm not sure why he thought we'd want it in the house.

Matt walked over and stared at it; if he'd had a stick I'm sure he would have started poking it.

"Two coyotes don't make a pack," Justin said. "I doubt they'll be any trouble."

"Tell me you didn't bait them."

"Don't worry about it."

"I told you not to do it, Justin."

He sat down on the couch in the living room, throwing his boots up on the wicker coffee table.

Fiona sighed, and of course she rolled her eyes. "You didn't take your boots off," she said. "How many times is that?"

"Real men don't take their boots off, sweetness," he said.

"Just take off the boots," I said.

He kicked them off, doing his best to spread more dirt than if he'd kept them on.

"So now we have two coyotes waiting just outside for their next meal," I said.

"How is that different than yesterday?"

"I don't understand why you can't just listen to me?"

"How long have you been up here, Baptiste? A couple of years?"

"Long enough."

"When I was five years old I used to go out and check the trapline with my uncle. What did you do back home in Toronto? Hunt for the lowest price on tampons? I'd say I'm more qualified than you to catch a few coyotes."

"That's not the point," Fiona said. "Baptiste is in charge."

"At least Justin gets results," Matt said.

"Kid's got a point," Justin said. "I do get results."

"The cockiness isn't helping," I said. "We've given you a chance here, Justin. After what you've done..."

"Don't start."

I knelt down and picked up the coyote with one hand. It was heavy enough for two, but I'd already committed myself to only using one. I carried it out and threw it onto the porch.

"So now you're the one baiting," Matt said. "What will that bring us, anyway? Bears?"

"I don't know why I bother asking you not to do something, Justin," I said.

"Don't bother," Justin said. "Because I'm going to do whatever it takes to keep us safe."

"That's not how it's looking to me. I see a guy who's doing his best to undermine me just for the fun of it."

He stretched back on the couch, wrapping his arms around his head. He was trying to show me just how not-worried he was.

"I'm not trying to undermine you," he said. "I'm honestly trying to help. Do you remember the conversation we had? I've got three guys lined up who are ready to go."

"Ready to go for what?" Fiona asked.

"For Stems," Justin said.

"Three guys," I said. "Not exactly an army. And how are you even getting in touch with Detour Lake anyway? Last time I checked they don't like using the radio."

"No," Fiona said. "You shouldn't be talking to them. Sara says —
"

"You shouldn't listen to Sara," Justin said.

"We're not talking to Detour Lake," I said. "At least I'm not."

I heard footsteps on the stairs. I turned to see Sara and I wondered how much she'd heard.

"Good morning, Justin," she said with a smile. "Brought your dirty boots in, I see."

"Uh, sorry," he said.

"What were you guys talking about?"

"Nothing important."

"They were talking about Stems," Fiona said. "I guess Justin doesn't want you included."

"And you're doing this here?" Sara asked. "Are you joking?"

"Kayla isn't here," Matt said. "She's out at the old Williams cottage, cleaning up Ant's shed or whatever."

"Alone?" I asked.

"With the dogs."

"It's not just Kayla I'm worried about," Sara said. "Frankly, I don't want to hear about Stems, either."

Justin shook his head. "We can't just stick our heads in the sand," he said.

"We talked about this," I said. "And we're done talking about it."

Justin laughed. "That's right. King Baptiste has spoken. No more talking about Ryan Stems. No more talking about what a goddamn joke the Supply Partnership has become. No more talking about how we hand over the best stuff we scavenge to a bunch of local morons and we get fucking bupkis back. All hail the great King Baptiste."

"You need to leave, Justin," Sara said.

"Don't worry... I don't mean to pick a fight. I won't beat up your old man."

"She's more worried about what I'll do," I said. "More than half this district would cheer me on if I hanged you from the yard light."

"More than half this district is dead. All I ever did was save a few lives."

"Get out," Sara said. "Now."

Justin gave another chuckle before getting off the couch and making his way toward the porch. "I'll take the coyote, I guess," he said. "I was kind of hoping Fiona would cook something up for us."

"Cook it up yourself," Fiona said.

For some reason that made me laugh.

The rain outside was getting heavy after breakfast so we decided to stay in for a few hours, in the hope that it would lighten up eventually. All of us except for Kayla, who went back to Ant's shed despite the rain.

Kayla's taken Ant's death the hardest, I think. They'd been friends from before The Fires, back when Ant was a new-in-town metal fab apprentice and Kayla danced at Fleshy's Inn. I think Ant was the first guy to take her seriously. Maybe that's why she won't let go of him.

Matt and Fiona went down to the basement to sort through a few yet-to-be checked boxes that we'd pulled from a shed up Kennedy Road, while Sara and Lisa decided to sort through Ant's stuff.

I've heard that some parents who suddenly lose a child end up leaving their child's room untouched afterwards, maybe for years. Now it's true that what I've heard may just be a pile of crap, and obviously Ant's not my kid, but it doesn't feel right to me for Sara and Lisa to be pulling out his clothes and stacking them on the bed in piles.

And it certainly doesn't feel right to have Graham standing by the door, licking his lips and hoping for a chance to take his old room back.

We need more time. The world needs to hold on for a little longer before things are allowed to start up again.

"Most of the shirts can work," Lisa said, "but the pants would be too short for Matt."

"They might fit Fiona," Sara said.

"I think we all have enough clothes," I said as I sat in Ant's old desk chair, flipping through some of his half-drawn comics; I know he had folders of finished work somewhere, but I wouldn't be surprised if Kayla or Fiona had already swept in to grab them.

"We'll show them to her, at least," Sara said to Lisa, not paying any notice to me.

Lisa held up a red hoodie with a long-fanged cobra. "Someone's going to want this," she said. She tossed it over to Sara.

It looked just like the hoodie Ant was wearing when he was shot. The one we'd buried him in.

"I want it," Sara said as she started to fold it. "But I don't really get first dibs, do I?"

"Kayla will want it," Lisa said.

"I think Fiona might want it, too," I said.

She'd always looked up to Ant. It wasn't just that both of them like to think of themselves as artists; Ant had a way of making everyone feel wanted, and that's something Fiona always needs a little more of.

"Good thing those two share a room," Sara said. "That'll postpone the decision for a few months at least."

"It'll work itself out," Lisa said. "One of them will shoot the other soon enough." She seemed to catch herself right after she spoke, looking over at Sara and then to me.

I'm sure Sara caught it; I saw a little ripple of pain wash over her.

"I wonder if Matt will be okay without a roommate," Sara said.

"He'll get used to it," I said. "We'll all get used to it."

"He asked me to move his stuff out," Graham said from his corner. "I don't think he wants to stay in here by himself."

"That's convenient," I said, not really thinking about what I was saying.

"What's that supposed to mean?"

"It doesn't mean anything. I just don't get all of the rushing around."

"He doesn't want to stay in this room," Lisa said. "Seems like a simple concept to me."

I shook my head. "Whatever... just pack Matt's shit up, then."

"That's what I'm planning on doing," Graham said. He sounded like a whiny little bitch.

"Then just fucking do it," I said.

I looked over to Sara, expecting one of her glares of disapproval, but she hadn't been listening. She was standing by Ant's bed, still gripping the red hoodie; she'd long stopped trying to fold it.

I started to sigh, but cut it short once I realized. I'd known this cleanup operation was a bad idea. Now Sara was falling back into it again. I heard her sniff a little before she started crying.

I wanted to pull her over to me. I wanted to comfort her.

But she can't keep doing this in front of everyone. She needs to be stronger than that.

"I'm going to check for some more boxes," I said.

I left the room as quickly as I could. I didn't want to risk getting sucked into that mood.

Someone has to hold us together. Someone has to move us along.

33

For some reason it always has to be me.

⤶

A little later on, I found Matt and Lisa arguing by the wiring trench, behind the cottage.

Well, there was no trench yet, actually, since they hadn't started digging it. They'd been out there for over an hour, and it looked clear to me that nothing had been done.

There was little worry we'd have the solar plant set up anytime soon.

"You'll settle this, Baptiste," Lisa said as I came over. "Matt wants to dig the whole trench by hand."

"By shovel," Matt said. "I'm not an idiot."

"I have trouble believing that you're in favour of more work," I told him.

"Well, we can't afford the fuel for the bobcat."

"But we're doing this to get more power," Lisa said. "That's the big priority, isn't it?"

I wanted to take her side. I really, really wanted to. But I couldn't.

"I think Matt's right," I said. "We're almost out of diesel, and Detour Lake won't be making their shipment until the spring."

"Assuming we get any of it," Matt said. "Which I doubt."

"Just shut up," I told him. He was right about our chances. "I'm sorry, Lisa, but we need to conserve what we have. We have way more wood and propane than diesel, so if the plant takes a little longer we can manage."

Lisa was staring at me, but I couldn't tell what she was thinking. For some reason it's impossible to know what Lisa is thinking until she opens her mouth or starts kicking your ass.

I waited a little longer.

"We're going to need more help," Lisa said. "I can't dig this trench by myself."

"I'm here," Matt said.

"Like I said... I can't do it by myself."

"What about Graham?" I asked. "Where's he? Out fluffing the goats?"

"Who gives a crap where he is?" she said. "He's almost as useless as this idiot."

"Hey," Matt said.

"I'll help," I said. "I mean, I can't every day... Graham and I are going into town tomorrow to find batteries for this thing... but I'll do what I can."

"I guess that's the best we can do," Lisa said.

"Uh... thanks."

She nodded.

Sometimes I wonder what it is about Lisa that makes me trust her the most.

❧

Sara disappeared just before dinner again, like she had on Sunday after Matt brought Ant home. I knew she was hiding up in Lisa's bedroom. She still likes to think she shares a room with Lisa, whenever she doesn't want to share a bed with me. When that happens I'm never sure if it's because she's angry with me, or if it's the only way she knows I'll leave her alone.

That last time she'd ended up staying in there all night, not appearing again until after we'd finished breakfast. I didn't want that to happen again.

I knocked on the door, but she didn't answer. I opened it slowly, trying to make my intrusion seem a little more polite.

She was lying on her old bed, the blankets pulled up to her shoulders.

"You just left," she said.

"I'm sorry," I said. I meant it. "I didn't want to get carried away with all of it."

"What the hell does that mean?"

"We need to be strong."

"Are you kidding me? Seriously?"

"What?"

"You need to support me, alright?"

I sat down on the bed beside her, running my hand through her half-curled hair. "I'm sorry... I should have stayed."

"Damn right you should have stayed," she said. "Christ... no one needs to see you acting like a goddamn robot. I know you're hurting,

Baptiste."

I shook my head. I tried not to cry.

"It shouldn't have happened," I said. "I should've been there to keep him safe."

"He was the one who chose not to be safe... that was Ant... not you." She brought up her hand and squeezed my thigh. She'd forgotten who was supposed to be doing the comforting.

"Do you think we made the right choice?" I asked her.

"We took him in and gave him a family," she said with a hint of a smile. "Ant was happy."

"I don't mean that... I mean by staying here. Maybe if we'd made the trip out over the summer we'd be down in Temiskaming or somewhere, and Ant would be out spray-painting stop signs and humping fire hydrants."

"We made the right choice," she said. "Staying here meant bringing in the Porters and the Tremblays, maybe saving their lives. As much as Justin pisses me off sometimes, I'm glad he's here and that he's on our side."

"That doesn't mean it was the right choice."

"Bad things happen. And they'll happen no matter what." She sat up and leaned in against me. "At least Ant wasn't alone when it happened."

"He was with Matt."

"Yeah, with Matt... his friend. And the rest of us are still here, Baptiste. And we're doing okay."

"For now..."

"No... we're not doing that. No more doom and gloom..."

"We're running out of fuel," I said.

"We'll talk to the Walkers. Or the Smiths... they must have some to share. They owe us for the extra eggs we've been sending them."

They owed us for far more than that.

"That's not how it works," I said. "No one shares fuel."

"We'll find a way," she said. Her voice didn't waver as she said it. "You'll figure it out, Baptiste. You always have and you always will."

I smiled; I was tired of talking about it, of fishing for reinforcement. It's not like I could just wave my hand and lose the guilt I feel about Ant... or about everything else.

"We're lucky to have you," she said.

"You're just sweet-talking me..."

She pursed her lips. "Is it working?"

I nodded.

"You're an easy man to please, Baptiste."

"And you're the perfect piece of tail to do it."

She giggled a little as she leaned over and kissed me.

I kissed her back and wrapped my right hand around the back of her neck, drawing her closer to me. And then I kissed her neck, listening to the slow deepening of each breath.

"I love you," she said.

"I love you..." I kissed her neck some more.

She moaned and it shot right through me.

I made sure to move us to the right bedroom.

TODAY IS FRIDAY, DECEMBER 7TH.

THE WEATHER was good, so Graham and I went into Cochrane today in the old grain truck. We skipped the weekly meeting and we did our best to put whatever shit's between us on hold.

Graham drove the truck and I was on lookout, both of us wearing as much protective gear as we have. If we know we're crossing the river, we'll start off with our riot suits; they're light enough that it's not that bad wearing them, except for a few hot weeks we had in July and August now that the sun's back. And once we cross the West Gate, the one on the road bridge, we'll strap our vests on over our suits and we'll throw on the helmets and goggles. It's a lot to wear, especially when we're lifting and hauling, but there's a big advantage to being some of the best equipped guys coming into Cochrane.

We reached the outskirts of town, passing by the industrial buildings along the highway as it runs along the tracks and into town.

"So... best place for batteries?" Graham asked. He was obviously eager to get started.

"I need to look for more pills first," I said. "I want to check Lady Minto again... just to be sure."

"You're serious? That's all the way across town."

"I'm serious. If we leave it for last we'll run out of time."

Graham winced like I'd kicked him in the nuts. "You can't just spring this on me, Baptiste. Plus... don't you think we should focus on what's best for the whole team?"

"Don't tell me my job," I said.

"That's not your job, Baptiste. Your job is security, not supplies."

"Well... when I die in six months I'll be taking on a new job as weed fertilizer. That sure as hell won't do you guys any good."

Graham shook his head. "You have pills for now. We don't have enough batteries."

I laughed. "There are probably three hundred car batteries left in

39

this town. We can pull those out once we're done checking the hospital again."

Graham started slowing down.

"We're going to the hospital," I said.

"There are a half dozen school buses over there," Graham said, pointing toward a gravel lot on the south side of the highway. "Let's yank those batteries at least... just to get started."

"You can yank whatever you like, Graham. But I'm taking this truck up to Lady Minto with or without you."

He turned to glare at me. I assume it was a glare; all I could see was his helmet.

"I'm not kidding," I said.

Graham seethed a little, but eventually he gave me a long sigh and a slow shake of his head. "It's selfish," he said quietly.

"That's your opinion."

He started us moving again, not saying anything more about it. I could tell that he was pissed, and I knew that he'd probably run right to Lisa when we got home to tell her what a big bad asshole I am. It doesn't make a difference what he says about me; he'll keep mumbling but we'll keep working, because that's really all there's left for us to do.

Graham pulled us into the empty parking lot of burnt-out Lady Minto.

Beside a curb.

We found her.

The first body of the season if you don't count Ant.

She'd been pretty once, early twenties, with short brown hair and thick purple-rimmed glasses, but her face was bruised and battered now. Someone had beaten her to death and I didn't know why.

"Pauline Yarrow," I said. "Wasn't she shacked up with the McIvors?"

I wasn't as horrified as I ought to be. As I used to be with this type of thing.

"I thought the McIvors left," Graham said.

"They did. Over a month ago. Guess she decided to stay behind."

I heard Graham sigh. I looked over and saw tears in his eyes. At least one of us still felt something.

I looked at the trail of blood that marked a path behind her.

"Looks like she stumbled over here from somewhere. She's been here a couple hours," I said, realizing that I'd become an expert on dead people.

"She thought she'd find help at an abandoned hospital?"

"I guess she wasn't thinking straight. You know, since she was slowly bleeding to death."

Although it was possible that she'd been hoping to find something to treat herself, like bandages or painkillers. If we'd left before sunrise, we might have found her before the end.

"I wish we had time to give her a proper burial," Graham said.

"I wish we had time to figure out who killed her." I climbed down from the cart. "Are you going to come in and help me look for supplies?"

"I don't need any heart pills."

"Maybe we'll find some pills that'll make you into less of a whiny bitch."

He ignored that. "I might go grab a few batteries."

I looked around the parking lot. There wasn't a single car.

"I wouldn't," I said. "It's not a good idea for us to split up."

"But it's a good idea to wander around looking for pills in a place that's been picked over by a hundred scavengers?"

"Just wait here, okay? I'll be back in... I don't know... twenty minutes."

Probably enough time for him to dig a shallow grave for Pauline; I hoped he wasn't stupid enough to try.

"Don't rush on my account," Graham said. "I wouldn't want you to overtax that fragile little heart of yours."

"Wait here."

I left the shotgun with Graham and made my way to what was once the emergency department; most of the building was burnt almost to the foundations, but there were still parts left standing, including an old folks' wing that was close to whole.

I was surprised to see what looked like fresh paper and garbage on the floor, floating on top of the ash and shards of burnt plastic and broken glass. I'm sure there have been other visitors to Lady Minto since the first time we'd scavenged there, people looking for painkillers and syringes and whatever else they thought they'd need for their homemade clinics. I was hoping that most people wouldn't even know what Laneradine is or why they might need it someday. Maybe they'd just tossed it off the shelves and I'd find a box of it lying under a soiled bedpan.

I still expect to see dead bodies there, which makes no sense since Lady Minto is about the only place in town where you won't find them, aside from poor Pauline out there in the parking lot.

We'd actually moved the patients out of Lady Minto a couple days before The Fires started; we'd known that the hospital was a tempting target for marauders, so we'd started moving people and supplies into the green zone, to a couple of doctor's offices downtown along with some of the equipment we thought we'd need. I know that decision saved some lives, but I wish we'd had enough time to bring over all of the drugs.

Of course, Fisher Livingston had commandeered all the drugs we had managed to store up, for his caravan of fools, so either way I'd still be up shit creek these days.

I searched through a pile of ash and what looked like pill boxes, by the remains of a nurses' station, glad to have a pair of heavy gloves designed to protect against stray needles. Antacids, laxatives, antifungals... nothing I needed... just every drug on the planet that wasn't connected to getting high.

The MDMA must've disappeared right away, likely before The Fires had even gone out. Some quick-thinking kids had probably realized the world was ending and had decided that it was the perfect time to throw a rave in their basement with the last few boxes of E.

I would've liked to try some.

I wasn't surprised that the first place everyone looked was cleaned out of the goodies, and I moved down the charred and roofless hallway towards the still-standing wing of the nursing home. That part of the hospital had made it through the fire for the most part, but it hadn't been treated well by the scavenging.

Graham and I tiptoe around when we scavenge, almost like it's a crime scene, trying to leave things just as they are. It's a waste of time and energy to make a mess, and you never know if what you glanced over today will be something to try and come back for tomorrow; it'll be easier to find if you don't leave a pile of crap in your wake.

But there are definitely a lot of guys who do things differently, with a heavy duty garbage bag in one hand and a crowbar in the other, wanting to make every place they visit look like the tent cities of San Diego.

All it would have taken was one visit by the worst kind of scavenger to make Lady Minto what it is today. There are holes in walls that serve no discernible purpose; someone just wanted to waste a little time and energy busting through drywall, and so they did.

But I had hope for the nursing home; people may have torn through the emergency room nurses' station and the pharmacy, but there was always a chance that they hadn't bothered with the old folk's portion, thinking that they had no need for pills to help them pee or build up their bone density.

Maybe I'd get lucky.

I found a set of wooden cabinets behind a desk; it looked more like a pantry than a nurses' station. The lock on it hadn't been broken.

Most of the locks I've picked are wafer locks, the cheapest of the cheap and the ones you get in most houses and offices. I've got a small set of lockpicks on my belt that lets me open a wafer lock in around ten seconds. But the cabinet was secured with something stronger, a heavy-duty tubular lock on each drawer; I didn't have anything to pick that.

I needed to take a page from the scumbag scavengers. I needed the right tools for the job. And I should have carried that right tool in from the get-go.

I jogged back toward the emergency ward. I could see the truck in the distance.

I couldn't see Graham.

I picked up the pace, sprinting toward the truck, jumping over the occasional two-foot pile of debris along the hallway. I ran out to the parking lot and looked around for any sign of him.

Pauline was still there, but Graham wasn't.

I shouted out a few swear words as I realized that he'd fucked off somewhere. It was a bad time for Graham to start acting like an idiot.

The truck was unlocked; I grabbed the sledgehammer and the crowbar. I made my way back to the old folks' wing and the locked cabinet, and then I started busting it up, smashing in from the side of the cabinet and jamming the drawers out from the inside. It took some time and a buttload of pushing, but eventually I'd popped each lock and launched each drawer open.

I emptied the drawers one after the other, throwing dozens of boxes and bottles and packets onto the counter. It made sense to take them all; most would come in handy eventually. If I do this job of mine well enough, there might even come a day when Fiona is old and crotchety.

But I didn't want to wait until I got home; I needed to know if there were any heart pills there. So I went through all of it.

And behind the anti-depressants and sleeping pills, I found a bottle of Laneradine. I felt my whole body seize up. The bottle wasn't that full, but it didn't feel empty. It took me way too long to figure out the childproof cap, my fingers trembling as I pushed and turned.

There were only three left. Three more days of happy heart health. Three more days to live.

I kept looking through the rest of the drugs. They'd be useful, someday, maybe... I could think of plenty of good reasons to stick a few sleeping pills in Matt's morning coffee.

I made my way back toward the truck with my pack filled with drugs, probably moving more slowly than I should have considering that we still had car batteries to collect. But it was hard to stay focused on the task when I'd just discovered what seemed like the mother lode, but ended up with just three more days of heart pills.

That wasn't worth much.

Graham still wasn't back when I got to the parking lot. I gave him a call on the handheld.

"Where the hell are you?" I asked.

"I'm looking for car batteries," Graham replied. "Looks like we might be too late. Over."

He was planning on carrying how many twenty-pound car batteries back to the parking lot?

"What's your location?" I asked.

"Just south of the elementary school. Over."

"Wait there. Don't move, alright?"

I climbed into the truck and started driving toward what remains of the English-language public schools. It was just over a block away, too far for Graham to be wandering off without backup. The whole idea is to have two guys with vests and guns. No matter how well-prepared he looks, one guy might still seem like a tempting target to the occasional gun-toting idiot.

Or to a guy with tiger stripes on his helmet.

I heard a gunshot from the south.

I kept going.

I reached the corner of 10th Avenue and turned to head toward Graham and the shot. I couldn't drive and hold the shotgun, and I didn't think I'd have much better luck aiming with the SIG.

I kept moving toward where Graham was supposed to be, hoping that he'd taken cover in time; there's no such thing as being completely bulletproof.

Another gunshot came, and I tried my best to place it. It sounded like a rifle; it wasn't coming from Graham. Still half a block away, but I didn't want to get any closer in the truck; whoever was shooting would see me coming.

I stopped the truck.

I grabbed the shotgun and made my way up the sidewalk, keeping my head down as much as I could while I ran.

There were no more gunshots as I came to the end of the block and crossed the road. I bent down behind a white pine, assuming that whoever had been shooting was still to the south of me.

I pulled out my handheld and pushed for Graham.

"I can see you," Graham said, his voice low. "Hold on."

I saw movement from a low bush a few metres along the sidewalk. It was Graham, crouched and walking toward me.

And then there was another gunshot.

I saw Graham fall; it looked like his vest may have caught the bullet, but I wasn't sure.

I pulled up the shotgun and pointed it down the street.

"Stop shooting!" I yelled at whoever. "Do you know who we are?"

I pulled the trigger, aiming at a white-panelled house because I didn't have anything better to shoot at.

Graham pulled himself over to me and my tree

"You okay?" I asked.

"It stings." He pointed to his gut.

"Didn't get through, right?"

"I don't think so. It just hurts... I don't feel like I'm bleeding or anything."

"We need to get back to the cart," I said. "Grab your SIG... we'll take turns with the cover fire."

We started moving backward as I took another shot. So far they hadn't replied.

"Where you aiming?" Graham asked.

"That ugly white house."

He took aim and fired too.

We made it to the collapsed chain-link fence along the schoolyard without hearing another rifleshot.

"I think they ran," Graham said.

"Maybe."

I fired again.

We reached the truck and Graham climbed in the driver's side. He seemed to be moving pretty well despite the hit to his vest. I hopped in the other side. I opened the window and held out the shotgun as he turned us around, but I held my fire and waited. I kept my barrel trained on 10th Avenue until we'd gotten far enough to the East that I couldn't see it anymore.

We'd left whoever it was behind.

"Turn left on 14th," I said.

Graham pointed the truck to the south. "You're going after him, aren't you?"

I nodded. "Dead Pauline, crazy guy with a rifle. You do the math."

I had Graham take us south to 6th Street.

"Wait here," I said. "Give me fifteen minutes after the first gunshot."

"Then I head for home?"

"Fuck you. Then you come save me."

I got out of the truck and made my way along Sixth, leaving the shotgun for Graham. I kept reasonably low, but I knew that — so-called Spirit Animals notwithstanding — most idiots dumb enough to take us on wouldn't be smart enough to see me coming.

I saw him at the corner with 10th Street, loading a couple of bicycles into the back of a pickup truck. He was not much older than Matt, and looked about as stupid.

I was tempted to shoot, but I knew I didn't need to. I walked up right behind him, to where his hunting rifle was leaning against the bumper of the truck.

I kicked it away.

He turned and saw me and my body armour, and gave me that look that's often followed by a change of underwear.

"You shot at us," I said.

He nodded.

I liked his honesty.

"Please don't kill me," he said. "I... I thought you were the guys who attacked Pauline."

"Who are you?" I asked. I wasn't sure if I recognized him.

"Jayden McIvor. Pauline was... she was with me."

"I didn't kill her."

"I know you didn't," he said. "I know who you are."

I don't think he could see much of me. But I guess our yellow-lettered OPP helmets and vests are pretty rare around here. It made me wonder why he'd shot at Graham in the first place.

"McIvor... didn't you guys leave town already?"

"Pauline and I stayed behind. We didn't think it was safe on the highway."

He wasn't wrong, but the town of Cochrane isn't any safer for tools like him.

"I need a ride back to my truck," I said.

"Okay."

He took a step toward the hunting rifle.

"Don't," I said. "I'll hold on to that for the time being."

He didn't argue.

We drove in the young man's pickup truck back to 14th. Graham was pointing the shotgun out the driver's side window of our grain truck, training it on the driver long before we were in range.

He kept the shotgun stuck on Jayden while the two of us climbed out.

"Says Pauline was with him," I said. "Have you two met?"

"I don't know," Graham said.

"I'm sure we've met," Jayden said. "It's a pretty small town." He turned to me. "Can I have my rifle back now?"

I started to unload the gun; you never pass it back loaded.

"We should bury her," I said. "We can't leave her out there in the parking lot."

"It might not be safe," Jayden said.

He didn't sound distraught. All I picked up from him was that he wanted to get gone.

It didn't sit well with me.

"There's three of us," I said. "We'll be safe."

"No... it's okay. I know she's gone. Burying her isn't going to change anything."

"It's no trouble," Graham said.

I could tell he was picking up on it, too.

"No... please... I just want to go home."

"Yeah, okay," I said. I waited a beat. "So the McIvors' place was cleaned out. The Marchands took the stove... but I think we have a couple of bottles of homemade wine that your family left behind... and that grand piano."

He nodded.

I had a feeling he would have nodded if I'd mentioned a leftover house hippo.

I wondered if the McIvors had actually left their grand piano behind. Or if they'd owned a grand piano. Or if "Jayden" knew anything about the McIvors.

"Where are you living now?" Graham asked.

"Does it matter?" Jayden said. "My girlfriend was just murdered in front of me. I just want to be left alone."

"Right in front of you?" I asked.

He paused.

I think he knew where I was headed.

"Yeah," he said. "Outside the motel."

"And you left her to stumble off to the hospital on her own?"

"Just give me my gun back."

"That's not going to happen." I looked up toward Graham. "Let's grab the fuel. We'll leave the truck here for now."

"What the hell do you think you're doing?" Jayden said. "You're going to steal from me?"

"We're leaving your truck here, stupid. We're taking the fuel to keep it from getting siphoned out on you."

"What about all the stuff I've got in there?"

"Don't worry... we'll bring along anything of value."

"There's no way I'm going to agree to this."

I sighed. "I don't know you, kid. Neither does my friend here. So we take you to someone who does. If your story checks out, we'll bring you and your crap back here."

"You can't do this."

"Just shut up for now, okay? You're not winning anybody over."

He glanced over at the rifle. Then back at me.

I knew he'd make his move eventually.

I pulled out one of the sets of plasticuffs from my belt. I pushed Jayden against the pickup truck and cuffed his wrists behind his back.

I saw the scrapes on his arms and the blood on his knuckles.

"This isn't right," he said.

I emptied his pockets. No wallet, no ID. Just a pocket knife and a package of chewing gum. I handed them to Graham, who stuffed them into one of the pockets of his riot pants.

We siphoned the pickup's diesel out, into one of our gas cans, and once that was done we unloaded a few things from the truck that we figured had some value: a flashlight, a couple boxes of breakfast cereal, and a can of evaporated milk.

No car batteries.

Jayden's haul wasn't much better than ours.

We found an empty cloth bag with a drawstring lying on the passenger side. It smelled faintly of sweat, but that wasn't going to be my problem.

I threw the bag into the cab with the rest of his stuff.

Graham helped me push Jayden in.

I bent over and picked up the cloth bag.

"What the hell are you doing?" Jayden asked.

I pulled the bag over his head like a hood, tightening it around his neck with the drawstring.

"Can you breathe?" I asked.

"This is bullshit," Jayden said. "You've got no right to do this to me."

"You had no right to shoot my friend in the ass."

"It wasn't my ass," Graham said, annoyed.

Jayden started to panic, kicking his legs. "Fuck!" he screamed.

"Calm down," I said. "It's a preventative measure."

I wanted him to think I hadn't made up my mind about him.

He was breathing hard and fast, but he stopped struggling. "Come on, guys... please let me go. Keep my rifle. Keep the fuel. Hell, I'll just walk home from here."

"No more talking," I said. "Do us all a favour."

He didn't respond.

I climbed in beside him, shoving him toward the middle of the cab.

He told me to go fuck myself.

We drove through the rest of town in silence, past the buildings on the northeast side that didn't get it as bad as the rest.

I stared out at what was left. It's hard not to stare.

Some say the flames topped fifty meters in parts of Cochrane. I'd been just north of town — by the airport — when they came; I'd never wasted any time measuring them.

We turned and headed south toward Highway 652 and home; I didn't see any other movement.

"This isn't going to end well," Graham said as we passed the old rec centre on our way out of town.

"Can we talk about this later?"

He shook his head. "We can't start taking prisoners, Baptiste. What are we going to do? Turn the chicken coop into a holding cell?"

"Just drop it."

"Whatever. This day's been a complete waste."

"I found all kinds of drugs. That's worth something."

"Well I didn't find a single car battery. Checked six cars. All had their batteries stripped out. The hoods looked like they were pried open or whatever, but after taking the battery they must've slammed it back shut. You can't even tell the battery's missing until you bust the hood open a second time."

"I guess that's the smart way to do it. No reason to leave the hood open and have the rest of the parts clog up with bird shit."

"Yeah, but it makes it harder for us."

"When did anyone make things easy for us?"

Graham nodded. "I guess someone's built a pretty hefty battery bank of their own."

"Anyone who wants to live past next summer will be building a battery bank." I turned back to look at Jayden and his cloth hood. "You got a battery bank, Jayden?"

"Eat shit and die."

I tried not to laugh.

"We're not sunk," I said to Graham. "It's a big district. Even if someone picked the town clean doesn't mean there aren't more batteries around here. We just need to keep looking."

Graham nodded. "That'll take a while. And a whole lot of diesel. Unless you know of a scrapyard around here."

I shook my head. "We'll ask when we get home."

I didn't bother asking Jayden.

"We could probably find a few batteries on our way back," Graham said.

"We can check, but let's not take too long. We should really get you checked out. You know, since you got shot and all."

"I'm fine."

"I'll believe that after you take off that vest."

Graham smirked. "I'm not stripping for you, Baptiste. So quit asking."

We started along Highway 652, eyeballing each driveway for cars. There could be cars locked away in garages or sitting out behind old sheds, but it would take at least fifteen minutes at each house, and there's a good chance that anything sitting out of the way is old enough for the battery to be in pretty bad shape. I'm not an expert on any of this stuff, but luckily Graham knows a whole lot more than I do. About quite a few of these things.

I still remember my shock when he explained that even gasoline goes skunky after a while.

It's that big electric engineer's brain of his that brought him to the wilds of Canada in the first place. Poor guy. But then again, he did find Lisa.

And she hasn't killed him yet.

We checked over three dozen yards between Cochrane and the Abitibi and ended up with eight 12-volt batteries for our trouble. Not a bad haul.

By that point we had maybe a half hour before the sun set. And we still had a murderer to deal with.

"Should we try the next concession road?" Graham asked.

"There are a few places on our side of the bridge," I said. "We should just check those and be done for now."

"We can grab those any time... we can send Matt up to do that...

or the Tremblays."

I nodded. "You're right... so we head home."

"Another hour and a half. That's all we'd need for the next one."

"We're out of time."

Graham grumbled a little but he didn't change the direction we were driving.

We soon arrived at the bridge. We've got four gates in total (including the unmonitored one on the bend on Kennedy Road, up by Sucker River), and the one that closes off the bridge is probably the strongest, made from cast iron that Ant welded together. He'd been taking metal fab in college before things went to shit, and I know he liked that there was something we needed done that he was best at, something other than growing weed or trying to blow things up in his "top secret" shed.

Those gates are important; they keep us safe and they give us control of any trade between Cochrane and the Ayn Rand-humping preppers up at Detour Lake.

I hopped out to open the three locks on the gate and deactivate the tripwire with the dongle. Once I'd finished, Graham drove through. I closed the gate and turned the battery-powered alarm back on before getting back in.

Less than five minutes later, we were home.

Sara and Lisa came out to greet us.

"Who the heck is that?" Lisa asked, nodding at the hooded man squished between us.

"Says he's Jayden McIvor," I said. "He lodged a bullet in Graham's vest."

Sara gasped.

Lisa gasped a little too, or maybe more of a seethe. Or a growl.

I was glad she didn't have a gun on her.

"I'm okay," Graham said. "It's just a little tender."

Lisa grabbed Graham by the arm, hard enough to give him a whole new injury. "Get your butt upstairs," she said as she pulled him out of the cab.

"Yes ma'am."

"I thought the McIvors left," Sara said.

"They did," I said. "Let's bring him inside."

Sara helped me with Jayden, while Lisa took Graham up to her room to check him out. I guess that makes sense; she must know naked Graham better than anyone else.

We sat Jayden down on the couch.

"What's the hood for?" Sara asked.

"It's part of the process," I said. "There's no reason to show him where we live and how we get there."

"I don't like it. It's dehumanizing."

"Make sure you fill out a comment card."

She glared at me.

I decided not to bother coming up with a better joke.

Fiona came downstairs with Lisa and Graham, her face showing a blend of curiosity and fear once she saw the man with the cloth bag over his head.

I wanted to tell her to go to her room, but I'm not her father. She doesn't have to listen to me.

I pulled off the hood and threw it on the couch.

"You people are fucking crazy," Jayden said.

"That's not Jayden McIvor," Sara said.

He gave her a hateful look. "What are you talking about? Of course I'm Jayden McIvor."

"I've known the McIvors most of my life. You're not a McIvor."

"He didn't have any ID on him," I said.

"What did he have?" Sara asked.

Graham reached into his pocket and pulled out the knife and the pack of gum. He placed the items on the side table.

Sara picked up the knife. "Homuth Lake Lodge," she said, reading the lettering on the handle. "I have no idea where that is."

I leaned in toward the prisoner, doing my best to intimidate him. "What's your name?" I asked.

"Jayden McIvor."

"Bullshit. Tell me who you are. I'm not above beating it out of you."

"Come on. Some crazy bitch says I'm not me and that's proof of something?"

"I know you killed her," I said. "You've got bits of Pauline on your freakin' knuckles, dumbass."

"What are talking about?" Sara asked, almost in a whisper, like she was hoping I wouldn't give her the answer.

"Pauline Yarrow. He pummelled the shit out of her and left her to die."

"I didn't touch her," Jayden said.

"Look at this," Fiona said, holding up the cloth bag. "Looks like blood."

"So you bagged her and then you beat her," I said. "Why not just leave the bag on her? Did you somehow know that I'd be coming for you?"

He narrowed his eyes. "I'm not scared of you."

I smiled. "I know you are."

"This is bullshit. I didn't kill anyone."

"Homuth Lake Lodge. Maybe we should see if you've been keeping your pocket knife up to snuff. I hear that those things can rust up pretty badly if you don't treat 'em right."

Graham glared at me. He wasn't about to watch me slice and dice someone on the couch.

That was okay. I wouldn't need to go that far.

"You must have hit her at least twenty times," I said. "At least. I wonder what it'll feel like when I slice a strip off for each punch you gave Pauline?"

"F-fuck you," the young man said. It sounded like he was ready to talk.

"Tell me your name."

"It's Caleb. Caleb Alden. I'm from Smooth Rock Falls. I did some work for the McIvors last summer."

"What kind of work?"

"Odd jobs... you know, built a fence, re-roofed their house."

"You're a marauder," I said.

"I'm not a marauder. And I didn't kill that girl."

"You mean Pauline... now you're forgetting her name?"

"They were going to kill me, too."

I heard the door open on the back porch. I looked over to see Matt and Justin. Kayla wasn't far behind; my best guess was that she'd been out at the shed again, and had heard them rushing by.

Justin strolled in like a man in charge. He nodded to me and stuck himself right smack in the middle of everything.

"Hoo-whee," he said. "Smells like some hot and fresh bullshit in here." He looked over to me and smiled. "Lisa called me on the handheld, said I'd better get my ass down here. Man I'm glad I did."

I glanced at Lisa.

She shrugged her shoulders. She apparently didn't think I could handle things on my own.

"Don't let me interrupt," Justin said. "Please continue your riveting account, kid."

"I'm not lying," Jayden — or Caleb — said. "There were three men with painted helmets, driving a grey pickup with a gun mounted on the back. They were chasing her down when she hopped in my truck."

Painted helmets. A grey pickup. A mounted gun.

He was describing the Spirit Animals, but that didn't mean he was telling the truth. Word spreads in strange ways.

"I thought she was your girlfriend," I said.

"I'd hooked up with her from time to time," Caleb said. "No big deal."

"What about the hood?" I asked. "And the blood?"

"They had the hood on her," Caleb said. "I guess maybe they were taking her somewhere but she got away."

Justin chuckled. "So she was running down the street with a bag tied over her head, found your truck and hopped in, and then you rescued her but somehow lost her right after?"

"We ditched the truck and ran into the hospital. We split up and I found a place to hide. They didn't look for me that long. They grabbed Pauline and walked out. Then I saw them kill her."

"Shit," Justin said. "You're lucky to be alive."

"I guess." He hadn't caught the sarcasm.

"I've heard enough," I said.

"I'm not lying," Caleb said. "Please..."

"He can't stay here," I said. "And we're not letting him run around the district looking for other people to kill."

"It doesn't make sense," Fiona said. "The McIvors have been gone for a month. What was Pauline still doing here?"

"Fiona the detective," Kayla said.

"You explain it, then."

"Pauline got into a fight with Jayden," Caleb said. "She stormed out and came to stay with me for a while."

"Or you kidnapped her," Sara said.

"That's ridiculous. I don't kidnap people."

"So why did you kill her?" I asked.

"I didn't kill anyone," Caleb said. "You have to believe me."

"Fuck it," Justin said. "I know exactly what to do. We take him outside and we shoot him in the back of the head."

"You're joking," Fiona said.

"He's a problem in need of a quick solution. We're not wasting an ounce of food or firewood on this piece of shit."

"Let's drive him out to Aiguebelle," I said. "We'll drop him off a couple clicks from the border and let them take care of it."

I expected Justin to argue.

I waited for it.

He gave me a nod instead.

"What's to stop him from coming back here?" Sara asked.

"Would you come back here, Caleb?" I asked.

"No fucking way," Caleb said. "I don't ever want to see any of you again for as long as I live."

Justin laughed. "I think we've got a plan."

"This isn't right," Graham said. "Aiguebelle has indentures."

"So what?"

"Don't we have a very specific policy of not allowing anyone to transport people across our territory for indenture? Didn't we almost get into a shooting match with Detour Lake last summer about this very same thing? Dropping him off in Aiguebelle means condoning slavery. I'm not willing to do that."

Justin shook his head. "Slavery? That's a pretty loaded word."

"What would you call forcing a person to sign their freedom away just so they can eat?"

"I call it two squares and a place to sleep," Justin said. "And if Caleb doesn't want that he can live out in the woods or something, catching fish with his gotch. Either way, he won't be our problem anymore."

"I won't fight it," Caleb said. "I have nothing to keep me in Cochrane anymore."

Justin smiled. "Beats the alternative... and saves us having to dig another grave."

"What..." Kayla said, her voice quivering, "what the hell is wrong with you?"

"Problem?" Justin asked.

"You're an asshole."

"And you're a slut. Are we all about labels now?"

"That's enough, Justin," I said. "You're over the line."

He sighed. "Shit," he said quietly. "You're right. I'm sorry, Kayla.

That wasn't cool."

"No, it really wasn't," Sara said, positioning herself in front of Kayla. "Look... I really think you should go home now, Justin."

The way he glared at her surprised me. I could see the red in his face. "I'm not going anywhere, Sara," he said. "Get used to it."

"We don't have any real proof," Fiona said. "There's some reasonable doubt here."

"Fuck reasonable doubt," Justin said. "I'm reasonably certain that the world will be a better place without this piece of shit."

"This isn't a debate," I said. "I've made up my mind."

Justin seemed pleased by that for once. "We can use my car"

"You have enough charge to make the trip?"

"More than enough."

"How has this been decided?" Graham asked. "This isn't right."

"Fuck," I said. "It's been decided, Graham. Let it go."

"All hail King Baptiste," Lisa muttered.

I'm not sure why everyone keeps calling me that.

Caleb didn't say a word as Justin drove us toward Quebec; he was still bound with the plasticuffs, and I'd put the hood back on.

The road to Aiguebelle was paved, but it hadn't been maintained much even before the comet and The Fires, with surface breaks and a shoulder that dropped away every few hundred meters.

It didn't take long for us to reach the junction at Wade Lake. If you turn left at that spot, it's a good two hours to visit the "objectivist commune" at Detour Lake. If you turn right and keep on for twenty minutes or so, you can get to Iroquois Falls, which used to be a small city before the plumbing went funny and people started puking their organs out.

We went straight, toward Quebec and the twin cities of Rouyn-Noranda and Val-d'Or, or Aiguebelle as they like to be called. Those fine folks tend to talk down to us savages from Ontario. Probably because they still have some semblance of civilization instead of a two-bit Supply Partnership that seems a little shy on the supplying.

About two minutes down that stretch, Justin pulled over.

He climbed out of the car.

I assumed he was going to take a piss.

He pulled up his seat and grabbed Caleb by the arm. "Time to get out," he said.

"Hold on," I said. "What the hell are you doing?"

"End of the line." He pulled Caleb out and pushed him toward the ditch.

"We're nowhere near Aiguebelle."

"This is as close as this kid's getting."

"Wait," Caleb said. "What are you doing?"

"That Aiguebelle stuff was all for show," Justin said. "A little bit of role playing for the ladies."

"No, Justin," I said. "This isn't the plan."

"Hold up... so you were serious? You were going to drag this sorry sack of shit to Aiguebelle? The borders are closed, Baptiste. They won't let anyone in these days, not even as indentures... and certainly not a goddamn murderer."

"I didn't kill anyone," Caleb said.

"Shut up," I said. "Since when are the borders closed?"

"Since I've been moving people for a long time, Baptiste. The last few loads Marc and I made to Quebec, before you guys made us quit... I had to sneak them past the border guards. This needs to happen. We need to kill him."

"No. This isn't how we handle things."

"It needs to be. If you don't have the sack for it..."

"I was worried you'd try to trade him off as some twink for Detour Lake... but not this..."

"He's worth nothing, Baptiste. And I fucking made you a promise, remember? No more trades outside your useless Supply Partnership."

"Yeah... you make a lot of promises."

"Seriously..."

"So keep your latest promise. Let's take him to Aiguebelle. He can stand at the border and beg for them to open it. Then he's their problem."

"We're not giving this asshole any more chances. You gave Ryan Stems a second chance, and look what that got us. Little Ant Lagace with three bullets in his chest."

"This isn't the same thing," I said.

"You're right. This time we know that there's no upside to second chances. This time it ends with a bullet to the brain. Now either shoot this asshole or give me your gun and I'll do it myself."

"Shit, Justin."

"Don't make me bash this fucker's head in with a rock."

I was losing control. "What the fuck is this? Do you think you can manipulate me into shooting someone?"

"I'm not trying to manipulate you... I'm giving you the facts. Only two of us are getting back in that car."

"Not a chance," I said. "We're taking him to Aiguebelle."

"We need to kill him."

"I'm not going to let that happen." I grabbed Caleb and steered him back toward the road. "We're better than that. We're not murderers."

"Fuck this shit," Justin muttered as he began to follow behind. He was pissed.

I was getting used to it. It's easier to keep track of the precious few who still like me than try to count all the people who'd feed me to the coyotes if they could.

I saw movement from the corner of my eye.

Justin grabbed Caleb's shoulder and pulled him backward.

I figured he was about to throw a punch. I threw my arm out, trying to grab his left elbow. It wouldn't stop his right from swinging, but I hoped it'd throw off his aim.

I wasn't able to stop it. Justin took Caleb down with the first blow. He started kicking him as I tried to pull him off.

"Come on, Justin," I said. "This is crazy."

He turned and gave me a shove. "You gonna stop me, Baptiste?"

It was a good question. I didn't know what to say.

"I'm done with this," Justin said. He started marching back toward the car.

I knelt down and worked to help Caleb to his feet. He slowly staggered up onto his knees. He was dazed; I'm sure the hood over his head wasn't helping.

I figured we were far enough from home.

I started to loosen the string that held the bag around his neck.

I heard Justin open his trunk.

I turned around to see the hunting rifle.

He was aiming it at Caleb, who was still on his knees and still blind.

"Don't do it," I said, trying to block the shot and hoping that would actually work to dissuade him from pulling the trigger.

He fired once.

Caleb fell back down.

A bullet to the brain.

Blood and grey matter on my pants.

"Who the fuck do you think you are?" I asked. I pulled my gun and pointed it at Justin's head.

"I'm the guy who handles shit. You can call me Justin."

"This isn't a fucking joke."

"This whole world is a fucking joke. Just look around you."

I was angry; I wanted to kill him.

I could say that Caleb got loose somehow, that he'd pulled my gun and shot Justin before I had a chance to react...

"I can't believe you did that," I said.

"I told you I was going to do it."

"You're a goddamn psychopath."

"Don't call me that. I did this to keep my family safe. And to keep you guys safe, too, Baptiste. Don't you dare treat me like a criminal."

"Then stop killing people."

"Do you know the difference between you and me? Aside from the fact that I've accepted that I'm an asshole, while you're still trying to be something else." He paused for a second. "No, don't worry... I'll tell you."

"Just shut the hell up."

"No. This is important. The difference between us. When I get home tonight I'll tuck my kids into bed and then I'll fuck my wife up the poop chute. When you get home you'll start thinking about how your wife and daughter are dead, and how you don't even know where they're buried or even how they died. How is that anything but the biggest goddamn joke in the whole fucking universe?"

"Fuck you."

"You'll change your mind about this," he said. "It was him or us, Baptiste. That's how it goes these days."

"I don't see how I can trust you after this."

"You're going to have to trust me. With that gimp heart of yours, it won't be long before you're dead and buried beside Ant and I'm the only one left to take care of things. Sara's going to depend on me. You realize that, right? Kayla and Fiona, too. Shit, Baptiste... I'm all you've got."

I lowered the gun. I wasn't about to use it.
I still needed him.

∽

I didn't tell anyone the truth about tonight.

Once we got back to McCartney Lake, I waited in the car outside the Porters' cottage.

Justin lent me a pair of clean pants and dropped me off at home.

Fiona was waiting downstairs, goofing around on her tablet. She asked me if I'd talked to anyone from Aiguebelle at the gate at Eades Junction, if I'd had a chance to ask if they had any of those artisan breadmakers to trade; I told her that there'd been two constables at the gate, but that they'd said they didn't have time to talk. Even if we'd gotten all the way there, I still wouldn't have asked about a god-damn breadmaker.

"I was worried about Justin at first," she told me. "That he wasn't good for us. But I'm glad there's another person around who has enough training to... you know... back you up or whatever."

I smiled and nodded; I was tempted to tell her the truth, to let her know that her instincts had been right, but I didn't.

It's enough for me to know what he's capable of.

And I didn't want anyone to know that I'd done nothing to stop him.

That I don't really have a handle on Justin Porter

There's no good that can come from telling people that.

2

TODAY IS SATURDAY, DECEMBER 8TH.

SINCE GRAHAM had a rabbit's foot and four leaf clover shoved somewhere between his close-cropped hipster asscheeks, we decided this morning to cross the river to find more batteries. Since we weren't going to be getting too close to Cochrane, it was a tough call whether we should take the truck or the horses.

In the end, my Scottish half won out and we hitched up the cart.

After passing through the gate and putting on our vests and helmets, we turned and headed south on Comel Road, just in from the banks of the Abitibi. There never was much of anything down there, just one house and an old rail siding; this part of the district emptied out long before the fires came, and now the only people who use that road use it to access the old rail bed that leads across the river to New Post.

"This place always creeps me out," Graham said as we passed a large expanse of burnt forest.

"You should be used to seeing this kind of stuff," I said.

"I'm not talking about the fires... these empty gravel roads. Every square inch of Ontario looks like the setting for a horror movie."

"You don't have gravel roads in Illinois?"

"Not like these, no." He grinned at me. "I come from a more civilized part of the world, you know."

"I come from the centre of the universe," I said. "We pave our roads in Toronto, too."

Graham shook his head. "It's hard to believe we ended up here... talk about some crappy luck."

"It's not all bad... lots of cute girls."

His face hardened again.

"What happened this time?" I asked. "You guys should try cutting out the fighting and move right into the make-up sex."

"It's not funny, Baptiste."

65

"Not funny to you, maybe..." I laughed.

He just shook his head again.

"Seriously..." I said. "What did Lisa do?"

"She's cheating on me again."

My mind went straight to Ant. But obviously it wasn't him this time. "Are you sure?"

"I'm pretty sure, yeah."

"So not really. Do you honestly think she'd be interested in Matt? The guy would lose a battle of wits with a watering can."

"Not Matt."

"Then who?" For a second, I wondered if he was about to accuse me. That would be ridiculous, obviously; it's hard enough to believe that Sara lets me touch her.

"I don't know..."

"So let me understand this," I said. "You are upset with Lisa because you think she's cheating with someone, only you don't know who."

"It's not Ant this time. At least I know that."

"That's not funny."

"You're right. Sorry."

"Don't apologize... you sound like a goddamn Canadian."

He smiled. "I need to confront her."

"You need to be sure first. You're actually pretty lucky, Graham."

"How's that? You mean because I got stranded up here? Or because I now have to hang around with you?"

"Yes... and yes... but mostly you're one lucky asshole because you've managed to hold onto Lisa for almost a year now. But once you start making accusations that you can't back up..."

"Yeah... I get it."

"If she really is cheating, you'll find out eventually. Trust me... I know all about this stuff." For some reason, I wanted to say more, almost like I wanted to brag about some of the things I'd done to Alanna... that when I'd come back from my last rotation I'd almost been obsessed with hurting her...

"I just want her to talk to me, you know?"

"I know. Lisa's not an easy person to get close to."

"There's nothing easy about her."

"She's not for beginners."

"Well, if she's not lucky I'll find someone of my own to cheat with."

"I'm not interested."

"Very funny."

"Well I don't think Kayla's into the whole facial hair thing you got going on. And I don't know who else is left."

"Suzanne Tremblay is interested in me," he said.

"You really are an idiot. Only you would pick a woman who'll get you killed. I can't imagine what Marc Tremblay would do to you if you banged his wife."

"I'll just make sure I wear my riot gear. I'll cut a little whole in the crotch area for easy access."

We both laughed at that.

A few minutes later we came upon a little two-door sitting alongside the road, not that far north of the gravel bed that led to the rail bridge at New Post; I wasn't sure I remembered seeing it last time we'd come down here, sometime during the summer, but it looked like it had been there awhile, with a flat tire and no other sign of damage. Graham hopped down and pried open the hood.

"Bingo," he said. He pulled out his wrench and got to work on disconnecting it. I realized that he was already getting faster since yesterday; sometimes Graham doesn't always seem all that mechanically inclined, which isn't what you'd expect from an electrical engineer. I guess there's a reason India's winning the tech race.

He pulled out the battery and started back to it with a whistle, but then something made him stop. He was frozen, his gaze locked on something in the ditch.

"Baptiste," he said slowly. "Come here."

I climbed down from the cart and jogged over.

Graham nodded toward a clump of orange and yellow flowers.

"Very pretty," I said. "Did you want me to pick some for you?"

"There's a body over there."

"Okay... so what's so special about that?"

I saw two bodies yesterday.

"I don't think it's been here very long."

I walked down into the ditch and saw him. He was young, maybe twelve, and he looked aboriginal to me. He was dressed in a black jacket but he was completely naked below the hips; someone had taken off his pants, his underwear, and even his shoes and socks. I couldn't see any blood; to be honest, I almost thought he was sleeping, or wished he was. But his eyes were open and his face was cold and pale. I knew he was dead.

And I knew what some goddamn pedo piece of shit had done to him.

I felt it... the anger, the sadness... the anxiety building up inside. It wasn't like seeing Pauline, who'd been just one more victim, like the charred corpses in Cochrane or the shot-up bodies along Highway 11. This was different.

I knew why.

"Do you remember this car being here before?" Graham asked. I realized that he was now standing only a couple steps behind me.

I thought about it for a moment. "Yeah... I think so."

"Me, too... I remember reading the bumper sticker. 'No on C-93.' So what was this kid doing out here?"

"This may just be where he was dumped," I said. "He probably came from New Post, whether he walked this far..."

"We should take him back there," Graham said. "They might be looking for him."

I shook my head. "If he's from New Post they'll find him soon enough."

"What does that mean?"

"We shouldn't get involved," I said. "The last thing we need to do is drive around with a dead kid on our cart. Hell, they might even think we're the ones who killed him."

"That's ridiculous, Baptiste."

"There's no upside... he's already dead." For a moment I wished that Sara was there to give a prayer or something; some kind of faith ought to surround that boy, and I knew it couldn't come from me. "Let's get going before someone from New Post shows up."

"No..."

I started walking back to the cart, picking up the battery on my way.

"Baptiste..."

I looked back at Graham and watched as he knelt down beside the body.

"Don't do it," I said. "I'm not helping you carry him."

"Then I'll do it without your help."

"Goddammit, Graham... I'm not fooling around. We need to go. You need to leave him here."

I stood by the cart and waited.

"So the coyotes can get him?" he asked.

"What difference does it make?"

I watched him stand up and walk to the back of the car. He took his crowbar and started prying open the trunk.

"What the hell are you doing?" I asked. "They're not going to find him if you leave him in the trunk."

"I'm going to put him in the back seat."

I walked back over to him. "Stop it... just give me the crowbar."

I reached out for it. He hesitated, but after a few seconds he handed the crowbar over to me.

"We need to go," I said.

He nodded, and we both went back to the cart. I took the reins and got us moving again. Graham went through the motions of being on lookout, but I knew he wasn't really paying attention.

"They'll find him soon," I said.

"If they're looking for him."

After a few more minutes we reached the concession road and a Ford hatchback that looked good for a battery; I was glad for a bit of work, so after I stopped the cart I put down the reins and hopped off.

"Pass me the tools," I said.

"That's my job," Graham said gruffly.

I nodded and got out of his way.

We made our way down the concession road past the morning and into the afternoon, taking the extra time to run up and down the other roads that led back up to Highway 652.

It was an even better haul than yesterday, with twenty-three batteries, including the one from Comel Road where we'd found the dead boy.

We didn't talk about the kid at all; we didn't talk about anything. Graham did the pulling and I did the driving, and there wasn't any need for us to speak. I know that Graham thinks I don't feel anything, that it meant nothing to me to see that kid lying there. He's an idiot for thinking that.

Every child makes me think of Cassy.

I felt the anxiety as we worked, and I tried to fight it off by stretching and yawning, an old trick that seems to help even if it makes me look like an idiot.

But all I could do was delay what I knew was coming. I just needed to make it through the day... I knew that was all I could hope to do.

We stopped before we reached Menard Lake Road, since that was getting pretty close to the Girards; it doesn't seem right to scavenge in someone else's backyard. Plus it was late enough that we had to start thinking about getting home for dinner, since there's nothing worse than getting back a little late and seeing that disappointed look in Fiona's eyes. For whatever reason, she cooks a full dinner almost every night, and it's a terrible idea to be that asshole who doesn't show up on time.

Graham took over the driving as we headed back up to 652 and started toward the Abitibi. That made me take lookout, which seemed like a good idea.

"Pretty good day," I said. "I didn't think we'd find this many batteries."

"And a dead kid."

I ignored that. "Do you think we have enough?"

"We can never have too many batteries."

We were almost at the bridge when I saw a cloud of gravel dust coming up from Comel Road. I swung the shotgun toward it.

"A cargo van," I said as it came into view.

"I see it."

"Electric motor... could be the Walkers."

"Could be."

Graham kept driving us along at the same pace as I kept my eyes on the oncoming vehicle. It was one of those white cargo vans from China, the large ones with self-drive that contractors use to carry things like power tools and a work table. There never were more than a handful of those electric vans around Cochrane, and I think the Walkers have the only one that's left. The fact that they can still run it means they must have a decent power supply to rely on and a battery bank that's bigger than what we've set up so far.

Maybe that's what happened to the car batteries around town. While we'd been wasting time on setting up the Porters and the

Tremblays, the Walkers had been building their operation for the future.

Probably a future that leaves us long behind.

"They're a long way from home," I said. "I wonder what they're doing out here."

"Does it matter?"

"Come on, Graham... don't you think it's strange?"

"Yeah... it's strange."

"Maybe they're giving us a push... stealing supplies from our territory... to see if we'll push back."

"Forget it, Baptiste."

"It's some kind of test."

"I don't think this is about us... they're not looking for some kind of fight."

"Well either way... they've found it." My pulse quickened and I could feel the surge of sling juice in my blood; it felt good to have somewhere to aim it.

Graham stopped the cart as the van approached. I kept the shotgun aimed at them; even if I trusted the Walkers, which I don't, there's always a chance their van had been stolen. It's crazy but I almost hoped it was; after all that's happened, Ant and poor Pauline and now that little boy, I wanted to fuck someone up. I'd be well within my rights to shoot some gun-toting, van-stealing marauder in the middle of a firefight, but I'm sure Sara would be pretty pissed if I brought back a couple of Walker heads to mount on the wall. Don't get me wrong... Sara hates the Walkers for how they treated her — and Matt and Kayla, and especially Lisa — but she's still too nice to consider the vengeance she ought to lay on them.

The van slowed as it neared, stopping about twenty meters away. Our team of horses was too experienced to spook but I appreciated that they'd given us a little space. Not that it made up for them being here.

I put the shotgun down where I'd still be able to reach it without any trouble. We both still had our helmets and vests on, and I kept my right hand near my pistol.

Two men came out from their truck.

The first was Dave Walker, tall, slim, forties or fifties and almost as bald as I am, armed with a hunting rifle slung around his shoulder.

The other man was someone I never thought I'd see again, a truly miserable piece of work, with a soft buttery babyface and coarse white hair.

"Livingston," Graham said. "I don't believe it."

Graham sounded more shocked than angry, and I guess to him there isn't as much of a reason for wanting to put a hole through Fisher Livingston's chest.

"That worthless sack," I said, wanting more than anything to pick up the shotgun and unload both barrels on him.

I have a reason.

"Hey there, boys," Walker called out as they neared the cart. "I heard about Antoine... I'm really sorry."

"What the hell are you doing out here?" I asked. "And with that asshole, no less?"

"Nice to see you too, Baptiste," Livingston said.

"Go fuck yourself."

Walker sighed; he looked pretty butthurt by how little his supposed sympathy had meant to me. "We had business at New Post," he said. "Not that it's any of your concern."

"We're all supposed to be working together, Walker," I said, "or did you forget?"

"Yeah... I guess I forgot. Maybe if you guys weren't hoarding supplies."

"That's quite the accusation." He was right, of course, since everyone hoards, but that didn't make a difference to how I was feeling. "If you've got a problem with us, Walker, bring it up at the meeting on Wednesday."

"Look... I don't want to argue, Baptiste. I know we're all a little edgy right now. We've all been feeling the pinch with supplies running out, and now with what happened to Antoine... but don't worry... I've got some of my best guys out there looking for Stems and his Spirit Animals."

"Out there looking for him? If he's really back around, you can just head up to Clute and I'm sure he'll find you."

"That's not where they hit the Girards," Walker said. "They ran into them on 11 South and were almost killed."

"Not everyone with a gun is Ryan Stems."

"What's that supposed to mean?"

Dave Walker really is an idiot. I'd have to explain it to him.

"A bunch of kids block the Trans-Canada with paintball rifles, and all of the sudden Stems and his men are in five places at once. Come on... I hope to hell you morons aren't in charge of anything."

"Watch it," Walker said.

"No, seriously... I think maybe I'll get myself a bike helmet and a BB gun and I'll stand out on Highway 11. And then you can come by and shit your pants for me. And then I won't have to keep telling you to stay the fuck out of our territory."

"Your territory?"

"If Stems has slipped over the Driftwood Bridge again he's working up by Clute, just like before, and exactly where he came after my guys."

"He didn't slip by us," Walker said. "We know how to guard a gate, Baptiste. We do a better job than you, by the way."

"Try to cross the Abitibi and see what I do to you, Walker."

"Okay," Graham said. "Everyone guards their gates."

"Clute's where you ought to be looking," I said. "You know, if your guys are actually looking for him and not hiding in ditches pissing themselves."

"Of course they're looking for him," Livingston said. "Somebody has to deal with a threat like Ryan Stems. I know I wouldn't want to be responsible for letting him get away."

I couldn't let that slip by. "Fuck you, Livingston. Seriously. The last thing I need is for you to mouth off to me about responsibility."

"Baptiste —" Graham said.

I shot him a glance and he got the message.

"Be reasonable, Baptiste," Livingston said. "We've all made mistakes, alright?" He shook his head. "I don't expect you to like me, but you need to at least hear us out."

"Hear you out? You guys didn't stop by to talk to us. We caught you scurrying around in our backyard like a couple of rats."

"I thought you said we were all working together," Livingston said. "We have every right to be here. And if we do stumble on anything we'll add it to our supply list."

"So now you have a supply list, Livingston?"

"Livingston works with us," Walker said. "He's in charge of our supplies."

"Bad idea," I said. "You know what happened the last time Livingston was put in charge of something."

"Yeah, okay," Livingston said. "I know I messed up. Goes with

73

the job, doesn't it? You don't need to keep crapping on me about it."

"If it was up to me you'd be hanging from a fucking jack pine. You're a goddamn mass murderer, Livingston."

"That's not fair at all. You know that's not fair."

I wanted to shoot him. God... I wanted to take his head clean off.

"We should search their van," I said to Graham. "I'd like to know just what they'll be putting on this inventory list of theirs. But then again, maybe we should just take the van. Since it's in our backyard I guess it's practically ours already. Does that thing still drive itself when there's no GPS?"

Walker gripped the forestock of his rifle. "You wouldn't dare —"

I'm sure he knew he had no chance against us, one gun against two men in body armour... but I really hoped he'd try. If he made any kind of move I'd be justified.

I could kill him right there. No one would be able to fault me for that.

No.

Even with my anger and the adrenaline, I knew that was bullshit.

I knew what Sara would say.

And I knew what Fiona would think of me. I'd never be able to justify it to her.

"Keep your van, Walker," I said. "But get the fuck off my lawn."

Walker looked me up and down for a moment before responding. "How generous of you, Baptiste," he said, nodding his head slowly. He held up his finger and shook it at me. "Now maybe you can tell me just what makes you the goddamn King of Cochrane?"

"What?"

"You hold up that shotgun and you try to scare us into putting up with your threats. But you know what? It's not going to work."

"It's not going to work? I think you're mistaken."

Walker turned to leave. "Why don't you go fuck yourself, Baptiste," he said as he started to walk away. "You'd better believe I'll be bringing this crap up at the meeting. See how many supplies you get when you're booted out of the partnership."

Livingston gave me one last look before following Walker's lead.

I turned to see Graham glaring at me, almost like he expected me to apologize for the fact that Dave Walker was telling me off.

I could hear Walker muttering something about me, and Livingston laughing back at him, that little laugh of his that's always made me sick.

They thought I was a joke, that I was all talk, that I didn't have the balls to do anything. They thought that Stems was back because I'd just been too much of a pansy to kill him the first time.

I'm not a fucking pansy.

Those assholes needed to know it.

"Make sure you've got a hold of the horses," I said to Graham.

"What's going on?" he asked as he firmed up his grip.

I pointed the shotgun at the van and aimed for one of the back tires. Twenty metres. An easy enough shot. I pulled the trigger and the tire burst.

The horses startled but Graham held on to them.

Walker swung around, tugging on his rifle but forgetting to unsling it.

"You're lucky I didn't aim for your lap dog," I called out to him.

"Goddammit, Baptiste," Walker said. "You're psychotic." He turned back around and picked up his pace.

Livingston turned back to face me. "You've made a mistake here," he said. "There are going to be consequences for this."

"Consequences?" I said.

"Yes. Consequences. As in people not putting up with bullying any longer."

"I hope you're living with the consequences. I hope you think about what you've done, every minute of every fucking day."

"Please... you know I think about it," Livingston said quietly. He turned his back to me again and continued behind Walker.

Graham sighed. "You shouldn't have done that," he said. "I think I should go talk to them, try and smooth things over."

"Go ahead," I said. "Maybe they can drop you off at the gate once you're done sucking dick. You can walk home from there."

Graham dropped the reins and climbed down from the cart "This isn't helping."

"It helps... we're safer if people know they can't push us around."

"We're safer if we don't get kicked out of the Supply Partnership. I don't know if you've noticed, Baptiste, but we're almost out of fuel."

"Everyone's almost out of fuel. Everyone but the Walkers and the Smiths, and they're both hoarding what they've got."

I couldn't believe it, but I was starting to agree with Justin.

"Come on, Baptiste —"

"This Supply Partnership is a joke. It makes morons feel like they're not alone even though they are."

"So I'm a moron."

"You might be. You're certainly acting like one."

Graham didn't take the bait. As much as I was hoping to keep lashing out at him, he wasn't going to let me.

I took a look over to the cargo van. Walker was back in the cab while Livingston was putting together the jack.

"There's something odd about that," Graham said. "Livingston changing the tire while Dave Walker sits on his rear."

It was odd, seeing the formerly well-heeled politician, on his knees in dirty clothes. "You should go smooth things over," I said.

"Are you kidding me?"

"Seriously. Go talk to Livingston, see if he needs some help with the tire. See what you can find out, but don't hesitate to shoot both of those assholes if you feel the need."

"I doubt they'll be in the mood to talk."

"Just start off with how much you hate my guts... it's a great ice-breaker."

"You're right about that."

"I'll head up the road a bit and wait for you. Tell them I've left you here because you're a sack of shit."

"What if they don't offer me a ride back?"

"Be glad you have a good pair of boots." I gave him a smirk. "Honestly, you're such a wimp about the cold. It hasn't even snowed yet."

Graham shook his head. "You're a fucking asshole, Baptiste," he said, loud enough for Livingston to hear. He jumped off the cart and walked toward the van, throwing me his middle finger.

It was a little more than I expected, but I liked it. It was about time Graham started acting like a real man.

Real men flip people off now and then.

I made my way up the road for about a klick and a half before stopping to wait for Graham, far enough that they wouldn't be able to see the cart or hear the hooves. It was dark and the stars were coming out; I knew that everyone back at the cottage would start to worry about us soon. I gave Lisa a call on the handheld and told her that Graham was talking to Dave Walker; I didn't bother mentioning Livingston or the exploding tire.

It had started to get colder, with the sun down and the wind picking up. It wasn't bad anywhere under the vest or my helmet, but even with the riot suit on, I was starting to get a chill in my thighs.

I gave it a good half hour before I started to think about heading back to pick Graham up. I could still see the lights from the van in the distance; they hadn't gone anywhere.

For a moment I wondered if something bad could have happened to him, but that seemed like a stretch. I'm pretty sure neither of those two would think of messing with Graham, not just because he's protected and packing, but because they know I'm not that far away.

After another few minutes I turned the cart around and started toward the lights. As I came within a klick or so, I saw the van moving away, heading back toward the south. Another light came on, the bluish glare of a headlamp.

By the time I reached Graham, he looked half-frozen; it was a wet cold hanging in the air tonight, and that's probably the hardest to keep off of you.

But still... the guy's a wimp. What, do they have palm trees in Illinois?

He climbed up and sat beside me on the bench.

"So what's the story?" I asked as I got us moving again.

"Livingston doesn't like you very much."

"I'll take that as a compliment. Any idea what they were really doing out here?"

"No idea. The only thing I know is that they're hiding something. I asked them point blank for a ride, and they said they didn't have time. No time to take me up the road?"

"They had something they didn't want you to see."

"I heard what they had... in the back. I heard someone coughing."

"Someone from New Post?"

"How should I know?"

"Well, why else would they want to keep it a secret?"

"They have plenty of people already," Graham said. "I've heard the Walkers have over three hundred indentures working for them."

"Bullshit. Where the hell would they find three hundred idiots dumb enough to sign their lives away?"

"From all over the district. Even further. They may have brought people over from as far away as Kapuskasing."

"I doubt Stems is pleased about Walker taking people from his fancy new nation."

"Justin told me that they're hoping to start exporting food to Souls of Flesh in Timmins... or down to Sudbury, even."

"That'll give them some powerful friends," I said.

"Yeah. All on the back of their indentures. The world's starting to look like the middle ages again. Manors and serfs. Well, worse, really."

"Then I guess it's no surprise Livingston's in the middle of it. He couldn't find any more babies to kill, so now he's turned to slave trading."

"A little harsh. You know it was an accident."

"He killed those people, Graham. Led them out into the middle of nowhere and let them burn. You can call that criminal negligence or whatever you want, but they're still dead because of that asshole. And I'm not about to forget that."

Graham shook his head. "I don't know what happened out on that road, and I don't know how Livingston could have made it out alive if everyone else was killed by the fires. But believe me... I could tell that Livingston's not the one to worry about. It's Dave Walker's show... all the way."

"Then they should both have their throats slit."

"Yeah, whatever... I just want to get home and have dinner. Apologizing for you has made me pretty hungry."

"You didn't apologize —"

"I'm kidding." He gave me a laboured sigh, before turning to stare off toward a line of trees at the side of the road, his headlamp bouncing against the fir needles.

We passed through the gate, Graham hopping off to let us through.

"We're so late I think we'll both go hungry," Graham said as he retook the seat beside me.

"Oh, they'll keep dinner warm for me," I said as I pulled off my helmet. "I'm the motherfucking king."

Graham laughed even though I'm sure he didn't want to. "You

still need to fix this. I'm not just talking about Livingston. You're not making any friends with the Walkers on this."

"Dave Walker probably doesn't like me pointing out that he's a coward and a thief."

"I don't know why these imaginary boundaries are so important to you. We go scavenging all the time in Cochrane, yet somehow you think you have a right to everything within ten miles of our place. I wonder what the guys at New Post think of these rules of yours."

"I know we can't enforce it. Not a hundred percent. But we're not like everyone else; you and I are outsiders here, and that makes a big difference. We need that buffer, to show these people we can't be pushed around."

"You know what we need? We need to keep some allies around here. No one's going to put up with us if you keep shooting out tires."

"Don't fret. We'll drop off a nice bottle of booze for the Walkers at Christmas. That should smooth things over a little."

"I frickin' hope so."

"Buck up, sugarpie," I said with a grin.

"You think that's funny? You know... I'm getting really sick of this."

"Sick of what, exactly?"

"You're out of control, Baptiste. Making threats, shooting at people..."

"Fuck, Graham... I didn't shoot at anybody."

"Seriously?"

"I needed to show them that they can't push us around."

"You didn't need to do anything. You want people to think you're tough? Too late. They already know that. So maybe now you should focus on getting people to not hate your guts."

"I don't need any more friends."

"You're not going to keep any of the ones you have if you keep acting like this. Starting with me, Baptiste."

I shook my head at him.

"I'm not joking," he said. "I can't trust you when you do things like that. It's too much."

He had a point.

"You're right," I said. I was already starting to realize how embarrassed I'd be if Sara were to find out how I'd acted. "I went too far...

I get that. Sometimes I lose perspective on this stuff."

"It's a problem."

"I know. That's why you're here. You balance us out, make people think we're not so bad. That's why we're a team, Graham." I put my hand on his shoulder. "That's why I respect you."

"Yeah... okay. Just... just tone it down, alright? I need to know I can count on you."

"You can count on me, Graham. You should know that by now."

"Yeah... okay." He turned back to the trees.

I didn't ask him not to tell anyone about the tire; I just hoped he'd only tell Lisa.

I was starting to feel the shame again.

We reached McCartney Lake a couple of minutes later. Lisa was waiting for us when we arrived.

I stopped the cart and looked over at Graham, waiting to see what would go on between them; I can't say I wasn't curious.

"You're late," she said.

Graham hopped down and walked over to her. "Blame Baptiste."

"I always do."

Graham gave her a hug and then a kiss. "I love you," he said to her.

They kept kissing.

I climbed down the cart and hurried inside.

I really didn't need to see that kind of thing right before dinner.

TODAY IS SUNDAY, DECEMBER 9TH.

WHEN I was growing up, so a long time ago, I used to watch all those movies about the end of the world. I stayed away from anything with zombies, partly out of respect for my father, but also because that shit is just so stupid.

But everything else was fair game.

I remember some of those movies pretty well. Most of them had Kevin Costner in them for some reason, and most of them were all kinds of suck. People would mope around starving and getting sick... that or they would just go out and murder each other. It was like those were the only two settings available for post-apocalyptic societies, sad sack or crazy-eyed killer. The end would come and civilization would drain away in an instant, people forgetting to bathe and wash their clothes, even forgetting how to use a goddamn fork at the dinner table.

None of it made any sense; I think the entire genre was just a refuge for wooden characters and plot holes you could drive a tractor-trailer through. I couldn't get into any story where there wasn't a plausible attempt to explain just how things got so messed up in the first place. Something more concrete than "global warming" or "monkey pox", something that set up a little thread of how we got from normal to fucked in X number of years. You'd be surprised how rare that kind of explanation is.

But there was one movie I liked, or at least it was better than the one about the mutant with fish gills or the one where Denzel Washington carries a crime-fighting bible. It was called *Testament*, and while it did have a little bit of Kevin Costner in it, it didn't suck like the others. It just made the end of the world suck.

In it the world ended with a nuclear war, and people began to die from the radiation, starting with the little kids. There weren't any grand adventures, or bad guys on Jet Skis, or idiot-savants with homemade helicopters. There was just an endless stream of bad things happening and no way to stop them from coming no matter how hard you tried. It's not like the main character actually has the power to fix the end of the fucking world.

In real life things happened differently than it did in any movie, but my world still ended. Things started spiraling out of control until one day we realized that we were on our own.

I'd come to Cochrane for the same reason I'd gone to every other little nowhere in Ontario, to consult on community safety, as if the problems in small towns are anything like what we'd gone through in big bad Toronto. I'd shown up and given a couple of presentations and gone to one of those useless community org luncheons, and then an army reserve regiment closed both highways to Timmins because of "disturbances". I wasn't going to make my flight home.

Things went downhill from there.

Over the next couple of days they called a state of emergency provincewide, to deal with the riots in Toronto. They transferred out pretty much all of the local police detachments, sending them down to reinforce the crowd control on Yonge Street.

I'd known the moment our airport shuttle was turned back that the chaos wasn't temporary. There wouldn't be any more police, or government, and there definitely wasn't going to be any more fuel shipped in. Whatever we had now was all we could hope for, and we knew that eventually what we did have would run out.

That all happened before the comet had even reached us, before they'd even tried (and failed) to divert the thing. The world was falling apart ten months in advance.

Cochrane didn't have it too bad at first, better than places like Timmins, where the wrong people took over, or Iroquois Falls, where they learnt first-hand just how bad cholera can get when you mix shitting and drinking. In Cochrane, we worked together and tried to keep people safe.

But that whole time people were dying, and they didn't stop dying... and not character actors and reams of underpaid extras, but real people, like Fiona's father, who used to coach her in hockey and had actually met Don Cherry at a restaurant in Montreal once, and Ant's older brother who used to drive an old Mustang and taught him everything he knew about being the centre of attention, and Sara's two little sisters who served as joint maids of honour at her wedding and — three years later — as joint shoulders to cry on during her divorce.

Those people and a crapload more are dead now, from disease, from The Fires, or by the hands of people who didn't have their own supplies but did have their very own guns.

But I think it's worse not knowing what happened to the people you love. Obviously the networks are down. Any phone that isn't equipped to talk to European or Nigerian sats is a brick as far as calling anyone; my fancy phone's useless since every satellite system on this side of the Atlantic has gone offline. Justin managed to get his hands on a phone that can reach the Nigerian array for voice-calls on a good day, for a few minutes at a time, if he angles it right... but that hasn't done much to get us out of the dark.

That means that Graham doesn't know about his parents, or his older brother or baby sister; he hasn't heard anything about what's happening in Illinois. And I don't know exactly what's happened to Alanna and Cassy, either... but I've seen enough to guess. And since the AM radio's full of static and we don't see planes in the sky anymore, I don't have any reason to change my mind on that. I don't need to listen to shortwave signals from New England to tell me that there's no silver lining out beyond the horizon, no life left for me back home on Sackville Street. All I have left is here.

Ant used to make breakfast every once in awhile. He made the best pancakes and french toast, but he always left the kitchen a mess once he'd finished, flour on every surface and sometimes even a pale yellowy goop dripping from light fixtures and window blinds.

But none of that mattered when it came time to taste what came out of his kitchen explosions; it was always worth the extra clean-up afterwards.

This morning, Fiona found me coming out of the bathroom and asked me if I'd play chef for once. I know she'd always enjoyed helping Ant when he was running the kitchen at breakfast time, but I'm not sure I can be the replacement she's looking for.

"I don't know what causes it," she said. "For some reason most men seem to have a talent for breakfasts and barbecue. I like that you guys are good at a couple of things."

"I used to be okay at making breakfast," I said. "But I was never as good as Ant. My specialty was eggs."

Fiona let out a little giggle. "Like frying eggs? Is that really something you can specialize in? A particular way of cracking the shells?"

"Omelettes, goofball. Sometimes I'd get up early and spend like an hour putting together the world's most perfect set of ingredients: red and yellow bell peppers, fresh spinach, never frozen... portobello mushrooms... some nice chorizo sausage if I'd remembered to pick it up the day before... there was only one problem."

"What?"

I smiled as I remembered it all. "Cassy hated omelettes. She never actually tried one, but she'd already made up her mind about them. But I wouldn't give up. I'd make those damned things every Saturday, and every Saturday she'd just have a bowl of cereal. I just thought if I kept making them long enough she'd finally feel obligated to at least take one little bite. She never did."

Fiona put her hand on my shoulder blade and gave me a little squeeze. "Will you make me an omelette?" she asked.

"I can do that."

"Good. I promise not to eat it. Not even a bite."

That made me smile.

She came with me into the kitchen, keeping me company while I put the ingredients together, with the added bonus that she knows where everything's kept. We talked about little things that didn't matter, like how we had two roosters but that they never fought, since one of them didn't seem to notice or care that there were hens around. I'd named that rooster Cock Hudson, but even I don't have a full handle on the reference.

Fiona's always good with that kind of conversation, keeping me interested while keeping it light. It's hard for me to back away from the heavier topics, but Fiona keeps me penned in and happy for it. She makes me into somebody fun for just a little while, and I love that about her. It's not that she doesn't know how serious life is; she just knows that I don't need to spend any extra time on the serious pieces.

Once my omelette bar was set up and stocked, Fiona guided everyone in one by one to place their orders. I felt like a short order cook, and maybe a little put-upon, but she stayed with me through it all, poking fun at Matt for saying he's allergic to red peppers but not the yellow ones, and laughing out loud when Lisa asked for one with just eggs and cheese and all scrambled up "if it's not that much trouble".

Once our customers were fed, I made Fiona her omelette, and she asked for everything in it, even though I'm pretty sure she doesn't like mushrooms.

She waited for me to finish making mine, and then we sat down and ate them together. It was a nice moment to spend with her, a moment I'd always wanted to have with Cassy, father and daughter and fried and folded chicken embryos.

But then again I guess I'd already had those moments, every Saturday from when Cassy was a baby, right up until that Saturday just before I'd left on my last trip up north. The two of us eating breakfast beside one another, with nothing else getting in the way. I'd already gotten what I wanted; it didn't matter that Cassy always chose to have cereal instead.

I took the mare out for a ride after breakfast. I conveniently forgot that I'd agreed to help Lisa with digging out the wiring trench.

I guess it isn't fair, with me prattling on and on about how no one should be out on their own, and then I grab my gunbelt and I take a trip by myself.

But you know what? Life isn't fair. I always wanted to be three inches taller and I certainly didn't choose to start growing my forehead at age twenty-six.

I gave Sara and Fiona their hugs goodbye before I left, with both of them shaking their heads at what a charming hypocrite I've become.

I took Nelson Road around the north side of McCartney Lake, riding by the cottages we set up for the Tremblays and the Porters, as well as the other half dozen houses that are sitting empty and slowly crumbling. I looped around the forest at the end of the road, taking the east route so I'd stay out of the shade, and then I was on the trail that curves up and around Coleman Lake and finds its way up to Highway 652.

The healthy trees end here and the destruction starts, with an old farmhouse that didn't survive the fires. I turned right and made my way to Murphy Road, just before the West Gate, and then I followed it north to that little marshy pond that always smells a little like gasoline.

I've gone further than this before, all the way up to the banks of the Sucker River, riding alongside it until I reach the little collection of burnt houses that used to be known as Florida for some stupid reason. I've let Fiona come with me a few times; she takes the mare and I take the gelding, since whenever he isn't hitched he has a strange walk that's always a little too close to a trot and it takes some effort to keep getting him to slow down.

Today I wanted to be alone. I didn't even really want to ride a horse, so I climbed off the mare at that cruddy little lake, and I took a whiff of that toxic smell that I've somehow grown to miss; you wouldn't think you'd miss the long lost smell of gas station. I slipped on the mare's halter and hitched her to a thin birch tree, and I started walking along the edge of the water.

That's when I saw something that didn't belong, a rubber glove lying in the muck. You get used to garbage when you grow up in a city, but up here you just don't see that much of it, and usually it's beer cans or fishing line or old shotgun shells from even older shotguns. A rubber glove is not something you expect out here. It's surprisingly rare to encounter such a thing as a deep woods enema.

I didn't pick it up or anything, since it's not much more appealing to touch than a used condom, and I kept walking until I found a second glove. That made sense in a way, two gloves for two hands, but it made the whole scene look less like an accident and more like waste disposal. And then I saw the broken glass. It wasn't cloudy like a beer bottle or thick like a mason jar; it looked more clinical than that, like something you'd want to test your urine with. It was enough to make me curious.

I started scouring the area looking for more, and it wasn't long before I found it, more glass, another set of gloves, and then something completely out of place, a two or three foot diameter well with some kind of hard plastic cover. I knelt down beside it, stuck my fingers into the grip holes, and then I slowly lifted it up and to the side.

It's times like that when I wonder how many other people get the urge to pee into a well.

But this wasn't a well; instead of a dark hole it was a hole down to something bright... well, not bright but certainly not total blackness. And the hole came with its own rope ladder.

If you'd have come upon something like this in Panjwaii District, the proper procedure would have involved lobbing a grenade down the hole, or, if you enjoy risking your life unnecessarily, you could always toss something down that's more in the stun and surprise category, and hope to climb down and disarm whoever's there before they shoot you. I wasn't equipped to do either, and I knew at this point that if anyone was down there, they were likely well aware of the idiot who'd just removed their manhole cover.

But it was probably empty, telling from the dirt and the spiderweb that had covered the lid, and the fact that I had trouble believing that anyone would be hidden underground so close by without us running into them at some point in the past eighteen months.

As I climbed down the ladder into the hole and moved toward the greenish light below, I knew that I was possibly on my way to making the dumbest mistake of my life, especially since I had a perfectly good set of body armour just a half hour's ride away.

What I found at the bottom was a light fixture of LEDs, inside what looked like a school bus with the seats ripped out. The windows were there, looking out on dirt and grass roots, while along one wall was a cheap laminate countertop on top of a bank of cabinets. I felt water at my feet and I looked down to realize that there was a good inch and a half of water along the floor of the buried bus. I guess one drawback to burying something in marshy land is that marshy land tends to be pretty wet.

My first thought was that it was some kind of shelter, a hastily constructed retreat that someone came up with when they found out the comet was coming. But it was too hasty for that, as if they'd just thrown an empty school bus into a pit and thrown some dirt over it. I wasn't even sure there was proper ventilation down there.

I opened one of the cabinets and I saw thick plastic bags of what looked like ice chips, or even crushed up icicles. I'd never seen that stuff before, but I knew what it was. And I knew there had to be some kind of ventilation in that buried bus if they were cooking meth in there.

There were at least twenty bags, each one weighing at least a pound. I checked the next cabinet over and found around a dozen more. The next cabinet had what looked like the cooking supplies, a full-on chemistry set along with various boxes and bottles. I checked the next cabinet over and found some burners and a few bags of President's Choice potato chips. The last cabinet had more plastic bags, but those held little yellow pills with embedded maple leafs. I had no idea there were people who cooked both meth and ecstasy, but then again, I didn't know people generally buried their drug labs in a marshy pit in northern Ontario.

I'd found what probably amounts to millions of dollars in illicit drugs, more the meth than the MDMA, since you can get some not-too-trippy government-issue ecstasy for cheap with a phony pre-scription. Well, I guess you can't get any of it now, since things like that disappeared from every pharmacy, clinic and hospital in the district long ago. So all of it's valuable now, not that drug dealing is part of my life plan.

But we're scavengers these days, and when you find something that has value, you take it with you. You don't just throw it away.

I grabbed a bag of each, just in case I decided on any show and tell, and I climbed out of the buried school bus and back up to the noxious pond. I took off the mare's halter and headed back to the cottage, her saddlebag carrying enough dope to cause some serious trouble.

I'm not sure if there's a way to make that trouble work for me.

LISA

ANT'S CAST of characters:

Lisa is trouble. I like trouble, but sometimes she's too much even for me.

She likes to drink, as per her drunken indian stereotype, and that works out well for me since she seems to like short French guys while under the influence of the old fire water. It's happened more than once and that's more than fine by me; I'm an equal opportunity sex god. I'm not so sure Graham would approve of me in-and-outing his on-and-off girlfriend, but as I have stated before categorically, Graham can go fuck himself.

I don't have a problem with him other than the fact that he seems to have a problem with me. I say live and let live, come sit down and have a beer with me. But there was some kind of horrible farming accident when Graham was a kid on his parent's goat farm down in Jesusland, and that metal rod must have gotten shoved so far up his ass that surgery was never an option. It's too bad, because I hear he used to play football or baseball or one of those lame-ass sports that isn't hockey.

But this isn't about Graham, it's about Lisa, although there have been a few awkward moments when I've got my fap on with Lisa doing her thing inside my head, and then she invites Graham in to say hello... I just tell that fantasy-blocking motherfucker to keep his hands to himself and to never look me directly in the eye.

Lisa is definitely a tasty treat; she has kind of short black hair and smoldering brown eyes, and probably the tightest ass in the entire Cree nation. She's from up in Moose Factory, right off James Bay, and she told me once that she shot and killed a rampaging polar bear. I know that's bullshit, since those poor bears are almost extinct, but I've seen her work a shotgun so I know that she'd probably be able to take out a rampaging Polar Bear Express train if she wanted to.

Have I mentioned how hot that is?

TODAY IS MONDAY, DECEMBER 10TH.

AFTER BREAKFAST, Lisa got back to work on installing the new solar power system and I actually decided to help for once, while Graham went down to the Tremblays to troubleshoot their water heater. I was a little worried about him being so close to Suzanne Tremblay and her apparent love of trouble, but it's not like I wanted to take his place. I'm older and I may be a little bit wiser, but I'm not really any better at resisting temptation; Suzanne Tremblay could have me within ten minutes if she wanted. Hell, the same could be said for pretty much any woman at McCartney Lake.

So I decided to stick to digging the line for the solar setup. Graham can be the one who digs a grave for himself.

It took less than five minutes for Matt to realize we'd started without him, and much to my disappointment, he rushed out to join us.

I wish there was a way to get him to have a life-threatening affair with Suzanne Tremblay.

If things go well and we find a way to keep Matt from fucking it all up, we could generate enough electricity to dump propane for good and get started on being self-sufficient; we wouldn't have to bother bringing home every half-empty propane tank we find attached to backyard BBQs. We've got a good number of batteries now and we've already collected enough spools of cable to hook them up. It feels like we're close.

We have passive panels on the roof of the cottage, and even a couple strips on the barn; from those we're able to charge up the basement battery bank enough that we don't even worry about things like our tablets or the toaster or the constant hum of hairdryers between the hours of 7 and 9 AM. (Not everyone has gone for the three showers a week idea.) But it's not enough power to replace all the propane or enough for us to charge up the two electric ATVs that have sat in a corner of the barn for over three months; it'd be nice to have ATVs that weren't using up that diesel we haven't found a solid way of replacing. And if we consider what we'd need in the spring for planting... let's just say we won't get far if we can't at least quadruple our current supply of electricity.

Back in July, Graham and I had stumbled on some crates inside one of the salt domes at the maintenance depot in Cochrane. I guess no other scavengers noticed them because they figured the dome would still be filled with salt; the rest of the maintenance depot was picked over pretty well.

Ant had told me once that he and some of the guys from his work had been the first ones to raid the depot, and that he'd found more than his share of his favourites, basically whatever could be used to blow something up.

We were pretty surprised when we found the crates, but even more surprised to find that the crates contained all of the components needed for a concentrated solar installation, something like a miniature version of the one they had at Darlington North. I watched over the dome, while Ant and Graham made several trips carting the crates over to McCartney Lake.

Graham and Lisa wired up some of the new batteries yesterday while I was out daytripping, and now we've put together a bank in the last two empty stalls in the barn, one that's six times the size of what we have in the cottage basement.

Installing the plant itself wasn't going to be easy since it's based on mirror fields spread out over half an acre, deflecting the heat into the thermal receiver. It took over two months of sporadic work to clear and level off the ground, and we didn't have the thermal tower mounted, and the turbine and condenser and the shed to hold them completed until early October. Then like everything else, the project was put on hold while we worried about our new arrivals, moving the Porters and Tremblays into their new homes and scavenging (and hoarding) any extra supplies we'd need to keep them going through the winter.

If we hadn't wasted time on that, Ant could have helped us big time and we could have had the system set up over a month ago. Now we'll have to do it without him. Graham and Ant complemented each other when it came to building, and while I know Kayla wishes she could take over for Ant, we won't be able to make up for what we've lost.

We have a week if we're lucky, before it's too cold to run the wiring underground from the solar field to the battery bank in the barn. We've learnt from some of Ant and Matt's previous sprinkler experiments in the garden that anything above ground will be chewed on by the local wildlife.

The ground's already started to freeze during the nights and staying somewhat frozen during the day, but with shovels, a little elbow grease, some trash bags and a pick axe, we've been able to dig over three quarters of the trench out so far.

I wanted it finished today.

So I got back to work on the hole, with Matt hovering around me with a shovel; every few minutes he'd give digging another chance before making a grunting noise and telling me yet again that the ground's just too cold to dig.

Lisa was in the barn running the insulated wire along the inside wall, and I can't say I wasn't jealous of how much quieter it was in there.

After three hours or so, the trench was finished up to the door of the barn, and I helped Lisa with the wiring, bringing it out the barn and along the trench to the generator shed at the edge of the field.

Once the generator was connected, we brought the hose over and filled the inlet for the exhaust pipe. Nothing so far has felt as strange to me as using a garden hose to kickstart a solar power plant. With the water in place, assuming we had put enough in but not too much, we pulled the tarps off of both mirror fields and powered on the tracking system with the propane generator. The three of us stood back and watched.

"What should we see?" Matt asked.

"You can see it now with the heliostats," I said, pointing at the hundreds of tiny bristles on the mirror sheets as they spun around to meet the sun. "They follow the sunlight."

"I know that. But what about the turbine? Should we see some steam coming out somewhere?"

"Tell me, Matt," Lisa said, "if the steam came out of the turbine, what would happen to all of the water?"

Matt looked to be thinking that over for a moment. "Shit," he said. "Just ignore me."

"Wish I could," I said with a smirk.

Now that we knew the heliostats were moving into place, we went into the shed to check the displays.

"I don't know what any of this means," I said as I stared at the numbers on the various displays.

"It's working," Lisa said. "We can check the batteries for charge. That will give us numbers we're used to."

We continued on to the barn, where we could see from the large and friendly LCD panel that the battery bank was charging, a large three percent taking up half the screen, above more numbers and letters that I didn't fully understand. I find there's something a little mind-bending about kilowatt hours.

"Three percent?" Matt said. "That sucker is charging up pretty quick."

"Up from around 2.7," Lisa said. "Usually batteries don't drain completely."

"Either way," I said, "it looks like we've got it working."

I offered my hand to Lisa, who gave it a brief and over-hard shake. Matt stuck his out, too, and Lisa and I both took it in turn.

"Great work, guys," Matt said. "I think Ant would be proud."

"We'll have to smoke a joint for him," Lisa said.

I grinned. "I'll bet ghost Ant is probably haunting his stash."

Lisa shook her head. "Not your best joke, Baptiste."

"Yeah... you're just not that funny," Matt said.

"And you're not that smart," I said. "But I don't hold it against you."

From what I could tell he thought I was kidding; that was probably for the best.

"Don't worry, Matt," Lisa said. "It's your good looks I hold against you. The stupid kind of makes up for that."

Matt flashed an insincere smile and skulked away. If I'd known it was that easy to lose him, I would've started the day off with a few choice insults.

"I don't know what we'll do if something goes wrong with this thing," I said. "Once we start relying on it..."

"Graham knows his stuff," Lisa said. "And for everything he's not sure about, we can fake it 'til we make it. And switch back if things go to shit."

"I hope it doesn't come to that."

Lisa gave me a smile, or as close to one of those as she ever gives.

"Shit comes weekly around here," she said. She gave me a quick pat on the shoulder and left the barn.

It's fleeting moments like that that make me think Lisa might actually think of me as a friend, and not just someone she's stuck with. That's assuming, of course, that Lisa believes in having friends; I doubt even she knows for sure.

∽

Tonight I stumbled onto people having sex.

I'd noticed that the door to the side veranda was open slightly, even though we'd already closed it off for the winter. I walked over to close it and I saw two naked bodies on the old lounge chair with the white and yellow flowers. Fiona's stained-glass loon dangled just above, and I'm sure she wouldn't have been pleased by what that little bird was seeing.

I wasn't trying to look, but I'm sure I was staring. The whole world has seen Kayla naked before, but Lisa was new to me.

"What the hell?" Lisa said when she saw me, pulling a ratty quilt over her breasts. "You're a fucking pervert!"

"Don't you have bedrooms for this kind of thing?" I said, pretending I was annoyed and not at all turned on. "It's a little cold in here to be naked, isn't it?"

"There's no privacy upstairs," Kayla said, standing up from the lounge chair and making no attempt to cover herself. She's one of those girls who's athletic without being too bony, always soft despite the tone. I'd seen her dance once, before The Fires, and before most people knew much about me; I almost got up the nerve to talk to her... almost.

I talk to her every day now. I still can't help but want her.

"You should have knocked," Lisa said. She already sounded less pissed.

"It's called 'sock on the door'," I said.

Kayla laughed. "I'll remember that. Can you give us a little privacy now, please?"

"You're not going to tell..." Lisa said. She'd moved on to being more worried than angry, and I almost felt bad for her.

"I'm not getting involved," I said.

"Thanks."

I nodded and turned away, closing the door. I made sure to lock it, too, using the little hook up top just in case one of the girls remembered to bring their key.

Then I gave them their privacy.

Luckily they had most of their clothes with them, so they didn't look all that chilled as they ran out and around to the front door of the cottage, barefoot in the December frost.

TODAY IS TUESDAY, DECEMBER 11TH.

MATT AND I spent the afternoon at New Post, helping to build a house. We call it helping but I think we sometimes get in the way, since the people we're working with have years of experience with that kind of thing. But they seem to appreciate the help, and I want to build up our relationship; it's not good to have neighbours you don't feel you can trust.

It's not easy trusting them; they're part of the Mushkegowuk Council, even if they're not officially members of Ryan Stem's little nation. It's hard to know if they've chosen a side.

I asked around about how things were going, hoping that someone would mention something about that boy we'd found on the other side of the river. But I couldn't just ask outright, so I didn't get an answer. All I knew was that everyone there looked worried. That doesn't really tell me anything.

I know they're probably running low on food these days, considering how many mouths they've got to feed.

Matt's like a movie star to the young women at New Post, and I've noticed that more of them are on the job site on the days I bring him with me. I'm pretty sure he could take his pick of the girls there if he wanted to, but for whatever reason he hasn't made his move. I think that he's so used to Kayla's take-no-prisoners flirting that he doesn't even realize when other girls like him; if a girl's not grabbing his ass or calling him her "sexy boy toy" he thinks she's frigid.

He's just as clueless about Fiona, who I'm sure would claim him in a minute if she thought she could.

Fuck, that pisses me off.

To be honest, I don't get it. I understand that he's young and good looking, that he's a whole lot younger and better looking than me. But it's still hard to believe that his looks make up for how goddamn stupid he is. Every day he does something that amazes me

97

based on the level of total idiocy.

Today his moment of stupid came as we were hammering in the joist hangers for the main floor. Both he and I were doing it, Matt because he's a moron who can't be trusted to do anything else, and me because it's my full-time job to make sure Matt doesn't accidentally nail his tongue to a 2x6.

So we were nailing the metal hangers while the rest of the crew was down in the basement doing everything else. Obviously they were wearing their hard hats and safety glasses, but I'm pretty sure they still didn't want to have anything dropped on top of them.

I think you know where this is heading...

"These nails are a bitch," Matt whined, as he worked on his first joist hanger. I was on my third, since I'm a normal human being with at least basic handyman skills.

"Just take your time," I said.

"Do we really need to fill all the holes?" He managed to drop a nail down into the basement as he spoke.

"All the holes."

"So like a Russian gangbang," Matt said, laughing.

"Focus on what you're doing."

"Jeezus, Baptiste... calm down."

I stopped hammering for a moment and turned to him. "Don't tell me to calm down. I'll calm down when you start taking the work seriously."

He sighed and took another swing at his hanger. "Shit!" he said.

I heard a yell from down below to match. I looked down and saw one of the workers grabbing her right arm.

"What the hell, guys?" she said. "I just got hit with a hammer. Do you even know what you're doing up there?"

"Sorry about that," Matt said. He looked over to me. "I guess I should have yelled 'fore'."

"That's it," I said. "That's enough. You're done here, Matt, alright? You're no good to this crew... that's for damned sure."

I expected him to say something back, maybe some weak excuse, but Matt just stared at me with a confused look on his face.

"Just find something to entertain yourself," I said. "We'll head home when I'm done. Don't be riding back on your own."

"Sorry," he said quietly.

He walked off the site and I lost track of him for the rest of the afternoon. It made the rest of my time there that much nicer. I think I even made some kind of contribution, once I no longer had to babysit.

Once the crew had stopped for the day, I walked back toward our ATVs with Gerald Archibald, the head councilor. He's not much younger than me, but with a full head of hair and a slight Cree accent.

"I guess you guys don't need any more housing," he said.

"Not enough baby making," I said. "There are probably three more cottages that we could make use of if we needed to."

"Probably won't have those cottages staying livable for much longer. You guys aren't doing any maintenance on them, eh?"

"We can't afford to. It's just not a priority for us."

"I'm not arguing with that... you guys have a lot to do."

"I'm sure you're busy, too. We haven't seen you in Cochrane lately."

Gerald sighed. "We don't go to Cochrane much anymore... not if we can avoid it. We actually had a close call on Friday... some retard with a rifle was shooting at everything that moves."

That sounded familiar. "A rifle? I think we ran into the same idiot."

"He actually took a shot at you, Baptiste? That takes a lot of balls." He gave out a little whistle.

"I didn't expect it... that's for sure." I didn't want to tell him anything more.

"No doubt, eh? You guys are probably the only ones around here who don't have to worry about being attacked."

"We have to worry," I said. "At least since Ant."

"What do you mean? What happened to Ant?"

I was surprised that Gerald didn't seem to know. I often forget just how separate the people of New Post are from the rest of us.

I guess Dave Walker and Livingston hadn't bothered sharing the news.

"Ant was murdered just over a week ago," I said. "The guys who did it called themselves The Mushkegowuk Spirit Animals. I'm not sure it was Stems."

"I can assure you that the Mushkegowuk Nation isn't involved in that."

"I don't know. Dave Walker says that no one's gotten past their gate, so I don't know what that means."

Gerald shook his head. "Sorry to hear that, Baptiste. I guess that's another reason to stick to this side of the Abitibi."

"I guess... but we all still need supplies. Unless you know of some-place that's better for scavenging? Iroquois Falls?"

"Bridge is down over there. Those idiots from Detour Lake dynamited it last month. I guess they don't want anyone crossing the river that far south."

"Detour Lake is worrying me more and more," I said.

"You and me both, buddy. They've been making up their own rules for far too long."

"So where does that leave for scavenging for you guys?"

"That's our big secret, Baptiste."

"Oh, come on. You can trust me, right?" I tried to sound like I wasn't all the serious, even though I really wanted to know the answer. Not just about where they get their supplies, but whether or not Gerald and his people actually feel like they can trust us.

He threw up his hands. "Keeping secrets means not telling any-one. We're running low on food, just like everybody else. But hey... you know us well enough to know that we wouldn't hold back supplies from you if you really needed them. Heck... if we ever find those heart pills you need... Laneradine, right? If we ever found some of those you'd be the first guy we'd call."

"I know," I said, nodding. Of course I didn't believe him, but there was no reason to tell him that.

I certainly don't hold any of it against him; we all like to pretend we'll look out for our neighbours and all that... but when things get tough, people close ranks. That's what it takes to survive. And believe me, I'll cut all ties with New Post at any point if it helps me keep my people safe.

I said goodbye to Gerald just as I found Matt waiting by his ATV.

"Ready to go?" he asked me, acting as if I wouldn't still be angry with him.

I nodded and climbed onto my ATV. The two men guarding the chain-link gate rolled open both doors, and we waved to them as we drove through.

We were driving our quads too quickly to talk to each other, which was fine by me. Conversation with Matt is like being trapped in an elevator with a talkative moron. He has nothing to say, but damned if he'll ever shut up.

We were just about up to the turnoff at Nelson Road when Matt stopped his quad dead. I slowed to check if he was alright; he had climbed off the ATV and removed his helmet.

He was trying to trap me into some kind of confrontation.

I turned around and drove over to him.

"Let's keep going," I yelled. "I have to take a piss."

"We need to talk about this."

"Fuck that... I'm going back."

"Please, Baptiste... you owe me that much."

That hooked me. I cut my engine.

"I really don't need this bullshit from you," I said.

"I don't understand. What is your problem with me?"

"There's no problem."

"You never take supply runs with me in the truck."

"You're not going to be doing any more supply runs. You know that."

That hit him hard, and I knew I'd been a little harsh.

I tried to soften my tone. "I shouldn't have let you and Ant go without me. That's my fault."

"That's not what this is about, Baptiste. You'll ride in the car with Graham but never with me. Why?"

"You're a terrible shot and you're bad with horses."

"Come on," Matt said.

"I'm not kidding. You're not an asset when it comes to scavenging. That might change someday... but that's how it is right now."

"Justin doesn't agree with you."

"Then you can ride with him. Why am I supposed to care?"

"But it's more than that. You don't really want to do anything with me. It's like you wish I didn't exist."

I shook my head. "Do you really want to do this? Do you really want me to tell you what I think?"

Matt nodded. He reminded me of a child now, a little boy who probably wouldn't even understand what I'm trying to say.

"You're a screw-up," I said. "You sit around and you make fun of me and Sara and everyone else, but when someone tries something on you..."

"Yeah, I get that."

"You need to grow up, Matt. Seriously... that's the best advice I can give you. Grow the fuck up."

"You say that, but that's not your problem with me. It's not about maturity at all. Half of Ant's jokes were about farting, but you didn't have a problem with him."

"Ant busted his ass. He only fucked around when the job was done... not before... not during... when it was done. You couldn't even hammer in a few nails today without almost taking some woman's arm off."

"Then give me a chance."

"I've given you a hundred chances. So far you're 0-for-100."

"And I guess Ant never messed up."

"Goddammit, Matt. You know he messed up... he's dead because of it. So tell me... if the guy who was way less of a screw-up than you are is buried out by the creek, what chance do you have?"

"That's not fair."

"Talk to Ant about that one. Ask him what's fair. But seriously, Matt... you know you can't just be some kind of replacement for him, right?"

"I'm not trying to be Ant," he said. "I just don't get why he was so important to you. You loved him like a son."

"What the fuck do you know?"

"That's how it is with everyone else, too. Fiona's like your long lost daughter, and you treat Graham like he can do no wrong. And since you're banging Sara we all know how you feel about her..."

"God, Matt... I need you to understand something here. I'm not your father, okay?"

"Screw you, Baptiste. That's not what I'm saying."

"That is what you're saying, asshole. And I'll tell you... I don't owe you some kind of fatherly affection. I'm not going to play catch with you out in the backyard, or teach you how to manscape your pubes. I don't owe you shit. If you can't contribute to the team, we're better off without you."

"Too bad Ant's dead and I'm still alive."

"Yeah, you know what? That is too bad. You're damn right about that."

I didn't bother to wait for Matt to find his comeback; I did want to make it home before next week. I turned the engine back on and drove on a couple hundred meters. And then I stopped to wait. I couldn't leave him out there no matter how I felt about him.

I couldn't leave that piece of total uselessness behind. Fuck.

I had to wait a few minutes before he finally started up again.

We didn't say anything else to each other for the rest of the trip, and when we arrived at the cottage I decided to make my way over to the amber rum. Fiona was close to having dinner ready, so that saved me from having to tell anyone about my day. I made it all the way to dinner without talking and when we all sat down I listened quietly to Graham as he talked about the goats, as he does most days if you don't tell him to shut up. Matt was quiet, too, and because of our combined silence Graham was at least ten minutes into it before Lisa finally closed down the topic with a cheery "I fucking hate those goddamn goats."

Then it was mostly silence.

TODAY IS WEDNESDAY, DECEMBER 12TH.

THE SUPPLY meeting this month was being hosted by the Marchands, so Justin Porter and Alain Tremblay joined Sara and I in our grain truck for the trip to the airport.

Cochrane's airport is pretty much the opposite of Pearson in Toronto, one single strip of runway and a terminal building that kind of looks like a small town radio station.

They used that airstrip mostly for the fire crews, the water bombers and the helicopters that would take the FireRangers to forward bases to fight the forest fires that would flare up every spring and summer. Last year, when the whole district was on fire or about to be, Graham and I came up here with a pile of other people, trying to keep one of the wildfires from reaching the airport by turning the concession road into a proper firebreak. Somehow we managed to save it, or rather Graham and the rest of them did, after I got cut off and surrounded with the lake at my back. In the end, there wasn't much point to saving the airport, since nothing's taken off or landed there since. We should have spent our time working to protect the town of Cochrane itself.

We only have three sets of protective gear, but that didn't cause any arguments since Sara almost always refuses to wear it. If she hadn't been chosen to chair the meeting, I'd have told her to stay home.

In the truck it's not that bad; we don't usually bother with the helmets in the cab, and I make sure we stuff Sara in the middle, with Alain driving and Justin on her right. I took a place in the back with the Mossberg, fully armoured and sitting in pretty much the same spot Ant had been sitting when those three bullets landed in his unprotected chest.

We got to the Marchands' roadblock around forty minutes early, which was just what I wanted. The two Marchand boys waved us through without bothering to ask any questions; I guess they know us well enough by now.

The parking lot was almost empty when we pulled in; I could see the Walker's white van and a couple of trucks. I knew Dave Walker was going to be a huge pain in the ass, and for some reason I was almost looking forward to it.

As if he had the guts or the sway to kick us out of the partnership.

I hopped out of the box with the Mossberg, motioning for the others to stay in the cab.

I found Fisher Livingston standing by the door beside a tall, skinny kid with a hunting rifle. Livingston wasn't armed, which didn't surprise me; I'd never seen him shoot off anything other than his big mouth.

"You can't bring your guns inside," Livingston said.

"Fuck you, Livingston," I said.

"He's right," the skinny kid said; I don't think he was older than sixteen. "No guns allowed inside, Mr. Jeanbaptiste. Same as always."

"I brought them in with me last time," I said. "And every time."

"They shouldn't have allowed that."

I sighed. I knew the rules and I'd never followed them. No one had ever called me on it before. "Well, I'm not comfortable leaving my guns outside."

"Then you can't come in," Livingston said.

I was about to tell Livingston once more to fuck himself when Sara joined us by the door.

"What's going on?" she asked.

"They won't let me in."

"It's the shotgun," the skinny kid said. "It's not allowed."

"Or the handgun," Livingston said.

"So leave them in the truck," Sara said.

I glared at her. "You know I can't do that," I said.

"Why not?"

I didn't know what to say. I couldn't get into an argument with her in front of everyone, in front of Livingston...

"Just leave the guns outside," Livingston said. "It's pretty simple, Baptiste."

"He's not leaving them outside," Justin called out from behind us. He had his rifle in his right hand. "And I'm bringing mine in, too."

"Hold on," the skinny kid said as he ducked into the building.

Another truck pulled up and I watched as a couple of the Girards climbed out, two of the brothers in their late forties both with poorly concealed holsters slipped into their belts.

I've never seen any of the Girards carrying handguns before.

"Sorry about Antoine," Denis Girard said to me. "He was a good kid." I know that Denis had always liked him.

"Thanks," I said. I nodded to his waist. "I see you guys aren't taking any chances."

"Things are getting bad out there... we ran into some trouble of our own."

"I heard..."

"It wasn't Stems, I don't think. *Dieu merci*. But we're not going to let it happen again."

The skinny kid came back out with Eva Marchand, the head of the family. She gave me a smile but I knew it wasn't a happy one.

"You can't bring the guns inside," she said.

"This was never a problem before."

"Look... everyone wants to bring in a gun now. We can't bend the rules for anyone."

"I'm not leaving my gun outside," Denis said. "We don't go anywhere now without protection."

"What are you all so worried about?" Livingston asked. "There are two men with guns blocking the road in. And there's this young man posted at the door."

"Not good enough," I said. "I need to know that I can keep my people safe."

"You're wearing a bulletproof vest."

"Sara isn't," Justin said. "And we're not going to risk her life over this."

"Justin will leave his gun outside," I said. "One of the Girards will keep a gun, and one won't. Maybe you can borrow one, Livingston, so you won't feel left out."

"We didn't agree to that," Denis said.

"That's the compromise," I said. "Take it or leave it."

"No," Eva Marchand said. "We're not allowing guns inside the building. That is the rule."

"Then we won't have a meeting."

"We don't need you, Baptiste," Livingston said. "You and Sara Vachon only get one vote anyway. And we'll just elect a provisional chair if Sara won't come inside."

"I don't give a fuck about voting. If we're not in there, there's no meeting."

Other families had arrived by that point, and they'd all gathered outside the door, fanning out behind Sara and me; I'm sure it was clear to everyone but Livingston that I had the crowd on my side.

"Please, Baptiste," Eva said. "Just leave the guns here and come inside."

"I'm not going to do that," I said. "You're going to need to give in on this, Eva."

"I won't do that."

"Then let's just have the meeting right here," Livingston said. "I'll start."

"That's not how it works," Sara said.

"Where is Dave Walker anyway?" I asked. "Does he know his lap dog has run away from home?"

"I'm representing the Walkers," Livingston said. "That's part of my role now."

"We'll need that in writing," Sara said.

Livingston reached into his jacket and pulled out a crumpled piece of paper. He shoved it at Sara with a cocky smirk.

"I need everyone's attention," Livingston said in that irritating toastmaster's tone he always used to trot out at meetings. "I'm here to let everyone know that the Walkers are withdrawing from the Supply Partnership, effective immediately."

"They can't just withdraw," Denis Girard said.

"We aren't even holding a meeting right now," Sara said. "Does anyone remember how these things work?"

"We're out of the partnership," Livingston said. "Now you know. I don't have anything else to say."

"What about your inventory?" Denis asked. "I'll bet half your supplies need to be redistributed."

"We're not redistributing anything. We're out of the partnership."

"That's not acceptable," Eva Marchand said. "The Walkers were a part of this agreement and they need to honour that. Their last inventory showed that the Walkers have more than their fair share of flour, beans, fuel... and many other things."

"We have more mouths to feed," Livingston said. "It would be irresponsible for us to continue handing out food to the rest of you, particularly as supplies are running low."

"Handing out?" I said. "I think what you're really looking for is for me to kick your ass."

"More threats, Baptiste? Is that the only thing you're capable of these days?"

I switched the shotgun to my left hand and grabbed Livingston by the sleeve of his coat.

"Hey... come on," he said. "Baptiste... please..."

I shook my head and let go. I wasn't going to hurt him; I just wanted to see if he still had a habit of groveling when reality shows him up. "You're a fucking joke, Livingston. You know that?"

"This isn't getting us anywhere," Denis Girard said. "The Walkers owe us supplies. We need to send our people to collect them."

"The Walkers are more than prepared to defend themselves," Livingston said.

"What is that supposed to mean?"

"It means what you think it means, Denis. If you attempt to cross the Frederickhouse River with bad intentions, people are going to get hurt."

"You can't really mean that," Sara said.

"What do you think will happen, Ms. Vachon? What would your friend Baptiste do if we showed up at your place threatening to take your supplies?"

"They're not your supplies," Denis said. "Those supplies belong to all of us. That's the deal."

"I need to go," Livingston said. "I'm expected back."

"You're not going anywhere," I said.

"You don't want to make this into something, Baptiste. I told you there would be consequences for your actions."

"We're getting those supplies." I turned to Denis. "Maybe a few of us should head back to Frederick with Livingston and pick up the first instalment."

Denis nodded.

"I'm coming, too," Justin said.

I heard the sound of automatic gunfire coming from the North. I grabbed Sara and pushed her toward the open door of the building.

"Take cover!" Justin shouted as he squatted down behind the engine block of the Girards' truck.

I made sure Sara was inside the air terminal building before I came out to join Justin. He'd already fired a few shots in response.

I couldn't see who was shooting at us, but I could tell that they were hidden in a line of evergreen trees, around forty meters away.

Denis crouched down beside us, as did his brother. Alain Tremblay was trying to clear everyone else out of the parking lot, pushing them into the building. It looked like the skinny kid with the rifle didn't want to go inside.

"We can use all the guns we can get," I said.

The boy smiled and I immediately regretted my words.

Alain frowned at me, but led the kid along the wall of the building, heading around the far side to guard our rear.

"Stems?" Justin asked.

"Sounds like it," I said. "Or one of his men."

"Just one?" Denis asked.

"Only one gun so far," Justin said. "But it's possible that it's a feint."

"Someone's probably sneaking around the other side of the building," I said. "That's why Alain is heading over there now."

"You guys are good," Denis said.

"We've been lucky so far."

I heard another gunshot, coming from the far side of the building. I nodded to Justin and I ran toward Alain's position.

He had the vest and the helmet; I was sure he was okay.

I poked my head around the corner of the building, and saw Alain and the skinny boy pinned along the wall. Alain had his rifle poking around the other corner, but I wasn't sure if he was actually able to see anything.

I made my way up the wall, finding a place between him and the boy, my back to a window; I knew it wasn't a safe place to stand.

"What's happening?" I asked.

"Someone was trying to sneak up on us," Alain said quietly. "I think I may have hit him."

"Let me see," I said, slipping in front of him. In the end, Alain's just good at hunting deer; he's never had to fight anything that shoots back.

I don't have the time or the energy to even begin trying to teach them all to fight a war.

I looked around the corner, relying on the helmet to keep my head in one piece. I couldn't see anyone; the only thing between us and the trees was a large piece of metal tubing. I knew that's probably where he'd taken cover; he could stay there all day without us being able to hit him.

A grenade would have been a good choice, if I'd had any.

Matt had told me there'd been three men that day out by Clute. I didn't know if Stems, if it was Stems, would have brought more people up with him from wherever he'd been keeping himself, but I knew that there'd be at least one more of them than we'd heard from so far. Maybe one of them was up with their truck, guarding it or something... but my gut told me that Stems would go all in on an attack like that.

"There's one more out there," I said in a whisper. "I don't want to take any chances until we know where that third guy is."

I heard more automatic fire, probably from that first position, in the trees. The shooter was trying to keep Justin and the Girards pinned down at their truck.

A second burst came, this one from the man behind the tubing. The shots slammed into the brick wall and shattered the glass of a full-length window. A few bullets came right through the building and cracked the window, only a few inches from the skinny boy's head.

"Move back," I said to him. "Keep away from the window."

He stepped back until he had cover by the brick.

"He's trying to keep us right where we are," I said. "So where is number three?"

"Where did they come from?" Alain asked.

"There's plenty of forest to hike through... it's not like the Marchands control anything north of here."

I heard the sound of a vehicle, but from where I was standing I couldn't see it; someone was driving up to the terminal building from the access road.

"Maybe that's the third guy," the skinny kid said.

More automatic fire came, from the trees to the north again. I heard the screech of tires followed by the opening of more than one car door.

"You guys hold here," I said.

"Will do," Alain said.

"And I need the truck keys."

Alain reached into his pocket for the keys, and once he'd fished them out he tossed them over to me.

I threw myself to the ground, crawling back toward the parking lot so the man in the grass wouldn't see me. I found my way back to Justin and the Girards, who were still crouched behind the engine block. I could see the two Marchand boys from the roadblock hiding behind their truck, too.

"I think Stems is sneaking up behind us," I said.

"I'll go with you," Justin said.

"No... I need you right here."

I held out the shotgun to Denis, who looked like he'd already emptied his handgun. "Try this," I said.

He took it and nodded.

I ran over to our truck, trying to keep as low as I could while I climbed in. I drove it down toward the runway, scanning the area for any sign of movement.

Stems could be on foot; I expected that I'd draw him out with the truck, that he'd pop out and start shooting, or maybe he'd just hold tight and wait until I'd driven right by wherever he was concealing himself.

I pulled onto the runway and followed it toward the west, moving closer to where the tarmac came right close to the edge of Lillabelle Lake. I hadn't seen anything, and it made me wonder if I'd made a costly mistake, if I'd gone south when I should have stayed up near the first two gunmen, so sure of myself that I'd given Stems and his Spirit Animals a chance to take everyone out.

I turned around and headed back toward the air terminal building, and that's when I saw something. Just a glint of reflected light... maybe nothing, coming from a small shed not far off the runway, between it and the parking lot. I tried not to slow down as I passed by. I watched out the rearview window and saw a man in a painted helmet and body armour poking his head out the door of the shed. No tiger stripes... a grinning shark.

I slammed on the brakes and pulled my SIG Sauer. I leaned out the window and took the shot.

He returned fire, spraying the truck with automatic bullets. I scrambled across the cab and out the passenger side door, making my way to the tail, instead of the engine block at the front. I hadn't even had time to turn off the engine.

My corps was protected, my head was somewhat safe, too... I

knew he might try to take out my legs, but they'd be tough targets to hit.

I reached the end of the truck and ran out toward the back of the shed, shooting at the door as I went. He hadn't been expecting me from that side, and by the time he swung his assault rifle around to find me, I was already crouched behind the shed.

I expected him to start shooting right through the shed walls, so I crouched as low as I could, hoping to hit one of his armour folds with my handgun before he had a chance to knock me down.

But he didn't shoot.

He'd already ran a good twenty steps before I realized he was heading to my truck.

He reached the truck before I had a chance to take aim. He climbed in the driver's side door and hit the gas pedal, without bothering to close the door on the far side.

I emptied the clip at the cab of the truck, but I don't think I hit him. I ran after him but obviously I couldn't keep up. As I worked to reload my gun, I watched the truck speed up on its way toward the terminal building.

I aimed for the tires on my second attempt, trying to slow the truck down. I managed to take one of them out.

The truck swerved as it neared the end of the parking lot.

I heard two shots.

The grain truck slammed into the back of the Girards' Ford F-350, splitting the pickup's bumper and lower frame from the box, which was thrown up onto the hood of our truck. Together the two vehicles careened forward into the corner of the air terminal building. The Ford pickup tore open a large gash in the brick, but that was as far as it went.

By the time I reached the scene of the collision, Justin was already there.

"Looks like Sharky is pretty fucking dead," Justin said.

The man hadn't been wearing a seatbelt, and he'd been thrown from the cab of our truck, through the windshield, and into the back of the F-350, just as it was being crumpled upward by the bumper from the grain truck. The helmet had kept his head intact, but the neck panels hadn't kept a shard of metal from slicing through his throat.

"I hope to god that's Ryan Stems," Justin said.

"I doubt we're that lucky," I said.

Justin leaned in and pulled off the helmet.

It wasn't Stems. His hair was too light of a brown, and his eyes were green. You could kind of tell that Stems was half-native, but this guy looked about as far from Cree as you could get.

I saw that Alain was still pinned to the wall, despite the hulking mess that was only a few meters away.

But the skinny kid was standing beside the wreckage, holding his hunting rifle like a trophy.

"Good shot," I told him. "And a lucky one."

I walked over to Alain.

"He's still out there?" I asked.

"I think so," Alain said. "I haven't seen any movement."

"No gunfire?"

"Nothing... nothing from the other guy, either."

"Okay... keep holding here, alright?"

Alain nodded.

I went back to find Justin, who was still standing by the wreckage. "We still have two more shooters," I said.

"I think they've run off," Justin said. "Been nothing since you left in the truck."

I saw Eva Marchand poke her head out the door.

"What is happening?" she asked. "Is everyone safe?"

"Just stay inside," I said. "We haven't cleared the area."

She didn't argue and disappeared back into the terminal building.

"Are you ready?" I asked Justin.

He nodded.

We slowly walked around the Girards' truck, me with my pistol and Justin with his rifle. We walked toward the trees, both of us crouching as low as we could. I kept my eye on the metal tubing, and as we passed far enough for me to see behind it, I could see that there was no one there.

We reached the trees and searched through them, and I found where the second shooter had been positioned, a pile of expended shells littering the forest floor.

"They're long gone," Justin said.

"They left a man behind," I said.

"Do you think Stems was one of the other two shooters?"

"I'm not sure... I'm not even sure Stems was involved in this. It all seems pretty amateur."

"Amateur? They seemed to have some pretty big guns for amateurs."

"Think about it, Justin... even with their automatic rifles we were still pretty evenly matched, especially since we have three guys in body armour. And the first guy opened fire too early, before the second was in position, and long before the third was close enough to take his shots."

"They still came pretty damned close to ramming that truck into us."

"Not that close. This just doesn't seem like something Stems would do. He's a pro."

We started heading back to the terminal building. I swooped down to pick up a couple of shells. They looked the same as the ones that killed Ant. They looked like .223s.

"They probably didn't expect us to be standing around outside with guns," Justin said. "They probably thought we'd all step inside for the meeting and leave our guns in our vehicles."

That got me thinking.

"That was the plan," I said. "Livingston would make sure that none of us were armed, including me... and then he'd deliver his message and sneak out early."

"The Walkers?"

"They'd only have to take out that one kid, and then they could just walk on in and kill every last one of us if they wanted to."

"And you think the plan fell apart when we wouldn't disarm." He shook his head. "I don't know, Baptiste... I just don't think the Walkers would try something like that."

"I guess we know who we can ask about that," I said.

∽

We returned to the air terminal building and found three of the Marchand boys keeping watch with their rifles. We went inside and found everyone else, sitting around a long meeting table. For a moment it felt like everything was just supposed to go back to normal. But that was silly, since normal probably doesn't include what I was planning on doing to Fisher Livingston.

But then I realized that Livingston wasn't there.

"Where the hell did he go?" I asked.

"I don't know," Sara said. "He never came inside."

I looked over to Justin.

"He wasn't outside," Justin said. "We would've seen him."

"He has to be somewhere," I said.

"Then we find him."

But we didn't find him. We searched for twenty minutes, checking broom closets, equipment sheds, and even an old Cessna that was parked off the runway.

Fisher Livingston and the Walkers' white cargo van had disappeared. That only made him look guiltier.

A couple of the Marchand boys gave us a ride back home, with Sara riding in the cab and the rest of us in the back of their pickup. We siphoned what was left from our truck into their tank as payment, and I think we probably lost some fuel at the end of it.

But at least no one had gotten hurt, aside from the idiot with the grinning shark helmet who came late to his own funeral.

I'm still not sure that idiot was one of Stems' men.

✍

I pushed for Lisa with the handheld once we reached the bridge. We had the Marchands drop us there, which is pretty much how things are handled these days; no one really lets other families get too close to where they live.

We met the cart not long after turning to walk down New Post Road. Graham was driving and Lisa was sitting beside him, and the back was so full that I wondered if there'd be room for four more of us.

Pretty much everyone hopped off when the cart had stopped. They gathered around us like we were something special.

"Thank goodness you're okay," Fiona said as she ran up to hug Sara. She glanced over at me, but glanced away once she saw me looking at her.

"Thank Baptiste and Justin," Alain said. "Those two are like superheroes."

"You were pretty badass, too," Justin said with a wide grin.

"We were lucky," I said. "That's all."

We all squeezed onto the cart, Alain sitting somewhat awkwardly on the bench between Graham and Lisa.

"You should have been better prepared," Lisa said.

"Was it Stems?" Kayla asked as she sat down beside me on the cart. She was visibly shaken.

"I don't know," I said, reaching around her with my arm and feeling her lean in against me. "Those guys certainly looked the part, but maybe that was just for show."

"It could have been anyone," Justin said. "I mean that. Anyone we didn't see at that meeting might have been hiding in the trees with a couple of semi-automatic rifles. The Lamarches, the Smiths... both those families didn't show up."

"But who has those kinds of weapons?" Fiona asked. "Can't be that many people."

"We have no way of knowing," I said. "It's not hard to believe that someone could have a stash of weapons they've been saving for a rainy day."

"I don't think so," Graham called out from up front. "We gathered up every gun in the district for patrolling. People were glad to help out."

"Legal guns, maybe," Justin said. "You don't honestly believe some outfitter with a secret AK-47 is going to offer it up for show and tell, do you?"

"Probably not," I said. "So we don't know who it was. Our best bet at finding out went flying through our windshield."

After we pulled up to the stable, Sara dragged me out to the dock. It seemed conspicuous to me, but maybe everyone else just thought she was wanting some kind of adrenaline-rush makeout session.

"Do you think it was the Walkers?" she asked once we were alone.

"Honestly... that's my best guess. If Stems had been running the op it wouldn't have turned into such a clusterfuck. That dead guy was wearing a helmet painted with a shark's head... it feels like someone really wanted to make that attack look like those Spirit Animal assholes. Not that Stems has ever mentioned the Spirit Animals. We don't know who they really are."

"I guess if Stems had been there people would have gotten hurt."

"I didn't say that. We weren't sitting ducks. We know how to protect ourselves."

"I know. I just don't believe it, you know? Dave Walker trying to have us killed."

"Or maybe if it was Dave Walker, he was just trying to scare the shit out of us, make us think twice before going after those supplies."

"No... that doesn't make sense. If they wanted us to be scared of them they would've been more obvious. Now everyone thinks it was Stems."

"That's a good point," I said. "So if it was Dave Walker, he probably was trying to kill us."

"That's comforting."

"Sure is... or maybe he was just trying to kill a few of us."

"Like maybe just you and Justin."

"Why me?" I asked, half joking.

"With you two gone I doubt anyone would go up against the Walkers. They'd have no issue keeping those extra supplies."

"It does sound crazy," I said. "Dave Walker outfitting his kids with big guns and telling them to go shoot people, just so they can keep more than their fair share of the kidney beans."

She leaned in and kissed me.

"Gunfights turn you on?" I asked with a grin.

"You turn me on, Baptiste. My Creole superhero." She giggled a little bit, which was adorable.

Sometimes I can't believe a woman like Sara would willingly sit on a dock with a guy like me.

3

TODAY IS THURSDAY, DECEMBER 13TH.

I WOKE up in the middle of the night to a full-blown panic attack. I'd been dreaming about gun battles, nothing that unusual for me, but this time it felt different, like I was protecting everything and everyone I loved and I was about to lose it all, and when I opened my eyes I felt ready to scream.

When it happens I feel the anxiety, but I also feel embarrassed, like I'm a wimp for not being able to handle a few scary dreams. I think that pushes it further, my panic starts to build and then I get even more ashamed of myself and the cycle repeats.

Fight or flight... what the hell do you fight when it's all in your head?

I climbed out of bed, doing my best to not wake Sara, and I found my way downstairs. From the darkness in the sky it felt like a long ways 'til morning... I knew that for me sleep was not going to be happening again any time soon.

I debated brewing myself some coffee, since I was dog tired but nowhere near wanting to go back to bed, but my mouth was dry so I decided to steal one of Graham's cans of cherry cola instead.

I sat down at the living room table, trying to calm myself by watching the lake, but the wind had picked up overnight and the water seemed more violent than usual, and all it brought me was more anxiety.

I took out my tablet and started trying to write out some more thoughts about what had happened yesterday, but for whatever reason it wasn't enough to beat back the stress.

I was breathing hard, and I could feel my heart pounding. I felt more adrenaline than I'd had in my system at the height of the attack.

It didn't make any goddamn sense.

It was like my own body wanted to kill me, like it wanted my shitty heart to explode like a block of C4.

I couldn't hold it off... I couldn't calm down... I couldn't keep going like this.

I went down to the basement, gripping the handrail more firmly than normal, because I felt like the whole cottage was shaking.

I bent down to the bottom of the pantry shelves and pulled out the red milk crate. I picked up the Dora the Explorer lunch box and opened it.

The ecstasy was what I wanted. At that moment I didn't care if it killed me.

I took one maple-leaf tablet and I swallowed it.

I went back upstairs and sat down at the table. And I waited.

It took almost thirty minutes before I felt anything, my heart still pounding and my mind racing. But slowly I started to calm down a little, and for a while I felt like everything was okay, like everything was happening for a reason, that I didn't understand why, but that I could accept it... and I could accept me.

It's hard to describe exactly what it felt like, especially now that the feeling's gone and I'm back to the same old Baptiste, always a little uneasy about the world around me. But for a few hours I was okay.

Really okay.

It wasn't the SSRI and beta blocker kind of okay, like I can barely function but at least I'm functioning... it was something more... something that I definitely need to feel again.

Sara and I took over the dining room table after breakfast, sending everyone else out so we'd have a chance to talk. It wasn't that we were trying to keep any secrets; we just didn't need people asking stupid questions, or trying to add their own uneducated opinion about how much rice we consume in a month. Sara knows better than anyone else; she keeps the counts, and she has the stats from a year and a half, broken down by person. It's a little creepy at first, when you realize that she actually has a different estimate for each one of us when it comes to how much toilet paper we use to wipe our individual asses. Matt uses the least, apparently, and Sara's marked herself down as the one who wipes her ass the most... I'm old enough to know that women wipe other places, too.

I think I'll attach some of her charts to this journal someday.

"We're running low on flour," Sara said as she stared at her tablet. "We'll be out by August 12th of next year."

"Is that just us, or the Porters and Tremblays?" I asked.

"All of us... assuming their counts are accurate."

I sighed. "You know they aren't."

"Everything's a guess," she said. "I just assume the Tremblays have less than they tell us and the Porters have more... so it all evens out in the end."

"August... that's a problem. A few weeks ago you were talking about eighteen months of supplies."

"I know... a few days ago we thought we'd be trading eggs and milk for some of the Walkers' grain."

"And I'll bet no one else has any grain or flour to trade."

She shook her head. "We can cut back on consumption," she said.

"Or we can eat the Tremblays."

She laughed. "But that's a good point, actually. We don't do much fishing... we could eat more meat and cut back on carbs. Probably not a bad thing."

"But either way... we're going to run out before next winter's over."

"Looks like."

"Goddamn," I said. "I really wanted one year to work on getting it right."

She reached out for my hand. "I know," she said softly. She gave me a smile that was almost relaxed; I knew that it wasn't, really.

"We don't even have the equipment yet... and we certainly don't have the fuel. Honestly, Sara, I don't know how you didn't see this coming."

She pulled her hand away. "Are you kidding me? I told you about this."

"No you didn't... I'd remember if you'd said 'Hey, Baptiste, we're all going to starve'."

"There was nothing stopping you from taking a look at the numbers. Everybody has just as much access to the data as I do. Don't try to blame me for the Walkers dropping out." She furrowed her brow. "Maybe you should blame yourself for shooting out Dave Walker's tire?"

"You heard."

"Yeah... we've all heard, Baptiste. I don't think anyone was all that surprised, to be honest."

"You weren't there... those assholes were walking all over us."

"It was stupid. What you did was stupid. So now instead of blaming me for knowing how to count, maybe you should focus on some kind of plan to get some crops planted in the spring."

"Yeah... I know."

She smiled again. I didn't deserve that, but it was nice to see. "So... a plan?"

"We'll have to start searching. Graham thinks that we should be able to find electric motors in just about everything we need."

"Just about?"

"It might be tough finding an electric combine. We don't have enough diesel to run one."

"But that's for harvesting," Sara said.

"Yeah."

"So we don't need it to get started. And if we can't harvest with a machine, we'll have to harvest by hand. We may need help from New Post, but trading away half the crop is better than letting it rot."

"This is all assuming we find everything else we need."

"I know... and assuming you guys don't run into any marauders. I think you and Graham should start bringing someone else along with you."

"I want Lisa to stay back... in case there's trouble at the cottage." And she was the only one who knew what the plan was if things went worst-case.

"I don't mean Lisa," Sara said.

"I'm not taking Matt. He'd end up shooting one of us before he hit a marauder." Or he'd end up spending the whole time blubbering about how I don't love him like a long lost idiot son.

"I don't mean him, either. Maybe Justin... or Alain..."

"I don't know about that," I said.

"Why not?"

"I don't know... I trust Graham... I know what he'll do... I can't rely on those guys the same way."

I'd once thought I could rely on Justin.

"Well you're going to need to get used to them," Sara said. "We're stuck together for the foreseeable future."

"I know what you're saying... so does that mean that we're no longer considering that first idea?"

"Which one?"

"Eating the Tremblays."

"Let's try our hand at fishing first."

I leaned over for a kiss. She didn't seem at all interested, but she still let me.

I like that about her.

∽

So I have a theory about Will Ferrell... the actor from the *Zoolander* and *Anchorman* trilogies, not the guy in Nevada who opened fire on a busload of migrant workers. Ferrell's better in an ensemble cast, rather than as a leading man; the stronger the other characters, the better Ferrell does. That's why he's remembered for movies where he isn't the only star.

I used to talk about this kind of thing with guys I worked with, but now I don't have anyone around me who'd watched a movie older than the moon base and the skinny glove fad. Sara won't even watch movies, which is about the most ridiculous thing I've ever come across. So I had two choices, to either watch the stuff that Ant and Kayla had collected, or show some of the classics to a new generation. Luckily, Fiona refuses to sit through most of Ant's slash-and-slice flicks, so that leaves plenty of room for our ongoing Will Ferrell Film Festival.

Tonight was *Zoolander 3*, where they shoehorned his Mugatu character into a plot about an award ceremony; I've always liked it better than the second one, but nothing beats the gas fight from the original or Hansel being so hot right now.

Fiona and Kayla joined me in the living room, and Matt was there, too, since I didn't have a dog kennel to lock him into. I was glad to see that the girls were laughing about as much as I'd hoped. I have a theory that if I get those two laughing together often enough, they'll start hating each other a little less, maybe even to the point of me not expecting their relationship to end in murder-suicide.

Then came the orgy scene.

"Isn't that you, Kayla?" Fiona asked, pointing at the screen.

"Where?" I said.

Fiona got off the couch and stuck her finger at a red-haired woman in one of the hot tubs, pausing the movie.

"My hair is blond," Kayla said. She already sounded unimpressed.

"Forget the hair," Fiona said. "It's the facial expression."

"That does look like you," Matt said.

I could see it, too. That scrunched up come-hither face Kayla makes that is significantly less sexy than her usual look, but hey... it's Kayla, so it still kinda works.

"So I'm just a dumb slut who loves orgies," Kayla said.

"Well, that escalated quickly," I said. But none of them had seen *Anchorman* yet.

"It's like I've got a fucking 'S' burned onto my forehead."

"Super Kayla?" Matt said.

"Just because I used to dance. As if that makes me... what... a prostitute?"

"There's nothing wrong with prostitutes," I said.

"Fuck you, Baptiste. I'm not a prostitute. And you guys shouldn't fucking treat me like one, alright?"

"What are you talking about?"

"I know how to weld," she said. "I know how to wire up a battery."

"Okay... still... what are you talking about?"

"You don't think I'm capable. You think that I'm just all ass and tits and good for nothing else."

"I never said that, Kayla."

"Well your girlfriend certainly has. I guess I'm not godly enough to contribute around here... unless I'm on my back."

"That's not fair," Fiona said. "No one's ever said that about you."

"Just hear what you want to hear, then."

Kayla stood up and left the room. I heard her stomp upstairs.

I looked over at Fiona.

She looked back at me.

"Do we just... let her go?" I asked.

"How should I know?" she said.

"I'll handle it," Matt said.

I decided not to stop him.

She yelled for a while, and after around twenty minutes he came back down.

"Can we take it back to the orgy scene?" he asked as he sat down beside Fiona.

"I'm fine with that," I said.

But when I saw the red-headed hot tub Kayla the second time, it wasn't funny. I felt bad. When someone tells you just how awful they're being treated, you always hope that you're not one of the bad guys being described.

But I was one of them; I wasn't looking past the beautiful blond girl who used to tour the handful of hotels between Hearst and North Bay that had a floor for dancing. I wasn't taking Kayla seriously.

And that wasn't her fault at all.

TODAY IS FRIDAY, DECEMBER 14TH.

THE TREMBLAYS were late to the meeting today as usual. Unlike the Porters, who always come as a unit even when I ask them not to, when it comes to dealing with the rest of us the Tremblays are generally just Marc and Alain. Sometimes I forget they both have wives and kids back in the long and flat one-story cabin up near the beaver dam, or at least I forget until I remember Marc's wife Suzanne and that sexy way she rolls her Rs. For whatever reason, the men are in charge over there, and though I don't know their wives that well, I'm sure it couldn't be any worse to put them or the coffeemaker in charge instead.

I think I've gone too far in the wrong direction sometimes, asking for consensus when I should have given orders. Based on the agreements Sara made, our cottage gets three votes, and the Porters and Tremblays get two apiece; I consider myself to have an unsaid veto, too, since there's no way in hell I'd let the newcomers override us on something that matters.

Our three votes mean that Sara and Graham make sense at these meetings, but most of the time Matt and Kayla come along, too, leaving just Lisa and Fiona to watch the cottage. More than three people is unnecessary as far as I'm concerned, but Sara doesn't really want me harping on that.

We were meeting at the Porters' cottage today; they had put out a full breakfast of eggs and pancakes, which would have been a bigger gesture if the eggs weren't all coming from our hens. But it still smelled good, and I certainly didn't hold back when it came time to refill my plate.

Sara chaired the meeting, just like she chairs the Supply Partnership, assuming it still exists. She doesn't do it because she likes the sound of her own voice, as lovely as it may be. She does it because she loves writing — and then following — the agendas, and she knows full well that the rest of us don't. I guess if she wasn't leading the discussion she'd be silently plotting mass murder.

"So that brings us to inventory," she said from her place at the head of the table, her eyes staring down on her notes. "I have a list from the Porters, but nothing from the Tremblay household."

"Sorry," Alain Tremblay said. "I'll drop something off in a few days."

"This keeps happening," I said. "This is becoming a problem. I don't like being a hardass —"

"You love being a hardass," Sara said.

"Okay then... I love being a hardass, so I can't stop myself from pointing out that you guys aren't taking your counts seriously enough."

"We don't see the value," Marc Tremblay said.

"Excuse me?" Sara said. "Did you really just say that?"

Marc just smirked while his brother Alain stood from his chair, looking as though he were preparing to give a speech. "We know there's value in it," Alain said, "but we have other priorities. We need firewood and we need fuel... that's most important to us right now."

I decided to stand up, too. "You also need food and medicine," I said. "We just don't know how much you need because you're not keeping track. Your priorities are screwed up, guys. If you run out of firewood sometime mid-winter we can give you some of the wood we're storing for next year, or hell... you can even go out and chop down some balsam fir and burn it the same day as long as you've still got hot embers in your stove." I looked over at Sara; she hadn't bothered to look up from her papers, so I kept going. "And if you don't have fuel for your truck, you just don't drive it. We have a cart and horses that never run out of gas, and the Porters have one of those tiny electric shitboxes that are so popular with the kids these days. We've all learned how to share with others."

"Just get your counts in as soon as you can," Sara said. "We need to stop thinking like we're three little silos. We need to start acting like one big team. We're all in this together, right?"

Alain nodded and sat down, while Marc muttered something that I couldn't make out.

I saw Kayla roll her eyes; I think she wanted Sara to notice, too, but I know Sara wouldn't have given her the satisfaction.

I sat back down while Sara continued on to new business.

Rihanna Porter raised her hand. Her husband was sitting beside her with a quiet but serious face, while her kids were messing around a little too close to the wood stove.

"What is it, Rihanna?" Sara asked.

"Some good news," she said. "Justin and I found a couple tanks of diesel fuel up by Silver Queen Lake."

"What were you doing up there?" I asked. I checked the map on my tablet just after I spoke, and I was glad to see that the lake was pretty much where I thought it would be. People around here know lakes and rivers the way I know the streets between Dundas and Bloor; I'm not sure how they remember them all.

"We went for a drive in our shitbox. We didn't think there was a problem with going up there."

"You'd said you were going to check for batteries on 2 and 3. Silver Queen is a long way from there."

"We went to visit the Smiths," Justin said. "I didn't realize we needed a permission slip."

"You need to stay safe. That's all that matters here. Maybe you don't remember when people tried to kill us two days ago?"

"Well, either way," Rihanna said, "the Smiths are gone. Took both their trucks and left."

"They left?"

Rihanna nodded. "They're gone." She didn't seem all that concerned.

"Did you get that diesel from their place?" Sara asked.

"They didn't leave anything of value there. Cleaned it right out."

"But with the Smiths gone," Justin said, "there's no reason not to start cleaning out the other cottages around there. There are over fifty homes on that lake... I'd say several truckloads' worth of supplies."

"How can that be?" I asked. "The Smiths must have gone through and taken everything they could get their hands on."

"The Smiths were lazy. They had the road blocked off to the rest of the world, so they just grabbed whatever they needed at the moment and left the rest right where they found it."

"We'd like to borrow that big diesel truck from the Tremblays," Rihanna said. "Justin and I can make a few trips to empty out those cottages. I'd guess there's a years' worth of supplies up there."

"I'm not comfortable with that," Marc Tremblay said.

"You're not comfortable with what, exactly?"

"With you taking our truck up to Silver Queen Lake. If anything, Alain and I will take the truck and one of you can squeeze into the cab and come with us."

"That doesn't make sense," Justin said. "We've already gone through and made a list of what's there. It'll be much faster for us to go grab it."

"It's too bad the smaller truck's gone," Marc said. "Maybe you guys should get your own damn truck... there are plenty of them sitting around in Cochrane." He sounded pretty pissy for a guy who used to make runs with Justin.

"We brought back the fuel," Rihanna said. "Just let us use the truck, please? We'll get it done more quickly if we use the team we're used to."

"I think that makes sense," Sara said. "They can retrieve the supplies while the rest of us get to work on the five hundred other things we need to get done before January hits."

"I'm still not comfortable with it," Marc said. "I think that should be the end of it. I don't owe you guys anything."

I couldn't let it drop right there; too much was being left unsaid.

"Sara's too nice to say it," I said to Marc, "but you're busy enough as it is. You guys are behind on inventory and your place is nowhere near ready for minus forty. If you think you're going through a lot of firewood now..."

"It's fine," Alain Tremblay said, his voice much friendlier than his brother's. "Take the truck. But I'm going to count the nickels in the ashtray." He gave a smile as part of his concession.

Rihanna laughed. "Actually, it's the air freshener we're interested in," she said.

"So that's settled?" Sara said. She received a few nods.

I had a feeling that nothing was really settled as far as Marc Tremblay was concerned.

After a few more topics that were more than a little boring, Sara called for adjournment, and we were soon on our walk back to our cottage. The Tremblays had driven over on their ATVs and they flew by us almost as soon as they had climbed onto their vehicles. They still use fuel like it'll never run out.

"I'm surprised you backed me up on that truck thing," Sara said to me as we walked along the rutted road.

"You shouldn't be surprised by that," I said. "I don't agree with you on it, but I wasn't about to argue."

"So you don't agree, huh? You know that Marc Tremblay was just being pigheaded."

"I know, but that's not the issue. There was something odd about the way the Porters were insisting on doing it all themselves. There's no reason for them to want to avoid sharing the work."

"You think they're trying to hide supplies from us?"

"It's not that. It's just a feeling that they're not being completely honest with us. I'm not sure I believe their story for being up at Silver Queen Lake in the first place."

"I get what they're doing," Graham said. "Marc and Alain can sometimes be more trouble than they're worth. They're always questioning every decision, pulling their passive-aggressive bullcrap whenever they're feeling underappreciated, which in their minds seems to be all the friggin' time."

"It doesn't get us any further towards working together," I said. "The best way to whip the Tremblays into shape is to get them used to how we do things around here."

Sara laughed. "You've walked into this one, Baptiste," she said. "Now you have no choice but to come with me this afternoon. We're going to help the Tremblays count their inventory."

"Help them? Who said anything about that?"

"It's called an ambush. It'll work better if there's no warning beforehand."

"Ah... I like the way you think," I said. "And the way you look... and the way you smell..."

Sara laughed again as everyone else seemed to groan. We soon broke into two groups, with Sara and I bringing up the rear, our bodies locked together with our arms. I gave her a quick peck on the cheek.

"I wish we had more privacy right now," she said.

"I like an audience," I said.

She pretended to be offended. "*Mon dieu,* Baptiste... you're a sick, sick man."

"I'm sick, eh? That's an excellent idea. I'll bet we can find a place in Cochrane that has just the outfit."

"I don't want to know..."

I leaned in and whispered into her ear. "Sara the slutty nurse. That might be my new favourite."

She pulled back and gave me a little shove. "You're a perv. Besides... you just had your birthday. I think you blew your chance."

"Your birthday's coming up."

She gave me her widest grin. "I already have a costume picked out for that."

"Sexy accountant?"

"Nope... beekeeper. My biggest fantasy is layers of protective clothing to keep you off of me."

"So... sexy beekeeper."

"Very *unsexy* beekeeper."

"I can still make it work. Remember, Sara... I reached puberty in an age when they still expected people to pay for porn."

"Keep it up, Baptiste, and you'll be magically transported back to the era of being a lonely virgin."

I laughed. "At least being a virgin again will cut back on some of the itching between my thighs."

Alanna and I never really had much sex. When you're as busy as we always seemed to be, you tend to look at the person you're shacked up with as some kind of adversary. If only she'd turned the dishwasher on, or remembered to move the wet clothes into the dryer... then maybe I wouldn't be so goddamned stressed... and then maybe I'd want to have a little bit of midweek action.

On most days the house was a mess, and as douchey as it was I just didn't have the energy to do anything about it, and by the time I was ready for bed, I was really ready for bed, and sex was the last thing on my mind. Well... sex with another person was the last thing on my mind. It's funny how, after a few years, sex becomes just a variation on masturbation that's often more effort than I felt like making. It was so tempting sometimes to just tell her I'm too anxious to sleep or to do anything else, so then I could go rub one off on the living room couch.

I remember the last time we had sex; it was the night before I left for up north, and we were so tired from packing that I think at first it felt more like a chore for both of us. But I started to kiss her neck and run my fingers along the line of her auburn hair, just above her right temple and the little divot from the frame of her glasses, and soon I was back to those days when we were first dating, when we were so horny for each other that we'd rush home and have sex on our lunch breaks, when things were so hot that I sometimes felt like my heart would explode and I'd die right then and there, young but especially happy.

So I kissed her some more and drew one finger down her cheek, and I listened to her breathe until I knew she was ready. I went down on her then, because I had the urge to do it and because she hadn't asked me to, and I was there with my tongue and my fingers, hearing her moans and feeling her body tighten and contract. On some nights that's enough to make her climax, and that's just what happened that night. I moved my body over-top of hers and I entered her and I looked her in the eyes and told her I loved her, and at that moment I meant it, and after a few minutes I finished... and then we laid together on the bed, both of us satisfied and for the moment, both of us happy with the other.

I think the sex with Alanna was better because of all those times she pissed me off. I think it was hotter because I spent half my time wishing she'd just leave me alone. I don't think good sex is driven by love; I think it's fueled by the kind of passion you get from occasionally hating the person closest to you.

I love Sara, but it's not the same; she still seems too good to be true, so I know we need a little more time for reality to set in. In many ways she's more sensual than Alanna, more willing to touch and be touched, as long as it's in the right places.

Back when I was married, the idea of being with someone different and not knowing where to touch them was something I would have given anything to experience again. But when I'm with Sara I think of Alanna, of the way she loved feeling my lips on her neck, the way she loved the tracing of my fingers around the little ridge of her belly button.

One day I'll probably start to be so accustomed to Sara's body and bringing her pleasure that there will be nothing left that surprises me. On the one hand I hope that it helps me recapture some of what I had with Alanna, but I also worry that I'll feel too guilty to enjoy it. It's funny, but I've never felt like I'm cheating on Alanna with Sara. I think I'll only start feeling that way once the sex really starts to pick up; one day it'll be the best sex I've ever had, and that's the day I'll feel like a cheat.

∽

After dinner we gathered in the living room as usual. I would have rather heard another selection from Ant's diary or played some poker, but I knew that it was time to talk about the problem everyone was hoping would go away.

"I'm concerned about the Tremblays," I said as I paced around the room.

"They're not pulling their weight," Lisa said. "Everyone knows that."

"Glad I'm not the only one."

"But what the heck are we going to do about it?" Graham asked. "When those guys aren't falling behind, they're crapping on every idea we have."

"I think you guys are being too hard on them," Fiona said. "They've had a rough time."

"We've all had a rough time," I said.

"But they came to us because they weren't going to make it other-wise."

"That's true," Sara said. "They weren't willing to take any of us in a year ago, so I can't imagine it felt good for them to show up here begging for help."

"I'm fine with charity," I said. "But at some point the charity stops and reality kicks in. There are seven people over there, using up supplies faster than the rest of us and providing very little in return."

"They know we don't have any options," Lisa said.

"What do you mean?"

"They know that you're too nice to force them out. So they don't have to work very hard. Hell, if they stopped working tomorrow I'm sure we'd still keep feeding them."

"And giving them our firewood," Graham said.

"Indentures aren't seeming so bad anymore," Lisa said.

"That's not funny," Sara said, almost growling as she spoke.

"I'm not joking... people like the Tremblays wouldn't last a week in Timmins. They'd have been thrown into a pit mine so that nature could take its course."

"We're not even going to discuss that kind of garbage," I said. "Let's just put them in a situation where they either have to do the work or they have to admit that they're not contributing. I seriously doubt they'd just give in and admit that they're useless. They'll have to come around."

"But they already have plenty of work they're not doing," Graham said. "You already went through the list with them."

"It's too easy for them to half-ass-it when they're working in their cottage. They could hide in that place all day pretending they're working and getting fuck all done." That made me think of weekends on Sackville Street, the todo lists I conveniently misplaced and the mancave I'd built in the basement that was less a workshop and more a masturbatorium. I felt myself smiling. "I know what that's like," I said, running my hand on my chin. "I happen to be an expert on that subject. My wife used to call me 'the invisible husband'."

Sara glared at me, probably more from surprise than anything else. She gets uneasy when I talk about Alanna, so I don't do it very often.

"Invisible husband?" Lisa said. "Probably a reference to your missing manhood."

I was surprised that she beat Kayla to the joke, but then I realized that Kayla wasn't even paying attention. She and Matt were staring out the window toward the lake. Matt was sulking, still butthurt over what I'd told him half a week ago, but Kayla just seemed vacant, like she'd checked out for the evening. I'd seen her angry; I saw that last night. But this wasn't something I'd seen from her before.

"So we need to send them out somewhere?" Sara asked.

"Marc and Alain, at least," I said. "I think they're the root of the problem. It's a safe bet that those guys aren't the ones doing laundry or food prep, either."

"So we do need to send them with the Porters," Graham said.

"I say we split them up. We'll send one to Silver Queen Lake and take one with us to start gathering up farm equipment."

"The Porters won't like that," Sara said.

"So that's one good thing about it," Lisa said with a smirk.

"It's a bad idea," Matt said from his place by the window. He'd been listening, apparently; I guess his pity party wasn't soundproofed.

"I'm afraid we'll need more than that for a counterargument," I said, trying not to sound like more of a dick than usual.

Matt looked right at me; he seemed more angry than hurt. "They hate each other," he said. "Putting the Porters and Tremblays together would be a disaster. Hell, I wouldn't be surprised if someone accidentally got shot or run over on that trip up to Silver Queen Lake."

"This idea is getting better and better," Lisa said.

I smiled and nodded at her; Lisa being witty is a rare treat, at least when I'm not the target. "But seriously," I said, "does anyone agree with Matt that we should keep spoon-feeding the Tremblays?"

"That's not what I said," Matt said, sounding a bit like a spurned toddler.

"Matt has a point," Sara said. "Some of the relationships here are starting to come apart. As hard as it's been trying to bring three families together, it'll be impossible to come up with some kind of mutual settlement if people start splitting off."

"Isn't that the same argument I gave for not letting them in?" I asked.

"The solution was never to let people die. We just need to make sure that everyone stays together. So we need to decide where the real risk lies. Are we better off pushing people together and risking some kind of feud, or should we let the Tremblays keep on with their crap until we all want to drown them in the lake?"

"Tempting," Lisa said, "but I don't really want to drown anybody. If we're going to run into trouble with people not getting along, it's better it happens now and out in the open."

"That makes sense," I said.

"It does," Sara said.

"Then I think we've got a plan. We'll push and push until someone loses their shit."

"This'll be fun," Lisa said. "It's like a psychology experiment."

"Like rats in a maze," Sara said.

I grinned. I had another memory from Ant coming to me and I took a minute to let it play. It was where he channeled George Carlin, about how a rat will do a lot of gross things but that he will never fuck a dead rat.

We'd all known that the mouse in the trap was dead, the bar having snapped its neck instantly. But Ant had posed that second mouse so well... so lovingly... for a moment I had thought old Carlin was wrong.

Sometimes I think anyone who never met Ant will start thinking he was a psychopath, since everything he did was at least a little crazy. But he was a good kid, and he would never have done anything to hurt someone.

That's more than you can say about me. Just ask Matt.

Some people call them pranks, but I think of them as life lessons.

So you thought that glass held some apple juice, but it was actually mineral water with a small sample of my freshly squeezed urine? Lesson: always give your drink a safety sniff before you pound it back.

So you cracked open your porn mag expecting some pretty girls, but some joker pasted in replacement parts from an old copy of Field & Stream? Lesson: if you don't lock up your fap lit you should come to expect that every playboy bunny you see will have been made into a tastefully-constructed reverse mermaid with the head of a lake trout.

My bro used to do the same for me, teaching sixteen-year-old Ant about life by jizzing in my shoes, and by pushing me to meet girls by sending them care packages consisting of a forged love letter and a pair of dirty gotch, complete with a skid mark of legendary size. I made a promise to both Almighty God and my child psychologist that I'd get my brother back one day.

That day was on his nineteenth birthday. Obviously being a good French Canadian Eduard had started drinking back before he had the need to shave, but we still had a family tradition of getting the birthday boy wasted on the cheapest beer available, and always on the first day it's actually legal to do so.

I planned the whole thing, and had him drive us a good hour away to friends in Val Gagne in his pride and joy, a 2006 Ford Mustang with the original gas motor, a V8. It was metallic blue with leather seats that had never seen a single stain. Eddie made it clear to me that there was no way in hell he'd let me drive us home afterwards; as far as he was concerned, we were in it for the duration, sleeping over even if we weren't wanted. That was fine by me; I'd worked it all out beforehand.

The thing about a really good single malt is that it tastes so bad to a beer drinker that they'd have no idea if you were to add a little something extra to the glass. That something was ipecac, and for those of you who aren't well-versed in inducing vomit, it made that feeling of "I need to puke" come to my brother much earlier and stronger than anyone would expect. It was so unexpected, in fact, that I was able to convince Eddie that we needed to get to the hospital. We took the Mustang... and I drove.

And for some odd reason, the trip was extra bumpy.

Eddie's car stank like nothing else for a good two months after that, and it's no surprise that I was never given a second chance to drive it.

But as my brother was kicking my ass the following evening, I could see in his eyes that he was proud of me. That's my favourite memory of him; not just because of how he looked at me, but because even eighteen hours after that very special single malt, he actually had to let go of my battered neck and run to the bathroom for one last puke.

That's a moment I'll never forget.

KAYLA

Kayla is a little bit slutty... not in the bad sort of hand job for a dollar way, but in the good friends with benefits way, where she makes you feel desirable without wasting time trying to convince you that you're any sexier than all the other people she's slept with.

At least that's the impression I get; I am sexy, so I'm not part of her target demographic. She's talked about sleeping with me, I mean, hey, she is a woman, but I've never taken her up on it... not yet, anyway.

But why not, you may ask... well, first of all, gentle reader... just shut up and let me do this. And secondly...

I like the idea of unconventional sex, which doesn't only mean doing it in a hot air balloon or various activities involving whipped cream and mayonnaise... it also includes seducing women who haven't really given much thought to wild and casual sex, women who really do call it "making love" or "being intimate"... Kayla never calls it that, since she'd fuck you for hours without actually letting you get to know her.

I get to know her by watching her strike the arc on the welding table, or strip a bolt, or trip over her own feet. I love that girl, but I laugh every damned time she falls flat on that pretty face of hers.

I don't think Kayla feels much of a connection with any of us; I get the feeling that she shut down that part of her life years ago, that she decided that she was too self-sufficient to worry about friends or family. My father used to call that kind of self-loathing feminism, saying that it all started with the birth control pill and that women have been getting more mentally unstable ever since, that they are trying to be like men while still being women. I think my father's full of shit on that and all other subjects of any importance, but I do believe that Kayla's got some serious issues in that slutty little brain of hers.

I wouldn't be surprised if one day we wake up to find her lifeless body hanging from a rafter in the barn, with a handwritten note that says "I came, I came again, and now I'm bored". People like Kayla don't usually live that long.

TODAY IS SATURDAY, DECEMBER 15TH.

THE PORTERS weren't happy with our plan to bring along one of the Tremblays, but they relented when I made it clear that it wasn't a suggestion.

They chose Alain, which didn't surprise me, since I'm sure he's less trouble than Marc.

The Porters left with their new helper early yesterday morning, while the sky was still dark. I saw them off before going back upstairs to sneak in a few more minutes of sleep.

Sara woke me up just after sunrise, and after a quick breakfast Graham and I hitched up the cart for the trip into town. We didn't have a truck of our own anymore, and while we may decide to look for a new one, I didn't want to do that just yet. We don't really have enough fuel to run our own truck right now, anyway.

Marc arrived just as we were about to go looking for him.

"So I'm your new pet," Marc said as he climbed onto the cart, a hunting rifle slung over his shoulder. "What happened to all the work I'm supposed to be doing around here?"

"This is more important," I said. "We want to find and bring over an electric tractor before the roads get any worse. We may end up trying to tow it somehow."

"You should have done it before winter, then."

"We were too busy saving your life," Graham said. "Maybe you should keep that in mind."

"Maybe you should watch what you say, motormouth."

"Maybe all of us should just shut up for a while," I said. "The best way to find ourselves in some real bad shit is to get so wrapped up in bitch-slapping each other that we're not keeping an eye out for trouble. As much as I hate the both of you, I hate the idea of dying with you idiots that much more."

That got them quiet, either because they were both thinking of how much of an asshole I am or because they'd realized once again that we're on the same goddamn team. If things go bad, and I know one day they will, we'll only have each other for backup. That's a pretty important thing to remember. People who forget that are the ones who don't make it back home.

The busy season for dead bodies is in the winter, and we were getting close enough to winter to make me nervous. The body count isn't just from people freezing to death in minus forty, but from bad guys who start getting a whole lot more active once the leaves fall and the snow starts to fly. Back in Toronto crime season was summer, and if there was ever a time when you'd lock your doors and be a little more careful where you went after dark, it was June 'til September. Around here those are the safer months.

Justin Porter told me once that marauders are a little like Vikings. He said that they'll come to your home and kill you anyway they can, and they'll gladly take your women if they get the chance, but that during the summers they act just like everyone else, growing vegetable gardens and mending fences. He said that you could work alongside a man for a whole summer and never suspect he's a marauder until winter comes and he slits your throat while you sleep.

This may sound strange coming from me, but I think Justin may have a problem trusting people.

Graham drove while Marc and I kept our eyes open for movement; I was on the bench beside Graham while Marc kept to himself near the back of the cart. He'd brought a travel mug along, and I'd noticed him nipping more than a few times already; I knew enough about Marc Tremblay to know that he had more than coffee in there.

The Porters had left the gate on Nelson Road wide open, and not for the first time. I hopped down and closed it behind us and made a mental note to kick their asses.

When we arrived at the bridge over the Abitibi, Marc hopped down to unlock the West Gate. He held up his hands like they were a catcher's glove and gave me his trademark smirk.

"I need the keys and dongle, boss," he said. "If that's okay with you."

I threw the key ring down to him.

"And you're a real pleasure to have along with us, Mr. Tremblay," I said.

He shot me the finger before tackling the locks.

It pisses me off how some people are about the damned keys. Everyone wants their own copy, but everyone has a chance of losing them. So I keep all of the keys and alarm dongles, and parcel them out as needed, kind of like how a car dealership handles test drives; if one goes missing, I'll know before the day is out, and I'll head over to the gate and change out whichever locks are compromised. Just like the safes, it's a pretty low tech solution, but like always those are the ones that work. Between the locks and the tripwire alarm, we've controlled the bridge for well over a year; aside from the sanctioned trade runs between the Walkers and Detour Lake, no one from outside our team has crossed through that gate since Ant put it up.

Marc unlocked the gate and waited, taking a couple shots from his mug, as Graham drove the cart through. He reattached all three locks and reactivated the alarm, then slowly climbed back up.

"Do you really think this will stop anyone?" Marc said as we got underway again. "I mean there's a dozen other ways to get across the river, especially once it's frozen."

"We can't stop people from crossing the river," I said, "but we can stop people from carrying much of anything across with them."

"I'm sure they can carry over enough firepower to finish us off."

"That's not why we put the gates up."

"Then what the hell are all these goddamn gates for?"

"If a bunch of marauders want to come over and try to kill us while we sleep, a gate isn't going to stop them. But it does stop a bunch of assholes from backing their truck up to our cottages and cleaning everything out while we're not home."

Marc just laughed at that.

We kept riding for a few more minutes in silence, but I knew that he hadn't really dropped it.

We passed by a stretch of scorched forest next to a small muddy pond; I remember the family that lived in the metal-roofed and fire-ravaged farmhouse beside it. They'd had four kids, two of them the funniest twin girls, about ten or eleven, who'd interrupt the town meetings and make a roomful of people laugh as they did it. That family had believed Fisher Livingston, when he'd said that there was a safe road that ran around the barricade Souls of Flesh had set up at Fletchers Lake to pick out indentures and kill the remainder, that if they followed him, they could make it all the way to Temiskaming, where good people were waiting with open arms and more food and fuel than they knew what to do with. They were out travelling on that so-called safe road when The Fires came.

They'd have been better off surrendering at the roadblock. I'm sure the father and his sons would have gotten dropped in the pit, but maybe those two little girls and their mother could have survived.

I think of those twin girls every time we pass by that burnt-out house, and I think of those girls every time I see that smug bastard Livingston's face. It still makes no sense to me that he could have survived when everyone who believed in him is dead.

I heard Marc give us a snort.

"So listen," he said. "You're telling me that we have no real protection against people trying to kill us?"

I didn't really want to get into it, but I couldn't exactly ignore him. "We have guns," I said. "Until we can find a rocket launcher that'll have to be enough."

"This is just one big joke."

"What the heck is your problem anyway?" Graham asked.

Marc's gaze shot over to Graham. "I have a real big problem with you, asshole. Do you think I don't know?"

"That everyone hates you?"

"You kissed my wife, you little shit. I should kill you for that."

"Why don't you guys kill each other later," I said. "We have work to do, and these little whine sessions aren't helping any."

"You know what?" Marc said. "You assholes deserve whatever happens. I guess we'll just keep building up a nice homestead for Stems to come and take over whenever he wants."

"I don't think you've done much building here," Graham said. "All you seem to want to do is whine like a little baby."

Marc's eyes widened as he glared at Graham, his face turning red. He stood up, dropping his mug, and started clambering towards the front of the cart, tugging on his rifle with one hand.

I put down the shotgun and jumped over the bench to stop him.

"Sit down, Marc," I said as Graham slowed the cart.

"You sit down," Marc said. "I don't think you have any kind of clue, you know that? You're just some big city asshole who knows nothing about security. It's no wonder your stupid Cochrane Protection Committee was a complete failure. And your goddamn Supply Partnership, too. A string of pathetic failures from a pathetic old man."

"Sit down or I'll sit you down."

"I'm not going to sit down. Fuck you, Baptiste."

I sighed. "Why does everyone keep saying that?" I said, trying to cut down the tension.

"Get out of my way."

"You need to calm down. Take a seat in the back and relax, okay?"

Marc placed his second hand on his rifle, lifting it upwards. "I'm not going to take a seat. Not while you and that idiot there are putting my family's life at risk. So we'll just sit back and hope no one shows up with bigger guns than us... great strategy. Maybe when they come we can offer up our wives and kids so they'll leave us alone... oh, yeah, that's right... you don't have a family to worry about. You don't have to worry about anyone but yourself, eh, Baptiste? I guess that's why you don't give two shits about keeping the rest of us safe."

"Don't piss me off —"

"So get out of my way, old man. You're not in charge of anything. I'm going to go up there and crack your little groupie's head open... and you're just going to have to deal with that."

He tried to push past me. I stopped him.

I don't remember much about hitting Marc Tremblay; I can remember that I hit the butt of my shotgun against his temple at a bit of an angle, and that his body twisted as he fell, slamming against the cart, his rifle falling over the side and onto the gravel shoulder. And I remember seeing the blood, and staring into his frozen eyes, wondering if I'd really knocked him out or if he was just in some kind of shock.

I felt Graham nudge past me and I watched him kneel down beside Marc.

I kept looking into those eyes.

"Holy..." Graham said. "What did you do to him?"

"I think I fucked him up." I didn't really know what I'd done.

"This looks bad, Baptiste... I don't think he's going to make it. There's a lot of blood here..."

I knelt down beside Graham to take a look. Marc's chest was still rising and falling and I could see his breath in the cold air. "He's still breathing," I said. "That's good."

"There's no way we can take him back home on this cart. The ride'll kill him."

"We don't have a choice. We can't just build a field hospital out of twigs and horse shit."

"He's going to die," Graham said.

"Neither of us knows enough to make that call."

"What do you think is going to happen here? What's the best thing that can happen? One of us stays here in the middle of nowhere with him while the other goes home and turns the Porters' little car into an ambulance? Then we drive him back to the cottage for treatment, after he's spent a couple of hours bleeding in the dirt?"

"We'll just have to risk taking him back in the cart," I said.

"He's going to die."

"Then we set up in one of those houses up the road. We can start some kind of fire to keep him warm."

"Okay," Graham said. "Let's try that."

I took some of the hay that was leftover from the hayride and tried to make a little bed. Graham and I moved Marc onto it, and I knelt beside him as Graham regained the reins.

The horses didn't know a slower gait, and in a way I was glad Marc wasn't conscious as we bumped along the road. Graham stopped us in front of the nearest house and joined me alongside the bed of hay.

By then I had regained some of my senses and I knew what Graham had been trying to say. I reached down and placed my fingers against Marc's neck. I waited for the pulse and it didn't come.

"I think he's dead," I said. I buried my head in my hands and started to cry.

Graham and I arrived back at the cottage around lunchtime, with our stories sorted out between us. We had Marc laid out on the hay, his eyes closed; we had nothing along with us to cover him, so it looked almost like he was just having a nap, until you noticed the blood.

Sara came out to meet us.

"Marc's family isn't here, are they?" I asked.

"Lisa's helping them put up some storm windows at their place," she said. "What happened?"

"H-he had an accident," Graham said, stuttering as he spoke

"He's dead," I said. "Tripped and hit his head on the side of the cart."

"*O mon dieu,*" Sara said. She climbed onto the cart and knelt beside the body. She lowered her head and whispered a prayer in French, her words quiet and quick.

"It was my fault," I said, unable to keep silent.

She wrapped her arms around me. "It's no one's fault."

I held her close to me and shut my eyes. I wanted to believe her, that I wasn't to blame. I could try and think that he'd provoked me enough, that he'd truly threatened our lives, that somehow I was justified in taking a man's life.

I wanted to believe that I hadn't just taken away a woman's husband, that I hadn't just stolen the father from two teenage boys.

But I don't believe any of that.

My dad died when I was fifteen. He wasn't murdered and it wasn't a tragic accident or some terrible run of bad luck; he had a bad heart and he didn't listen to his doctor. They didn't have emergency defibrillators back then, at least not at the supermarket, and when he collapsed he pulled an entire display of mandarin oranges down with him. He died long before the ambulance could reach him through the mess of evening rush hour along Dundas Street.

He left me that bad heart of his, along with his temper, and I'm not sure which one has cost me more.

Graham and Sara went together to see the Tremblays; I didn't have the balls to go with them. I'm sure Sara gave a good reason for my absence, and I doubt me being there would have made it any easier.

I spent the rest of yesterday in my room, not reading, not sleeping... not really thinking that much about it, either.

I can't change what's happened.

I can't change what I've just become.

Kayla came to see me after the sun had set. I guess Sara hadn't gotten back from the Tremblays, since she hadn't come up to check on me; I wondered if Alain had arrived home yet, to hear the news about his brother.

Kayla knocked on the door, but she came in before I had a chance to answer. I hadn't bothered to turn on my lamp, and I think she was surprised to find me sitting on the bed, fully awake. I turned on the light to let her know she was welcome.

"I brought you some food," she said. She spoke slowly and gently, in a tone I'd never heard from her before. She put a plate down on the nightstand, with two slices of untoasted bread covered in dark red jam. "Home-baked bread and raspberry jam... it's always been my version of comfort food." She reached into her back pocket and pulled out a small silver flask bearing the inlaid outline of an eagle. "And some comfort drink," she said with a slender smile.

"Thanks."

"Fiona made it with her new breadmaker. The one Graham got from Marc." She sighed. "It was nice of Marc to find that for her."

I nodded. I hadn't heard any of that before, and I didn't want to hear it then.

She sat down beside me, putting her hand on my knee. "You're a good guy, Baptiste."

"That's what they tell me." But I didn't believe a word of it.

"I haven't been the same old Kayla lately... I'm sorry for that."

"I don't know why you'd need to be sorry."

"I... I just feel like I haven't been able to add much to the group."

"Don't ever doubt how much you do for us, Kayla. Or how much you mean to us."

She leaned over and kissed my cheek. "Thank you," she said. She took a deep breath and squeezed my knee. "I've never told you about my older brother."

"No, you haven't."

"He died when I was seventeen... around five years ago. He rolled his car on Highway 101 just outside of Timmins. He wasn't drunk or anything... it was just icy and he lost control..." Her words trailed away as she took another breath, tears starting down her face. "That's who the tattoo is for."

"What tattoo?" I asked, not that I didn't know about it.

She pulled her shirt down off her left shoulder, showing it to me: a bald eagle clutching a rose, under a banner that read "My Heart, Undone".

"I like it," I said. "I always have."

"It was just so icy. He was tired, too; we both were. He'd driven me down to Timmins to pick up Mom's car... first time I'd taken it out of town and I'd had to leave it there when the battery went. We were driving back home and I was following right behind him..."

She dropped her head into her hands, her whole body shaking as she started to cry.

"You don't have to tell me," I said.

"I couldn't bring myself to get out of the car. I just pulled over and sat there. I didn't call for help or nothing... I just stared at his license plate, reading those upside-down letters over and over again. He was already dead, but I didn't know that."

"I'm sorry... I'm not sure why you're telling me this."

"I don't know... I just thought it might help you to hear it."

I put my arm around her shoulder. "It does help," I said. "Thank you."

"I've never wanted to be that girl who lost her brother. Maybe I try too hard to be someone else... I don't know. I know it's not the same for you, since you didn't know Marc that well... but I just... I don't want you to carry it."

"I don't have a choice. Every time we lose someone I'm going to carry it. But I'll be okay... really."

"Are you sure?"

"I'm sure. It was just an accident."

It had been an accident. I had just wanted to stop him; I hadn't meant to lose my temper, to hit him so hard...

She leaned in and kissed me on the cheek. "Take care of yourself, Baptiste."

"You, too."

She smiled once more as she left the room.

I didn't feel like eating, but after all she'd shared I felt like I couldn't risk her thinking I didn't appreciate what she'd done. Once

I'd finished the bread and jam, I started in on whatever was in the flask. I think it was rye, and it wasn't very good. But as I fell asleep, I was grateful that Kayla had trusted me enough to be herself with me, if only for a few minutes.

TODAY IS MONDAY, DECEMBER 17TH.

YESTERDAY I decided to ride up to Silver Queen Lake with the Porters. I didn't want to be anywhere near McCartney Lake and the mourning Tremblay family.

I remember Justin and his wife Rihanna from before the fires, when they would come to the town meetings at Tim Horton Centre, and sit near the back. I hadn't known more than their faces, since they'd never raised their hands to speak and they'd always left right when the meeting adjourned, ducking outside before most people had even stood up from their chairs.

I think the first time I'd spoken to either of them was on the morning they'd come to the gate, asking for our help. I didn't even know that Justin had served in the Forces, and I certainly had no idea what he was capable of. Back then, I hadn't ever known about the things he and Marc Tremblay had done.

It's over an hour and a half to Silver Queen Lake, and the route the Porters took was on gravel that was in pretty bad shape. We skipped Cochrane entirely, but we didn't have the same option for Clute; there's only one road to Silver Queen Lake and it goes through Clute, and whatever roadblock that might be there. It's the same road Matt and Ant were taking on their way to bring eggs to the Smiths, the same road where Ant was killed and the man with the tiger striped helmet laughed his head off.

I wasn't sure those supplies could be worth the trip.

The Tremblays' truck had only the front bench, so it was pretty tight up there with all three of us, especially since we all wore riot suits and I insisted on keeping all three helmets and vests up front along with my shotgun and their hunting rifle.

We'd be ready to suit up and fight through whatever opposition or barricades we found.

But Clute was quiet, and we continued on.

We listened to Green Day, of all things, on the way up, with Rihanna quietly starting to sing along every once in awhile as she drove, before she'd catch herself and glance over to me, with a slightly embarrassed look in her eyes.

We didn't really talk at all, and I was okay with that. The truth is, I know full well that Justin and I would still get along if I wasn't careful, that I'd start forgetting how much I wanted to stay angry with him. I remember how much I hated them both before, when all I knew of the Porters was that they'd turned Sara away when she'd begged them for help.

Justin hadn't even made his standard offer, to take her and her group somewhere else, to trade them for diesel or a couple boxes of condoms. I still wonder why he hadn't. Maybe he'd thought Sara and Kayla weren't worth much, but no one could be that stupid. More likely he'd known enough about Lisa to stay clear of the whole bunch.

I know Sara's done her best to let the past go, not that it doesn't flicker back from time to time. At first I'd hated them as much as humanly possible, like I was hating them double because Sara didn't. But it didn't take long for Justin to start acting like a friend, and after a little while, I guess we were friends.

I don't want the same shit happening again. I'll work with the Porters, sure, but I can't afford to like them.

Silver Queen Lake is a lot bigger than McCartney Lake, and it has enough cottages that I was already feeling winded when we arrived, thinking of how much work there was to do. Usually when you scavenge, you spend more than half your time just wandering around looking for stuff, especially these past few months, so there isn't that much lifting and loading in a day; it's more like a scavenger hunt than helping someone move. I had a feeling the latest job was going to be quite a bit more intense in the amount of hauling.

"We've been working from the north shore around to the south," Rihanna said as we dressed in our gear inside the cramped cab of the truck; she'd stopped at the junction right before the woods gave way to cottages. "We've done six, so that leaves just over fifty to go."

"You're kidding me," I said. "There's no way we'll be done in the next few days."

"It's taking longer than we expected," Justin said. "That's good, actually. We're finding more than we first thought."

"I thought you already took inventory of the supplies."

Justin laughed. "We checked out a couple of cottages, sure. But we haven't even been inside more than a dozen so far."

"So we don't even know what's inside."

"That's what makes it exciting," Rihanna said. "Maybe we'll find some videos or books or something. I'm getting pretty tired of watching the same six movies on my tablet."

"To be honest, guys," I said, "I'm worried about safety here."

"You weren't worried before," Justin said. "Isn't that what the helmets and vests are for?"

"How sure are we that these cottages are all empty?"

"The Smiths had a roadblock here. A big old Dodge truck. They would have noticed if there were other families trying to get in and out."

"We don't know enough about how the Smiths handled things," I said. "We don't really know what was happening up here."

"We know the Smiths pretty well," Rihanna said. "I've known that family all my life."

"That's not what I mean. There are probably two dozen families left around here right now. How do we know that someone else didn't know the Smiths well enough to know they were leaving? Maybe someone else has already laid claim to these supplies."

"We were here first," Justin said.

"So you think. But I doubt that would stop anyone either way. And considering that the Smiths weren't at the last Supply Partnership meeting, I'm sure more than one person has wondered if they took off."

"So what is it you want us to do?" Rihanna asked

"Let's take a tour around both sides of the lake, check for any vehicles, or signs of life. Maybe we'll be able to tell if there are different sets of tire tracks visible."

"Other than ours?" Justin said. "There's no way to know for sure if someone's been here."

"Well obviously. Look, just humour me for an hour, and then we can get back to work."

"I didn't realize bringing you along would suck up so much of our time."

"I'm such an asshole wanting to keep us alive."

Rihanna laughed. "Good point," she said. "Guess I'd better check if we've got something to listen to that isn't Green Day."

We followed the road along the south shore of Silver Queen Lake, our vests strapped on and our helmets on our laps. There appeared to be more than a few sets of different tire tracks along the road; I climbed out at a few points and checked the impressions from the treads. There were at least two different vehicles, maybe more. It was hard to tell. And for all I knew they were from the Smiths. I just didn't know.

It didn't look to me like anyone had stopped in at the first few cottages. The first one had an overturned tree blocking the front driveway that would have been too big to drive over, but small enough to move. A good number of them had their doors and windows boarded up, with no sign that anyone had tried to pry the boards off.

It made me uneasy. If another family had come to scavenge, I would have expected them to have stopped at the first cottage, or if the impromptu tree barricade had scared them off the one, they would have tried the others. I didn't make sense to bypass the boarded up buildings; those had the best chance of having the most supplies.

In my little notebook I keep a list of all of the families we know about, whether they're part of the Supply Partnership or not, along with where we think they're living, and what vehicles and weapons we know they have. Sometimes we've visited other families ourselves, particularly around Christmas and New Year's, but other times all we know about a family is second- or third-hand knowledge. And even with that, I know we don't have a full list.

There could be other families that we think are long gone, or new arrivals from Smooth Rock Falls who aren't big on Ryan Stems and his Mushkegowuk elders, or even refugees from Timmins who'd rather scrape by up here than sign their lives away to Sons of Flesh back home.

I checked the pages for any mention of families up near Silver Queen Lake. The Barrs, the Shiers, the Vezeaus... all of them were stationed somewhere around here, but like Justin had said, the Smiths were supposed to have had full control over Silver Queen Lake.

"Could be the Chapleaus," Justin said as he looked over my shoulder.

"I think they live on Bentley Lake," Rihanna said.

"No, no... Bentley's where the Barrs live now."

"I don't think that's right..."

"It doesn't matter," I said. "There's no way to be sure. But if someone's living up this road, we'll find out soon enough."

"I think this is a waste of time," Justin said.

"I don't care. We're doing it."

"Let's just do it," Rihanna said. "It'll be fine."

Rihanna kept driving, slowly enough that we had time enough to scan each yardsite. Over a dozen empty cottages so far; I knew we'd be at the end of the road soon.

"There," Justin said, pointing out ahead of us on the right. "A pickup truck."

I looked at the truck, an old gray Toyota pickup, parked in front of a two-story A-frame cottage with a glass front. The bed of the truck was covered with a large green tarp, and under it was an uneven bulge that reached higher than the roof; it reminded me of Afghanistan, and of a very different time. I already knew from what Matt had described that there was probably a machine gun mounted under that tarp.

"Looks like an old-fashioned technical," Justin said. "That's gotta be Stems."

Rihanna stopped the truck.

"Put on your helmets," I said.

Neither of them argued with me.

"They probably know we're here," I said.

"What do we do?" Rihanna asked.

"We need to go," Justin said. "We're not prepared for a fight."

"Keep your heads down," I said. "Let's see if they come out."

I couldn't detect any movement, aside from smoke rising from the chimney.

"They aren't just scavenging," I said. "It looks like they're living here." My gut told me they'd been here for a while, maybe even several days. "So do we really have a reason to think this is Stems?"

"I think the Chapleaus have a Toyota pickup," Rihanna said.

"Are you just saying that because you think the Chapleaus live around here?"

"I'm not sure. I think that's their truck."

"It's Stems," Justin said. "I know it is."

"I guess it doesn't matter who it is," I said. "I'm going to assume they're dangerous."

"We need to go."

"This isn't worth getting killed over," Rihanna said.

"We'll go back and bring up a second vehicle and some help," I said. "We throw up a roadblock of our own on the north shore while we empty out those cottages."

"So we waste more fuel we can't spare?" Justin asked. "Let's just go back to the north shore. There's plenty of stuff up there."

"It's not safe."

"It was safe enough before you came along."

"Sure it was... do you even remember if there was smoke from that chimney yesterday? Or the first day you were up here?"

Justin shook his head. "We need those supplies."

"We need to do this right."

I started to think it over in my head. The little electric car could make the trip, but I'd feel safer finding something more sizeable to bring up. A new grain truck or maybe even bigger. And then we could fill one truck up while the other stood guard, and then we'd switch. Five or six people could get the work done quickly enough.

But I wondered if I was being overcautious. If Justin and Rihanna hadn't noticed the Toyota and the chimney smoke before, whoever was there may have just arrived in the past day or so. Perhaps by the time we returned they'd have their own roadblock set up.

And I didn't know for sure what was under that tarp.

But the outline was too familiar.

"I need to know more," I said. "Rihanna, turn us around and head back up the road... slowly."

She nodded and turned the wheel.

"I'll meet you guys up at the mile road," I said.

"Don't do this, Baptiste," Justin said. "You're no good to us dead."

"Have a little faith in me." I looked to Rihanna. "Turn us around... please."

As Rihanna drove the truck away from the cottage, at a snail's pace, I slowly opened the passenger door and lowered myself out onto the gravel, taking my pistol but leaving the shotgun behind. I ran in a crouch toward the trees, across the road from the cottages and the lake.

I waited there until Rihanna and Justin were well past the next few cottages. Then I threaded my way through the woods, until I was about two hundred meters from the cottage. There, I crossed the gravel as quickly and quietly as I could, sheltered from sight by a sharp bend in the road.

I wrapped my way around the garage and the shed, until I was crouched beneath a small window on the east side of the cottage. I waited there, listening for the people inside.

I heard a door open, and then several sets of boots, walking down the wood steps. I peered around the corner to see two men walking toward the Toyota, dressed in black armour, with painted helmets.

A tiger and a bear. Two of the men who'd shot Ant.

Both men had what looked to me like AR-15s slung over their shoulders. I was pretty sure they were the same guns used on Ant and at Cochrane Airport.

One of them pulled off the tarp, while the second man climbed into the box, placing his weapon down. The gun mounted on the back of the truck was much heavier duty than I'd expected; I didn't recognize it, and it looked closer to an anti-aircraft gun than something like what we used in Afghanistan. The first man then climbed into the cab, and backed the truck down the driveway toward the road.

They were headed after the Porters, just far enough behind that Justin and Rihanna wouldn't know what was coming.

I grabbed my handheld and pushed for Justin.

"Justin... you there? Over." I tried to speak softly in case someone was left in the cottage. There was likely another one in the cottage. A man with a shark helmet had died at the airport, but what about the other one Matt had described, the one with the coyote?

"I'm here. Is everything okay there? Over."

"The Toyota's coming for you. They've got a bigass machine gun mounted on the back. You need to get out of there."

"You're kidding."

"I'm not kidding. Step on the fucking gas. Over."

"Shit."

I readied my pistol and rushed the door of the cottage. I swept through as best as I could remember to do, checking each room on the main floor before making my way upstairs.

The first bedroom was empty. The second was not.

I recognized both girls from before The Fires. Tabitha Smith and

Natalie Girard; the two of them were only a few years older than Fiona. Both had their wrists ziptied to the bedframe and neither of them had a shred of clothing on their bruised bodies.

"It's okay," I whispered as I held my finger to my nose.

Tabitha started to cry.

I left them there, while I cleared the rest of the second floor.

I then came back, and cut them loose with my leatherman.

"How long have you been here?" I asked.

Neither of them answered right away. I wanted to ask if they were okay, but the question seemed ridiculous.

"It's been around three days," Natalie said.

"We... we were headed back to my parent's place," Tabitha said. "But everyone was gone when we got there."

"They left?" I asked. "Uh... without you?"

"I don't know what happened... the house was empty. They didn't even leave a note. It doesn't make sense." She began to cry again.

"It's going to be okay. We've got to go."

I had the girls wrap themselves in bedsheets and I rushed them downstairs. There was no sign of their clothes or any boots, and oddly, no sign of any clothes in the entire cottage, so I had them wait on the front steps while I made my way to the garage.

The door was locked, so I kicked it open. There was nothing inside, no car, no ATV.

"Dammit," I said. I walked back over to the porch.

"Don't you have a car or something?" Natalie asked.

"I had a truck. But things have gotten a little messed up."

I grabbed my handheld and pushed for Justin again.

"Justin? Rihanna? Are you okay? Over."

I hoped that the silence was only because they'd driven out of range.

"Are you there?" I asked. I turned to the shivering girls, standing barefoot beside me. "We need to get moving."

I led them silently across the road and into the trees, and we ran farther up the road, the wrong direction from where I'd said I'd meet the Porters. Of course, I didn't expect them to come back anytime soon, assuming they were still alive.

After five minutes of running in the woods, I knew the girls would need to get out of the cold; it wasn't winter yet, but it was cold enough to hurt.

I took off my riot suit and clothes, everything short of my under-wear, and parceled it all out as best as I could between the girls. Each girl took a sock on one foot and a boot on the other. I had them lean together, hidden against a tree, and the two of them stood like shiver-ing flamingos as I made my way to the nearest garage.

I approached in a straight line up the driveway of an older cottage, right to the overhead door of the small single garage. Once there, I reached down to see if I could pull it up, but it didn't surprise me that it was locked. I made my way towards the side door

It looked old and flimsy enough that I might be able to bust it down. I had to take a running start, however, as I threw my shoulder against it, since I no longer had a boot left to kick the door in. I had to launch myself against it twice more before the door gave way; by that point I could barely move from the pain of repeatedly smashing my shoulder against the wood.

Inside the garage, I didn't find a car or an ATV, but I did find a riding lawnmower. I wasn't sure if that was worth anything to me. I also found a smelly pair of work boots on top of a toolbox that I was barely able to squeeze onto my near-frozen bare feet.

I went back and retrieved the girls, each one limping across the road with one boot and a wet sock, and we found our way inside the cottage with the help of a crowbar from the toolbox.

I didn't know if the Spirit Animals would be able to find us, but luckily I still had a contingency holstered on the belt I'd hung over my shoulder, since I was no longer wearing pants.

After scrounging up some musty clothes for Tabitha and Natalie to wear, and some less than appetizing food for them to eat, I found myself a pair of binoculars on the lakefront veranda and I peered out over the lake.

The way the shore wrapped around a bay, I could see a corner of the A-frame cottage, and I could make out a thin wisp of smoke still rising from the chimney. I hadn't taken the time to check, but my guess was that the stove was wood and not propane, and the small amount of smoke likely meant that they hadn't returned to throw more wood on the fire.

It was still three hours until dark, so I had no reason to expect any lights to come on as an indicator; the wood stove was the only sign I had.

I could expect once they'd returned that they'd come looking for the girls; and if they came looking, I'd see the truck. But if they didn't give a shit that those girls had gotten away... well, then I guess they'd just get back home and stay there.

Either way, I wasn't sure how we were going to get past them. It was too far to expect the girls to travel with me on foot and through the woods, until we reached the nearest family I felt I could trust; even by car, the Marchands were a half hour away. And trying to crowd three people onto that riding lawnmower would be even more ridiculous.

Our best chance would be to wait until I knew they'd left their cottage again, and start looking for some other form of transportation, hoping to find it and then to escape before they returned.

Of course, I couldn't actually see where their truck would be parked from where I was standing. All I could see was that little billow of what I'd guessed was wood smoke.

I went from the porch back into the cottage, to check on the girls. It was warmer there than it was outside, but since we couldn't light a fire without giving ourselves away, it still wasn't much above zero.

Tabitha and Natalie were huddled together on a couch, neither of them doing much, other than shivering.

"You girls doing alright?" I asked.

"We're okay," Natalie said. "Thanks."

"I wish I could be more help right now... this isn't really going according to plan."

"I just wish I could have a shower," Tabitha said.

"I'm sorry," I said. "I could probably try heating some water with the lawnmower battery, but I think there's a good chance I'd set myself on fire."

Both girls nodded ever so slightly; neither one seemed close to a smile.

"I'll get you girls out of here. It's just going to take me a little while."

"We know," Natalie said. "We feel safe with you, Mr. Jean-baptiste... probably safer than we'd feel with anyone else right now. I know you'll take care of us."

I nodded, unsure of how to respond. I certainly didn't want those girls to know just how little faith I happened to have in myself.

I heard the noise of an engine at least an hour after the sun had set. I looked outside to see the pickup truck, its lights off, barely visible aside from the glint of the moonlight.

The girls were sleeping; I felt no need to wake them. We were better off being as quiet as possible.

I watched and waited as the truck drove by, not slowing down or stopping as it passed us by.

Once it was gone, I waited by the window, knowing that it would come back our way soon enough, as they turned around at the end of the road.

It was back within twenty minutes, but by that point they'd sped up and the headlights lit up the road in front of them

The rest of the night passed, and morning came without any further sign of the Spirit Animals and their Toyota. The wood smoke had faded completely now, and it was starting to look like they had not bothered to stay.

Natalie found us some cereal for breakfast, and even some powdered milk and bottled water to complete the meal.

"This tastes much better than it should," I said, as I sucked up the last of the milk.

"I've been drinking powdered milk for months," Tabitha said. "I'm not sure I'd even like the real thing anymore."

"Well, all we've got is goat's milk," I said. I quickly realized that I sounded like a jerk. "Just ignore me."

"We've got goats, too," Natalie said. "But we still use powdered milk to make up the difference. And like everything else, we're starting to run low on it."

"I've wanted to ask you girls about something, but I don't want to make you uncomfortable."

"Go ahead," Natalie said. "Just ask us."

"Did you know the men who attacked you? Did you recognize them from before?"

"I didn't know them. Normal-looking guys... uh... white..." She looked over at my half-Haitian face. "Not that white is normal..."

"I'm just special," I said.

"I don't think they were from here," Tabitha said. "I wouldn't be surprised if they came from another province. Or even the States."

"Why do you say that?"

"I don't know... they just seemed different."

"Different how?" I could see that she was becoming more upset. "You don't need to answer right now."

"I think I know what she means," Natalie said. "Everyone around here walks around like they're still a little in shock. We all lost people in the fires, even those of us who still have our families. But these guys... they seemed more excited than heartbroken... like this was almost a game to them. A game where they seemed to have learned the rules long before the rest of us."

"That explains their equipment," I said.

"What do you mean?"

"They might be ex-military. I've known guys like that. Sometimes the guys who come back really aren't okay..."

"Like PTSD?" Natalie asked.

"Kind of... we all lose something when we've been deployed. Some guys never really came back in. This might have seemed like an opportunity for them."

"An opportunity," Tabitha said. "So that's what you'd call it."

"I'm sorry. I don't mean to minimize what they've done."

"It was a roadblock," Natalie said. "After we realized that Tabitha's family had left... we were almost back through Clute when we ran into them... they had those animal helmets on, and one of them, with the tiger helmet, was standing in the back of the truck, pointing that mounted gun right at us. He started to laugh, and he took off his helmet so we could see the grin on his face. That's when I knew they weren't going to let us go."

"They would take shifts," Tabitha said.

"But one of them liked to wear his helmet," Natalie said. "Visor tilted to dark. He kept it on the whole time, like he was the only one who didn't want us to know who he was. Maybe we would have recognized him from before The Fires. I'll never forget that helmet. The coyote..."

"I'd know him if I saw him again," Tabitha said. "I'd know."

I wondered if I'd know him, the man with the coyote helmet. Was it Ryan Stems himself? It's no secret that he's always liked the younger women; everyone in the district knew that.

"I don't want to be an ass," I said, "but why were the two of you out there on your own?"

Tabitha shook her head. "It was stupid. I got into a fight with my parents and I took off on my bike."

"Your bike?"

"My bicycle... I know, I'm an idiot. I rode all the way into Cochrane, telling myself that I'd be better off on my own. That's when I ran into Natalie's uncles. I stayed with the Girards for a couple of days, and Natalie was driving me back home. Since I hadn't run into any trouble on the way down, we thought we wouldn't run into any problems heading back."

I turned to look at Natalie. "And your parents just let you go off on your own?"

Natalie's cheeks turned red. "I didn't tell them we were going. I was going to take Tabitha home and then I was going to head over to see you guys."

"To see us? Why?"

Natalie blushed some more. "To see Antoine. I wanted to see how he was doing."

"Ah." I felt my heart drop.

"How is he doing?"

I hesitated. "Oh, Ant? He's doing good."

"Has... has he mentioned me at all?"

"Let's talk about that later. Right now I think we should think about getting out of here. I think those guys left last night, and I'm not sure when they'll come back."

"So they've just given up on finding us?" Tabitha asked. "Don't they care that we know what two of them look like?"

I didn't feel the need to answer that. "We need to find a car or an ATV... something that can get us away from here."

"I think I know where there's a car we can use," Tabitha said. "The Blackwells left a couple of old cars at their place... it's only a few minutes away."

"What about keys?" I asked.

"I'll bet the keys are just where I last saw them. On their key rack."

"And fuel?"

"They're both gas engines... we were going to eventually drain them for one of our generators, but we never got around to it. There should be something left in the tanks."

"That's probably all too good to be true," I said. "But I'm overdue for some good luck."

"We all are," Natalie said.

And I felt like an idiot all over again.

We travelled together on foot to the Blackwell's old cottage, Natalie and Tabitha a few paces in front and to the left of me, closer to the trees.

We passed by the cottage where the girls had been kept, but the truck wasn't there. There was no sign that the Spirit Animals had stayed the night.

We got to the Blackwell's without seeing or hearing the Toyota, and once I broke in, we found the keys just where Tabitha had expected them to be. After some impromptu siphoning from one car to the next and emptying a half-full gas can in the garage, we had a rusty old Honda Fit with three quarters of a tank.

And we were lucky enough that the gas hadn't spoiled enough to keep the engine from turning over.

I had Natalie drive, while I sat in the passenger seat, staring out with the binoculars I kept from our hideout. Tabitha laid down in the backseat, clearly exhausted but nowhere near sleep.

I wasn't just looking for the Toyota; I was watching for any sign of the Porters, but not sure I wanted to find anything. Hopefully they were back at McCartney Lake, telling the sad story of how I got left behind, and doing their best to make sure that no one came rushing back to find me.

As we neared the bottleneck near Clute, I could see Natalie tensing up.

"Don't worry," I told her, "if they're up there, I'll see them long before they know we're coming."

"I know," she said. "I just can't help it."

I put my hand on her shoulder.

"Please don't do that," she said sharply.

"Sorry."

I went back to scanning the road ahead.

"Something's there," I said.

"Oh, god..."

"It's not a roadblock... I see a couple of vehicles..." I strained my eyes to see more. "A white van and a green truck." I knew both of them. "That's our truck... and I think the other is the Walkers."

"Are you sure?"

"I know that I'm not looking at a gray Toyota. I'm sure about that."

I heard Natalie sigh. She looked over to me and shot me the slightest of smiles.

I wasn't surprised to see that it was Dave Walker and Fisher Livingston who were eyeing us as we approached. Justin and Rihanna were there, too, standing alongside the other two and looking no worse than before.

"You girls don't need to get out of the car," I said. "You can just wait here if you'd like."

I climbed out of the passenger seat and walked over to the Porters.

"You guys are okay," I said. "I really didn't think you would be."

"Thanks for the vote of confidence," Justin said.

"Ryan Stems," Livingston said. "A gray technical with a mounted machine gun." I was expecting more sneer from him.

"Only saw two guys in helmets," I said. "With AR-15 rifles and that big mounted gun. Did you know they carried those kinds of weapons?"

"I thought you knew, Baptiste."

"Who are those girls?" Dave Walker asked.

"Natalie Girard and Tabitha Smith," I said. "They were being held against their will up there."

"You saved them."

"I guess I did."

Dave Walker frowned at me. I could tell that he wanted to keep hating my guts.

I appreciated the effort.

"So what happened, Justin?" I asked. "Did they come after you guys?"

"They started to," Justin said.

"There's no way you could have outran them."

"We didn't... we outgunned them."

I almost laughed. "Bullshit."

"They turned around once we got in sight of the Walkers," Rihanna said.

"They just let you go?"

"I don't think they're stupid," Livingston said.

"What is that supposed to mean?" I asked.

"If they know who you guys are, they would have known that you wouldn't be an easy target. Once they saw us coming up the road they must have decided not to take on an even larger group. I'll bet they're a little scared of you, Baptiste."

"They have two semi-automatic rifles and an anti-aircraft gun, Livingston... even with my armour they could have turned me into confetti. Had I even been there."

"I doubt that," Dave Walker said. "I'm sure you would have taken one or both of them with you."

"They're not about to risk being wiped out," Livingston said.

"It doesn't make sense," I said. "Ryan Stems decides to cross the Driftwood River and start a war with just two or three of his closest friends?"

"Who knows?" Livingston said.

"Well, we have no proof either way that it was Stems," Dave Walker said. "Not yet."

Not until I run into the man in the coyote helmet.

"Is that what this roadblock is for?" I asked. "Are you hoping they'll just fall into this clever little net of yours?"

"It's not a roadblock," Walker said. "Not yet."

"We were actually trying to figure out if you were worth saving," Justin said.

"You guys've been here all night?" I asked.

"The truck's been here all night," Rihanna said. "We don't really have enough diesel to be tromping around the district. But Fisher drove us home last night."

I wasn't pleased with the first-name basis. "So how did you get back? Don't tell me Livingston stayed the night."

Rihanna chuckled. "You didn't notice our little shitbox," she said. She pointed to their little electric car parked a little up the road. I noticed a familiar idiot sitting in the front seat.

"And you brought Matt," I said.

"He wouldn't stay put."

Say what you will about Matt, he still seems to want me to like him, enough that he'd want to help. Or perhaps he had just hoped to see my lifeless body for himself.

"Don't tell me you guys were actually planning on coming back for me," I said.

"We weren't going to leave you there," Livingston said.

"You'd have loved that, eh, Livingston? Saving my ass so I can't keep telling you to kiss it?"

"That was one of the perks."

I shook my head. "I respect the idiotic sentiment." I looked back to the little rusted Honda. "I've got to take those girls home."

None of us spoke as we made our way south towards the Girards.

I had Natalie take the extra long way around Cochrane, since I didn't have the energy to deal with whatever we might find in town.

I knew I had to deal with the two or three remaining Spirit Animals. It wasn't about revenge, for what they'd done to Ant, or to Natalie and Tabitha; those men would strike out again at someone else... probably not us, not yet... but someone.

I won't be able to sit by and hope someone else kills them first.

At one point I'm pretty sure I could hear Tabitha snoring, and I was glad that at least one of the three of us was getting some sleep.

"I need to ask you," Natalie said to me as we neared Bondy Lake. "What is it?"

"Would you ever consider letting us come live with you?"

"Why would you want to do that? You have your family."

"I don't want to be with my family."

"Hold on... when you were on your way to see us... were you hoping to move in with us?"

She started to cry. "I don't know how Antoine feels about me...

169

but I've always wondered if he loves me."

"I don't — "

"I don't expect you to know if he actually loves me," she said, giving me a warm smile. "I just want a chance to ask him."

It broke my heart. Where she hoped to go was a place that no longer existed, not the way she wanted it to be.

"I need to tell you something," I said.

"What?"

"Why don't you pull over for a minute, so it's easier to talk."

I waited until the car was stopped; I then reached over and pulled out the keys.

"What's going on?" she asked.

"It's about Ant," I said. "We lost him."

"What do you mean you lost him? Where did he go?"

"There was an accident, Natalie... Ant didn't make it."

She collapsed against my shoulder, pounding her fists against me. Then she started to weep.

And I wept, too.

I don't know if I've ever felt worse for anyone.

I don't know why that is.

4

TODAY IS TUESDAY, DECEMBER 18TH.

JUSTIN AND Rihanna stopped by just before lunch, their two kids in tow. My first thought was to try and figure out how to keep them from staying over to eat, but Fiona seemed perfectly happy adding a few extra mouths, so we extended an invite and they accepted.

I can't tell if they're trying to win me over.

Having somewhat reliable electricity with the new solar plant has made a big difference for how we eat. Last year we had one small upright freezer on the geni, and we treated the microwave like a luxury item, only using it when we had no other choice; that meant the most meals were planned to provide just enough, with no expectation of leftovers, and oftentimes that actually ended up being not quite enough for everyone.

But now Fiona always makes extra at dinner, and seals the remainder into one of over a hundred unused plastic food containers in our stockpile, adding the date and her own four-star rating before shoving it into one of the three chest freezers we now have on the go in the basement.

So while she still loves to cook, or at least she tells me she does, there's about a 50/50 chance these days that lunch will be "a la carte", as she puts it, and we'll all just grab our own entree from the freezer and wait our turn to heat it up. We should probably bring over a second microwave.

The Porters are lucky that today happens to feature a fresh meal of grilled cheese sandwiches and cream of vegetable soup. I don't think they realize just what that entails; first Graham milked the goats, then he and Fiona made the cheese, and while they did that, Kayla kneaded and then baked the bread. And I think Matt may have opened the soup can.

I don't think the Porters could ever begin to put together a meal like that.

We sat down around the long pinewood table, and with the four Porters we filled up every chair but Ant's.

By now everyone seemed to have gotten used to what had happened yesterday, but I could still tell that there was a strange reverence for me — from a few people — that I didn't really deserve. I tried to keep the details of what happened unsaid, particularly when Kayla and Fiona were around... I just told them that there were two girls who were stranded up there, and left it at that. I know there's something patronizing and maybe a little bit sexist about my urge to cover things up, but I'm not sure I'm sorry for it.

"So there's a reason we stopped by," Justin said as he eyed me eating my soup.

"I figured," I said. "I just assumed it was something about Silver Queen Lake."

"Yup..."

"I haven't really had a chance to process it all. Right now I'm having trouble imagining how we can get at those supplies without exposing ourselves too much."

"I know. It's not something we can handle on our own."

"I wasn't expecting you to say that. I thought you were coming here to convince me that we needed to go back today."

"There's no way you're going back," Sara said.

I sighed. "We need to get those supplies somehow."

"I think you guys know about my phone," Justin said.

"The phone you won't let us use?" Lisa asked.

"I called everyone's numbers. You know that. The networks were down all over the continent. I can barely get a signal, and we're a lot closer to the Eastern Hemisphere than most people."

"That was two months ago," Graham said. "I'm sure someone's working to get things going again."

"Then we'll try again soon, okay? But that's not really the issue right now."

"What is the issue?" I asked.

"I got a call from Dave Walker. Nice long message."

"I didn't know you two were phone buddies."

Justin sighed. "There are around a dozen people in the district with working phones. I talk to all of them."

"And keep the details to yourself," Lisa said.

"So what did Dave Walker want?" I asked.

"He made us an offer," Justin said. "He told me that they'd be willing to work together with us to retrieve the supplies... that we could split everything up 50/50."

"That's hard to believe," Lisa said, her hand covering a mouthful of grilled cheese.

"They've decided to take over the Smiths' old roadblock," Rihanna said. "They brought up a camper and a couple of trucks."

"I placed a call to D'Arcy at Detour Lake," Justin said. "He's already gotten back to me with a nice counter-offer."

"No," Sara said. "We're not working with Detour Lake."

Justin shook his head angrily. "You're not in charge."

"We're not working with them," I said. "They're more trouble than they're worth."

"You need to rethink that policy, Baptiste."

"I'm pretty sure I don't."

"Wait," Graham said. "If we team up with the Walkers we're pissing on the Supply Partnership. We shouldn't even be talking to them at all after the stunt they pulled. Not until we get our fair share of their inventory —"

"Good luck with that," Justin said.

"When do they want to start?" I asked. "ASAP?"

"They don't want to start emptying the cottages until we can get up there with a couple trucks of our own. They want two of us to help man the roadblock, and two to help with the loading. And they want you on the roadblock, Baptiste."

"It isn't right," Graham said.

"And we're going to somehow split everything up without any arguments or dirty tricks?" I asked.

"What's the other option?" Lisa asked. "We either take what we can get or we're left with nothing."

"But I don't understand," I said. "Walker said he'd never work with me... what's changed?"

"He must have been struck with a rare bout of common sense," Rihanna said. "You and Justin are the most highly-trained guys in the district."

"I think Stems has me beat on that."

"I know I have you beat," Justin said.

"We'd be betraying our friends," Sara said. "The Marchands and the Girards. The Lamarches..."

"There won't be any Marchands or Girards or Lamarches soon," Justin said.

"So you're planning on some more people snatching?" Lisa asked.

"Fuck you."

Lisa stood up from the table. "How about I grab a broom handle and we see just who gets fucked?"

"Easy guys," I said. "We all know you hate each other. There's no reason to keep reminding us."

"We can't agree to this," Sara said. "They betrayed all of us by dropping out of the partnership. We can't reward them for that."

"Come on," Kayla said. "No one cares about the stupid Supply Partnership."

Sara groaned. "No one asked you, Kayla —"

"Maybe someone should start asking me... maybe you guys should stop treating me like a goddamn child."

"What are you thinking, Kayla?" I asked. I had to start somewhere.

She seemed surprised at the question. She looked around as though she was waiting for someone to jump in. "We need to show the Walkers that we're not people they can take advantage of," she said. "As long as we keep on with this stubborn attitude that we can't work too closely with Detour Lake, the Walkers will know that we don't have any choice but to deal with them."

"That's it," Justin said. "Exactly." He was almost bouncing in his chair; I guess he's not used to people agreeing with him around here.

"If we teamed up with Detour Lake we'd be stronger than the Walkers. We'd be stronger than New Post, too... and probably Stems."

"I don't know about that," I said. "Underestimating Stems is a bad idea."

"Do you even know what you're talking about, Kayla?" Sara asked. She sounded annoyed. "Those people up there are incredibly unbalanced. We can't trust them."

Kayla groaned. "They're unbalanced, are they? Just because they were smart enough to plan ahead?"

"From what I've heard," I said, "they have a whole lotta men and a handful of women. That'd make any group unbalanced. Add on some cabin fever and the various mental... uh... conditions that come from being a prepper..."

"No," Kayla said. "That's not fair. These guys weren't up there waiting for the Rapture or something. They knew what was happening and they acted. That's not crazy... that's smart."

"I think you wish you'd been a prepper," Justin said.

"I was a goddamn prepper."

"You were?" I asked. "For real?"

"Yeah, alright? A full-on survivalist nutjob. And if I hadn't caught my boyfriend humping the town skank of Kapuskasing I'd be living up at Detour Lake right now."

"Some rivalry there, eh?" Sara said. "You couldn't let that bitch get away with it... Kayla the Town Skank of Cochrane has to represent."

We all turned to see what had just happened. I'd never heard Sara speak like that before.

Kayla gasped along with the rest of us.

"If you guys are going to call the Walkers," Sara said, "do it on the radio in the Tremblays' truck... not on Justin's phone. No more phone calls behind people's backs."

"What about the message this sends?" Lisa asked. I couldn't tell if she was honestly wondering, or just trying to poke Sara.

Sara slammed her hands down on the table.

We all started paying attention.

"I don't care about the message," she said. "I am so sick of carrying this. If you guys don't think the Marchands and the Girards matter... then fine. Do what you want to do."

She stood up and walked out to the kitchen. The pans started clattering; she was pretending to do the dishes.

"What is her problem?" Lisa asked.

"I don't know," I said. "A lot of bad news and not much good, I guess." I turned to Kayla. "Are you okay?"

"I'm fine," she said. "Whatever."

"It's not too late to do this right," Justin said. "We team up with Detour Lake and send Walker packing."

"We're not starting a war," I said. "We team up with the Walkers and we go from there."

"I'd rather be the one who starts the war than the poor bastard who's caught by surprise."

"There won't be any surprises. I don't trust the Walkers any more than I trust the guys at Detour Lake. We get in and get the supplies and we get out. No one's getting married here."

Kayla stood up from the table. "We might as well be marrying them," she said. "They've already got us on our back with our legs in the air."

As she walked over toward the stairs, Justin gave her a smile.

She nodded, but didn't smile back.

That was still more than I wanted to see between the two of them.

∽

Since our smaller grain truck was still in a heap at the airport, we needed to find a second truck in order to carry our half of the haul we were expecting. The nice thing about being the last few stragglers in what was once a half-decent community is that there are still quite a few trucks left behind.

Graham and the Porters and I piled into the Tremblays' truck and headed up 652. We picked up a gravel truck at a yard just outside Cochrane, the first truck we saw, actually.

It felt strange taking two trucks up there, not just because we had to siphon our scant diesel, from the Tremblays' grain truck to the new one, but because our homes at McCartney Lake would be down four people at a time when we're not feeling particularly safe.

With Graham and I gone, Lisa's the only one at our place who has the know-how to use a shotgun; we left both of the big guns at home, but Matt's still working on holding them properly. I don't have the patience to train him, so Justin's taken that on. I've given Kayla and Fiona a few quick lessons, but neither of them are the least bit comfortable holding a weapon.

I know I need to push them harder, get them to understand why it's so important that everyone knows how to defend themselves. And Sara makes it that much harder for everyone when she refuses to even look at a gun.

There are a surprising number of Tremblays who know how to shoot, so I wasn't worried about them, but the Porters' kids had to come up to our place since we certainly couldn't leave them all alone. That leaves one cottage completely empty, but since there's probably ten times more supplies at Silver Queen Lake than we have at the

Porters, I decided that it was worth the risk.

We reached Silver Queen Lake by late morning, and I was glad to see that the Walkers were there waiting for us, with a large open-top grain truck.

"We figured we'd start along the north shore," Livingston said, as I climbed out of the truck and started to suit up.

"You're in charge of the scavenging?" I asked.

"Pretty much."

"And the divvying up, too, I'll bet."

Livingston nodded to Graham as he joined us. "Your man will be there too," he said. "Everything's 50/50, Baptiste... as best as we can make it. And just to be sure you know there are no hard feelings, I'll make sure you guys get first pick."

"How nice," I said.

"Look... I know you still have a problem with me. I get that. But for the time being, it would be a lot simpler if we just try to get along."

I nodded; that was about all I was willing to give him.

I turned to Graham. "I think you know what we need most," I said.

"Don't worry," Graham replied. "I've got us covered."

"Good man... and if there's anything you're not sure about, just give me a push on the handheld. I aim to please."

He smiled. "Will do, boss."

Justin and Rihanna walked over to us, each carrying a riot suit, vest and helmet.

"You need to actually put that on," I said to Justin. I turned to Livingston. "We've got a set for you guys, too. You'll have to pick who gets to wear it."

Rihanna held out the gear; Livingston took them and held the vest close to his face, as though he were evaluating the exquisite fabric of a fine Italian suit.

And people wonder why I hate him.

He placed the gear down in the near-frozen muck.

I let it slide; I wasn't the one who'd have to deal with how cold that riot suit would be.

"Where are your people, anyway?" Justin asked Livingston.

"We've got one shooter in position," Livingston said. It sounded like he was trying to impress me.

"What does that even mean?" I asked.

"A sniper."

I laughed. "Good one. But seriously, do you really have some ass-hole hiding in the trees somewhere?"

"I *was* hiding," a woman's voice called out.

I turned to see her, about mid-thirties, dressed in camo. I recognized the face; I remember pretty much every woman in Cochrane who falls into a certain... uh, range.

"I'm sorry," I said, trying not to laugh again.

"I know," she said, "I look ridiculous."

"No... you look pretty good, actually. I certainly didn't notice you when we were coming in."

She chuckled. "That's because I was in the camper taking a piss." She pulled off a glove and held out her hand. "I'm Katie," she said. "Don't worry... I washed my hands, more or less."

I shook hands with her. "I'm Robert Jeanbaptiste," I said with a smile. "Please don't *ever* call me Bob."

She laughed. "Don't worry, Baptiste... I know who you are. There's a photo of you on my father's dartboard, right next to the Biebers."

I glanced over to Livingston.

"Dave's daughter," he said.

"And to think I was starting to like her."

Katie gave me a friendly shove.

"So where's the rest of your team?" I asked her, glad to have someone other than Livingston to ask.

"They'll be back in a few minutes."

"They've already started, haven't they."

She seemed to hesitate. "No..."

"We forgot to bring up some stuff for the camper," Livingston said. "So we sent a truck back to grab it."

I knew him well enough that I assumed he was lying. Fisher Livingston had once made a living doing just that. And for a while back then, I'd put up with it, always pretending that I'd never noticed.

Always letting Ant smooth things over between us.

And as much as I didn't want to, I decided I'd have to start pretending again, at least for the time being. I wanted to wait and see exactly how Livingston and the Walkers were screwing us.

∽

The rest of the Walkers' complement arrived within the half-hour, pulling up in their little electric van. We helped them unload some boxes of food and equipment for the camper.

I guess Livingston had been telling the truth; they came up the same way we'd come. Even a stopped clock is right twice a day, and Livingston's still an asshole.

With the van emptied, one of the new arrivals, who looked like a younger Dave Walker, hopped in the grain truck with Livingston without giving us more than a glance, while the other, a tall native man with a long ponytail, joined up with us at the roadblock.

As the two scavenging trucks drove away, I offered the man my hand.

"Good to meet you, Baptiste," he said.

"I think we've met before," I said, trying to place him. My first thought was that I'd seen him around New Post. "So you live with the Walkers?"

"I work for the Walkers."

"Like Livingston."

He chuckled. "Yeah," he said, "like Livingston."

"So which one of you is dressing up in our extra gear?" Justin asked.

"I'm still planning on cowering in the trees if anyone comes," Katie said. "So I guess that leaves Sky."

"Sky?"

"That's me," the native man said. "I like to think it's a badass name."

"It's pretty badass," I said.

"So do we just stand around here waiting for something to happen?" Justin asked.

"We usually sit in the camper," Sky said. "The kitchenette faces out to the road, so it's not like we'll miss someone coming."

I turned to look at Katie.

She grinned. "I have no problem with staying warm," she said.

"Well... I have a problem with it," I said.

"That doesn't surprise me," Justin said.

"If someone wanted to take out a roadblock, they'd either come at us full on with superior force, or they'd sneak up on us, on foot. If I was going to do it, I'd go with an ambush."

"And staring out at the road might not do us any good," Katie said. "Mr. Baptiste, I'm glad you're here."

"I like you."

"But we'll take shifts, right?" Justin asked.

"Two shifts," I said. "One Walker with one whatever the hell we call ourselves." I looked over to Katie. "What do people call us?"

She laughed. "Did you want the polite version?"

"Let's stick with that, yeah."

"My father calls you guys 'Baptiste's crew'. Well, 'F-ing Baptiste', usually."

"Are you serious?" Justin said. "That's ridiculous. I've always called us 'The Justin Porter Gang'."

"Who's Justin Porter?" Katie asked. I'm not sure she was joking.

Justin chuckled. "Ouch," he said.

"Just kidding... I've seen you around. If you really want, we can all think you're badass, too."

"I *am* badass."

"I believe you," I said. "That's why you and Sky should take the first shift."

Katie made us some instant coffee and we sat down at the kitchenette in the musty camper. It was one of the older styles, bulky and fully furnished, from the days when people thought it made perfect sense to try and put a house on wheels. I'd never actually been in that kind of camper before; growing up, we lived by my father's rule that camping always had to involve a tent, and for whatever reason I'd kept the tradition alive with Cassy, while Alanna stayed home with the indoor plumbing and frozen pizza.

"My father says some pretty strange things about you, Baptiste," Katie said as she dumped several tons of sweetener into her mug.

"He thinks I'm an asshole. I think he's right."

"I like assholes... they're the only people who know how to get things done."

"So you're an asshole, too?"

"Nah... I'm a treat. I just, like, admire you guys from afar."

I laughed.

She smiled and gave me a look that I knew well enough. I guess there's something alluring about men your father can't stand.

"I'm a little surprised that you're out here," I said.

"Sorry... I didn't realize shooting people was men's work."

"I guess that sounded bad... it's more that you're Dave Walker's little girl."

"His little girl, eh? Wow... facetious and flattering. You know that I'm like older than this camper, right?"

"And only half as musty."

"Ha! Well, truth is, my father doesn't really like me being here. But my little brother Zach's just gone up the road with Fisher, so it wouldn't make sense to tell me I can't help out. And let's face it... my life is pretty damned boring. I basically just sit around all day."

"Yeah, right. I'm sure there's never any work to do."

"You'd be surprised. I don't like to get my hands dirty, or my fingernails scuffed..."

"But seriously... what are things like for you guys?"

"It was harder last winter. Especially since it went on until, like, June. And it was just the six of us trying to run a farm. When we first took it over I didn't know which end of the chicken lays the eggs."

"You guys have grown since then... how did you manage it?"

"Same way you guys have... people show up and ask to be a part of the group. Sometimes it feels like we're not getting things quite right, but compared to most people we're killing it."

"What about indentures?"

She began to look uncomfortable. "What about them?" she asked.

"Do you have any?" I already knew the answer.

"What difference does that make?"

"Come on, Katie... I'm sure you can guess how I feel about that crap."

"Oh, that's right. Baptiste the abolitionist. No indentures allowed. Must be tough being stuck up here with the backwards hillbillies." She threw her hands up in the air. "It's nothing to do with me. I didn't make the decision."

"I know you didn't," I said, trying to sound like I could relate. "I just don't know how you guys do it."

"You have no right to judge us..."

"That's not what I mean. I just don't understand how you can even make that work. Why bother getting someone to sign their life away? It's not like that piece of paper means anything."

"You'd be surprised," Katie said. "Those damned indenture docs have a lot more power than you'd think." She turned and looked out the window at the endless gray. "It runs both ways, you know... it's a promise from both sides."

"Yeah... I've seen that kind of paperwork before... ten years of service in exchange for ten years of food and shelter. Just no specifics on what that service might be."

"Can we not talk about this, please?"

"I didn't mean to make you uncomfortable."

"Bullshit... you want to make me feel guilty. But you have no idea what it's like for me."

Katie didn't seem like the type of person who cried easily, but I could see that she was on the edge of something.

"I'm sorry," I said. "I was out of line."

"Yes, you were." She tried to smile but it didn't take. "Like some kind of asshole or something. Let's just find something else to talk about."

"Sounds good to me." I smiled. "So... do you know much about Stems?"

"Wow... another great topic."

"I'm just asking. I'm a lifelong learner."

"Stems is a problem that doesn't have a solution. He shoots at us one day and pretends he's our best friend the next."

"If he's the one doing the shooting."

"Are you saying that we're shooting at him?"

"That's not what I mean. I have a feeling that someone's been doing their best to make it look like they're killing on behalf of Ryan Stems and the Mushkegowuk Nation."

"Why?"

"I don't know. Do you?"

"Of course not." She was getting upset again.

"I didn't mean anything by it, Katie."

She took a sip of her coffee and scrunched her face from the taste. "So, like... a false flag," she said.

"Impressive..."

"Oh, I forgot... little girls don't know how to read books or any-thing..."

"Yeah... okay..."

"It wouldn't make sense for a gang of marauders to go to the trouble, would it?"

"Probably not. It's not like we'd be so intimidated by painted helmets that we'd just start packing them some care packages."

"So who? One of the families around here? Someone further away?"

I shrugged. "Sons of Flesh?"

"Or Detour Lake?"

"There's too many shitheads to choose from."

"It's great to be popular. Either way, it's backfiring."

"What do you mean?"

She looked away. Her fingers started tapping on the table. "I don't know..."

"No... you know, Katie."

She gave me a slow and heavy sigh. "My father's been talking to Stems."

"Talking?"

"Protection. I don't know if we'd be a full-on part of the Nation or whatever..."

"You can't be serious. All the work you guys have done and you're just going to hand it over?"

"All the work we did with our indentures, you mean."

"I can't believe your father would do that."

"I don't know. I'm not at the meetings. I'm not in charge of any-thing, Baptiste. For all I know, I'm just talking out of my ass..."

I couldn't help myself. "Tell me more about this ass of yours..."

I heard Graham's voice on the handheld. "Baptiste... you there? Over."

I grabbed it and pushed to talk. "What's up, Graham?"

"You need to get over here... over."

"Okay... north shore, right?"

"North shore... probably four cottages from the end of the road. Over."

I turned to Katie. "I guess we should both head over there. You okay with that?"

"Okay," she said. I could tell that she was worried.

I was, too. But I didn't want her to know that.

"I'm sure everyone's okay," I said.

She nodded. "I hope you're right."

∾

Graham was standing by the road when we arrived. From what I could see, everyone else was still hard at work.

"What's going on?" I asked him, as Katie and I stepped out of the Walkers' van.

"You guys aren't being honest with us," Graham said, glaring at Katie.

"What do you mean?" she asked.

"Come on... we're not idiots." He looked over to me. "They've already gone through these cottages, cherry-picking the best supplies."

"How can you tell?" I asked.

"They did a crap-poor job of hiding it. Every cabinet and cupboard I've seen has been ransacked... what's left is obviously less valuable than whatever they've already taken."

"That's a pretty big accusation," Katie said. "Even if stuff's missing, how can you be so sure that we're the ones who took it?"

I didn't know what to think. I didn't trust the Walkers, obviously, and certainly not Livingston. But Graham seemed to be making some pretty big assumptions, with nothing concrete to back them up.

"Can I talk to you for a second, Graham?" I asked.

"I'm going to go inside and look around," Katie said.

Once she'd left, Graham grabbed me by the arm.

I've rarely seen him that angry.

"You don't believe me, do you?"

"I don't have enough information, Graham."

"So you can't just trust me on this."

"Come on, man... I know Livingston's a shit, but I still don't see how you can know for sure that they're screwing us."

"You *know* they are."

I nodded. "But maybe it's not going down how you think. And confronting them like this... I'm not sure it's the right move. What did you say to Livingston?"

"I called him out on it. I told him that I could tell he was trying to put one over on us."

"Dammit. You've put me in an awkward position here."

"What's awkward? You need to back me up."

"I don't think I can, Graham. Now isn't the time for this."

"You're kidding me."

"Nothing's changed... even if you're right, we need to take what we can get here. Anything's better than jack shit."

"It's not worth it. We can't just sit here and take it up the rear for a few measly bags of rice."

"It's more than just a few bags of rice... there's no way they managed to empty out everything of value from fifty-some cottages. Look... you need to drop it."

"Come on, Baptiste."

"Please... just drop it. You don't need to play nice... just don't be a dick about it."

"No way... I'm not going to drop it. This is bullcrap and you know it."

I grabbed him by both of his arms just below his shoulders. "You need to drop it, Graham. Trust me on this. Please."

I could see that he wanted to keep arguing with me; I just held onto his arms for a moment, looking him right in the eye. I wasn't trying to intimidate him; I know Graham better than that. I was trying to show him just how important it was for him to let it go

He shook his head and sighed.

"Please," I said again.

"I can see you don't have my back on this. Too busy chasing another woman who's young enough to be your daughter."

I didn't say anything else. I just waited on him.

"Whatever," he said. "Just don't expect me to put any effort into making friends with these jerks."

"I don't expect any miracles. But seriously, Graham... thanks."

"Just go back to the roadblock before Justin accidentally shoots himself."

I nodded.

Katie came back outside just a few seconds later; I had a feeling she'd been listening in.

That's the way it is with the Walkers, I guess. They've got it bred into them.

Katie and I didn't waste any time getting back to the camper. We found Justin and Sky outside, both of them leaning against our truck.

"Anything exciting happen?" I asked as I walked over to see them.

"We saw a bald eagle," Justin said.

"That's something."

"So I guess it's time to relieve you guys," Katie said. She grimaced. "After I go to the ladies' room, though. To relieve myself…"

"I've got a few minutes of standing left in me," Justin said. "Maybe enough for you to get those hands washed this time."

She chuckled, and then she and Sky made their way into the camper.

I was sure they'd be talking about us the second the door was closed.

"What happened?" Justin asked me.

"Graham thinks they're ripping us off… he thinks they've already taken out some of the best supplies."

"What did Rihanna say about it? She'd have a better idea since she's been in a few of those cottages before."

"I didn't get a chance to talk with her… but I don't think it really matters if they did it or not. We can't do anything about it either way. We just have to take what we can get."

"So we're their little bitches, eh?"

"I'm not happy about this either."

"Well… fuck 'em. And if you ever leave me with a goddamned indian again…"

"Is that some kind of joke?"

"What?"

"Take a look at me, Justin… what do I look like?"

"Come on…"

"If you want to be a goddamn bigot, just keep it to yourself, alright?"

"Shit… it's not like —"

"Shut up," I said. "There's nothing you can say that's going to make you look like less of a racist fuck right now."

"Fuck you, Baptiste."

"Yeah… fuck you, too. Now you don't have to go into the trailer, but seriously, just get the hell out of my sight."

That got me a nice middle finger.

He chose to head back to the trailer, and as he was going in Katie was coming out. She gave him a warm smile, and he nodded back.

"He looks pissed," she said to me as she met me by the truck."

"Don't worry," I said. "He's pissed at me."

"That's good... so what was going on with your friend Graham?"

"He doesn't trust you."

"Oh."

"I'm sorry, Katie, but I don't really trust you guys, either."

"My father told me you shot out one of his tires a week ago."

"He deserved it."

"No, seriously... like, fuck your pissing matches. The only thing that stands between where we are right now and where we ought to be is every man in the district and their tiny little penises. First it was just that garbage between you and Fisher Livingston... and now it seems to be you versus everyone else."

"You seem to know me pretty well," I said.

"I'm sorry," she said. "I didn't mean it to come out like that. It's not your fault... well, it's not *all* your fault. It is what it is, I guess."

"It's a bad situation."

"It doesn't have to be like this. Why do you think my father asked for your guys' help on this?"

"I assumed we were working up to a bromance."

"It's time to get things back on track. We need to work together."

That sounded strange, considering the dump Dave Walker had taken all over the Supply Partnership. But maybe I was just pissed that he was the first to kick it when it was down.

The partnership hadn't been working. Walker was just the first to accept it.

"I'm willing to work together," I said. "To try.."

"I believe you." She laughed. "See? Now there's one Walker who's starting to trust you."

"I want to trust you, too, Katie."

"That's good."

"I just need you to tell me the truth."

"The truth?"

"You know... did Livingston screw us over? Did he poach some of the supplies before we got here?"

"We weren't here very long..."

"That's not what I asked."

She turned her head towards the camper. "There's no right way for me to answer your question."

At least she wasn't lying to me.

Livingston had sent one truckload back before we'd arrived, and I'd probably never find out just what goodies had been loaded up for the trip.

And all I had left to do was try and make sure they didn't sneak a few more loads out without us knowing.

But I dropped the subject right there, since I didn't expect her to tell me anything more about it, and we spent the rest of the day talking about anything else, from my stories about Toronto and the glamour of being a community safety consultant, to her descriptions of what things were like in Cochrane before I got here. It's funny how little I know about the way things used to be up here.

I've never really talked about Cochrane with anyone, since I've always felt like it's a first class ticket to a depressive episode. But Katie was different... she seemed detached as she talked. She didn't seem the least bit emotional as she told me about her time waiting tables at the one and only fancy restaurant, or about how the first boy she ever kissed was the first man to be killed by marauders. It was like she was describing a movie to me, like it was all from a life that had happened to someone else.

And she didn't ask me about my family.

I guess she knew, since the whole area knew. There wasn't a person in Cochrane who truly believed I'd ever see them again.

I'm just glad I didn't have to have that same old conversation all over again.

By the time the other two trucks came rolling up behind us, I was pretty sure I'd made a friend. That sounds pretty trite, but I don't make a lot of new ones these days.

TODAY IS WEDNESDAY, DECEMBER 19TH.

THIS YEAR'S snow finally came, starting last night, just after dinner.

It's lasted all through the day today. By noon, we were up to around twenty five centimeters, with no end in sight.

It's always like pulling teeth to get Graham and Matt outside when it's cold or snowing, so Kayla, Lisa and I did the chores, with Lisa giving me a quick lesson in milking the goats, and Kayla running off the names and laying habits of each hen; I'm pretty sure she was rounding up the egg count, in an attempt to keep some of the stragglers from finding their way into Fiona's stewing pot.

I went down to the Tremblays with Lisa, to raise the Walkers on the UHF rig, and they made it clear that the snow would keep them away from Silver Queen for at least a day, since they'd have to make sure they had enough trucks to plow closer to home. I don't see why they think that's more important, but I knew we'd have trouble getting up there ourselves. We agreed to talk again tomorrow morning.

And I did my best not to think about how easy it would be for them to be lying, to be sneaking out a few secret loads from Silver Queen Like while they pretended they couldn't ever get up there.

It's not like I could change the weather. Other than the five hundred metric tons of carbon dioxide I've gladly pumped into the atmosphere over the past fifty-some years.

We had a few days like this last winter, so I already have a good idea of just how long we can put up with each other in a confined space. Last March saw a spring blizzard that kept us inside for two days straight, and resulted in no less than three physical altercations; the fact that all three were between Kayla and Fiona didn't ease the tension as much as you'd think.

This time around, Sara decided to use up the day in baking. which kept Fiona occupied as well. I sat in the kitchen with them for over an hour just after lunch, listening to their conversation and generally just enjoying the warmth of the oven and the smell of sugar and caramel. Sara doesn't believe in baking bread when she could make treats instead.

But I knew I couldn't sit around all day; snow means that our little island has become less safe. The Abitibi isn't frozen yet, but soon it will be, but even before that we'll need to start worrying about snowmobiles.

Snowmobiles.

Starting today.

Last winter there wasn't much snow compared to most years, but there was still enough to make our original roadblock on Nelson Road — a wood fence with two rickety gates — pretty much useless. Anyone who had a snowmobile or a tracked ATV could have come up on us from any direction.

And they did.

The first time was last December, before Ant had come along, and long before the Porters or Tremblays, back when the seven of us were just getting used to working together.

Lisa and Graham were stringing up a makeshift extension on the fencing around the goats, since the snow was already banking high enough that any of the more enterprising animals would be able to find their way out.

The goat pen is across the driveway, probably about as far from the cottage as you can get and still consider yourself on the homestead. I guess that'll change if we ever plant those crops.

I heard the snowmobiles from right by the cottage, where I was splitting firewood with Matt. For a moment the sound didn't even register as anything I needed to worry about.

By the time I realized that I needed to check it out, I could see them coming, two machines heading up the unplowed driveway.

They were moving toward our Lisa and Graham and the goat fence; I guess they had it in their heads that they were dealing with a solitary couple.

Lisa had noticed them, too, and as she hadn't worried about bringing a rifle out with her, she hustled Graham toward the trees at the far end of the clearing.

She was counting on me to take the heat.

I grabbed my gun belt and strapped it on, and debated running into the cottage to grab my armour. I turned to Matt instead.

"Go inside and put on the body armour," I told him. "Helmet, too."

He nodded and started toward the front door.

I grabbed his arm.

"Other door," I said.

He went around back while I walked out onto the driveway.

The snowmobiles slowed. If they were armed, they'd have little chance of getting a good shot off while moving. They were wearing balaclavas, but since one had a scarf on as well, I couldn't be sure they were trying to hide their faces from anything other than the cold.

"Private property," I shouted.

"Don't shoot," one of the snowmobilers said.

He turned off his machine and climbed off, pulling up his balaclava to reveal his face.

I didn't know him.

"You have any guns?" I asked.

"Yes," the man said. "Handgun in my saddlebags. My wife has a knife, but it's none too hazardous."

I nodded to Graham.

He and Lisa walked back and Graham checked both sets of bags. One pistol and one knife. No surprises.

Lisa took the gun from him and checked it over.

"I guess you can see this land is occupied," I said. "I should tell you... next time you come to a homestead and find it's not empty, you'd be better off just turning around. People have been shot for less."

"You've shot people for less?" the man asked. He seemed to be sizing me up.

"Where are you from?"

"Hibbing, Minnesota... originally. You know... Bob Dylan. My family comes from Kapuskasing, though." He stepped toward me.

I let him.

He held out his hand and I shook it.

"I'm Ryan," he said, "and this is my wife, Juliette."

She waved but didn't come closer. And she still had a balaclava covering her face.

"You're headed the wrong way," I said.

193

He smiled. "I'm taking an inventory."

"There's no way we're telling you what we've got."

"Not supplies... people."

"Still not telling you."

He nodded. "I'm sorry... I didn't mean to pry."

"I'm pretty sure you mean to," Lisa said.

"What's your last name, Ryan?" I asked.

"What's the difference? For all you know I'm just making shit up."

"That's what I was assuming. Thanks for clearing that up."

"It's Stems. Of the Kapuskasing Stems. On Maple Drive."

"Clever," Lisa said, "but we're all filled up on douchebags right now."

"You been to New Post yet?" I asked him.

"No... is that a town?"

"It's a bunch of people with guns and a big gate. Good bunch, though. I recommend you go visit them instead."

"You're a tough crowd."

"You want it tougher?" Lisa asked.

He chuckled. "I'm good. If you're willing to put our weapons back in our bags we'll be on our way."

I nodded to Lisa and she handed the handgun back to Graham, who repacked them in the saddlebags.

If it had been me, I would have unloaded it and kept the ammo.

Juliette waved again as they drove back up the driveway.

It took almost a week for the news to reach us. Ryan Stems and his lovely "wife" had kept going, crossing the bridge and then trying to rob the Lamarches at gunpoint.

Juliette had been keeping a gun in her jacket.

The Lamarche family lost both of their sons.

Ryan Stems lost Juliette, who the Lamarches guessed was somewhere around seventeen years old.

I should have searched them. And I shouldn't have let them leave. It doesn't matter what so-called good Ryan Stems thinks he's doing for the Mushkegowuk Nation; he'll always be the man who came here as a marauder, the man with the blood of those two Lamarche boys on his hands.

The same goes for the blood of that teenage girl he'd called his wife.

❧

Everyone else — everyone aside from me and Sara and Fiona — came up with a more liquid way of passing the time during the storm, and I'm pretty sure that the four of them were drunk before they'd finished lunch.

Kayla and Lisa are surprisingly unfun when wasted, while Matt just gets stupider. The only one of them who is the least bit interesting as a boozer is Graham, who seems to turn his prissiness down a few notches.

"You guys are the best," I heard him shout from the living room.

"I like him better as a drunk," Sara said as she rolled the dough out on the laminate counter.

"It's like there's this little fun-time Graham who's only allowed out once a year," Fiona said.

"It's for the best," I said. "Lisa wouldn't put up with him if he was happy all the time."

I heard the sound of broken glass, followed by a rousing cheer.

"We'd better witness whatever this is," Sara said.

We walked out into the living room to see a pile of broken glass and Graham, standing over it with a bloodied hand.

"What the hell happened?" I asked. "Did you cut yourself?"

Graham held up his other hand. "I think, maybe," he said.

"Someone ought to bandage that," Lisa said. "Or at least cut up the other hand, so it matches."

Kayla and Matt started to laugh, and Graham soon joined in, even though it was clear that he was past understanding the joke.

I turned to see that Sara was laughing, too. I didn't get it. "That's funny?" I asked her.

She nodded. "Nothing wrong with a little bit of fun."

"Goddammit," I muttered. "Fiona, can you help me out here? Get me something to wrap up his hand?"

Fiona rushed back to the kitchen.

"I swear, Graham," I said as I reached for his injured hand. "If I get blood on my clothes I'm going to open up a few more veins."

"Don't worry so much," Graham said. "You know... you worry too much, Bat-piste."

"Sounds like a bat taking a piss," Matt said. "Bat piss! Bat piss!"

"Yeah," Kayla said. "How do you explain that, Baptiste? Why are you named after bat piss?"

"This is getting out of hand," I said, looking to Sara for some kind of assistance.

"Fiona and I can bandage him up," she said, putting her hand on my back.

"What about the rest of these idiots?"

"Who you calling an idiot?" Kayla asked. "Who's the one named after bat piss again?"

"Don't let them get to you," Sara said. She gave me a kiss, but it didn't help to calm me down.

"This is ridiculous. Every one of them is drunk off their ass."

"But it's a fine, fine ass," Kayla said. She stuck it out at me and gave it a little wiggle.

"This can't happen again," I said as I made my way upstairs, leaving the noise behind.

I think I was angrier at myself for letting it happen.

❧

"Your anger was disproportionate, Robert."

I'd had a therapist back in Toronto who'd told me that pretty much every time I'd talk about the latest thing that made me lose my temper.

Guys like me... we're great when the shit hits the fan, or at least we like to think we are, but when things are going so-so and something gets on our nerves... watch out.

It doesn't make sense for me to want to beat the life out of Matt, or to want to scream my head off at Kayla. It's disproportionate. It's out of whack.

So I'd put a bag of pills in my pocket when the snow started coming down, those pills with the little maple leafs; I'd expected to need one yesterday, but I'd never gotten to it. For some reason, I needed it today.

I sat down on my bed and I gently tossed a pill from one hand to the other.

I knew that it was a bad idea, that I was the only person there who was both sober and experienced enough to shoot a gun. If this pill took me out of commission for six or seven hours...

196

Stems might have snowmobiles or he might just use snowshoes. He and the Spirit Animals could come back to take us out once and for all. If he cared to. If he hadn't really changed from the first time we'd met.

Or... maybe some other, random guys could show up at any moment, with no real purpose other than to totally fuck us up.

That doesn't sound any better.

I couldn't afford to take that pill.

Fiona came to see me in my room a little while later.

I was reading a book on my tablet, lying on my bed in my boxer shorts; she didn't seem to care that I was somewhat close to naked.

"Are you okay?" she asked, as she planted herself on the bed beside me.

"I'm fine... thanks." I sat up and gave her a smile.

She put her hand on my bare knee; I don't think she meant anything by it.

"I didn't think it bothered you when people drank," she said.

"It usually doesn't. But there's a limit, you know? Things are a little out of control downstairs."

"There's not much else to do around here today."

"See what's happened to you? You hated people drinking when you got here."

"I was fourteen when I got here."

"Well, it's not a good idea for more than half of us to be drunk. What if there was some kind of emergency?"

She grinned. "Like what? Yeti attack?"

I laughed at that. "Possible... or zombie snowmen?"

I loved hearing her giggle.

She arched her eyebrows. "Homicidal Christmas elves?"

She gave me a funny look that made me crack up.

"You're awesome, Fiona. You really are. You remind me so much of my daughter... have I ever said that?"

She seemed to be taken aback. "Um... Sara's told me that before. That you think I'm a lot like Cassy."

"Well... you are."

She looked down for a moment. "Does that bother you at all?"

"What do you mean?"

"I don't know. With me being here all the time... does it make you miss her that much more?"

I realized then that she was crying. Forgetting my bare chest, I leaned in and wrapped my arms around her. "I miss her with everything I have, Fiona... but that's not any worse because of you. If anything, you make it a little bit easier for me."

"I really want to meet her someday. I'm sure she's a wonderful person."

"She was a wonderful person," I said.

"Sorry... I didn't think..."

"I can't spend every day hoping. It's too hard."

"Sorry..."

"I love you, Fiona... so very much."

"I love you, Baptiste."

I gave her a squeeze and a kiss on the cheek.

It didn't feel like holding Cassy.

"I found something," Fiona said.

I looked down at my crotch. Could she...?

"That breadmaker that Marc said he found," she said.

"Where did he find it?"

"He said it was from a house on the way to Gardiner or something."

"Are you sure?"

Ant and Matt had checked every house on Kennedy Road back in the spring. They wouldn't have missed something that important to Fiona. I might have, but not them.

"I'm sure he said that," she said. "And that's the thing. I found a recipe card in the instruction manual."

"He even had the manual?"

"'Grandma Lamarche's *Pain Québecois*'."

"Shit."

Marc had lied.

And because some bald idiot had managed to kill him, the truth had died with him.

Unless Justin knew.

Not that he'd tell me. Not that I needed to hear it.

He and Marc had gone back at it.

"Marc took that breadmaker from the Lamarches' place," Fiona said.

"Looks like."

"So the Lamarches are gone now."

"I think so."

"Did Marc and Justin have something to do with them leaving? They'd driven people to Aiguebelle, and to Detour Lake before…"

"I don't know," I said. "I need time to think this through."

Both families had missed the meeting, the Lamarches and the Smiths. And now both were gone. And Marc had gotten hold of some of the stuff that was left behind. Or he'd taken it from them.

I don't know if Justin had been at it again. But it seemed like Marc had gone back to work. And I hadn't noticed. Despite holding onto the keys and the alarm fobs, and trying to keep tabs on everyone, Marc had been smuggling people off as indentures again.

And Justin was the one who no longer needed to borrow a fob from me…

"Let me know what I can do to help," Fiona said.

"I will." I gave her a smile. "We should head back downstairs… see what they'll break next." I climbed off the bed a little too quickly.

She nodded. "I'll bet it's another chunk off of Graham."

They weren't sober, but they were less drunk by the time dinner came around. So as we ate, I decided to give them the speech, the same one I gave at the start of last winter.

"Winter is the most dangerous time of the year," I said. "And this year may end up being worse."

"People are trying to kill us," Sara said.

"We don't know that," Lisa said.

"We don't," I said. "But we do know that there are two guys, with AR-15s and a very big machine gun, who need to be handled."

"So fucking handle them," Kayla said.

"I will."

"Good. You go kick their asses, you… asskicker."

"Come on," Sara said, "can you at least pretend that you're not a drunken whore for two minutes?"

"Sara," I said, "come on..."

"Yeah, Sara," Kayla said.

"My god, Kayla," I said. "Just shut up for a minute. This is serious, okay?"

"She's right," Lisa said. "We should take them out. Right now."

"Right now?" I said. "Or did you want a shot of Drambuie before we leave?"

"The snow's still falling. If it's still falling in a few hours —"

"Once you've sobered up..."

She nodded. "We head up to Silver Queen Lake and we find them."

"They could be anywhere," Sara said. "There's no way to know if you'll even find them."

"That's true," I said.

"But if we get there and find nothing," Lisa said, "it won't be a wasted trip. We'll still get to balance things out with the Walkers a little, take a few choice items for ourselves."

I don't know why, but at that moment I knew I wanted to do it. Maybe because I needed somewhere for the venom to go.

"That might work," I said.

"It'll work."

"Seriously?" Sara said.

"So you guys want to try and hook the plow up to the new truck and drive all the way up to Silver Queen Lake?" Graham asked.

"You can drive us," I said.

"What about Justin?"

"What about him?"

"You're going to want Justin," Lisa said. "I hate the fucker, but even I think we should bring him with us."

I shook my head. "No... this is an internal operation. No Porters and no Tremblays. Just us." There was no way I could trust Justin.

"So you want me to stay behind with one of the shotguns?" Matt asked, despite his mouth being stuffed full with a bit of goat cheese and potato perogy.

"You and Kayla," I said. "Six-hour shifts with the shotgun and the handheld, round the clock, until we get back. If this goes bad, you call Justin for backup."

"I don't think this is a good idea," Sara said. "Kayla's never even held a gun."

"I've held a gun," Kayla said. "You don't even know me."

"This may be our best chance," I said.

"You really think we're in danger?" Fiona asked. "You really think they'd come here?"

"They wouldn't come here," Graham said. "We're too strong."

"You're overconfident," I said. "But you're probably right. There are way easier pickings out there. For now, at least."

"What do you mean?" Fiona asked. "You think they'll go after Natalie and Tabitha again?"

"I doubt it. The Girards have too many people and guns."

"Now who's overconfident?" Lisa asked.

"Well, either way," Graham said, "we're not at risk."

"But someone is," Fiona said. "Right?"

"Yeah," I said. "Someone is. So we go up to Silver Queen Lake and we take these guys out. And we do it when they least expect it."

"Tonight," Lisa said. "Midnight."

I nodded.

Sara shook her head.

"We'll be careful," I said.

"It's a bad idea, Baptiste," she said. "It's a really bad idea."

"It's a calculated risk. "We'll stay safe. I'll make sure of it."

"Please, Baptiste."

"I'll keep us safe."

"You'd better," she said quietly.

I didn't really need an excuse to get Sara alone after dinner, since I'd be leaving with Lisa and Graham just after midnight. I'd be leaving her along with Matt and the girls, and I needed to make sure they could rely on each other. That they wouldn't be so busy sniping at each other that they let something bad happen.

So I took Sara for a walk down to the barn, and I reached out for her hand at great personal risk.

She took it, but she didn't seem too happy about it.

She'd been overruled. She'd learned that she had no strange veto power over me. I don't think she wanted to accept that.

"I want to talk to you about something," I said as I caught the first whiff of the horses. "But I don't want to make it a big deal."

"What a spineless way to start an intervention," she said. "Just tell me."

"What's the deal with you and Kayla?"

"There's no deal. I don't like her."

"That's not like you, Sara. You're known for liking people."

She shrugged. "I've known Kayla longer than you have. I've known her long enough to know what she's about. And I've known girls like her for much longer than that."

"What does that even mean?"

She let go of my hand. "You really don't get it, Baptiste. No man ever does. Women like Kayla go through life expecting to be treated special because they're pretty."

"I'm not sure if you've noticed, Sara, but you're not ugly."

"How romantic."

"You know what I mean. It's not like you aren't treated better because you're attractive."

"We're all treated better because we're attractive. Do you think a newcomer like you could have been voted onto the Protection Committee if you'd looked like pig crap?"

"I do have some actual experience..."

"But being pretty is not enough. We built this family with hard work and by taking care of each other. Kayla comes along for the ride because she has blond hair and perky boobs."

I sighed. I knew what I wanted to say, that Sara was blinded by some kind of prejudice, that the only reason she couldn't see all the good in Kayla was because she was putting all her energy into ignoring it.

But what could I say that would change her mind? What could I come up with that would actually make a difference for Kayla?

"I've been pushing Matt away," I said. "He's been getting on my nerves and I haven't been working hard enough to let it go."

"I'm aware that you're an asshole," she said. There was a hint of a smile.

"I need to accept that I'm putting my crap onto him. That whatever faults he has are nothing compared to how I build them up in my mind."

She shook her head. "This isn't the same thing, Baptiste. Matt's a bit of an idiot, but he's a good kid. Kayla's not. And now this prepper garbage..."

"I'm going to work on it. I'm going to do my best to go easier on him." I took her hand and brought it up to kiss. "I'd be really grateful if you'd try to do the same for Kayla."

"I can't do that."

"If we keep pushing them away, they're going to move closer to Justin."

"So?"

"So come on, Sara. You don't see what's happening here? Justin is becoming a problem. We can't risk giving him a couple of new allies just because we're stubborn."

She nodded slowly. "I know. I'll try."

I leaned in and gave her a kiss. "I love you, Sara."

She smiled.

"What?" I asked.

"You meant it that time."

"What?"

"Sometimes it sounds like you're just humouring me, like you feel you should say it because we just had sex or you just said something stupid. But that one was real."

"Okay..."

"I love you," she said.

She always meant it.

TODAY IS THURSDAY, DECEMBER 20TH.

GRAHAM AND I hooked the plow up to the truck, just before midnight, without more than a small amount of trouble. Lisa joined us a few minutes later, carrying the beat-up leather guitar case I'd kept in the basement.

"What the heck is that for?" Graham asked. "Baptiste's gonna sing these guys to death?"

"Sing them to heaven with some Mumford & Sons," I said.

"It's not a guitar," Lisa said.

"Oh," Graham said.

She handed the case to me.

I put it in the cab of the gravel truck, behind the bench.

"Well," Graham said, "what is it?"

"Not here," I said.

Graham drove us through the first gate and then to the bridge, almost hitting 80 kph in the snow. There's no way I would have been comfortable taking it that fast.

He stopped at the gate and I opened the door to hop out.

"Hold on," he said. "What's in the case?"

"A gun," I said.

I hopped out and unlocked the gate.

Graham didn't drive through at first, so I waved at him to get going. He shook his head and drove up past the gate.

I climbed back into the truck.

"What kind of gun?" he asked as he started driving toward Cochrane. "You have a hunting rifle or something?"

"A C12 light machine gun," I told him. "It's no anti-aircraft gun, but it does the job."

"What... the heck?" He turned to Lisa. "You knew about this?"

She nodded.

"But... we could have been using this," he said. "The whole time...

the attack at the airport..."

"We didn't need it," I said. "It's for emergencies only."

"If that wasn't an emergency —"

"It wasn't. And now we're going to use it on those two cunts at Silver Queen Lake."

I watched Graham cringe at the language. I made a mental note to say 'cunt' more often. Alanna used to say it all the time; she said that it was part and parcel of being a post-feminist, whatever the hell that meant.

"I can't believe you guys kept this from me," Graham said. "You don't trust me?"

"It's not about trust. It's about needing to know. Lisa and I are both trained to use it —"

"Wait... you showed her how to shoot it?"

"It's not that hard," Lisa said. "Just hold on tight and shoot."

"So I know that if something happens while I'm gone, Lisa's back at the cottage with the C12. That's why she and I never scavenge together. Well... that and the sexual tension."

Lisa smiled.

"This..." Graham said, "I'm not happy about this."

"You're allowed to be angry," I said. "You're allowed to think I'm an asshole."

"That ship has sailed."

"Just don't tell anyone."

"Why? Why is it a bad thing to have more people who know about that thing, and how to use it?"

"I don't want Justin to know I have it."

"Why?"

"You're like a two-year-old," Lisa said. "So many goddamn questions."

"Justin's a problem," I said. "That hasn't changed."

"So why do we keep him around?" Graham asked.

"Because he doesn't need a light machine gun to do the job. And just because he's trouble doesn't mean he isn't useful. It just means that we can't trust him."

"I don't get the hatred," Graham said.

"It's about trust," I said. "That's all."

"So it stays a secret," Lisa said. "That's why we're taking a risk here. This is the first time in over a year that we've left people behind with no real protection."

"So what if Stems attacks?" Graham said.

"He won't," Lisa replied.

"He probably won't," I said. "But these guys will show up eventually, if we don't take them out. So we take the chance and hope to hell that we're not making the biggest mistake since 3D television."

Graham nodded.

He still seemed pissed. By that I mean angry, but I'm sure he was also still a tiny bit drunk.

We drove through Cochrane with the lights off, relying on the glint of the moonlight against the snow. If there was anyone there they'd hear us, but they wouldn't be able to see that much.

We didn't run into anyone; all we saw were forgotten and dead buildings, covered in a fresh blanket of snow. Most of the buildings in Cochrane were damaged in the fire; the south and west sides were hit the hardest, and looking around those neighbourhoods now looks like those old photos of Hiroshima after the A-bomb fell, blackened skeletons of brick and concrete that used to be churches or schools or hockey arenas, and every once in a while there'll be a tree or a hydro pole that's still standing, and you wonder just how it survived when even the cars burned up so much that they just look like bundles of metal sticks.

The rest of town didn't get hit as badly, but there aren't that many buildings that didn't catch some of it. Sometimes when we scavenge I'll walk up a flight of stairs wondering if they'll collapse from some unseen damage, or I'll walk through the front door before realizing that a back wall has caved in and there's nothing left inside but rubble.

The polar bear habitat is still standing at the southeast edge of town; we walked through it once and could still see where someone had shot and butchered the four bears that had been housed there. The whole town looks like a carcass that's been picked over.

We turned north on Western and head up to Clute, where we found a trailer at the bottleneck just like the one the Walkers had brought up to Silver Queen, but it was dark with a drift of snow blown halfway up the door.

"Guess they weren't lying," I said. "They're sticking close to home."

"No tracks anywhere," Graham said. "No one's out today."

"So if we're lucky those Spirit Assholes are bundled up by the fire," Lisa said. "Just waiting for a couple of pretty little head shots."

"We're not going to pose for photographs with their bodies," Graham said. "We're not savages."

"That was totally something Matt would say," I said. "You sure you two aren't related?"

"Shut up," Graham said.

We kept on driving toward Silver Queen Lake, along a road that was as lifeless as everywhere else.

Once we were at Silver Queen, I told Graham to take the south road, without any solid reasoning; I had no evidence they'd go back to the cottage where I'd first found them, since most of the cottages there had enough supplies leftover to keep a couple of murderers comfortable.

"So let's keep it simple," I said. "I'll take the front with my SIG and Lisa will take the back with the Mossberg. You've got your SIG, Graham, and a one-ton means of vehicular homicide. You see anyone you haven't slept with..." — I motioned to Lisa — "or wish you could be just like..." — motioning to me — "you know what to do."

"What about the C12?" Graham asked.

"It's not an emergency yet."

"*Takay*," Lisa said. "Stop the truck."

Graham took his foot of the gas.

"I told you to stop," Lisa said.

"Hold on," Graham said. "It's not as simple as slamming on the brakes. This plow messes up the whole weight of this thing."

He let the truck slow for a moment before I could feel the brakes slowly kicking in. It took about thirty seconds and an extra hundred meters, but we stopped.

Lisa elbowed me in the ribs. "Get out," she said.

"What is it?" I asked.

"Snowmobiles. Saw the lights out in the trees to the south."

I nodded and climbed out.

"Are you sure?" Graham asked.

"I grew up in a town of five thousand, with less than a hundred cars. I know what a goddamn snowmobile looks like." She turned to me. "They should catch up to us any second."

"What do you expect us to do?" I asked. "Shoot them?"

"I don't know... maybe."

"Okay." I lifted my SIG and fired into the air, toward the north. Whoever it was should get the message, not to fuck with us.

"You're a terrible shot," she said.

"Not sure they'll even hear it."

I could see the lights now, poking out from the trees. Two machines.

And then I heard the engines slowing.

We took aim.

"Don't shoot," a voice called out.

"Why not?" I yelled back.

"Baptiste?"

"Yeah?"

"It's Zach Walker... Dave Walker's son. Sky's here, too."

"How do I know you aren't full of shit?"

"It's a badass name," a second voice said. "Isn't it?"

I lowered my gun.

Lisa followed my lead.

"What the hell are you guys doing out here?" I asked as they stepped out of the forest.

"Looking for you," Zach said. "Justin called my father and said you were on your way up here."

I wasn't sure who told Justin, but I could take a guess. And I could kick Matt's ass halfway to Quebec when I got home.

"What do you want?" I asked.

"Justin wanted us to turn you around, and send you home. He says you're going to get someone killed."

"I don't take orders from Justin Porter."

"And neither do we. We want to help. Reinforcements."

"So wait... your father sent his kid up here to fight?"

"I'm not a kid."

"Sure you are."

"We don't need any help," Lisa said. "We'll handle this."

"No," Zach said. "You won't. This is a partnership. We'll do it together."

"That's fine," I said. "We could use another couple guns. But I'm in charge of this operation, so you'll defer to my judgement."

"Absolutely." He gave me a grin.

Exactly what a kid would do.

⁓

I had Zach and Sky ditch the snowmobiles and hop in the back of the gravel truck. They both had hunting rifles that they'd slung over their shoulders.

Graham took us farther up the road, toward the bend.

I could see the woodsmoke in the moonlight.

"They're here," I said. "We'll come in quick, since they may have already seen or heard us. Assuming they're not drunk or fucking..."

I realized what I was saying. I thought of Natalie and Tabitha, and the bruises on their wrists, from trying to free themselves from the bedframe.

"Fuck," I said quietly.

We turned the bend and I saw the gray truck. And two more of them, three in total, each with a snow-covered tarp wrapper over the guns in the back.

"There's three trucks?" Lisa said. "What the hell? How many guys —"

"Shit," I said. "Turn us around, Graham."

"Hold on," he said. "It's not easy..."

"Come on... turn us around..."

I reached behind the cab and pulled out the guitar case. I laid it out on my lap.

"There's no time," Lisa said.

I opened the case and pulled out a magazine. I grabbed the C12 and loaded the ammo, and then I aimed it out the window.

Lisa reached over and pressed the button to open it.

They shot at us first.

I couldn't see from where.

I aimed for the front window and started shooting.

"Hold on," Graham said as he started to turn the truck.

I heard the wheels spinning.

"Shit," Graham said. It had to be bad if he was swearing. "We're stuck."

"Holy fucking shit," Lisa said. "This is a goddamn nightmare. What do we do?"

"We shoot," I said. "We shoot and we hope Graham can get us moving again."

I heard the sound of bullets slamming against the side of the truck; we had our helmets and armour, but they weren't foolproof. And the guys in the back didn't have anything.

I hoped to hell they stayed low.

I emptied my first thirty bullets and reloaded. I only had eight mags total. Only seven left. I kept firing. I had to pin them inside the cottage until Graham could have us moving again.

The wheels spun some more.

"You're digging us deeper," Lisa said. "You don't even know how to drive in snow."

"I'm doing my best," Graham said.

"It's not good enough."

"It's not the tires... it's the plow... it's stuck in the snowbank. I can't get it out."

"What does that mean?" She was almost screaming at him.

"We'll have to dig it out."

"Do we even have any goddamn shovels?"

"What if we removed the plow?" I asked.

I had to reload again.

"I can remove it," Graham said. "Take me thirty seconds or so. Then I'll give the bumper a shove and we should be able to get out."

"I'll do it," I said. Out of habit, mostly.

"No... I'm faster. I've got my gear on... I'll be alright."

Graham opened the door and climbed out, with Lisa taking his place. I ramped up the firing as he got into position; he was mostly covered by the engine block.

There was a good chance he'd be able to pull it off.

He threw his gloves off into the snow and pulled at the plow, disconnecting the hitches and moving on to the wires.

I reloaded again.

"Start reversing," Graham yelled.

Lisa slammed on the gas. The wheels spun.

"Hold on," Graham said. He bent down and started digging into the snow with his bare hands, moving to the right.

The engine block wouldn't be covering him anymore.

I shoved two magazines into my pockets.

I opened the door of the truck and jumped out, hoping to draw fire. I ran toward the back of the truck, firing as I went.

Their bullets followed me.

I felt a prick in my left leg. I kept moving.

I turned the back corner and reloaded.

"Baptiste," Graham called. "Move out of the way."

I ran back in between the cottage and the truck, heading for the passenger side door. My left leg was slowing me down.

I took another hit, in the side. The vest seemed to have stopped it.

I climbed into the cab just as Lisa slammed on the gas.

The truck rocked backward and soon pulled out of the snow.

Lisa slammed on the brake.

Graham made a run for the cab as I emptied another magazine.

Lisa shoved herself against me as Graham climbed in.

We were on our way.

"Do you think they'll follow?" Graham asked.

"I don't know," I said.

I heard a tap on the back of the cab.

"Sounds like they're okay," Lisa said.

"Thank goodness," Graham said.

The knock came again. Harder.

"We can't stop now," I said.

"I know," Graham replied.

The road was poorly plowed, of course, but it was enough for us to get through in the one-ton gravel truck. We kept on past the first of the Walkers' empty trailers, not stopping until we reached the second at Clute.

I expected Zach and Sky to hop out and walk up to the door.

They didn't come.

Instead there was another tap on the cab.

I got out of the truck and walked over to the back, Lisa right behind me.

Sky was lying in the truck bed, his foot kicking the cab, while his hands were gripping Zach's chest.

Lisa climbed into the back without a word.

She threw off her jacket and tore one of the sleeves off her shirt.

"Find the first aid kit," she told me as she worked to stop the bleeding.

I went back to the cab to get the kit.

By the time I came back no one was hurrying.

"He's gone," Lisa said.

Zach Walker's eyes were still open, staring at me.

It reminded me of Ant.

Sometimes the anxiety gets so bad that you feel like you're not even able to breathe anymore, like the stress is actually going to kill you.

I guess now that I'm over fifty and on heart pills for life, that stress might just finish the job.

So tonight, just after ten, once Sara had fallen asleep, I took another tablet with the little maple leaf. I could say it was for the bullet hole in my leg that Lisa had half-heartedly patched up, but that was just an excuse.

About forty minutes after I swallowed it, I went down and sat in the kitchen, in the dark. I didn't want anyone to find me like that.

When I was seven I got lost at Canada's Wonderland. I remember being nervous at first, once I realized that my father had lost track of me. I stood under the Skyrider for what seemed like hours, watching the loop where the people strapped standing up would go completely upside-down, my little seven-year-old brain trying to figure out why there wasn't a spray of coins and keys every time the roller coaster car would reach the top.

And I wondered why no one had stopped to ask the little brown boy with the curly hair if he was lost; I'd been too scared to actually ask anyone for help.

My father found me, and I think in the end I was only lost for twenty minutes or so. When he grabbed me by the shoulders and brought me in for a hug, I could see the absolute panic in his eyes. That was the first time I realized that my father could be afraid of something. It didn't make me think of him as more human or more relatable; seven-year-old Baptiste just thought his dad was weak.

There's so much crap we wish we could take back, things we did or things we said... I wish I could take back how I felt about my father at that moment.

I've known for a long time now that there's nothing wrong with being scared. It's been thirty-five years since I came back from the work in Panjwaii, and there are times when I'm still scared, when the weight of if comes back like I'm twenty years old all over again, on a mission that sounded noble but didn't work out that great.

I don't remember what it's like to not have that in me. When I try to remember being a kid and what that felt like, to be innocent and naive, the feelings I remember are from that day at Canada's Wonderland, the fear of being lost forever and the shame of seeing my father afraid.

When the light to the kitchen went on, I froze, as if I hoped that I wouldn't be seen if I just... didn't... move.

"Why are you sitting in the dark?" Kayla asked me.

"Migraine."

She walked over and leaned up against the table beside me. "Sara's still up?"

"Nope. I couldn't sleep. Sometimes the yard light bothers me."

She walked over to the window and looked out. "The yard light isn't on, Baptiste."

"Then I should head up to bed."

She smiled. "Or you can cut the bullshit." She walked back to the table and sat down beside me.

She put her hand on my lap and squeezed.

"It's okay, Baptiste," she said. "It'll be okay."

"Okay."

She nodded. "I'm not that good at this stuff. Would you like a handjob instead?"

That made me laugh.

"You seem off," she said.

"I'm tired... and I got shot... and I got someone killed today, so..."

"Come on..."

"I know... don't blame myself and all that garbage."

She gave my thigh a tap. "That's it," she said. "You're drunk."

"Do I smell like I'm drunk?"

She took a whiff. "No..."

"Am I slurring my words? Do I have a bottle of Jack in front of me?"

"It's something..."

I wrapped my hand over hers. "Look, Kayla... I'm actually wanting to be alone."

"I don't care. I'm here. So share whatever you've got or this will get way more awkward."

"It kinda feels like you're hitting on me. Do I need to pull out my rape whistle?"

"I think that's a euphemism... I think you're sexually harassing me..."

"You're the one with your hand on my thigh."

"You're the one with the bulge in your pants."

I looked down and saw it. If I hadn't already started feeling the effects of the E I would've been embarrassed.

Kayla put her hand in my pocket.

"Hold on," I said. "Kayla..."

I didn't really want her to stop...

"What is this?" she asked as she pulled out the plastic baggie. "Maple leafs..."

"Vitamins."

"I've seen these before... hell... I've used these before."

"What?"

"Seriously, Baptiste? You've been holding out on me."

"Kayla... you can't tell anyone..."

"Don't worry. Where did you find these, anyway?"

"Scavenging somewhere. I didn't know what they were at first."

"And so what? You just decided to experiment?"

"I don't know."

She grinned. "You must realize, sir, that I have a rather highly tuned bullshit detector."

"They were Ant's."

"Fine. Don't tell me. I don't care."

"Who did you get yours from?"

"I don't have any."

"I mean from before."

She leaned in and whispered into my ear. "A little unbalanced, don't you think? I show you mine and you give me fuck all?"

"What did you want?"

She squeezed my thigh again. "What do you think I want?"

"Are you serious?"

Kayla laughed. "You're hilarious, Baptiste." She gave me another slap on the thigh.

"I don't think I am."

She stood up from the chair. "Don't get too high, alright?" She dropped a hand on my shoulder. "You're a pretty great guy, Baptiste."

I nodded. "And you have terrible judgement."

She started to walk toward the door, but then she stopped.

"I got mine from Zach Walker," she said. "We all did. Zach and his big brother."

"The Walkers are drug dealers?"

"Some Walkers were. It's a booming business, providing you have some initiative and the backing of The Souls."

"You're kidding."

She smiled. "Toronto isn't the only place with a drug problem. You're not the first junkie in town.

TODAY IS FRIDAY, DECEMBER 21ST.

STILL SNOWING.

Even if it wasn't, I don't think the Walkers would be up to working at Silver Queen Lake.

Dave Walker's son is dead, and it's partly my fault.

And the assholes who did it are a hell of a lot stronger than I'd realized.

So I guess it's completely my fault.

This week's meeting was set to be held at the Tremblays; that was the last thing I wanted to do this morning.

That's just what I said to Sara when she woke me up.

"You're kidding me," she muttered, as she sat up in bed.

"I'm not going," I said, turning onto my side and away from her. I was acting like a child; I felt like a child.

"I can't believe I'm sleeping with a five-year-old."

"I'm just not ready for this."

She stood up and walked around to my side of the bed. "You're coming with me, Baptiste."

"I'm not coming."

"We're in crisis here. None of us have any idea what's going to happen now. Don't you think you oughta be at the freaking meeting?"

"I'm not coming."

"Baptiste..."

"I'm not coming."

"This is ridiculous. If you want to hide out here, go ahead. But I'm not going to cover for you. If people ask me why you can't be bothered to show up and give some kind of guidance... or you know, leadership... I'm just going to tell them that you're lying in bed like a sad little puppy."

"Thanks for nothing, then," I said, closing my eyes so I wouldn't

217

have to see the look on her face.

"You're disgusting."

I stayed in bed until I knew she'd left.

Sara came back an hour or so later, and I was still in bed, half-awake.

She stomped around the room a little, opening the blinds and making her side of the bed, all the things she does when she's trying to get me to talk to her without, well, talking to me first.

I didn't take the bait, so she disappeared again, and by the time I went downstairs she wasn't there.

No one was.

Lunch had been eaten and there were still dishes in the sink.

I didn't see anything left for me, but for all I knew it had been one of those single-serve, leftover lunches.

I didn't check the pile of dishes too closely; I didn't want to find out that Fiona had made something fresh and no one had come to get me.

Well... I guess Sara had come to get me... and stomped around...

I found Kayla and Matt outside on the dock, dressed in full winter gear and sitting in snow, staring out over the wintry lake, an oversized bottle of spiced rum cupped into the snow between them.

"Looking to freeze to death?" I asked Kayla.

"It's warm out, silly," she said. "Are you still feeling sick?"

"Sick?"

"Sara said it was coming out of both ends," Matt said.

"We didn't want that much information," Kayla said.

"I'm fine," I said. "Where is Sara?"

Kayla shrugged. "Fuck if I know."

"Thanks for the help."

I saw a series of footsteps heading over to the barn, so I followed them.

Sara and Fiona were in the barn, Fiona sitting on a small step ladder while Sara brushed the mare.

"Hey Baptiste," Fiona said as I walked inside.

Sara didn't turn to look at me.

"What are you guys doing?" I asked.

"Sometimes it's nice to get outside. You feeling better?"

"I'm fine."

"You should take a shower, Baptiste," Sara said, still giving the horse her full attention.

"What?" I said.

"Whenever I'm starting to get better I make sure I wash up. It helps."

"I don't need a shower."

She put down the brush. "I'll take you back," she said.

She walked right past me and out the door.

"I think you're supposed to go with her," Fiona said with a grin

"I know."

I followed Sara back to the cottage, then up the stairs, and into the bathroom.

She closed and locked the door behind me.

She started to undress.

"Aren't you angry with me?" I asked.

"I want to strangle you. Take off your clothes."

I hesitated.

"Get naked," she said.

I did as she told me.

She motioned for me to step into the bathtub. and she followed me in, standing between me and the tap. She turned on the water to the lower faucet and got it up to her favoured temperature, before she pulled the knob to bring it up to the showerhead.

Like always, the water was too hot. Just like Sara liked it.

Alanna had liked it hot, too.

I don't think I've known a woman who didn't.

She handed me a bar of soap. "Do my back," she said.

I started lathering her shoulders.

"You need to talk to Alain about his brother," she said. "And you need to make a call to Dave Walker, offer your condolences for his son."

"You know I'm not ready for either of those."

"I don't care. Make yourself ready. We need you to be ready."

"I'm not good right now, Sara."

I finished with the soap on her back and she turned to rinse herself off. Sara really is a beautiful woman. Too beautiful to be there with me.

"I need you, Baptiste," she said. "I can't hold this family together without you."

"I'm the problem... I'm the reason things are falling apart. If I hadn't got it in my head that I could take those guys out... if I hadn't gone up to Silver Queen with the Porters... if I hadn't killed Marc Tremblay... if I hadn't left Ant to be murdered on the road..."

My legs felt weak.

I sat down in the tub.

"This isn't you," Sara said. "This isn't the man I fell in love with. You're stronger than this, Baptiste. You're not the type of man to let bad luck and a few accidents stop you in your tracks."

"You know what the worst part of this is?"

"What?"

"The way you all still delude yourselves into thinking that I'm some kind of leader."

"I'm not listening to this crap." She stuck her head under the stream of hot water.

It was probably the most wasteful shower she's ever taken.

"Katie Walker called Justin this morning," she said. "There's a memorial for Zach tomorrow. They expect you to be there."

"We can't all just take off for a funeral."

She pointed at her ears. "Hold on."

She pulled her head out from the water.

"I couldn't hear you," she said, "but I'm sure I can make an educated guess. And the answer is that you're going. You and me, Baptiste."

"Just us?"

"Just us. I doubt they'd want to see Justin and Graham, and I'm not sure anyone else had ever met Zach."

"Kayla knew him," I said. And regretted. "Like an acquaintance or something."

"Oh. No surprise there. He did have a pulse and a penis, right?"

"I don't think she'd want to go."

"Good. And when we get back, we'll stop off at the Tremblays."

"Isn't that enough for one day?"

"Be a man, Baptiste. You're acting like Alain's going to bite your head off because you couldn't save his brother from slipping on some ice."

"Fuck, Sara... you don't know what happened out there. He didn't slip... I hit him."

"What do you mean? You got into a fight with him?"

"He was drunk... he was angry... I just wanted to stop him from going at Graham. I hit him the wrong way. Obviously I didn't mean to kill him."

"*Mon dieu*, Baptiste..."

She looked down at her hands.

I wanted to reach out and touch them, but it didn't feel like the right moment.

She shook her head. "I can't believe you lied to me."

"I'm sorry, Sara. I didn't know how to tell you."

"That doesn't matter. You can't be keeping secrets from me. That's not allowed."

"Not allowed?"

"I won't accept that from you. Do you understand me?"

"I understand."

"I'm serious."

"I know."

She wrapped her arm around me. "Does Alain know what really happened?"

"No... and I don't think there's a reason to tell him."

I gritted my teeth and waited for the argument.

"You're right," she said. "There's no reason. As long as you're okay with him not knowing."

I nodded. "There's a lot about Marc that I'll bet he doesn't know."

"Like what?"

"I think Marc and Justin were at it again. They took supplies from the Lamarches."

"Isn't that a good thing?"

"How did they know the Lamarches had left? How come they didn't tell us?"

"We all had a feeling they'd left."

"But Fiona's had that breadmaker for how long?"

"I don't know."

"They didn't tell us about the Lamarches because they were involved."

"You think they made a deal."

"Those assholes cornered the market. The only guys north of

221

Timmins who could sneak people across our territory. They were just using us."

"It's not that simple."

"How can I give Alain my sympathy when his brother deserved what he got?"

"You'll figure it out."

"I don't know."

"You will." She leaned in and gave me a kiss.

Then she turned off the water and grabbed a towel.

5

TODAY IS SUNDAY, DECEMBER 23RD.

ZACH WALKER'S memorial service was today.

Sara and I went, with our body armour stowed and my SIG and belt on; Fiona had wanted to go, but I told her it wasn't worth the risk. She gave me a full dose of teenage indignation, but she eventually stormed off and let it drop.

We took the gravel truck, even though we have less than a quarter tank left; I know there are three crews out there who want me dead, and their Toyotas would be tough to handle with a wooden cart and two tired horses.

Sara and I arrived at the Walker's rail bridge around a half hour early, which was later than she'd wanted and earlier than I'd hoped for; the last thing I needed was awkward conversations with grieving Walkers.

We parked the truck and got out, the two men at the bridgehead nodding as we walked by. I didn't recognize either of them, and I was surprised that they hadn't said anything about the gunbelt.

"You'll do the talking," I said to Sara as we crossed the frozen Frederickhouse river; we'd never been allowed to cross the river before.

"This isn't that hard," she said. "Just look sad and nod and be prepared to hug people you'd never hug in real life."

I groaned.

"This is important," she said.

"I know."

There was a white tent set up on the west bank of the river, one of those tents you'd use for a wedding.

Livingston was standing by the white plastic door. Sad country music was floating out from inside.

"Ms. Vachon," he said. "Baptiste..."

"I'm sorry, Fisher," Sara said. She reached out and gave him a

225

hug.

"Thank you."

"How are they?"

"Not bad."

"That's good."

Livingston turned to me and offered his hand.

I shook it and gave my best sad and sympathetic face.

It wasn't easy.

"I appreciate you guys coming," he said.

I nodded.

He motioned for us to walk inside.

Sara took me by the hand and led me in.

There were dozens of chairs set up, maybe over a hundred, and most were taken. Over half of the Marchands were there, as were Gerald Archibald and what looked like over a dozen people from New Post.

I was starting to wonder if we should have brought a few more bodies.

Eva Marchand waved us over, and the mass of her family shifted over to open two seats to her right. Sara sat next to her, and I took the next chair over.

"It's good to see you two," she said. "*C'est terrible.* Are you okay, Baptiste?"

I nodded.

"I heard it was an ambush."

"Not quite," I said. "I made a series of bad decisions."

"It's not your fault." She said it in a way that made it clear that it was.

"Are the Girards not here?" Sara asked.

"Not yet," Eva said. "No one's been able to reach them."

"They might be out of fuel," I said. "We're certainly running low."

"We'll swing by on our way home," Sara said.

I wasn't going to argue with her in front of Eva Marchand and everyone else.

I felt the draft of an open door.

I turned to look, expecting to see a handful of Girards.

Instead I saw Ryan Stems.

I stood up and pulled my gun.

"Baptiste," Sara said. "Don't..."

"No guns," Livingston called out. "Please."

Stems wasn't holding a gun.

I wasn't even sure he was armed.

I put my SIG back in its holster. "What's he doing here?" I asked.

"Apology accepted," Stems said.

The Marchands started shifting seats again. One for Stems, and one for his latest companion, a young native woman. Much too young for him.

As per usual.

Stems sat down beside me.

"Mr. Jeanbaptiste," he said.

"Why are you here?" I asked.

"To pay my respects. Like you."

"Do you have any respect to give?" I felt Sara's elbow. I ignored it. "You've got some nerve coming here, Stems."

"No more than you."

Sara cupped a hand over my knee and leaned in "It's good to see you, Mr. Stems," she said. She smiled at the young woman on the other side of him. "I'm Sara Vachon. From McCartney Lake."

"Sorry," Stems said. "This is my beautiful wife, Anna."

"How many 'wives' do you have?" I asked.

"Baptiste," Sara said. "Don't..."

"Just the one," Stems said with a grin. "How 'bout you?"

"*Pardon,*" Eva Marchand said, "I did not invite you to sit with me so you can create a scene."

"Sorry," Sara said.

"I'm sorry as well," Stems said.

I groaned.

"Are you still living over in Smooth Rock Falls?" Sara asked

"We are," Stems said. "Anna's family lives in Kapuskasing, so we try to visit them when we can."

"Taking any field trips to Silver Queen Lake?" I asked.

"Come on, Baptiste," he said, "you're smarter than this."

"Excuse me?"

"You know it wasn't me. This is the first time this year I've crossed the Driftwood River. The Walkers control that bridge, remember?"

"Sure... I'll just start taking you at your word, then... like it's worth anything."

"Robert, please," Eva said. "You're embarrassing me."

"I think we should find another place to sit," I said.

I stood up.

Sara didn't.

I glared at her.

"Find a place in the back," Sara said. "Maybe stand with Livingston by the door."

As I walked away, the Marchands all shifted back a seat.

The Walkers came in a few minutes later, sitting down in the empty rows at the front. Katie was walking with Sky, who had his arm around her.

Dave Walker looked around after he sat, over to the back row where I was sitting, but I couldn't tell if he'd noticed me. I'm not sure he was noticing anything, really.

Once the family was seated, Livingston walked up the aisle.

I expected him to sit with the Walkers.

He walked up the front and turned to address us all.

"There is nothing more heartbreaking than the loss of a loved one," he said, "especially when that loss is sudden, and the loved one has so much life left to live. Zach was a good guy. That's the consensus. And all of us are a little less whole without him."

He kept on for a while, before inviting the family to speak. Katie went first, with Sky still draped around her, talking about growing up with her little brother and how he used to be so much stronger than he looked, how at age seven he'd picked her up — his fourteen-year-old sister — and carried her down two flights of stairs, because he was playing fireman, and that's what firemen are supposed to do.

Then she told a story about Zach's first date, when he'd been so nervous that he'd called his big sister from the bathroom at the restaurant for advice.

Funerals would be a hell of a lot easier to sit through if you didn't have to start thinking of the dead guy as a real person.

After Katie it was Dave Walker's turn, and I was tempted to sneak out the back, just in case he started talking about the day his son was killed.

But he didn't mention it; he just talked about how much he loved his son, and how he's now lost two of his boys and that if it wasn't for the children he still had left he wouldn't know what to do with himself.

When Dave Walker started to cry... it was too much for me. I looked around, hoping no one would notice my tears.

I'm not even supposed to like these people.

The last person to stand up to talk was Zach's girlfriend, a pretty blond girl with a cute french accent, and everything good that goes with it.

The one thing I remember about my father's funeral was that it was the one and only time I'd forgotten to check out all of the girls.

"I love Zach," she said. "I can't believe he's gone. I can't believe he lost his life for no good reason." I think she was looking right at me. "I can't believe that so many people are dying for no good reason. And the people responsible just sit here like there's nothing wrong with that."

I wasn't sure if she meant that just for me. Just for me, or just for Stems, or just for both of us.

Or for every person in that tent.

"We're all the same people," she said. "Five years ago we were friends and neighbours. Now we don't trust each other. Now we shoot each other."

I noticed Katie inching toward her.

"I'm not finished," the blond girl said. "I have more to say... about Zach."

Katie put her hand on the girl's shoulder. "Tell us about Zach," she said.

The blond girl tried to smile, and then she talked about her boyfriend, for long enough that she seemed to forget about assholes like me.

After Katie helped Zach's girlfriend back to her seat, Livingston came back up for a closing prayer.

He started in English, but said every second line in French, like they sometimes used to do in elementary school. Livingston's French is even worse than mine.

Once he was done the prayer and invited us all to the table of refreshments, I heard what was a huge sigh of relief from pretty much everyone, in both official languages.

And then I found my way to the coffee.

And Katie Walker found her way to me.

"Baptiste," she said as she came in for a hug. "I'm so glad you came."

"I'm sorry," I said, the first time I'd said it. Because I meant it.

"I wish you could have kept him safe. I know you did your best." She paused. "You weren't sitting with Sara..."

"I wasn't sitting with Ryan Stems. I'm not up for that."

She nodded. "I don't like him, either. My youngest sister grew up with the Lamarche boys. We haven't forgotten."

"He's never made amends, has he..."

"Let's not talk about that."

I nodded. "I don't know what to talk about."

She smiled. "I don't, either."

The pause was a little awkward.

"So you and Sky..." I said.

"Me and Sky. We're engaged, actually."

"Since when?"

"Since last Wednesday. Bad timing... but what else do you do when you're snowed in?"

"That or Scrabble."

"I'm awful at Scrabble. I keep making up words."

"That probably makes you good at it. You just need to find stupider opponents."

"I don't have time to play against you right now," she said. "Maybe later."

Sara found me then, putting on her fake smile as she approached. She was still pissed at me.

"Did I hear you're engaged?" Sara said as she gave Katie a hug. "Congratulations."

Katie held out her left hand for inspection.

"What is this?" Sara said.

"What?" I said.

"That's my ring."

I took a look at the ring on Katie's finger. It wasn't too big, just a diamond, jutting out of a twisting gold band.

"Are you sure?" Katie asked. "Maybe it's just the same model."

"It was a custom design," Sara said. "My ex-husband had it made in Montreal. Where did you get that?"

"I... I'm sorry," Katie said. "I didn't know... you can have it back."

"No... but thank you. I don't want it back. That's why I gave it away in the first place."

"So you sold it?"

"No... I gave it to one of my sisters." Sara began to cry. "I told her to hold onto it in case I ever thought about getting married again."

"Your sister..."

"She died at Carman Lake. Both of them did."

"So maybe she left the ring in town," I said.

"She used to wear it," Sara said. "On her index finger."

"I'm sorry," Katie said. She began wrenching on her ring finger.

"No, please... keep it. I like the idea of someone being happy wearing it."

"I don't know..."

"Think about it... don't decide right now. But do you know where you got it?"

"Sky found it... at Silver Queen Lake, I think. In a jewelry box. I should go get it for you... in case you recognize anything else..."

"Not right now," Sara said. "Don't worry about it."

"We'll be back at it after Christmas," I said. "We'll talk about it then."

"Okay," Katie said. "Thanks, guys. I'm going to go check on my parents."

She leaned in and kissed me on the cheek before leaving.

I turned to Sara. "Are you okay?"

She shook her head. "No..."

I gave her a hug.

"Not here," she said. "Not now..."

"Okay." I took a deep breath. "Guess we'd better talk to the rest of the Walkers."

We made our way to Dave and his wife.

"Thanks for coming," Dave Walker said. "I do appreciate it."

Sara gave him a hug, and then one to his wife. "I'm sorry," she said.

I shook Dave Walker's hand.

Then he turned away.

I didn't mind.

I hated me a little bit, too.

We left the tent after another twenty minutes of awkward mingling and solemn nodding, with Sara's eyes so puffed out from emotion and exhaustion that I was worried she'd collapse.

I felt a hand pull on my shoulder.

It was Livingston.

"There's a problem," he said. "You guys can't leave."

"What are you talking about? I need to take her home."

"Our men have spotted three pickup trucks up the road. I think they're waiting for you, Baptiste."

"Shit."

"You're not prepared for them."

"I have stuff back at my truck."

"But is it enough?"

"You're loving this, aren't you?"

"No, I'm not," Livingston said. "Those are the men who killed Zach Walker."

"Then get your men and let's take care of this."

"You're expecting us to pick a fight before Zach's even buried?"

"I expect you to want some kind of revenge."

"They're probably not after us."

"There we go," I said. "There's the Livingston I remember."

"Just stay here for now... they'll give up eventually."

"That's a joke, right?"

"We should stay," Sara said.

"And then what? If they're looking for me they won't just give up."

"Then they'll get their chance another day. When we have backup."

"We ought to have backup right now. If this wuss won't help us I'll find someone who will."

I found Eva Marchand, standing with the skinny Marchand boy who'd fought with us at the airport.

"I'm sorry," Eva said when I asked, "we're not ready for a fight."

"They'll kill us," I said. "Me and Sara."

"We can take Sara with us... we can keep her safe."

"And so they'll just kill me."

"You don't have to cross back over the river," Eva said. "You can stay here for now. The Walkers will keep you safe."

"And I'll leave my own people exposed. You know the Walkers should be fighting beside me. And you should be, too, Eva."

"That's the wrong choice. I won't risk my family... sorry."

"I won't forget this."

"You can be angry with me, Monsieur Baptiste... but let us take Sara. We can get her home safely."

"Okay..."

But that wouldn't be enough.

I needed help.

I would need to ask Dave Walker. At his youngest son's funeral.

"Baptiste..."

I turned to see Ryan Stems and his little wife.

"We can help you," he said. "I have two men at the bridge. That makes five of us."

"Five?"

"I can shoot," little Anna said.

"We won't need to shoot," Stems said. "We drive out together, with a truck from the Walkers..."

"The Walkers will help?" I ask.

"I'll handle it. These guys won't engage if we're three on three."

"That's three on three plus mounted anti-aircraft guns. Not that equal."

"Still... these guys are cowards."

"You sound pretty sure..."

"I am. When you dropped in on them the other day, Thursday night —"

"Why are you so well-versed in this?" I asked.

"When you dropped in on them, did they come after you?"

"No..."

"They knew you could put up a good fight. Once you took off, they said a little prayer and cleaned the shit off their thighs. They didn't come after you."

"You know an awful lot about this..."

"Sky told me what happened. I do have friends around here."

"Bullshit."

"Okay... maybe not friends..."

"So your entire plan rests on a hunch that these assholes will turn tail the moment they see I'm not alone?"

Stems nodded.

He was cocky about it.

"How do I know this isn't a trap?" I asked. "These guys told Matt they're the Mushkegowuk Spirit Animals... friends of yours..."

"You're smarter than that, Baptiste."

"Explain it like I'm five."

"They want us to distrust each other. We've had raids on our side of the North Driftwood, too. Except on our side they wear OPP helmets and they like to pretend that they're from something called the Cochrane Protection Committee. Sound familiar?"

"Then who do you think they are?"

"I know who they are. Detour Lake."

"How do you know?"

"Can we just get this done?"

I'd have to either accept his help or I'd have to bunk with the Walkers.

And since Sara was pissed and Katie was engaged, I'd probably end up canoodling with Livingston...

"Okay," I said. "Let's do it."

"Alright... you're welcome, by the way."

"I didn't thank you."

"That's right... maybe you should..."

"Fuck you, Stems."

He laughed. "Close enough."

Stems did get a truck from the Walkers, complete with two more men and their hunting rifles; those men weren't Walkers, so they might very well have been indentures. I didn't ask.

I took the gravel truck in front, with Stems in the passenger seat and both of us wearing body armour; it certainly fit Stems better than it would Sara.

Behind us was Stems' black half-ton, with his two men and his young bride, who ended up with a shotgun that was almost as big as she was; that being said, it was clear from the moment she'd taken it over from one of Stems' men that she knew how to use it.

I guess Stems has a thing for girls with guns. I'll be sure to keep him away from Lisa.

The Marchands waited behind, with their two Ford pickups and Sara; we all switched to the same unencrypted band, so once we were sure it was safe, Stems would be able to call Sara on his handheld and give the Marchands the all-clear.

I drove up the road slowly, as Stems scanned the distance with his binoculars.

"I see them," he said as we neared the rail crossing. "Two trucks."

"Only two?"

"I'm not sure if the other's behind, or off somewhere else."

"Could be another bad maneuver," I said. "At the airport they tried to sneak up behind us."

"There's no behind us, is there?"

"Not yet... once we cross the tracks..."

"The tracks will be the 'behind us'."

"Maybe..."

"So we stop?"

"Couldn't hurt."

I put on the brakes.

We waited.

"No movement," he said.

"I can see that."

"Now what?"

"I'm in no hurry," I said. "Sometimes the key to victory is knowing when to sit back and wait."

"I'm from the US Army," Stems said. "We're not so good at waiting."

"Or nation building."

"Or communication."

"Or coming under budget."

"Hah!" Stems said. "Sometimes I forget how much you and I hate each other."

"I don't forget."

"Yeah... that's not really your deal."

"You're still a criminal in my books."

"I know." He didn't sound surprised. "They're moving."

"They're coming?"

"Nope... they're going. Still just the two... heading east."

"Luring us?"

"I doubt it."

"I guess we'll find out," I said.

I started moving forward, even more slowly than before.

"Step on it," Stems said.

"Why?"

"I want to see how they react."

"If they're even watching."

"They're watching."

I sped up, kicking up snow with the tires and making the engine roar.

"They're off," Stems said. "They're pissing themselves."

"No one is pissing themselves."

"I am... a little..."

The Toyotas were speeding away, faster than you'd usually see on concession road in the middle of winter. They didn't want us to catch up to them.

We reached the rail crossing.

I glanced to the left, and then to the right. "Nothing," I said.

"So where's lucky number three?"

It felt like the airport all over again. Two in front, a third hidden somewhere...

"Maybe I'm not the target," I said.

"Who's the target then?"

"They want us to give the all-clear. They want us to chase them toward Cochrane or Clute or something, and then the third truck will take its shot."

"At the Walkers?" he asked.

"At the Marchands, maybe... or Sara... or both."

"That doesn't make any sense, Baptiste. You're the one who tried to kill them."

"And they're doing a piss poor job of trying to kill me back."

"What?"

"Call Sara and tell them to stay put. Don't mention anything else."

"Yeah, I know," he said. "Clear channel."

He pushed for Sara. "Sara and Marchands, this is Stems. Stay where you are. Repeat. Stay where you are."

There was no response.

"Sara and Marchands. Come in."

Nothing.

236

"Shit," Stems said. "Does she know how to work a handheld?"

"Something's wrong. If she's not responding... something's happened."

"Could be jamming."

"But if they want us to give the all-clear..."

"They knew we wouldn't. I said they were cowards... I didn't say they were idiots."

"So we turn back."

"No, wait... I think I see the Marchands."

"She couldn't get through to us and so they decided to come looking?"

"I never said the Marchands weren't idiots."

I stopped the truck. "We'll all go together, I guess. I'll ride with the Marchands."

I hopped out.

The first of the Marchands trucks slowed to a stop; the second passed in front before slowing down a little further ahead.

Eva rolled down the passenger-side window. Sara was crammed up beside her.

"What's going on?" Eva asked.

"I'm riding with you," I said.

"There's no room."

"I'll take the back."

"But you're the one they're after."

"We were chasing two trucks. We're not sure where the third is. So I'm with you until we find it."

She nodded.

I walked around to the back and climbed into the bed of the pickup.

The skinny kid was there, holding his hunting rifle with a serious look on his face.

"Together again," I said.

He nodded.

I tapped on the cab and the truck started moving.

Stems took the lead, rushing ahead with his three trucks.

The other Ford pickup started up as well, falling in behind us.

We drove past the first concession road, with no sign of the third Toyota. For all I knew, there were three gray pickup trucks a ways in front of Stems, and I was just wasting our time. But I couldn't think of a downside to a little extra caution.

A minute or two later, we reached the junction with Highway 579. We couldn't see the Toyotas.

To the right was Cochrane.

To the left was Clute and Silver Queen Lake.

Stems turned left.

We all followed.

I saw a cloud of snow coming from just left of the road. A truck coming up a driveway, heading toward us.

Too big for a pickup.

A gravel truck.

Stems kept going; he apparently hadn't done the size comparison.

The gravel truck pulled out right in front of him.

Stems slammed on the brakes.

His second truck didn't stop in time; it swerved around Stems' pickup, then rammed right into the gravel truck.

Stems' third pickup drove into the ditch.

I was almost tossed over the cab as the truckbed I was standing on lurched to a halt.

A gray Toyota technical pulled onto the road, a man in armour and a helmet — painted like a bald eagle — standing in the back with the mounted gun.

He pointed it at Stems' three trucks, but didn't fire.

A second Toyota came out to the south. It turned onto the highway and drove toward us. As it closed, I could make out the helmet of its AA gunman, painted with leopard spots.

The Marchands slammed their two trucks into reverse. The boy and I did our best not to fall right out of the box.

We sped backward to the junction, toward that second technical.

It pulled to the side, letting us pass.

Hoping to separate us from Stems.

The second Marchand truck was first to reach the junction, reversing onto the concession before switching back into drive and heading back onto the highway, to the west toward Cochrane.

I braced myself as our truck did the same.

The second technical had turned around as well; it was following behind us, and closing in.

I turned to the skinny boy beside me. "It's up to us," I said. "We need to hit the driver or the tires. Both difficult targets."

He nodded. He wasn't smiling like I'd remembered from before. I think he was starting to understand how quickly it could all go to suck.

I took out my SIG and knelt down by the tailgate, as close to the driver's side as I could get.

"You need to stay lower," I said. "Let them aim at me. No... move more to your left."

He laid down on his stomach, probably in his best imitation of a sniper. He was in way over his head.

The gunman in the back of the Toyota opened fire.

His aim was not nearly as good as I'd expected it to be. Few of the rounds were even hitting the truck, and so far none had come close to my head.

I waited for the Toyota to come close enough, and then I started firing back. From the back of a moving pickup, my aim wasn't much better.

The skinny kid took a few shots as well, staying low as I'd told him.

I heard a loud blast from in front of us. Our truck pulled hard to the left and I lost my balance, slamming into the bed of the truck.

For a moment I thought we were about to roll, but the roll didn't come, and we landed upright, in a ditch full of snow.

I looked for the second truck. It was in the ditch on the other side of the road, blown onto its side, the hood and at least half the cab on fire.

"Get everyone out of the truck," I yelled. "Stay low in the ditch."

I turned to the skinny kid. "Get into the snow. Take a shot every ten seconds or so. How much do you have left?"

"I don't know," he said. "Two or three rounds."

"Shit."

I hopped out of the truck bed and landed in the snow, the skinny kid right behind me.

I had eight rounds. That's not much against guys with as much body armour as you.

The Toyota stopped less than five meters from us.

The gunman opened fire on the truck.

I opened fire on the gunman.

There are still two weak spots on most sets of ergonomic body armour, after years of so-called improvement: the delts and the kidneys. The delts are harder to hit, and less lethal if you do.

I aimed for the kidneys.

It took three rounds before I got one.

The gunman fell from his mount.

I charged at the truck.

The driver slammed it into reverse.

I took two shots just to keep them moving.

With the Toyota flying up toward Clute and Silver Queen Lake — and their friends, and Stems' three trucks — I had the skinny kid stay in position with the two other gun-toting Marchands while Sara, Eva and I checked on the burning truck.

It looked like something out of my past.

The bomb had been crude and it had been dirty, either radio-activated or weight-triggered... I had no idea which. The five Marchands inside had been ripped open by thousands of pieces of shrapnel, probably screws and nails and any other scraps of metal you can find at Home Hardware.

They weren't wearing helmets or armour. They hadn't stood a chance.

❧

It didn't take long for Stems to show up. I didn't do a headcount or anything, but it looked like they were all in one piece.

One of Stems' men was once a medic out of Petawawa, and he looked over all five bodies, not that he could do anything about them.

Two of the surviving Marchand boys were throwing snow on the fire; I guess they needed to do something. The skinny kid remained on watch. Eva Marchand stood still, staring into the flames like she was sitting in front of a campfire.

Sara took her by the hand and led her back to the other Ford pickup.

"I hit the gunner," I told Stems. "What about you guys?"

"Nothing," he replied. "When the explosion happened, they just drove off."

"You just let them go? Even the one on your six?"

"Hey... we came to help you."

"Help me with what? Counting the bodies?"

"Screw you, Baptiste. This is all on you. Running around like you think you're a goddamn one-man army... what did you think would happen?"

"Harsh criticism coming from a murderer who fucks little girls."

I felt an arm grab at my elbow.

Sara pushed her way in between us. "What the hell is wrong with you two?" she asked, almost in a whisper. "Have you already forgotten what happened here? *Mon dieu.*"

"Talk to your boyfriend," Stems told her. "Tell him to go home and leave this to the professionals."

"I'd choose Baptiste a thousand times over you," she said. "You know, I feel sorry for the people who've put their trust in you."

"You're just as delusional as he is. You two are beyond hope."

Stems shook his head. He shoved the truck keys at Sara and walked back toward his own vehicle.

"That's my body armour," I said.

He started tearing it off, tossing each piece down into the snow.

Sara clasped my hand. "This wasn't your fault," she said.

I'm sure she was just trying to help.

TODAY IS MONDAY, DECEMBER 24TH.

THE ONE-MAN army took a day off today. I've done enough damage, I think.

Sara was insistent that we check on the Girards at least, if not the Marchands; I was equally insistent that we stop wasting fuel on ridiculous errands. After almost twenty minutes of bickering, some of which made both of us laugh, we compromised: we'd take the cart, only to the Girards and back, and Sara would wear the helmet and vest from the moment we crossed the Abitibi River

I think she hates that armour more than the possibility of getting shot.

Last Christmas Eve, Sara and I had taken the truck (the old truck that's still sitting smashed-up at the airport) and gone to each family between us and the Walkers, dropping off little treats that Sara and Fiona had baked, along with some apple ice wine that I've never liked.

Fiona had even done up a funny little Christmas card for Sara to hand out, with a group photo and a modified quote from an old comedian: "Christmas at McCartney Lake is always at least six or seven times more pleasant than anywhere else. We start drinking early. And while everyone else is seeing only one Santa Claus, we'll be seeing six or seven." That's not what you'd expect from a Mormon girl, but Fiona's always been a little different.

Last Christmas Eve we spent seven hours on it, visiting around two dozen families, with maybe ten minutes with each. This year we can't risk going out and visiting the last few families we still know about.

There were around fifty families left after The Fires went out; that was down from probably three hundred when the shit first slammed into the proverbial fan. At least fifty more had taken Livingston up on his death march to Temiskaming, with just enough setbacks and delays to put them in the middle of the worst place to be, and at the worst time, of course.

I'd told them not to go; I knew what would happen.

I should have done more.

∽

When we came to the junction off Menard Lake Road, the Girards' wood and metal gate was left open, with no one in sight.

The Girards aren't known for making mistakes like that.

"Do you think they're okay?" Sara asked.

"I think they've left."

I've probably run into Denis Girard and his brothers more than anyone else over the past couple of years, and they've always been among the best to talk to. Denis has told me before they'd never leave, and I'd always believed him.

"You want to check?" Sara said.

"I do."

"Okay."

We had the twelve gauge and my pistol, but I knew that Sara would never touch a gun. If we ran into trouble, like one or three gray Toyota Tundras with mounted machine guns, I'm pretty sure that trouble would be more than capable of outgunning me.

As much as Sara would support my decision, it wasn't hard to tell that she was hoping I'd turn the cart around.

"We'll come back on Boxing Day," I said. "It's Christmas Eve and I don't feel like doing any heavy lifting."

We rode back home as the sky grew dark, eating and drinking the gifts we no longer expected we'd be giving away.

I'd made sure not to have too much ice wine, which was helped by the taste of it, but Sara was getting pretty drunk.

"I loved Christmas," she said as we made our way home.

"You don't anymore?"

"What Christmas?"

"Come on... you can still find something to love about it. Ice wine?"

"I can drink ice wine anytime, Baptiste. We used to sneak it into school."

"Elementary?"

"High school," she said with what may have been a little burp. "I used to pour out bottles of apple juice and fill them up with the good stuff... you can't really tell the difference unless you look really closely."

"I would have loved to see Sara Vachon in high school."

"Sure... perky breasts... well... they're still pretty good."

I laughed. "I know they are."

"I wasn't cool in high school, Baptiste. Not like now."

I laughed again.

"What's so funny?" she asked. "Anyway... I'd share the ice wine so people would like me more."

"I'm sure they liked you enough."

"They called me Tampon."

"What?"

"Vachon *Tampon*... it rhymes."

"I don't get it."

"I used to stick myself into the middle of things, always trying to keep the peace..."

"Used to?"

"Shut up. Sophie Minot used to tell me that whenever I showed up, I plugged up all the fun."

"That doesn't sound good."

"She's a bitch." She sighed. "She was a bitch. I'm sure she's dead now... I think she moved to Toronto."

"Good riddance, I guess."

"She wasn't all bad. She had the tightest ass..."

I didn't know what to say to that.

"I'm kidding," she said. "Now don't go and plug up all the fun."

"I like you, Sara the Tampon."

"That's Vachon *Tampon* to you."

∽

We found that everyone at the cottage had been drinking too, even Fiona at long last, though she seemed aloof from the others, sitting at the dining room table and flipping through a magazine about cottages and whatever. Everyone else was carrying on in the living room, making enough noise that it sounded like there were fifty of them.

There was too much drinking. It wasn't safe.

But I was too tired to be angry.

"Have a drink," Kayla said as we came inside.

"The Girards are gone," Sara said.

"They left just before Christmas?" Matt said. "That doesn't make much sense."

Sara threw her hands in the air, flopping them left and right before landing them on her hips. "I'm going to bed," she said.

She started towards the stairs, her steps uneven. I wrapped my arm around her and helped her up the steps. I took her to her bedroom, instead of mine, but found that Lisa had converted the second bed to a place to keep her clothes in neat little stacks.

"Looks like you're bunking with me again," I said. "I didn't realize we'd officially moved in together."

She gave me a sloppy kiss. "You can't get rid of me, mister," she said in a yelling whisper.

I laid her down on my bed and pulled the covers over her.

"Good night," I said before kissing her forehead. She was already asleep.

I came back downstairs for a Christmas toast. I swooped into the dining room and gave Fiona a smile; she followed me out to join everyone in the living room, even though she didn't seem happy to do it.

The mood had already changed among the drunkies. They still had their drinks in hand but their smiles had gone. The only person who even bothered to look up when Fiona and I walked in was Matt, and I know he wasn't looking at me.

"There's not many of us left," Kayla said. She was standing and staring out the window toward the frozen lake.

"There's still the Walkers and New Post," I said. "Those are some big numbers right there."

"With everyone else taking off," Graham said, "you gotta wonder if they're onto something." He was on the couch with his arm around a sleepy-eyed Lisa, who slowly nodded in agreement.

"We'll need to head back out there and have a look," I said. "We don't know anything for sure."

"Sounds good," Graham said. "Maybe they left something worth taking."

"There's that bright side," Matt said.

"Then let's have a toast," Kayla said, turning around and trying her best smile. "Someone needs to do one."

"Ant did it last year," Fiona said. She didn't need to remind us.

"I'll do the honours," I said. "I think I remember some of what Ant taught me."

"You need a drink," Kayla said, making her way to the kitchen. She came back with a glass that held a straight shot of something golden.

I took the glass with a nod and held it high. "Here's a toast to all the pretty ladies. The rest of you motherfuckers can all go to hell. *Santé!*"

"*Santé,*" the others said in reply, as we all took a drink.

TODAY IS TUESDAY, DECEMBER 25TH.

SARA ENDED up having the bed to herself last night; I woke up Christmas morning on the living room floor. Fiona greeted me with a Merry Christmas, a warm hug, and a cup of black coffee.

My head throbbed a little, but I've had worse ways to start the day.

We decided as a group, last winter, not to exchange gifts; it's not really fair when Graham and I can find all sorts of useless crap in Cochrane, while most everyone else is left to fashion gifts from twigs and frozen dirt.

But Fiona broke the rule last year, giving each of us another homemade card, so I wasn't surprised when she cornered me again this morning, after breakfast.

"Sorry," she said, as she handed me a large envelope.

"We're getting a divorce?" I asked.

I opened the envelope and pulled out a piece of sketch paper.

"I didn't frame it yet," she said. "I wasn't sure if you'd like it."

It was a charcoal drawing; I recognized the scene from pretty much the only printed photo I have. Me, Alanna and Cassy, standing together at Niagara Falls. Fiona had taken my little wallet-size and turned it into something beautiful... there was more of my wife and daughter in the faces she'd drawn, than in that old wrinkled photo.

"It's perfect," I said, as I pulled her close to me. "Thank you so much, Fiona. It's just... perfect."

"I've sprayed it, but I just need to find the right frame."

"Don't worry... I can find something the next time I'm in town." I kissed her on the cheek. "It's wonderful."

"I didn't get anything for anyone else this year."

"Ah... okay." I wasn't sure how to feel.

"Sara's birthday is coming up in February... I'll make something for her then. I've just been busy lately, you know?"

"I know, Fiona. You do a lot around here."

"No, you do a lot, Baptiste. I don't remember me rescuing two stranded girls on the side of the road."

"Two stranded girls?"

"Now you've blocked it from your memory? It's a damned good thing you found those two before someone else did."

I'd forgotten the story I'd told. To Fiona and Kayla those girls were lucky; in that version, they'd been cold and scared... and that was all they'd felt.

I didn't regret the lie.

"I guess so," I said. "I got to say, Fiona... your work has really gone far. You've got a real talent."

She blushed a little. "I always wanted to be an artist. Well, that and a supermodel."

I chuckled.

She smiled at me. "I figured by the time I was sixteen I'd have run off to join one of those eco-collectives, do the whole off-the-grid artist thing."

"Off-the-grid artist and supermodel, you mean."

She laughed. "Yeah. They had a few places like that right around here. I wonder if some of them are still around."

"Maybe it's not too late for you to live the dream. But make sure you warn me before you go." I gave her cheek another peck. "And thank you, again... really."

"You're welcome."

It was nice to feel special.

❧

"I want to show you something," Fiona said after lunch.

"I know how to find the sink," I said, "I just choose not to wash dishes."

"Funny. But seriously... come on a walk with me."

"Outside? In the snow?"

She smiled. "Yeah... in the snow... you big baby."

We put on our jackets and boots, and I followed her out the front door.

Des and Juju came along, too. They always will, unless you make it a point to block them on your way out.

"I wasn't sure I should show this to you," she said as she led me toward the path that runs around the lake.

"Oooh... a dead body..."

"That's not funny."

"Sorry."

As we walked around the bend, I kept an eye out for any new tracks in the snow. I might as well dampen the day by finding out that the coyotes were back after us.

"This is it," Fiona said, stretching her arms out in front of her.

"It is...?"

"This." She tapped her hand against a maple tree.

"A sugar maple. Didn't know there was one so close to home."

"Look closer," she said.

I stuck my face an inch from the bark, sticking my tongue out at the same time.

"See the initials?" she asked.

I did. They were carved deep into the bark.

"RB + FR," I said. "Who's that?"

"You don't know?"

"No. Well, I assume you're 'FR'."

She rolled her eyes. "I'm not *the* 'FR'... just like you're not the original 'RB'."

"My last name's Jeanbaptiste," I said. "Remember?"

"Close enough," she said.

"Okay..."

"It's supposed to be funny, stupid."

"It is?"

"*Ugh.* Someone carved these years ago, and it's funny because you're like old enough to be my grandpa."

"Harsh."

"Well... it's biologically possible, isn't it?"

"There's a lot that's biologically possible."

"So now you're hitting on me?"

"That's not funny."

She laughed. "Yes it is."

I laughed, too. "There's no one else who's as big of a goofball as you."

"And there's no one else old enough to use a word like 'goofball'."

"Well? What word would you use to describe yourself?"

"Smart... beautiful... sexy..."

"Uhh..."

"I'm getting cold," she said. "Walk me home, Robert Baptiste."

"*Jean*baptiste."

"Who cares?"

"I don't."

She leaned in and gave me a kiss on the cheek. "You're blushing."

"No... I'm freezing to death."

She laughed.

I wasn't sure what to feel.

Justin Porter stopped by, just before dinner. Since it was just him, I knew that he wasn't going to be bringing any cheer.

Sara came with me to greet him. Graham was fidgeting with the stove, but he stopped and looked up.

"I knew it," Justin said as he stepped inside, bringing the snow with him.

"That you're a douchebag?" I asked.

"Dave Walker just stabbed us in the back. Listen to this..." He held up his phone before he started to read. "'We're not interested in continuing arrangement at SQL. We've taken on a new partner.'"

"They're backing out of Silver Queen Lake?"

"He's telling us to back out."

"Fuck that. We're not giving it up."

"Don't tell me... tell him."

"Well... call him."

"I have. He's not answering."

"Then leave a message."

"I have. I don't think it's his phone not getting a signal. I think he's avoiding us. I guess he's a little miffed that you got his son killed."

I wanted to punch him in the mouth. "Is that a joke?"

"There's no joke here, Baptiste. Just a series of fuck-ups. Believe me... no one's laughing."

"Go home, Justin."

"Why? You going to get me killed, too?"

"I just might. You think I don't know what you've been doing?"

"You're a mess, Baptiste."

"Get out."

He gave me a smirk before walking out the door.

I don't know why he felt he needed to fuck up my Christmas.

"What are you wanting to do?" Sara asked me as she wrapped an arm around my hip.

"Besides shoot him in the head?"

She nodded.

"I want to go to Silver Queen Lake tomorrow to get our supplies."

"It's not safe," Graham said. "It's not worth it."

"He's right," Sara said. "We've had way too many close calls."

"So we just give up?" I asked. "We let Dave Walker shit all over us and take everything while he's at it?"

"Yes," Sara said. "We do. We back off and we stay alive. We have other things to worry about —"

"I'm not scared of Dave Walker. You know that."

"You have too many enemies," Graham said. "I... I told you this would happen."

"You told me?"

"Look... we need to take a breath. Things are getting out of control."

"Out of control? You mean, more out of control than the end of the fucking world?"

"We can't risk it," Sara said. "And what about the Girards? I made a promise to check on them. Aren't you going to back me up?"

"I like this new tactic," I said. "Everyone just piles on to old Baptiste."

"Is that what you think this is?" Sara asked. "Some kind of personal attack?"

"That's what it sounds like. Baptiste is an asshole... everyone hates his guts..."

"Dammit, Baptiste... this isn't about you. Can you just listen for once? The remaining supplies at Silver Queen Lake aren't worth any of us dying. We have enough to make it —"

"We don't have enough, Sara. We don't have nearly enough. We're short of flour... we're short of fuel... how the hell are we supposed to plant crops in the spring when we don't have any of the equipment or even the goddamn seed?"

"There's no farm equipment at Silver Queen Lake," Sara said. "No fuel, either... just a little bit of food and apparently a whole lot of stolen jewelry. Whatever's up there isn't going to save us. We need to look elsewhere. We *will* look elsewhere. Don't give up on us, Baptiste."

"Then you don't give up on me," I said.

"I haven't."

"No one has," Graham said. "We're just scared."

"So Justin's scared, too?"

"Yes," Sara said. "If Justin honestly thought he could do a better job than you he'd go ahead and do it."

"So what do you expect me to do?" I asked. "Just let Dave Walker win?"

"If everything we do is based more on winning some undeclared war... my god, Baptiste... then we're screwed."

"I can't let him win —"

"He's not going to win. It's a long time before this is over."

I nodded.

And I gave her a kiss.

"What," Graham said, "nothing for me?"

"Kiss the stove," I said. "I heard it's hot for you."

Sara groaned.

That was nice to hear.

TODAY IS WEDNESDAY, DECEMBER 26TH.

I KNOW that Justin wants to go back to Silver Queen, with or without me; part of me hopes he won't come back.

I decided to take Graham and Matt with me, to Bondy Lake to check on the Girards. I wasn't about to take Sara back there, and I knew that she and Kayla and Fiona would be safe with Lisa and my magic guitar case.

After breakfast, the three of us left in the cart; three guys, three sets of armour... we'd save the diesel for farming, if that ever happens.

Bringing Matt would be an irritation, and it left less room for whatever we found and wanted to take back with us, but I wanted to make sure my only job while we were there was to keep a hand on my gun. Matt and Graham would handle the lifting.

We went through the open gate, and after another couple of minutes, we reached the house.

I noticed right away.

"Someone's been up on the roof," I said, pointing to the bare wood where shingles should have been.

"They had solar shingles," Graham said. "They must have stripped them down to take with them."

"That's a heavy load."

"Probably too heavy," Matt said.

"Someone took them," I said. "But I doubt it was the Girards."

Aside from the stripped shingles, the old Girard house looked like it always did, aside from the fact that the door was propped open. It wasn't until we got inside that we noticed that some of the pipes had burst; whatever heat had been in that house was long gone, especially with the front door wide open. The damage was minimal, though, and it didn't get in our way.

The dining room set was still there, a beautiful hand-carved oak table that I found pretty tempting, along with eight matching chairs, six around the table, and two lined up along the wall.

There was no food left, and aside from the furniture, the only other items that remained were too large and heavy for us to bring home. There was also no sign of their ATVs or the two-ton diesel truck they'd used, whenever they could get it to start on homebrew.

"At least they weren't killed by marauders," Matt said, as he and Graham checked some cupboards in the mud room.

"Lot of clothes left behind," Graham said.

I saw what he was talking about; there were winter clothes still hanging on the wall. Some of it was in childrens' sizes.

"They had a few kids, right?" Graham asked.

"Two or three," I said.

"Does that mean something?" Matt said.

I nodded. "If the clothes are out here and hanging up they probably still fit. It's only getting colder out there, so you'd think they would take all of it with them."

We went upstairs to check the bedrooms. I was pretty sure there was no one else in the house, so feeling the urge to pee, I found the bathroom. It smelled like the last visitor hadn't flushed, despite the window being wide open and the cold outside air finding its way in. When I lifted the toilet lid, I saw that the bowl was filled with a clean and clear block of ice; my guess on the source of the stench was that stuck somewhere along the pipes in the wall would be a very shitty flavour of homemade popsicle.

I was pretty sure their pump wasn't running anymore, but I took a piss in their frozen toilet anyway, watching the warm stuff melt a little divot in the ice; it wasn't like they were around to complain.

I felt a little dirty after, since there was no water to wash my hands, and when I checked the medicine cabinet for disinfectant, all I found were a few scented soaps and an old toothbrush on the top shelf.

That got me thinking.

I realized that the toothbrushes were still out in a little holder on the sink, even though the toothpaste was missing.

People usually pack up their toothbrushes for a trip.

I guess it didn't mean anything, really, since they wouldn't be doing much brushing on the road. They might have been saving some new toothbrushes to take with them.

I still had the feeling that something was off.

As I closed the mirrored door to the cabinet, I caught a patch of dark in the porcelain tub behind me. I turned around, pulling my gun from its holster and holding my breath.

It was a pile of brown and black fur.

Two dogs.

In a shallow puddle of frozen blood.

I pulled the shower curtain closed and then I left the room.

I found Graham in the hallway.

"Check for blood," I said.

"What?"

"Blood. There are two dogs in the bathtub. Looks like they were slaughtered."

"Why would they kill their own dogs?"

"I don't think they would."

We checked the upstairs first, looking for any sign of violence to go with the dead dogs. We didn't find anything up there, but I noticed that there were too many things left around that people wouldn't usually leave behind. There were family photos in each bedroom, and on a toddler bed — that was still covered with a pink unicorn comforter — I found a cute little plush kitty.

I remember what it was like to have a kid; the stuffed kitty wasn't an item you couldn't find room for. There's not a parent on earth who'd make that mistake. If that little girl's favorite things were left behind, chances were that she was left behind, too.

Once we were done in the house, I took a quick look around the grounds. There was no sign of a fresh grave dug into the frozen soil, but it wasn't a given that they'd have taken the time to dig a hole in winter. It was hard enough for us to bury Ant when the ground hadn't been fully frozen.

Like everything else I'd seen, it told me nothing for sure.

We loaded up the dining room set and started back home while we rode we talked things out, trying to understand what could have happened.

"Maybe the little girl was mauled to death by the dogs," Graham said. "They wouldn't have wanted to bring those dogs with them after something like that."

"Sounds like too much of a coincidence," I said. "The dogs kill her right around the time they decide to leave?"

"There's no way the Girards were murdered," Matt said. "They're armed to the teeth. If there had been any shooting we'd have seen something... broken glass or shell casings... something, at least."

"That's true," Graham said.

"I know it doesn't make any sense," I said. "But there's no way they would pack up the supplies, leave all their keepsakes behind, then slaughter their dogs and toss them in the bathtub."

"People do crazy things," Matt said. "It sounds messed, but I think it's the simplest explanation. Do you really think a gang of marauders is going to somehow trick the Girards into leaving their house so they can kill them all without making a mess?"

"And why bother going to so much effort to hide it?" Graham asked. "Why hide the bodies?"

"There may be a way to find out," I said. "I think we should go back and take another look."

Graham and Matt were just as curious, so we returned to the Girard homestead. They followed behind me as I wandered around the yard, poking my head into the chicken coop and doing a quick inspection of the barn.

"There's nothing here," Graham said. "There aren't even any footsteps left to see in the snow."

"One more place to check," I said as I walked over to the root cellar that was dug into a little rise behind the barn. I scraped the snow off the door, but it was frozen and I couldn't get it open; I began to kick it. After several tries my boot smashed right through, creating a gash in the door but not pushing it open. I peered inside, but it was too dark to see. I pulled my headlamp from the pouch on my belt and pointed it through the hole, like a flashlight.

"I guess that's it," Graham said.

"Hold on."

There was something in there, like burlap sacks...

Maybe potatoes... maybe worth taking back home if they weren't rotten.

My light bounced along, running along the lumps in the cellar. Then the light reflected back to me from a set of frozen eyes.

"Oh my god," I said. I'm not sure it was loud enough for anyone to hear.

I kicked on the door again, widening the hole. The winter sun came in enough for me to see clearly what I was looking at.

I recognized most of them, Denis and his two brothers... and an old man... and two old women, and three young children. Their hands were bound behind their backs, their bodies lifeless and bloodied. I could see well enough that they had been beaten to death rather than shot. Whoever had done it had chosen not to waste any bullets; they probably used something like the butt of a shotgun to do the job.

Just like I'd used on Marc Tremblay.

I saw then what they'd wanted me to see: the bodies of two young women, bruised and cut.

Natalie Girard and Tabitha Smith.

Both girls were bound like the rest, but they had been stripped naked. Their throats were cut. And drawn onto Natalie's stomach, in black marker, was a message, just for me.

YOU DID THIS BAPTISTE.

I could feel my chest harden as I fought to breathe.

Graham pushed his way through to look. Once he had seen, he turned his head away. I heard him vomit.

"What the hell?" Matt said. He shoved his way forward as well. I watched his knees buckle as he fought to stay on his feet. "What does that mean?"

"They killed them," I said. "Because of me."

"I don't get it," Matt said. "How did they manage to get the Girards to give up and let themselves be murdered?"

"They're not all here. Some are missing."

"Maybe they got away."

"Maybe..."

"But how —"

"Hostages," I said. "They grabbed a few of them... maybe the kids... told the rest to give themselves up."

I knew what had really happened. The two girls. The two chairs against the wall. They'd been torturing them, using their pain as a bargaining chip.

I couldn't bear to admit it out loud.

"It still doesn't make sense," Matt said. "So they've got my kids or whatever, and they're going to kill them. So I hand over my guns so they can kill the rest of us?"

"Safe passage," Graham said.

We both looked over at Graham. His face was still pale and I could tell that he wasn't feeling any better.

"Maybe they promised them safe passage," Graham said. "Whoever did this may have convinced the Girards that all they wanted were supplies, that if they cooperated they'd let them leave."

"You think anyone would be stupid enough to believe that?" Matt asked.

"I'd believe them," I said. "I'd believe anything that would make it stop."

I'd have done anything to save those two girls.

I should have brought them to live with us.

"As if," Matt said. "You'd just build a little sniper nest and you'd fuck them up with your shotgun."

"You don't know me as well as you think you do."

Matt looked at me, bewildered. He had no idea.

"So they're not all here?" Graham asked.

"I think a few are missing," I said. "Natalie's sister, for one."

"And Michelle Girard," Matt said. "We went to school together. Well... different schools, but I knew her."

"So that's two missing persons. Both young women."

"You think some of them got away?" Graham asked.

"No... not really. You don't just leave family behind." I wondered what Cassy would have thought of me saying that.

"My god," Graham said. "What's stopping them from coming over to our place and doing the same to us?"

"I don't know," I said. "Could be we have better security, or it's because they figure we're better armed. Or it could just be that they're saving us for last."

I'd left the girls wide open. If those assholes were out to hurt me... Lisa on her own couldn't protect against whatever this was.

"We'd better get back," Matt said.

I'd already started running.

We threw the dining room set off the cart and headed back, as quickly as we could get the horses to move; I could not help but think how much faster we'd be moving if we'd had enough diesel to run our truck.

I couldn't keep my mind from slipping into a bad place.

I started to think of what could be happening to the women I had promised to keep safe, that they'd be taken like Natalie and Tabitha were, stripped and bound and terrified, with the man in the coyote helmet getting off on all of it. They'd be hoping desperately that we would come home to help them, but frightened to death of what might happen once we got there. I couldn't stop from picturing them, tied to chairs in our dining room, with Sara trying to focus the attention on herself, hoping desperately to deflect the violence away from the young women she wanted so much to protect.

And then I thought of my wife and of Cassy, and for an instant I saw them too, screaming in terror and pain, wondering why I'd never come back for them.

But then it kicked in, the single-mindedness, the discipline, that had kept me alive when I needed it most, and I was able to take my focus away from the fear and move it over to what I needed to do.

Graham was driving those horses as fast as he could; he didn't need any help from me. I would come up with a way to take the Spirit Animals out before they even saw us coming.

We reached the bridge over the Abitibi. I could see no tire tracks on the road back, no sign that any Toyotas had come this way.

And the gate was still locked. We saw no sign of tampering.

That was nothing close to a guarantee; there were other roads and other bridges, and the river itself was frozen enough in places for a hardened pickup to cross over the ice.

We stopped the cart not far past the junction with New Post Road; there's nothing quiet about a team of horses Matt didn't argue about being left behind with Graham's SIG, as Graham took the shotgun and followed me.

We wound our way through the woods, to the back of the barn. He stayed on the ground as I climbed up to the loft; I'd done it enough times that I could do it without making a sound.

I reached the top and I peered down into the kitchen. I could see Fiona there, leaning over the stove and stirring a pot that was close to boiling over. I couldn't see the others, but I could hear Kayla laughing from wherever she was.

I snuck back down the ladder just as quietly as I'd climbed it.

"We don't want to surprise them," I said, finally feeling myself breathing again. "Lisa will mess us up."

We made our way back to Matt and the horses. He could see from our faces that everything was okay.

As we brought the cart up to the cottage, Sara and Lisa came out to greet us, neither one having bothered to put on a coat.

"What did you find out?" Sara asked.

"Not much," I said, rushing to give my reply. "Everything's gone. Looks like they bugged out."

"Bugged out?" Lisa asked.

"They've left," Graham said. "Didn't leave much behind."

Matt added nothing as we went inside.

Fiona was bringing dinner out to the table, and we ate in silence for the most part. I hoped that the ladies would think the tension was only fatigue on our part.

When dinner was done, Graham tugged on my elbow as I rose from the table.

"Thanks for dinner, ladies," he said. "You'll help with the dishes, Baptiste?"

"I guess," I said, trying to sound a little rankled.

We went into the kitchen and Matt followed. That was suspicious, I know, but it might have been even worse for Matt to be left sitting at the table, craning his neck in the hope of eavesdropping, while trying to act like nothing is wrong.

We put the stereo on and played *Music @ Work*, one of The Hip's better albums for covering up a secret meeting. You don't want to use *Road Apples* for something like that.

"So we're not telling people?" Graham said, in a low voice, as he poured water from the jug into the canning pot.

"I don't know yet," I said. "It's not something we should just blurt out over dinner."

Graham took the pot out to sit atop the wood stove; we'd have some time before we could do any actual work. Usually at that point I'd get a little pissy waiting for the water to heat up, wishing that Ant would have had the chance to install a more efficient water heater; this one time I didn't mind the delay.

"We shouldn't tell them," Matt said. "What good will it do to scare the bejesus out of them?"

"We need to be honest with everyone," Graham said.

"Let's be honest with ourselves, here," I said. "We all know how this will work. I'm going to tell Sara later tonight, and Graham, I'm pretty sure you'll tell Lisa. And let's assume that Kayla will find a way to extract the information from Matt, through some kind of sucking and/or fucking motion..."

"Funny," Matt said.

"So this really comes down to whether or not we're going to tell the Porters or the Tremblays."

"We shouldn't tell them," Graham said. "Not yet, anyway. It's not like they can contribute anything that's productive at this point. Justin hasn't seemed exactly... stable, lately."

"I agree," I said. I left it there. "And let's leave Fiona out of this, too."

"Why bother? Who cares if she knows or not?"

"It's important to me. Just don't talk to her about it, and tell that to anyone else you're blabbing to. She's still just a kid."

"I don't think she'd like you calling her that," Matt said.

"Doesn't matter. Just leave it to me."

Graham went to retrieve the water, and then we started in on the dishes.

Matt mostly stood and watched, using his dish towel as a tool for fidgeting.

"So what is our plan now?" Graham said. "Obviously we need to get the hell away from here."

"I don't think so," I said. "It's not going to be any safer out there."

"It can't be more dangerous than this, Baptiste. There can't be that many targets left on their list. And you're the one they're really after."

"So we throw away a good defense in hopes that we can outrun these assholes?"

"Baptiste's right," Matt said. "We're stronger here. Home ice advantage."

"We'll play things safer," I said. "No more delays. No excuses. Everyone learns to use the guns. And no one leaves the house without having someone with them who's armed and ready to shoot."

"Not good enough," Graham said. "I say we pack up whatever we can and we slip out at night. We could be halfway to Lake Timis-kaming by morning."

"We don't know where these assholes are based right now, or how many there are, or what else could be waiting down the road for us. It's too risky."

"So you want us to stay here and wait to die."

Graham's attitude was starting to piss me off.

"We can defend ourselves," I said. "They come for us, we'll take them out. It's that simple."

"What if there are too many of them?" Graham said. "We have what, a dozen people who can shoot... maybe five or six who can actually hit anything? Assuming we have enough guns, which we don't."

"They're not sure they can take us out. That's probably why they haven't come for us yet. They know they can't beat us."

"You're overconfident."

"This place may not look like much but they'd need an army to take it from us. They know they'll spill a lot of their own blood to get in here. So they're stalling, and when they come for me, it'll be because they've gotten desperate. They'll be hungry and tired and unsure of themselves, and we'll get them."

"There's no way to be sure of that," Graham said.

"Listen to me, for once. I know what I'm talking about. You're not the one who's actually had to do this kind of thing before. This isn't a game, Graham. You have no idea how any of this shit goes down in real life. So don't start acting like you can even have an opinion when it comes to keeping us safe."

Graham didn't back down. "You're gambling with the lives of every person in this house. I don't know what you want out of all this, but I actually want to live through it. I'd like a chance to start a new life or something, you know, raise a family... and I'm not going to throw it all away because you want one last chance to relive your glory days."

I dropped my dish towel and left the kitchen, knowing that I wouldn't be able to stay another minute without punching him out.

Sara found me before I'd dressed to go outside, and by the time the two of us were out past the barn I'd told her everything, about the Girards, about Natalie and Tabitha, about Graham. She didn't say she agreed or that she disagreed with anything I'd said. She just held my hand and listened.

As I talked I felt like I was a child again, back when I would get so upset about something that I could barely breathe and I couldn't even talk, my whole body heaving as tears would run down my face.

And I realized I was crying, because I knew that everything was falling apart. We'd lost Ant and I'd killed Marc Tremblay, and now we had two less people to face an enemy that would come for me eventually. That was assuming that we'd only stay two down, that we wouldn't lose Graham, too, that he wouldn't pack up and leave, taking Lisa with him. And maybe taking everyone else away from me, too.

But then I found that I was crying because I missed my old life, where I got to be an asshole just for kicks, not because I was trying to keep people alive.

I don't think I can protect this so-called family anymore; even if I'd been there in Toronto, crouched by the front door of our own house with a baseball bat, telling Alanna and Cassy to keep the noise down... even then I wouldn't have been able to save my family from the chaos that would swallow them.

I've spent so much time blaming everyone else for being trapped away from home, blaming travel restrictions and fuel shortages, like those were the things what kept me from saving my daughter and my wife... but the truth is so much easier to understand: I just didn't have it in me. I wasn't the hero, or even a good father, and I was certainly never a good husband. I was just a fool who liked telling people what to do. And I was angry with Graham, because he'd finally grown enough of a backbone to point out what a phony I'd become.

"I can't do this anymore," I said.

Sara gave me a hug and kissed my cheek. "Don't believe your doubts," she said. "You can't trust yourself right now... you can't listen to anything your mind is telling you. Listen to me instead."

I didn't interrupt.

"You are a good man," she said. "You've saved the lives of over a dozen people. You led us to make this home together. It isn't your fault that Ant is dead, and at least he lived his last year with his new family, and not by himself. And Marc Tremblay's death was an accident, no matter what you think you did. And what happened to Zach Walker, to the Marchands and the Girards... there was nothing you could do. And the rest of us are still here, Baptiste. What do you think would have happened to us if you hadn't been here?"

"You would have figured it out."

"That's not true. You know it's not true. You've seen what the Walkers wanted me to sign. Ten years of service. And they wouldn't even take Kayla because of her goddamn ex-boyfriend."

"You never mentioned that —"

"I guess there was also that stranded work crew near the airport, but they'd only take us girls, and only if we didn't mind spending most of the time on our backs in trade."

"Those idiots didn't last long..." (We'd lost track of them before the first Christmas at McCartney Lake.)

"And I'm sure the Tremblays and the Porters would have tried their luck on the highway if we hadn't helped them."

"Now that's more of a missed opportunity for us."

"Yeah, yeah... but what about Fiona? If you hadn't taken her on, where would she be? She was fourteen years old, Baptiste... no parents, no friends. She wouldn't have had a chance."

I shook my head.

"Don't bother arguing with me," she said. "I know you don't agree with me right now. But all I want you to know is that I've always believed in you, and that doesn't go away, even when you've lost faith in yourself. You're our best chance by far, Baptiste. I'd say that's obvious to everyone but you, apparently."

I knew she meant it.

I leaned in and gave her a kiss.

"We should get back," she said.

By the time we'd come back to the cottage, the dishes were done and everyone had gone about their evening routines. It was like nothing had been said.

Lisa glared at me, though, so I knew that Graham had already talked to her. Lisa doesn't believe in hiding her feelings.

That's something I've learned to respect.

Neither Lisa nor Graham said anything to me.

Matt and Kayla seemed to be avoiding me, too, while Fiona seemed oblivious to all of it, as she sketched in her notebook.

It was all for the best.

I was still upset, and I knew that the anger would come out, either in tears or in blind rage. Crying in front of everyone was not something I was willing to do, and I couldn't afford the other.

But at the same time, I know that I need to make Graham understand. He needs to know that there's no room for discussion when it comes to our safety.

It's my responsibility... it's my decision to make.

I went upstairs with Sara. The two of us laid together in bed, Sara with her reader and me with my tablet, writing an entry in my journal that I'm not sure how I should end.

At least I have Sara.

Having her beside me makes this bearable.

❧❧❧

6

❧❧❧

TODAY IS THURSDAY, DECEMBER 27TH.

ANT WROTE this last August:

It's hard for a guy like me to talk about love; I've spent my time on this earth in pursuit of a full variety of the storied Canadian beaver, and truthfully, falling in love gets in the way of that.

But love is something that sticks with you, like a bad cold or genital herpes, and sometimes it gets even worse as time goes on. Sometimes it won't go away, no matter how much you want it to, no matter how much time you spend fapping to other girls.

I miss Natalie. It was impossible being with her, after being with her sister for so long, but that doesn't really change anything for me. I think she misses me, too, not that we can send each other texts or try to run into each other at the grocery store. We might as well be a thousand kilometers away.

I left the Girards without any time to pack or really say goodbye; all I had time for was to tell Natalie that I loved her. She smiled in that way she always did when she heard my usual bullshit; I don't think she understood what kind of love I was talking about.

One day I'll get up the nerve to go back and explain it to her.

The night I'd dropped off Natalie and Tabitha, I took that little Honda back to McCartney Lake and parked it at a cottage up the road. It still had just over half a tank that hadn't gone totally bad, but I didn't really have any plans for how to use the gas that was left.

Last night, after Sara had gone to sleep, I decided to drive back to the Girards, in that little car. I brought along a vest and a helmet, but I didn't feel like putting them on. I even took off my belt, stuffing it on the passenger seat beside me. It all felt like too much to carry.

I almost got stuck a few times in the snow, and at those moments I felt pretty stupid that I hadn't brought along a snow shovel or some sand. But luckily that little car had more guts than I'd expected, and I made it all the way to Bondy Lake.

I'd forgotten to bring the tarps, too.

I went back into the empty house and gathered up the bed sheets. Then I brought them down to the car and spread about half of them in the back; I folded down the passenger seat as well to get a little more room.

Then I took the rest of the bed sheets and I went to the root cellar. I strapped on my headlamp, which felt strange strapped directly against my scalp and not onto my helmet, and I lowered myself down to where the bodies lay.

I'd been worried about coyotes finding the frozen bodies, not that I was sure if they'd be able to do much with them without a warm stove to heat them up. But most of the dead Girards looked just as they did before. There might have been some rodents down there; I didn't look that carefully.

Natalie and Tabitha probably looked exactly like they did on the day they died.

I knew it wasn't fair to leave Tabitha there, away from her family and then away from her best friend, so I wrapped the two of them up with the sheets.

I carried Natalie first, and I didn't know how to feel as I balanced her over my shoulder like a surfboard, her body rigid and cold. I placed her in the car and then I went back for Tabitha.

I felt a little guilty leaving the rest of them there, but I knew it would be hard enough with two.

I drove them back to McCartney Lake, to the place near Wright Creek that we'd chosen when we lost Ant. I laid them both out in the snow, Tabitha wrapped in a sheet of yellow and green flowers, and Natalie covered with pink unicorns.

I decided that one day I would go back to the root cellar, for the children at least.

I gathered some logs from our firewood pile, along with two bottles of lighter fluid, since I didn't have any kindling. I lit the fire and I waited a few minutes for the flames to grow hot. Then I grabbed my steel shovel and shoved it into the fire.

It took much longer to dig those two graves than it did to bury

Ant, and the sun had already risen before I had finished filling them back in.

I was just glad that my heart had kept up with the digging.

Kayla found me there.

"Sara's looking for you," she said.

I tried to give her a smile; I'm not sure it worked. "Thanks for letting me know. You're not going to ask me what I'm doing?"

She gave me a look that surprised me, like she understood exactly how I was feeling.

She wrapped her arm around me. "I know what you're doing... and I know that he'd appreciate it, Baptiste. Ant really did love her."

"That's what he wrote."

"He told me once. One night when we were out together by the lake. I asked him if he wanted to kiss me, and then he just blurted it out like he was confessing to murdering someone. 'I'm in love with Natalie Girard,' he'd said. And then he gave me a hug and a kiss on the cheek and said that a blowjob would be perfectly acceptable, however." She started to laugh. "I can't imagine what it would be like to be in love with someone like Ant. It must have been so frustrating most of the time."

"That's what love is, Kayla. If you're not frustrated you're doing it wrong."

"I've never thought of it that way."

"I'd rather you didn't tell anyone about this."

I really didn't want to explain why I did it. I'd cared enough to drive two dead girls up from Bondy Lake, but I'd never ever bothered to ask where the Tremblays had chosen to bury Marc.

"Don't you think they'll notice?" she asked.

"Just don't tell them for now, okay? Let them find out another day."

"Okay."

"Thank you, Kayla." I gave her a kiss on the forehead.

She giggled. "That means you love me," she said.

That made me smile. "Yeah... that means I love you."

We walked back together. And when Sara asked, Kayla told her that she'd found me out on a walk.

I doubt Sara has any idea what I was doing out there near Ant's stand of sugar maples.

She didn't ask me.

Today was the day for limbing and splitting the birchwood.

We'd cut down around two dozen birch trees during the late summer, while there were still enough leaves to suck moisture out of the wood. Now it was time to revisit the fallen trees and turn them into firewood. We also have around twenty balsam firs on the ground, just off the road, but they'll have to wait for sometime next week, after we've sobered up from New Year's.

When we first moved into the cottage at McCartney Lake, we'd run our stove off of hastily-cut fir and whatever pre-split bundles of firewood we could find. Some of it was too green, but we made it work. Graham had done his best to tell us about hardwoods versus soft, and how his father used to swear by Pacific Madrones for their firewood, which didn't mesh well with them living on the banks of the Mississippi River. Based on his advice we made sure to cut some birch as well that summer, piling it on the metal racks to season for the following winter.

Now we're hooked on birch, and it's been easy enough to find; you just go to wherever there was a forest fire ten to twenty years ago, and there you'll find your firewood. We've seen colonies of young birch trees all over the district now, but it's the older trees we need, the ones where the bark has already turned white, and the closest acreage of firewood-ready birch is on the far side of the lake. That's where our fallen trees were waiting.

One of the only good things about the breakdown of society is that — for the first few months, at least — there was plenty of really good equipment sitting around, waiting for you to take it all home; that's made the job a whole lot smoother.

After being up all night, all I really wanted to do was sneak upstairs and go to sleep, but I had to set an example, or at least make sure Matt didn't look better than me. (Ant was gone, so someone needed to take his slot.)

So five of us piled onto our three tracked and gas-guzzling ATVs, leaving Kayla and Fiona back home with the dogs and a shotgun, and headed off to our woodlot. Sara and I pulled the utility trailer, while Graham and Lisa dragged the splitter behind them. It took three times as long with snow on the ground, the trailer and splitter wheels getting stuck in a few patches of powder on the way.

I would have liked to bring Des and Juju with us, but I wasn't comfortable leaving just two people back at the cottage without some kind of backup. If someone came along we'd be able to hear the barking echoing out over the lake.

As expected, it was Lisa and Graham who worked the hardest out there, taking the bucked logs and setting them up on the splitter. Matt did his best on limbing with one of the chainsaws, but as always, his coordination was a little off. Sara loaded the split logs onto the trailer while I did a little of everything.

I just couldn't keep up with Lisa and Graham; I wanted to, but there's no way my heart would be able to take it, even if I'd had a full night's sleep. As hard as it was to do, I made sure to take a break every five minutes or so. As much as I was glad to have brought the defibrillator along in the trailer, I wasn't hoping for a chance to use it.

We heard the dogs barking just before lunchtime. We all stopped working and listened. No gunshots, no screams, just the dogs. I was sure it was just a local pest running through the yard, maybe a squirrel or a Tremblay. But we still needed to be sure, so Lisa and I hopped on an ATV and headed back to the cottage to check, while Graham stood watch at the woodlot.

As we reached the back of the cottage, we could hear voices. We climbed off and readied our guns, Lisa with the shotgun and me with my pistol.

"Baptiste!" a man's voice called out. "Your girls won't let us come inside."

I came around the corner to see a black half-ton with Ryan Stems standing in front. He didn't seem to be armed, or that's what he wanted me to think, but a man standing by the passenger side door had a shotgun aimed right at me.

I was way too tired for that shit.

I didn't have my vest and I didn't have my helmet. There was no way I could take them both out before they got me. And I knew there'd be a third man somewhere. Maybe crouched around the corner of the porch... maybe up in the loft...

I pointed my gun at the man by the truck. I noticed that Lisa had done the same.

Kayla and Fiona were behind the screen of the front porch;

despite the small bits of training I'd already given her, and her claims to the contrary, Kayla was holding the shotgun like someone who didn't know how to use it.

I turned to Kayla and Fiona. "Are you two okay?" I asked. They both nodded. Kayla kept the gun up and aimed, her arms shaking.

"I didn't mean to frighten anyone," Stems said.

"Bullshit," Lisa said. She started to angle her barrel towards him.

"Why did you come here?" I asked him.

"I wanted to tell you in person. There are going to be some changes around here.."

"You're leaving? Have a good trip."

"Fucking hilarious, Baptiste." Stems shook his head. "After what's happened the last few weeks... this can't go on. You need to stay on this side of the river."

"Like a time out?"

"There are too many guns in Cochrane District. Too many guns and too many murders."

"Don't forget the explosion," I said.

"This isn't a joke. I don't find dead bodies as funny as you do. I guess you laughed like a hyena when you found the Girards."

"What happened to the Girards?"

"Don't screw around, Baptiste."

"How do you know about the Girards?"

"You should have reached out to me," he said. "The moment you found them."

"You should have reached out before you killed them."

"Still not funny. It's Detour Lake. I know that. Running around and pretending they're me. You know they killed those two girls because of you. And the rest of 'em, I guess. And I'm not willing to see the same thing happen to the Walkers or the Marchands. Or to your people."

"What is that supposed to mean?"

"We're taking over. The Mushkegowuk Nation. From the North Driftwood River to the Abitibi, from James Bay to Timmins. And our borders are closed."

"I don't think we can agree to that," I said.

"We don't need you to agree. We have more guns than you."

"Are you sure about that?"

"I know you like playing the heavy. But try to remember who

you're talking to."

"Who am I talking to? Some idiot from Minnesota who thinks he's tough because he was stupid enough to join the US Army?"

"I'm the only reason you're still alive, Baptiste. Remember that."

"I don't have a problem with shooting you in the head. Try to remember that."

"Someday you may get your chance."

"I do hope so."

"But for today, just shut up and listen. We're cleaning up the district... well, a part of it, at least. The Nation is sick and tired of having a shit sandwich on its border. And you've made it pretty clear that you're part of the problem."

"Fuck you, Stems."

"I'm doing this to protect your people, Baptiste. To protect them from those assholes in the Toyota technicals *and* to protect them from your bad decisions."

"The only bad decision I made was not shooting you in the head when we first met."

"I'm not happy about this situation, either. I want you gone."

"Then get me gone."

"Don't tempt me, Baptiste. My orders are to leave you be as long as you stay on this side of the river. If I have to drag your corpse over the bridge just to cover my ass... well, I'll do it with a smile on my face."

Stems was playing it wrong, trying to scare me, but really just pushing Lisa to the edge. I didn't have to look over to her to know that she was pretty close to losing her cool... I knew that if she took a shot I'd have to take mine, too. If I was lucky she'd take out the man by the truck, and I'd have a few milliseconds to guess where the third man was positioned. I focused my vision on my far left, trying not to move my pupils.

I couldn't tell if anyone was up in the loft. There was no way to be sure.

I knew that the best thing for us was to do nothing.

"We're willing to stay on our side of the river," I said. "As long as you keep to yours."

"Not a problem," Stems replied. "Sounds like you understand the situation."

"Yeah. I understand."

"Then make sure you share the rules with that piece of shit Justin Porter. You know I'd be happy to deal with him myself if I catch him crossing the Abitibi."

"I'll tell him."

"Good. Just remember... I'm doing this for all of us."

He backed up to the truck and climbed into the front seat. The second man climbed in, and Stems put the truck into reverse. As they pulled away from the cottage I finally caught a glimpse of the third man, running out from his hiding place behind the corner of the porch. He hopped in the box with what looked like a C9 rifle on his shoulder.

Stems had brought a bigger gun than I'd expected. A gun from the Canadian Forces. Almost as fancy as mine.

I kept the shotgun on them, until I could no longer see the truck. And then I waited another couple of beats, just in case.

Lisa and I made our way onto the screened-in porch. Lisa gave Kayla a hug, while I wrapped my arms around Fiona.

"I thought that was it," Kayla said. "My god... I really thought they were coming to kill us."

"You guys did good," Lisa said. "I'm so proud of you two."

"Yes... really good," I said.

"Why weren't you here?" Fiona asked me.

"I was out splitting wood."

"But you should have been here."

"I know... I should have been here."

I hadn't been thinking straight.

I should have stayed behind. Or Lisa. One of us. Always.

That was how it was supposed to work. That's how I said it would work, from here on out.

I was too tired. I'd fucked up.

"And all this talk about keeping us safe," Fiona said. "Seriously..."

"Take it easy, Fiona," Lisa said. "Everyone's okay."

Fiona started to sob.

I didn't know what to do. I let my arms drop from around her.

She ran from the porch and up the stairs.

We all glanced at one another for a moment. Lisa still had that berserker look in her eyes, Kayla was still shaking with fear... none of us seemed particularly well-equipped to follow Fiona up to her room.

"I guess I'll go," Kayla said to me. "She's too mad at you to

278

bother with me."

I nodded as she left.

"She's right," I said to Lisa. "I should have been here."

"I know," Lisa said. "You should have been. You won't make the same mistake again."

✂

Graham and I went out in the truck, to check the damage to the gate on Nelson Road. The locks were busted open, but that wasn't a surprise.

"How did this happen?" Graham asked. "The tripwire should have triggered the alarm."

I knelt down and took a look. "Everything's intact."

"So we should trip it?"

"We should trip it." So I did.

Graham grabbed the handheld and pushed for Lisa.

"Alarm's sounding," Lisa said. "Gate on Nelson Road."

"So the hop's working," I said. "So what went wrong?"

"I don't know," Graham said. "I'm more of a hardware guy, and this might be a software problem."

"Or jamming."

"Maybe... I don't know. You know who needs to check on this."

"Shit." I didn't want to hear it. "Do me a favour. You ask him."

"I can," Graham said. "But it'd mean a heck of a lot more coming from you."

"Who are you, Sara now?"

"Just pointing out the obvious."

"I know."

✂

I found Matt chopping wood, or playing with an axe, which is probably a more accurate description of events.

"I need you to check the hops," I said. "Particularly the one on the Dougalls' roof."

"You want me to climb up on the roof? That sounds like a bad

279

idea. That place is going to cave in."

I had to sigh. "First off, it's not going to cave in... otherwise we wouldn't have put a hop and panel up there. Second... just shut up and start checking for viruses or whatever."

"Viruses or whatever?"

"You know... breaches. I want to know if someone has compromised our network."

"Someone like Stems."

"Yes... like Stems. Can you just do this for me?"

"Yeah, alright. I'll check it out."

I didn't want to say it. But I had to. "Thanks," I muttered.

✧

We decided to stop our wood splitting for the day; it felt like we'd be tempting fate if we divided into two groups again so soon.

Everyone stayed close to home. While we all acted like we were getting things done, I know that every one of us was too busy wondering what we should do next.

"We should have some kind of meeting about it," I said to Graham as I passed him by the chicken coop. He was collecting the eggs, which was not something I remember him ever doing before.

Carcassonne was following by his heels; I think that big dog was just as surprised by Graham as I was.

"Actually, I was meaning to talk to you," Graham said. "I've been saying that we'd discuss this over dinner. Maybe come up with a few options, and have some kind of vote."

I wasn't so much surprised as annoyed by the way he seemed to be taking charge. "That's a strange thing for you to be taking the initiative on."

"Someone needed to."

"I'm sorry... was that a joke?"

"I'm not joking," Graham said. "I think it's time we made some tough decisions."

"Okay now," I said, "you need to think this through for a minute, Graham. It's good that you're taking an interest —"

"An interest? You gotta be freaking kidding me. I'm getting a little sick of this patronizing attitude of yours."

"Watch yourself."

"You're not the boss, Baptiste, and you and Sara aren't the only grownups around here. It's time you start listening to the rest of us."

"I listen," I said. "But just because you have an opinion doesn't make it right. I know you want us to leave. I'm not an idiot."

"It's not about me wanting anything... it's about what makes sense for us as a group. And staying here doesn't make sense anymore. It's just not safe."

I shook my head and sighed; I was being a prick, but I felt it was the right approach to take at that moment. "I don't want to have the same stupid conversation with you over and over again. We are safer right here. If we leave, we won't survive."

"You don't know that."

"You're right... I can't promise that you and Lisa and the rest of us will be shot up and skullfucked somewhere along the highway... or thrown into the big pit by The Souls and left to die. It's not definite... it's just highly likely."

"More scare tactics from the master," Graham said. He turned to walk away.

I grabbed his arm. "I need to show you something."

He glared at me for a moment, like he was about to stay on the attack, but I think he could tell that I was about to let him in on something that mattered.

I took Graham down into the basement. I led him past the half-dozen shelves, overflowing with aluminum cans and boxes of dry goods, past our three chest freezers with Fiona's leftover collection, and over to a tower of six long and deep plastic boxes stacked up along the dampest of the damp concrete walls.

I pulled off the top three boxes, one by one. I could tell I was already pushing my heart too hard.

I moved on to the fourth box. I pulled out one of the white and gray binders I'd saved from the committee. I let the binder fall open to the middle, and I flipped over until I found the right page. I began to read.

"Beginning in the month of February, approximately five hundred and twenty people left Cochrane for neighbouring areas, including Timmins and Aiguebelle. A public plea was made for all evacuees to make contact with us, in any way open to them, to assure us that they were safe and that the road was clear. As of March 31st, we have not received a single message confirming that any Cochrane residents have arrived at a secure destination."

"That could mean anything," Graham said. "Phones and networks were down more often than they were up. And I doubt most people know much about making calls on the radio anymore."

"I was sent down toward Timmins to see if I could find any trace of our people. I found some of them."

"And they didn't make it."

"They didn't make it. They were slaughtered, sometimes by marauders, sometimes by The Souls. Bodies lying on the paved shoulders like roadkill. Who knows how many more ended up in some big pit. Sometimes the marauders would burn the bodies to keep down the stench, but other times the corpses rotted where they were left; they didn't bother to hide the mess, and they certainly didn't bother to dig any graves. It's here in hard copy, Graham. The committee took each one of my photos and printed them out. Take a look."

I handed him the binder, and watched as he flipped through several pages of photographs. I hadn't shown these to anyone before, and I doubt I'd share them with anyone else in that cottage. To me and Graham, these were just unfortunate people who got caught up in something terrible. To everyone else these could be neighbours, or friends... in Sara's case, there was always the slim chance they could be her sisters. No one else needed to see them.

"This was over a year ago," Graham said. "I'll bet the majority of those marauders have moved on. And I'll bet The Souls have better things to do these days. Those highways are empty now... there aren't enough people traveling on them to justify lying in wait. I really don't see how this changes the situation."

"That's why you're dangerous, Graham. You've made up your mind."

"What, about you? You seem pretty stuck on digging in, no matter what it costs us."

"I think I'm starting to understand. This isn't about how many guns we have, or whether or not it's safe out on the highways. This is about how you're so scared of having to fight that you'd rather pin all of your hopes on running away."

"That's not it."

"That's *so* it, man. I thought you were naive. Turns out you're just chickenshit."

Graham made some kind of growl and shoved me square on my shoulders. I felt my head strike the wooden staircase.

"Don't start something with me," I said as I took position with my fists out.

"You're right. I've seen what you're capable of. I don't want to end up like Marc Tremblay. People seem to keep dying around you, Baptiste."

He turned away again, and I didn't say a word as he walked back up the basement steps. I looked up the stairwell to see Lisa waiting for him at the top. I'm sure she heard some of it.

I found an old wood step stool and sat down. I wasn't ready to go upstairs, not yet. I wasn't ready to face any of them.

∽

Sara chaired the meeting between the seven of us, apparently hoping that if everything seemed official, that we'd all spend less time yelling across the table at each other.

We all sat around the pinewood table, Sara at one end and Graham at the other, and the rest of us clustered around them based on our little orbits, Fiona and I on one side and Lisa at the other, with Matt and Kayla smack in the middle.

"Things might get a little heated," Sara said. "I know a lot of us have pretty strong opinions on the topic of whether to stay or go. So let's all raise our hands like in school, without any interrupting." She said it in a half-joking way, but I think everyone knew not to fuck with her. "I'm going to start."

Graham raised his hand.

"You can go next," Sara said. "All I really want to say is that we all have our jobs around here. I'm in charge of inventory and Fiona runs the kitchen. That doesn't mean that Kayla can't speak up if she thinks we're too low on firewood, or that Matt shouldn't care if we don't have enough cutlery. But what it does mean is that each of us owns a specific part of our collective responsibilities... and in that one area that person will have the final say."

Graham was shifting violently in his chair, but he held his tongue.

"Baptiste is in charge of security," Sara said. "That's his expertise and I don't think anyone here truly questions that role. But we've had a series of incidents lately that have made us all a little uneasy." She paused for a moment, biting her bottom lip. "Ant wasn't doing the most he could to be safe, and it killed him. Marc Tremblay slipped and hit his head, and he didn't make it, either."

I glanced back to Graham. He was staring directly at me. I couldn't tell what he was thinking, if he was considering telling the truth about Marc and what had really gone on out there.

"We know what happened to the Girards," Sara said. "And we have reason to believe that the same thing may have happened to the Smiths and the Lamarches. And now Ryan Stems is trying to close us in to this side of the river."

"And Ryan Stems was able to sneak up on us," Graham said. "And could have killed every last one of us if he'd wanted to."

"Hold on, Graham... I'm almost done. Stems came when we were vulnerable, when maybe too many of us were away from the house at the same time. That's something we'll need to fix going forward."

She nodded to Graham.

"I respect Baptiste," he said, "I really do. He's done a lot for all of us. Just as we've all done a lot for him. But it doesn't matter how much you like or respect someone... if a situation is unsafe, it's unsafe. Baptiste can't change that, no matter how hard he works at it. It's not safe here... so we need to find somewhere that is. It's that simple."

Matt spoke next. "I really don't know who's right on this," he said. "Today was too close. Too fucking close. I don't know what I would've done if something had happened to... the girls. Maybe that's all of our screw-up, not just Baptiste. I should have been there —"

"The point?" I asked.

Sara scowled at me, but all I gave in return was a shrug of my shoulders. Someone had to remind Matt that we were all just humouring him.

"I think we should listen to Baptiste," Matt said. "He's the expert around here. He was on the Protection Committee, so he's got to have a better understanding of what we're up against. If he says it's not safe to leave... well, I believe him."

For a second I almost felt bad for being hard on Matt; that happens sometimes, but usually he'll remind me just a few minutes later why I want to hit him on the head with a mallet.

It was Lisa's turn next. "If Baptiste wants us to listen, he needs to give us something to work with." She looked straight at me. "If you have information that you're not sharing, you can't really blame us for not trusting your judgment."

I knew Graham must have told her, and now she wanted everyone to know.

Fiona stuck her hand up, waving it much too eagerly.

Sara gave her a quick nod.

"That's not fair, Lisa," Fiona said. "Baptiste isn't hiding anything from us. Well, not from anyone who isn't me. But he's not pretending that there's no risk to staying here."

I stood up as Sara nodded to me. "I'll lay it out for everyone, okay? There's no question that most of the families that left town and tried to make it to Temiskaming or Timmins or Aiguebelle were killed en route. The Protection Committee expected some violence, but we believed that it would be limited to a few incidents, and it wasn't like we were going to force people to stay in Cochrane. We'd thought there were a handful of marauders, at most But reports were coming in much faster than we could check them. We revised our estimates upwards to the point that we believed that there were over two dozen armed groups in total, including The Souls and Hells Angels, most in and around Timmins and the rest along Highway 11. At their height, there were probably over one hundred marauders in the area, responsible for as many as fifteen hundred deaths."

I heard the gasps from everyone, as Graham rose to his feet. "How many marauders do you believe there are now?"

Sara bristled, but she didn't intervene.

"There are probably six or seven groups left around Cochrane," I said, "but I'll bet half of those are copycats, and aren't doing much of the killing. I think these three Spirit Animal crews with the Toyota technicals are the only major marauder threat left within thirty klicks of Cochrane."

"They're a pretty big threat, aren't they?" Graham asked.

"They are, but it's no better farther down the highway. We know that Timmins is fully run now by Souls of Flesh. I'll bet if it wasn't for the Protection Committee having organized people into patrols in the early days, we'd have had them taking over up here. That same thing probably happened in a lot of other towns. I wouldn't be surprised if half the towns left in Ontario are being run by criminal organizations."

"What are you saying?" Sara asked. "Is there really nowhere left to go?"

I took a deep breath. "I don't think there is," I said.

"What about Temiskaming?" Kayla asked. "It's safe there, isn't it?"

"We don't know... there's nothing to prove that Temiskaming isn't just as bad as everywhere else. If we could even get there."

"They're pretty quiet," Matt said.

"What do you mean?" Sara asked. She'd apparently given up on any semblance of order.

"On the radio... in the Tremblays' truck. If you scan the channels you only get a few groups here and there... and none of them talk about Temiskaming."

"That doesn't mean much," I said, wondering why Matt was spending so much time playing with the radio. "I doubt people mention their location often enough for you to pinpoint it. And that radio is digital; you wouldn't even pick up on any encrypted chatter."

"You think people are using encrypted radio signals?" Lisa asked.

"We use them on our handhelds, right? And I'd guess The Souls are using them in Timmins... otherwise Matt would be picking up on their conversations. Same for Aiguebelle. You'd probably need an analog scanner to even notice the signal."

"Well, there's no mention of Temiskaming on shortwave, either," Matt said. "Whenever they talk about us on the BBC or that news station out of Boston, they talk about Toronto being a mess, obviously, but they also mention Sudbury and even Aiguebelle once in a while. But no Timmins, and no Temiskaming. It's a black hole out here."

"They talk about places that are getting aid," I said. "They probably have people on the ground in Aiguebelle to distribute food or fuel, and a correspondent here and there. I don't think they'd bother with a place as small as Temiskaming. It's probably no different than the way it was in Cochrane before The Fires, just a few dozen families trying to hold on."

"They're out there," Graham said. "And we can make it to Temiskaming if we go now, before the next attack."

"They're not going to attack," Matt said. "They're not strong enough."

"They want to attack," I said. "But they'll wait until we let our guard down... until we stretch ourselves too thin."

"Like this morning," Lisa said. "We're lucky it was Stems and not those assholes pretending to be him."

"We got back in time... and I won't let that happen again."

"So you know they're coming for us," Graham said. "But for some stupid reason you still want to stay?"

"We're stronger than they are," I said.

"That's not true."

"Trust me. We play it safe and we wait. That's our best chance."

"I can't let this go," Graham said. "We aren't safe here."

"We should vote," Kayla said.

"It doesn't matter what everyone wants," I said. "It matters that we stay safe."

"We're taking a vote," Sara said. "But you're still in charge of security, so you're in charge of whether or not we stay. You'll make the final decision."

"Then what's the point of voting?" Lisa asked. "He's already made up his mind."

"Someone make a motion."

"I'll do it," Kayla said. "I move that we stay at McCartney Lake."

"Okay," Sara said. "There's the motion. Show of hands... all in favour?"

I didn't know what to expect. I raised my hand and watched as the other hands shot up, Fiona, Kayla and Matt, four against two.

"Motion carried," Sara said.

"Tell me, Baptiste," Graham said. "What would you have done if they'd all wanted to leave?"

"I'm not sure," I said. "But I don't think I would have given up. I don't think I'd ever be willing to take us on the highway."

"So we'll never agree."

"We don't have to agree on everything. I'm not against looking at this again in the spring."

"Whatever," Graham said.

"No, seriously, Baptiste," Lisa said, "I cannot wait until the snow melts, so we can talk and talk all over again, while you just ignore us and do whatever the hell you want."

"I think we should adjourn," Sara said.

But by the time she'd said it, Lisa and Graham had already left the dining room, on their way upstairs and away from the rest of us.

"It'll blow over," Kayla said.

"I don't think it will," I said.

"It has to," Fiona said.

"I know."

I left for my own room, and I think for the first evening since we moved into that cottage on McCartney Lake, the whole downstairs emptied out, as everyone went to hide from everyone else.

TODAY IS FRIDAY, DECEMBER 28TH.

THE WEEKLY meeting was held at our place, which is exciting and wonderful if you're Fiona, and no one else. She'd baked up something she called a dutch baby, and she'd laid out the fancier plates, alongside cloth napkins folded in triangles.

Kayla told her to stop trying so hard.

I hadn't seen Alain Tremblay since before his brother died. I hadn't given him my supposed sympathies, and I certainly hadn't apologized for the "accident". Since he hadn't dropped by since, I was starting to get the impression that he was perfectly content with the idea of never seeing me again.

But when he showed up with Marc's wife Suzanne, he smiled and extended his hand.

I didn't know what that meant.

"I hope you're feeling better," he said to me. "I know it's been a rough couple of weeks."

I nodded. "It hasn't been fun for any of us."

I heard Fiona's laughter from the dining room. I turned to see Matt leaning against the table, chatting her up.

Suzanne came in for a hug and a peck on the cheek. "Baptiste... it's good to see you," she said. She smelled amazing, in that way where you aren't really sure that it's something that could have come from a bottle.

"You, too," I said.

"Just waiting on Rihanna and Justin," Sara said as she came over to greet our guests.

"My nephew's gone down to babysit," Alain said. "They should be here soon. It smells wonderful in here... Fiona is a wonderful chef."

"And supermodel," I said.

"What?"

"Uh... bad inside joke." I felt like an idiot.

289

Sara was glaring at me.

"Should we eat?" I asked. "I'm sure the Porters won't mind."

"We can wait a few more minutes," Sara said.

I nodded.

I didn't know what we were going to do while we waited.

All I knew was that it would be all sorts of awkward.

Alain sat down on the couch; Suzanne sat beside him, almost touching, but not quite.

Sara sat down on the rocking chair, leaving me the recliner.

"That's my spot," Kayla said as she appeared out of nowhere. "And no... we can't share." She threw herself down on the recliner, throwing out the footrest as she landed.

Sara glared at me again.

I'm not sure why that was my fault.

I thought about standing, milling around the living room while everyone talked about whatever, but that would have been even more awkward, so I sat down beside Suzanne.

She gave me a tap on the thigh.

I didn't bother looking at Sara.

"So you had a visitor yesterday," Suzanne said.

"News travels fast," I said.

"It does," Alain said, "whether you want it to or not."

"We were going to bring it up at the meeting," Sara said.

"Sorry... I didn't mean to sound rude."

"No," Kayla said, "you have a right to know."

"Where's Graham?" Suzanne asked.

"Hiding," I said, forgetting the audience. "Uh... another stupid joke. I think he's feeding the goats. Lisa's with him."

Suzanne smiled. "He loves those goats."

"His family raises goats," Sara said. Present tense, I noticed. I guess there was no reason to make unpleasant assumptions. "Boer goats... for meat. I think they have over fifty head."

"Graham told me eighty," Kayla said.

"He told me one hundred," Suzanne said.

"Should be five hundred by New Year," Alain said with a chuckle.

The front door opened without a knock.

It was Justin and Rihanna.

"Good morning," Sara called out.

"Morning," Justin said.

"Are we late?" Rihanna asked.

"We haven't started eating yet," I said. "So I guess you're just in time."

"Good... I'm starving."

I hate it when people say that.

⮾

We ate breakfast without Graham and Lisa, since even Sara seemed to agree that they had no legitimate excuse for not knowing what time it was.

Alain handed out a boatload of compliments, mostly to Fiona and her breakfast, but also a comment on Sara's beauty and a mention of Kayla's sharp wit. He was trying a little too hard, but I guess that's better than the opposite.

Once the last few bites of Fiona's sweet, doughy contraption were taken, Sara got right down to business.

Graham and Lisa still hadn't arrived.

I think Sara preferred that, after yesterday's fight.

"So I'm sure by now everyone's heard about Stems and his message," Sara said.

"Tell us again," Justin said. "I want to hear it from you." He looked over to me. "Actually, I'd like Baptiste to tell us, since he's in charge of security around here."

"Stems snuck over the river yesterday," I said. "And through our gate. He busted the locks and somehow he didn't set off the alarm."

"Somehow? You don't know?"

"Actually," Matt said, "I found something. It looks like there's a problem with our detection system."

It was Matt's perfect timing. Rather than mentioning something to me beforehand, he had to blurt it out in front of everyone.

"What kind of problem?" Justin asked.

"It's wide open. Anyone on our network has the ability to disable the alarm. And someone did... just long enough for Stems to pay us a visit."

"Can't you figure out who disabled it?"

"Nope. We didn't turn on auditing for user actions. Just the event log."

Justin scoffed. "Didn't turn on auditing? What kind of security system doesn't have full auditing by default?"

"It's better than your non-existent one," I said.

"So you're saying that someone at McCartney Lake is working with Ryan Stems?" Sara asked.

"I guess so," Matt said. "My money's on Graham. He's not here, right?"

"That's ridiculous," I said. "Don't just throw out accusations, Matt. You look like an ass."

"And that's a ranking from an expert in the field," Justin said.

"We need to lock it down," Rihanna said. "Can you do that, Matt?"

"I already have," Matt said. "Only me and Baptiste can change it now."

"You and Baptiste?" Justin said. "How does that make sense?"

"You still have that goddamn dongle, remember?" I said.

"Why does he have a dongle?" Sara asked.

"I gave him Ant's," Matt said. "I thought it made sense."

"Without asking?"

"Asking who?"

"Asking me," I said. "You know... the guy in charge of security."

Matt gave me a smirk. "Hey, guy in charge of security. Who knows how to configure the detection system?"

"This isn't funny, Matt," Sara said. "You can't just ignore the rules whenever you feel like it."

"Wow," Justin said. "Then how about this rule? Don't leave a couple of young girls unprotected at your cottage while you trounce around on the other side of the lake."

"It was a mistake," Kayla said. "It won't happen again."

Justin groaned. "Let me give you guys some tips, since you apparently don't fully get the idea of security. Number one: don't let people sneak in. Number two: use your goddamn dinosaur brains to figure out who caused the breach. Here's a hint: it was fucking New Post."

"New Post?" Matt said. "Why would you say that?"

"Come on, Matt... we share the hop at Blackwell Road with them. They have access to our network. And they probably have people who are professionals when it comes to things like hops and detection systems."

"I'm professional."

"I mean trained... certified..."

"Oh."

"Where's the proof?" I asked. "You want it to be New Post because you hate them. But you can't prove it."

"No, I can't," Justin said. "Because apparently we don't audit things around here. But tell me something, Baptiste... have you taken a drive up to the bridge on 652?"

"Not yet..."

"Well I have... and the gate's intact. Stems didn't drive his truck over that bridge. And the gate up by the bend in Kennedy Road is intact, too."

"It's a half-ton pickup truck," I said. "It's not impossible to off-road a little."

"Come on... why risk getting stuck in the muskeg in hostile territory when you can take a nice old rail bridge controlled by your friends at Taykwa Tagamou?"

"He has a point," Alain said. "There's a very good chance that Gerald Archibald let Stems through."

"We need to confront him," Rihanna said.

"I don't know," I said.

"Ooh," Justin said, "more indecisiveness... keep it up, Baptiste... you haven't killed us all, yet."

I wasn't going to take that. "Enough, Justin. I'm not going to put up with your shit for another second. Either you're a part of this team or you're not. You can't sit there sniping at me every thirty seconds and pretend that you've got my back."

"I don't 'got' your back. I don't support you. I support the idea of keeping us alive. And that's pretty much at odds with your leadership."

"I think you should go, Justin," Sara said.

"That's your answer to everything. Someone makes a good point? Just kick 'em out."

"Come on, Justin..." Alain said.

"No, Alain. You need to pick a side here."

"That's not how this works," Sara said.

"This doesn't work," Alain said. "This is one-man rule, and it is failing us."

"What one-man rule?" I asked.

"Who chose to attack the gunmen at Silver Queen Lake?" Justin asked. "And who did it without wanting me to know?"

"I wasn't hiding it from you."

"I think you were," Matt said.

"Shut up, Matt."

"Don't tell him to shut up," Justin said. "He has as much a right to speak as anyone else."

"Don't do this, Justin," Kayla said. "Please..."

Justin ignored her. "Speak, Matt. Tell us why Baptiste likes to keep secrets."

"He doesn't trust you," Matt said.

"But why?"

"Because you're using us," I said. "You came here begging for help, and then you and Marc Tremblay kept on with your little indenture shuttle. That's why you wanted that goddamn dongle... so you could take the Lamarche daughters and sell them to Detour Lake... so you could rob the Smiths blind in exchange for some indenture contracts. How can anyone trust you?"

"*Calisse de crisse,* Justin," Alain said. "You're doing it again."

"Fuck, Alain," Justin said. "You drank the booze. You ate the fucking belgian chocolates... you knew what we were doing."

Alain shook his head. "And with Detour Lake again? After what they've done? To the Marchands... to Antoine... they tried to kill you. Did you forget?"

"They weren't after Justin," I said. "They don't shoot their hired help. They just wanted to put a hole in the Supply Partnership, I'll bet. Maybe put a hole or two in me."

"They wanted us on their side," Justin said. "They knew what Stems was up to, that he's going to come for all of us eventually. You needed to pick a side, Baptiste. But that's always been too hard for you."

"I can't believe you and Marc would betray us," Sara said. But she was staring at Suzanne. That's who she meant.

"I didn't know," Suzanne said.

Sara shook her head. "You're lying... you're all guilty. Every last one of you."

"*Ta guele! Tu m'invites ici, puis tu insultes moi... et mon mari mort!*"

"*Ton mari meurtrier.*"

"*Chienne.*"

"Picrelle."

"Enough," I said. "This is way out of control."

"Then reign them in, Baptiste," Justin said. "You know, Baptiste-style. Bad-choice them to death."

"Are you a fucking ten-year-old?"

I heard a chuckle from the living room. "You all sound like ten-year-olds," Graham said. "What the heck is going on in here?"

"Sara's lost her shit," Lisa said. "This is the moment I've been waiting for."

"We should adjourn," Sara said, trying to sound calm; it wasn't working. "Maybe we can try again tomorrow."

"I'm going to New Post," Justin said. "I'm going to get some answers."

"I'm pretty sure they hate you at New Post," Lisa said.

"I should be the one to go," I said.

"Oh?" Justin said. "Well... uh, sorry Baptiste... I wasn't clear. I want someone to go to New Post and not fuck it up. So you're out."

"I'll fuck you up..."

"You'll both go," Alain said. "But take someone with you... maybe someone they don't hate."

"I'll go," Lisa said. "I'm the right colour."

"I think that might be racist," Graham said.

"It's only racist when you say it."

"Yeah," I said. "White people, eh?"

Lisa nodded. "You're still half-racist, Baptiste. Never forget."

"Enough goddamn chit chat," Justin said. "I'll be outside in twenty minutes. Bring me a vest and helmet. There's no way we should show up without our gear."

"Agreed," I said.

"If that's decided," Sara said, "I think we're done."

"You mean adjourned?" Lisa asked.

"Whatever."

She stormed upstairs before Justin had the chance to stomp out through the living room.

You know things are messed up when Lisa starts looking like the calm one.

"So what do we do about him?" Lisa asked me.

Justin was outside, waiting to go. Apparently his strategy was to pretend like we had no reason to hate him.

"What can we do?" I asked. "Can we shoot him?"

"Make it look like an accident?"

"We still need him."

"He tried to kill you, Baptiste."

"I don't think he did. It's not like he's been giving orders to Detour Lake. He's just under the mistaken impression that we can work with them."

"He can work with them," Lisa said. "You and I are the ones who can't. Unless those assholes want to give us some kind of 'honourary Aryan' badges. They never say it, but you know they think it. I honestly think we should make sure Justin Porter has an accident. You already threw a nice one for Marc Tremblay."

"I don't know..."

"He's going to cost us. More than we can pay."

"Once he's gone, he's gone," I said. "That'll weaken us."

"We need people we can trust."

"We need people who can shoot." I picked the third riot suit up out of the chest. "At least for now."

Justin, Lisa and I were in full gear when we took the Tremblays' truck to New Post. There was still enough diesel for the trip (but not much more), and I wasn't sure I liked the idea of Ryan Stems and his guns tearing through what little horse flesh we have.

They were expecting us, with almost a dozen people waiting for us at the New Post gate. I counted six hunting rifles and a shotgun, and a couple of council members standing behind the engine block of a pickup.

No sign of Stems.

We got out of the truck and walked towards them in a line, our guns at our sides, but ready. Justin looked just as comfortable with his rifle as I was with the Mossberg, while Lisa actually seemed the shakiest for once.

Gerald Archibald stepped around his hiding place and walked up to us.

I guess he didn't think we'd shoot him.

"I'm sorry, guys," he said as he held out his right hand.

I wasn't about to shake it. "What kind of arrangement do you have with Ryan Stems?" I asked.

"Stems has guns. That's the extent of it. He came to the rail bridge yesterday morning and we had to let him through."

"What's the point of even having gates?" Lisa asked.

"Do you really think we were going to fight a war because a fellow member of the Mushkegowuk Nation wants to pass through our land?"

Mushkegowuk Nation. He'd never included New Post in that before. They'd always been arm's length...

"I don't believe you," Lisa said. "Ryan Stems isn't a threat to you. Don't bother with this 'under duress' garbage."

"So what happens when Stems asks you to go to war with us?" Justin asked.

"No one's going to war," Gerald said.

Justin took a step closer to Gerald, sizing him up. "I'm ready. I want you to know that."

"Is that a threat?"

"No one wants threats," I said. "I just don't know how we can trust you."

Gerald nodded toward Justin. "And you trust this guy?"

"What's not to trust?" Lisa said. "He steals, he lies..."

"Watch it," Justin said.

"Go ahead," I said. "I'd love to see what happens when you take a shot at Lisa. I'm guessing it'll end with your face in the snow."

"I can't promise to support you against Stems and the Mushkegowuk Nation," Gerald said. "I can't. I'm sorry."

"We get that," Lisa said. "But it was pretty shitty for you guys to deactivate our alarm system."

"What are you talking about?"

"We have the logs, Gerald. You guys turned off our alarm so Stems could sneak up on us." She was convincing; I almost believed her.

"It's an act of war," Justin said. "You know that, right?"

"I'm sorry," Gerald said. "I don't want this to get in the way of

297

our friendship."

"There's no friendship here," I said. "You stabbed us in the back, and you've just admitted that you'll do it again and again."

"That's not what I said."

"There's no point in talking about this. There's no point in us even being here. We need to get home and take care of our own."

"I'm sorry, Baptiste," Gerald said.

"Don't bother," I said.

Justin opened his visor and spit on the ground. He then marched off, headed back towards the truck.

Lisa backed away slowly, keeping her shotgun ready.

I turned my back to leave, trusting that they'd have no reason to shoot me.

We got back to the Tremblays' truck and made our way back home.

I told Matt to cut them off from the hop. I wanted them nowhere near our network.

I'll be happy if I never see or hear from another one of those New Post assholes again.

TODAY IS SATURDAY, DECEMBER 29TH.

SARA AND I decided to spend some time after breakfast going over the inventory. After a cursory display of helping clean up the dishes, I went out to the table to find that Sara had already unfolded her tablet to widescreen.

"Ready for business, eh?" I said.

"I've sent you something," she replied.

I took out my tablet.

"You'll need to go bigger," she said.

"So detail-oriented," I said. "*Très* sexy."

She didn't smile. "Let's just get started."

I unfolded my tablet to the wider screen. "Inventory list? Don't I have this?"

"It's a new version," she said. "For your eyes only."

I chuckled.

"It's not a joke, Baptiste."

I opened the document. "Four scenarios?"

"Just read."

"None of these sound too promising. Porters and Tremblays leave with over half our supplies? A 'cold war' with New Post? Wow, Sara... you're supposed to be the optimist."

"There's an optimists' scenario. The one marked 'rainbows and unicorns'."

"What's gotten into you? What is this?"

She groaned. "It's reality, Baptiste. Things are going from bad to worse, and I don't see how we're going to turn it around."

She'd given up on believing in me...

"It's not that bad," I said.

"Justin's about to do something stupid. I just don't know what. And Stems won't put up with us scavenging across the river any-more..."

"Put up with us? Like he has a choice..."

"We don't have many friends left, Baptiste. It's getting pretty close to us against everyone else."

"And that's my fault, right? That's your big lesson here?"

"What do you want me to say? You want me to pretend that every decision you've made was the right one?"

"They all seemed right at the time. Like you could do any better —"

"That's not what I'm saying..." she turned away from me.

"Then what are you saying, Sara? Please... tell me..." I grabbed her hand and gave it a little squeeze.

She yanked her hand away. "Don't."

"What is it? What's the problem?"

"You're my problem. And I'm stuck with you. You run around flirting with every woman in the district, and I just have to sit back and take it."

"What are you talking about?"

"Suzanne Tremblay... Katie Walker... Kayla Fucking Burkholder... what is it with you?"

"I haven't done anything!"

"Maybe... maybe not yet..."

"Are we going to talk inventory or not?"

She grabbed her tablet and stood up from her chair. "Just read, Baptiste. And message me when you're done. I don't want to be around you right now."

Sara stormed back up the stairs.

That's about all she ever does these days.

⌘

After an auspiciously Sara-free lunch, I decided to help Kayla outside. It was probably the nicest day since the snow had fallen, so that was a bonus.

"Do you really check the water every day?" I asked as she headed into the chicken coop.

"Twice a day, actually," she said. "But only in winter. Can't let it freeze."

"You'd think Graham could wire something up for that. A thermometer..."

"Some things are just better the way they are. Nice and simple."

"Simple. Sounds nice..."

"I already said that," she said with a grin. "No eggs... I would have thought there'd be some since this morning. Our hens are getting older."

We started walking over to the goat pen.

"I'm thinking we can try again this year," Kayla said. "Throw one of the roosters in and let nature take its course."

"I think it was the weather. Bad air, bad food... this year will be better."

"I hope so."

We checked the goats' feed and water.

"So Graham lets you handle the goats now?" I asked.

"He doesn't like it. But whenever Suzanne Tremblay beckons, Graham goes running."

"He's still doing that?"

"She's French. . he'll always do that. Until Lisa kills him."

"I don't get that. What's so special about French women?"

"Says the guy who likes to canoodle with Sara *Vachon*."

"Yeah, sure. But what does Suzanne Tremblay have over Lisa... or you?"

"Or me?"

I think I was blushing. "Come on, Kayla... you're... I just don't see what's special about Suzanne."

She stuck her finger out and poked me in the nose. "You'd fuck her."

"No comment."

She laughed. "Women suck, Baptiste. You know... other women. They get all pissy whenever their guy's eye starts wandering... like it's a personal affront to them that he'd ever think about doing what his body's programmed to do."

"Like fuck strippers?"

She glared at me.

It took me a moment to realize what I'd said.

"You'd fuck me," she said. "Even if I was a filthy stripper."

"I'm sorry... it was just another stupid attempt at a joke."

"It's okay, Baptiste. You don't need to apologize to me. I get you, you know?"

"Yeah..."

"Goats are good. It's all good. We should sit on the dock and get wasted."

I was tempted to say yes. Wouldn't Sara love that, seeing me sharing a bottle with Kayla Fucking Burkholder.

Maybe she'd realize that her jealous bitch routine was the quickest way to get me down to that dock with Kayla.

"I should get going," I said. "I have some reading to do."

She smiled. "That won't stop me from getting drunk on the dock."

"I know. That's what I like about you Kayla... you're nice and simple."

She punched me lightly on the shoulder.

I waved goodbye.

It's been a year and three months since the day that Sara and Lisa showed up at our door.

It was late September, not that it was recognizable. The ash clouds seemed just as thick as they'd been since the comet, and the ground was frozen but barren of snow. There hadn't been much of anything, not much rain... the only thing that even reminded us of normal weather was the wind, and by late September, that wind was getting colder.

Sara was dressed for the coming winter, like she'd expected a blizzard at any moment. She smiled at Graham as he opened the door; I doubt she even noticed that I was poking upstairs, through a half-open a bedroom window, or that I had a shotgun trained on her chest.

Not that I was sure I'd be able to pull the trigger.

Lisa knew I was there; she couldn't see me, but she knew. She was holding an old Winchester that looked like it hadn't been fired in fifty years; there was no way it was serviceable, and from the way she was holding it, I could tell that she knew enough about guns to know that all she had with her was a bluff for idiots.

And she knew we weren't idiots.

"My name's Sara Vachon," Sara said, as she held out her hand.

Graham took it. "We've met," he said. "I think..."

"Well, you're Graham. Ellie..."

"I guess I'm famous."

"You're not famous," Lisa said.

"This is Lisa," Sara said. "Lisa Wesley. She's in charge of charming people."

Graham offered Lisa his hand.

She glared at him like he'd just pulled down his pants.

I did my best not to laugh out loud.

"Is there something I can help you with?" Graham asked.

"We heard that Fiona Rees is with you," Sara said. "That you took her in."

"Sorry... I don't know her."

"You're lying," Lisa said.

"You're charming."

"Look," Sara said, "we need your help. We've got nowhere to go."

"It's just the two of you?"

"Four," Lisa said.

That set me off. They'd expected us to take them in, but they were hiding half their people out of sight.

"Husbands?" Graham asked. "Kids?"

"Just two more mismatched socks," Sara said.

"Where are they?"

"They're in position," Lisa said.

"Oh... to take us out?"

"To keep us safe."

That was too much for me.

I laughed.

"What's so goddamn funny?" Lisa asked, looking upstairs to my half open window.

"Your gun can't shoot and I can see your car up the road," I said. "With two people cowering inside."

"Glad we're entertaining you," Sara said.

"Who are they?" Graham asked. "The other two."

"Does it matter?"

"It matters," I said. "We're not really looking for more liabilities."

That set Fiona off; she was supposed to stay in the basement stairwell, quiet as a mouse, but instead she marched out to the front porch, pushed past Graham, and walked right down the steps to the gravel walk. She looked up to face me.

"I'm a liability?" she asked. "Are you kidding me? Who cooks your meals, Baptiste?"

"Get inside," I said.

"Hello, Fiona," Sara said.

"Fiona! Get inside."

"We don't know anything about you," Graham said. "How can you expect us to just let you come in?"

"We don't expect you to," Lisa said.

"We don't have any other options," Sara said. "You guys are it."

"So what are you offering?" I asked.

Sara glanced upward, trying to get a look at me. "We're not offering our bodies. I can tell you that."

"I mean supplies. Do you have any supplies?"

"No."

"That makes it easy."

"Not funny," Fiona said.

"You guys must bring something to the table," Graham said. "Right?"

At the time I'd figured he was interested in Sara; I'd certainly been drawn to her.

"We're willing to work," Lisa said. "And I can hunt."

"Matt is strong," Sara said. "He can help with that kind of thing."

"What about you?" Graham asked.

"I'm not as strong, but I'm alright."

"And the other one?" I asked.

"Kayla," Lisa said. "She's... she's something."

"Something?"

"You'll like her," Sara said. "Every man does."

"Maybe you should have led with her," I said.

"You're an asshole," Lisa said.

Graham laughed.

And I realized who he was really interested in.

"Bring the other two up here," I said. "Then we'll talk it over."

I already knew how I felt about them.

Sometimes being pretty isn't enough.

7

TODAY IS SUNDAY, DECEMBER 30TH.

THE TRIPWIRE alarm on the Abitibi bridge sounded this morning, before anyone was up. It was the first time I'd even heard it since the Porters had arrived at that gate. I knew that it could be the Spirit Animals, but a frontal assault didn't seem likely. They'd try to sneak up on us.

Lisa and Graham were downstairs before me, Lisa with armour on and her jacket piled overtop, and Graham checking the shotguns.

"The Spirit Animals?" Graham asked.

"I doubt it," I said.

Lisa and I took the truck. We'd be able to make the trip in less than five minutes; to me, that's worth the diesel it takes, for as long as we have it. I'm not sure how long it would take someone determined enough to break through the locks on our best gate, but I knew it would take longer than we'd give 'em.

I could hear ATVs revving up the road from the north shore cottages, probably the Porters. I wasn't sure if we really needed backup, not that there was much I could do to stop it.

In the end, Lisa and I got to the gate in less than four minutes.

Standing by the gate was Eva Marchand.

"This is new," Lisa said.

I threw my helmet on and climbed out of the truck, while Lisa readied the shotgun from her seat.

I left the door open so she could hear.

Eva's gloved hands were clasped in front of her. Her red pickup truck was waiting on the far side, off the bridge completely, with the skinny kid and one of her thirty-something sons, standing beside it with their rifles.

"What are you doing here, Eva?" I asked. I wasn't unfriendly.

"Ryan Stems came to our house," Eva said. I could tell that she was trying to sound unperturbed, but it wasn't really working.

"He stopped in to see us, too."

"He told us we had two choices; sign indentures with the Walkers or cross the Abitibi."

"Or what?"

"Or he'd disarm us... by force if he had to. And take our supplies. And take us to the Walkers anyway."

"When did he start doing Dave Walker's dirty work?"

"I think it's the other way around," Lisa called out from the truck.

"I think she's right," Eva said. "Stems told me that he's already chased those Spirit Animal men out of the area. He said they won't be coming back."

"He sounds a little too confident."

"He said they were from Detour Lake."

"I'm not sure I believe that," I said. "If they were coming in and out of Detour Lake, we'd have seen them."

"There are always ways around you, Monsieur Baptiste. There are more backroads than you think there are. I don't think there's any way to know where those men are. That's another reason we couldn't stay where we were. There are too few of us left."

"Well, there's not much out this way, Eva. Aiguebelle's closed its borders. And the bridge is out at Iroquois Falls, from what I hear. Not sure that's true, though, considering the source." It wasn't like I could have any faith in what Gerald Archibald had told me.

Of course, for all I knew Aiguebelle's border was still open, and Justin was full of shit... or, *somewhat more* full of shit...

"I've heard that, too," Eva said. "From the Girards."

I wasn't sure she even knew what happened to them. "Well, you can still cross at Twin Falls Dam if you're headed to Temiskaming, but... I wouldn't recommend the trip."

"We want to join you. I'm hoping that you'll consider taking us in. We... we have supplies. And weapons. And quite a bit of ammunition, too."

"Lisa," I said, "bring me the keys, will you?"

Lisa climbed out of the truck, slinging the shotgun over her shoulder. She handed me the keys and I began to unlock the gates.

I didn't bother with the dongle. The alarm had already gone off; we knew they were here.

Two weeks ago, I would have done my best to turn the Marchands away. I would have tried to come up with a list of convincing reasons why we shouldn't have anything to do with people who'd never done much to help us.

But that was before I buried Natalie. And before Eva Marchand had to bury five of her children and grandchildren.

Everything feels different now... there are so few of us left. The anger... what's happened in the past... it's all drained out of me. I'm just too damned tired.

I heard ATVs pull up. Justin and Rihanna.

"I can't promise anything," I said to Eva, "but I'll do my best."

Eva smiled. "Thank you so much, Baptiste."

"You're good people." I wasn't lying. "That's what counts around here."

Sara was not happy with me.

"They are not good people," she said.

Almost every one of us were crowded around the dining room table, Tremblays and Porters included, since the ship had sailed on keeping it a secret; the Marchands were waiting up the road, Lisa and Matt keeping an eye on them.

"Good people don't turn other people away," Sara said. She stopped for a moment, biting her bottom lip. Then she almost started to laugh. "I know... I'm a hypocrite."

"You were the one who wanted to have people join us," I said. "What's changed?"

"I'm not saying no to the Marchands... I just don't want us glossing over what they did last winter."

"So you must hate us, too," Alain Tremblay said. "That's good to know."

I expected the Porters to join in, but Justin and Rihanna just sat silently, listening.

"I don't hate anyone," Sara said. "But that doesn't make what you did okay. I asked for help, and you gave me none. You left us to die." She turned to look at me. "And honestly, Baptiste, I don't understand this big turnaround with you."

"We'd be stronger with them," I said. "Besides, I'm no better than they are," I said. "If it had been up to me, we wouldn't have taken anyone in."

"That's silly," Kayla said. "You took *us* in. That counts for something."

I realized that I was about to say something that could change a lot of people's opinion of me. I wasn't sure it was a good idea to talk about it, but I felt like I should. I felt like I was done holding onto it.

"You don't understand," I said. "I wouldn't have taken anyone in. We had to take Fiona, but after that..."

"Don't say it like that," Fiona said. "Like I'm a stupid burden to you."

"Fiona... you know what I mean. There's no way I would've left you there by the lake. You know I'm glad I found you." I turned back to Sara; I had to explain. "Graham and I aren't from here... so we've been thrown together from the start. Hell, we've been a team since even before The Fires. And when we decided to take Fiona with us, we knew that we were it for her. So when we met you —"

"We didn't know if we'd found the right place to live," Graham said. "We didn't know if we'd be able to get enough food and firewood together to make it through the first winter. So when you guys came to us, it felt pretty impossible to add four more mouths to feed."

"So I said no," I said. "I told Graham and Fiona that we couldn't risk everything on a bunch of people we barely knew."

"So you were really going to let us die?" Kayla asked.

"It's not like you were helpless. I mean, there were four of you, and only three of us. You could have struck out on your own."

"It wasn't safe," Sara said. "You knew that. You knew that we had no way of protecting ourselves. You had all the guns, Baptiste."

"I'm glad that Fiona and Graham changed my mind. I'm glad we took the risk. But as much as it pisses me off that people turned you away, I understand why they did it. Family comes first, every time."

Or it should.

"I guess it's lucky we're family now," Sara said. "That's assuming that we are, and that we're not just a bunch of strangers hanging around you and Graham and Fiona."

"That's not fair," Fiona said.

"I don't care," Sara said. She stood up and left the table. "Do whatever you want with the Marchands. I really don't care." She was up the stairs before anyone had a chance to respond.

From there we continued the meeting, no one really taking over as chair, but Graham leading things, for the most part.

No one else had a problem with the Marchands; since they had able-bodied people and the supplies to feed and arm them, there was really no reason not to take them in.

The only other thing we discussed at our emergency meeting was how best to move their supplies and equipment from Lillabelle Lake over to our cottages. After some argument, I won out on using the cart for all of it, saving what little diesel we still had left for a real emergency. We'd stick to the back roads, three men in armour, away from Cochrane and well away from Clute. And we'd throw in the Tremblay's UHF rig and a battery pack for good measure; the Marchands had one in their truck, so there'd be a way to stay in touch the whole distance.

It was a risk, but I felt it was worth it.

We gave Alain Tremblay and Lisa the task of surveying the empty cottages around the lake; I doubt Lisa would have agreed to her partner had she been at the meeting, but she didn't argue with the decision. For all her bluster, she's probably the most reliable person we've got.

Graham took charge of the supply transport, taking Matt and the skinny Marchand kid on the cart, each one of them fully dressed in riot suit, vest and helmet; we only had the three sets, but either way I doubt we'd have wanted another body taking up space on the trip. Graham assured me that if they saw any signs of gray pickups, or painted combat helmets, or pretty much anyone at or on the way to the Marchand homestead, they would drop everything and come back home.

I spent the rest of the day in the living room with Eva Marchand, telling her a little bit about our security setup and finding out as much as I could about the way things were on the west side of Cochrane.

Eva was convinced that they and the Walkers were the only families left.

"Do you really think Stems would attack you?" I asked.

"He attacked the Lamarches once. I know you haven't forgotten."

"He's changed... I think..."

"He said he'd force us to move. So an attack could happen. And between him and Detour Lake, I wasn't willing to risk my family on it. And I knew that we'd be safer here with you."

"But how did you know we'd take you in?" I asked.

"You took the Porters and even the Tremblays. They had nothing to give. Together we are all stronger."

"What about the Walkers?"

"What about them?" The mention seemed to upset her.

"I have trouble believing that they would expect you to sign on as indentures."

"Why not? We're no different than anyone else they've enslaved."

"There's Fisher Livingston... if they let that scumbag join them..."

"He didn't join them. He signed the paper."

"I doubt he'd do that."

"He was scared and alone. What else could he do?"

"Curl up and die? That would be my holiday wish."

"I see you're still blaming him."

"That won't change."

"I think you should consider forgiving Monsieur Livingston, Baptiste. We've all made terrible mistakes over the past couple of years. I certainly hope you won't hold mine against me for eternity."

"I can't hold on to anything forever," I said. "But I'm not ready to let Livingston off the hook just yet."

Eva changed the subject, asking about our plans for growing crops. I told her as much information as I felt she needed to know, nothing more, and she smiled and nodded politely. By the time I was done talking about it, I could smell fried fish in the kitchen.

Soon after that, Fiona came out to make sure that the Marchands were joining us for dinner. I guess for them it was either that or opening a couple cold cans of corn in their truck; they really didn't have much of a choice.

I went to see Justin Porter for the first time in what seems like forever. We used to be something close to friends, once. Now I know how often he's stabbed me in the back.

I ran into him on my way to his place; he was on his snowmobile, and he stopped to talk to me with the engine still running, like he was ready to make a quick getaway.

"Cut the engine," I said.

He shook his head. "I'm meeting someone. Don't have much time."

"This is important, Justin."

He turned off the machine. "Takes a big man to resign his post," he said.

"Not funny."

"Who's joking?"

"It's true what Stems said, isn't it? Those guys with the Toyotas and the big guns are from Detour Lake. The same Detour Lake that you were hoping we'd go steady with."

"That's not true," he said, so quickly that I couldn't tell if the notion had come as a surprise.

"It makes sense. No one screams 'we like to pretend we're real soldiers' like Detour Lake."

"There's no way. I know those guys. They're good people."

"The same way you're good people?"

"You really think I'd want us to partner up with them if I suspected for one second that they were behind the attacks?"

"I don't know what to think. You've been running people to Detour Lake behind my back. I know that. You know that I know that."

"I'm not doing that anymore. I haven't done a deal since Marc died."

"That doesn't make you any more trustworthy."

"Then it's all out in the open, is it, Baptiste? Good. Well, I think you're incompetent. And I want you to admit that you're beyond hope here, and that I'm a better choice for keeping us safe. That's it. No other motives... no schemes... just me wanting to keep my family alive. And your people, too... if I can."

"Fuck, Justin. I won't trust you, so you can forget about it happening. But I'll tell you right now: if I ever find out you're making deals with Detour Lake again, I will kill you."

"Leave the threats to people who can carry them out," Justin said. He turned on the engine. "I'm not scared of you."

And then he drove away.

Sara didn't come down for dinner, and as much as Fiona tried to cover it up, I noticed when she snuck a plate upstairs.

I did my best to take Sara's place in the conversation, asking questions about Eva and her family, hoping that I wouldn't accidentally trigger some tidal wave of grief, but knowing that I had to keep going with it... because that's what you're supposed to do.

I wanted to ask about one of her daughters-in-law, particularly about the bulge in her stomach, but I didn't. The Marchands seemed careful not to hint at pregnancy; I'm not sure why they'd think it would change anything for us.

I don't mind babies as long as they're not living in my house.

After dinner I excused myself, asking Graham and Lisa to organize the sleeping arrangements, and then I went upstairs to my room to find Sara. I opened the door without knocking, wondering if she'd fallen asleep with the lamp on again, but she was awake, sitting against the headboard with Ant's journal in her hands.

"Do you remember the day he came to us?" she asked.

"Last Christmas," I said, as I sat down beside her.

"He never told me what he had done. I know it must have been something pretty bad to make him leave the Girards' on Christmas Eve."

"I know what he did."

"What was it?"

"He fell in love with Natalie Girard."

"I don't really remember her. Wait... she was one of the girls you found up at Silver Queen Lake."

The way Sara described her felt strange to me, like Natalie was just a "+1" on the dead neighbours list. Natalie meant more than that to me... and she'd meant far more than that to Ant.

"She was a really nice girl," I said. "But Ant wasn't actually dating Natalie... I'm pretty sure he was dating her sister..."

"That sounds like Ant."

"It does."

"And now they're all gone. *Mon dieu*... I never thought I'd see so much death."

I put my arm around her shoulder, but she quickly pulled it off.

"Don't," she said. "I'm still mad at you."

"I know."

"You let him in... no problem. Ant showed up, shivering and a little drunk, and you and Fiona had the couch made up for him before he even had his jacket off."

"I remember... he was more than a little drunk."

"Why him? Why was Ant okay, but not me? And why was Fiona just fine? Was it that they have something special, or is it just that there's something wrong with me?"

I almost thought she was kidding, but I could see the tears welling in her eyes.

"I love you, Sara," I said. "You're the one who's special to me."

"No, Baptiste... you didn't want me. Now that I'm here, sure... you'll take me. You'll let me stay in your room... you'll let me be your fuckbuddy."

"Come on, Sara..."

"So what's the plan, buddy? Are you going to move on to Kayla Fucking Burkholder once you're bored with me?"

At first I felt bad for her.

"Sara..."

"Oh... sorry... I guess maybe you want to get in on Suzanne Tremblay first, before she gets any older. She's even older than me .. and maybe you'll make a play for Katie Walker, see if you can squeeze her in before her wedding day... but then... I know you'll circle on back to Kayla. You want her... do you think I can't see it? Every time the two of you are together... *mon dieu*... it makes me sick."

I was losing my temper. I didn't deserve to be treated like that. "You're being ridiculous —"

"And once Kayla's old news, how long until Fiona's ready to go? Will you at least wait until she's eighteen before you bend her over the kitchen counter? Can you do that for me? Wait until she grows up *at least*?"

I never hit Alanna, not once in the thirty years we'd known each other; I'd never come close. And I'd certainly never hit Cassy, either. But there are times when you lose it, when it's like you're on the outside watching, not really able to do anything to stop what you're about to do. Maybe that's what happened when I hit Marc Tremblay... I don't know.

I hit Sara, my open hand against her temple, like I was just trying to shove her away. I hit her and then I pulled back, shocked that it could happen so quickly.

"I'm... I'm sorry," I said. I climbed off the bed, pulling away from her.

She looked just as surprised as I was, staring at me while she gingerly felt her face with her hand.

"I don't know why I did that," I said. "Honestly, Sara... I don't know what just happened."

"Get away from me," she said.

"Sara..."

"You need to leave this house right now. Get out of here... or I swear to Almighty God I will get a knife and I will slit your throat."

She didn't sound angry. She sounded more self-assured than anything else.

I left the room.

I went down the hall and grabbed a pillow and a couple of heavy blankets from Lisa's closet.

Tonight I'm testing out the wood stove at a cottage halfway between us and the Tremblays, the one we've chosen for the Marchands. Luckily Lisa and Alain had already brought over enough firewood, and all I had to do was clean the stove and wipe down the dusty sofabed.

I think tomorrow morning I may be eating my breakfast out of a can.

FIONA

FIONA IS like a girl in a Norman Rockwell painting. She has those rosy cheeks, that pretty brown hair, and those next-door looks that make you feel like you have the hots for your baby sister.

I think I could see my way past the guilt on that.

Fiona stands away from the rest of us, much like Baptiste. If we were all planets, Baptiste would be Jupiter, all big and gassy, and Fiona would be Pluto. Not even really a planet, like the rest of us. Something else... something a little erratic. Sometimes she dips out so far that you barely even notice her. (I'm Uranus, naturally.)

From what Kayla told me, Fiona had only been in Cochrane for a couple of years before The Fires came. Apparently her parents were Mormons, which is odd since they only had the one kid; maybe that had made Fiona an outcast in Brampton, too, since she certainly fell into the role pretty easily when she got here. Kayla knew her from around and never liked her; to be honest, I don't think Kayla's ever given me a reason for it that makes any sense.

Fiona's just as smart and funny as anyone who isn't me, and she doesn't have any odd ticks aside from the occasional God and Jesus schtick. But she is a little too attached to Baptiste... it's pretty weird... and I've never been sure if she wants him to be a father to her or just fuck her. Either way, I'm sure she'll end up disappointed with the result.

Maybe one day when she's a little older I'll let her know that I think she's more than fuckable. Obviously I'll find a better way to say it... I'll probably feed her some bullshit about her eyes.

Church girls love compliments about their eyes. I think it's because they're too repressed to appreciate God's good word on their tight little asses.

TODAY IS TUESDAY, JANUARY 1ST.

I WOKE up yesterday morning to a visitor. She brought Irish coffee and some kind of impromptu egg and cheese breakfast sandwich.

"Thank you, Fiona," I said, giving her a smile, despite how cold and depressed I was feeling.

She sat down on the pulled-out sofabed right by my legs, which wasn't surprising since every other surface in the cottage was still filthy. "I figured you needed a friend," she said.

I pulled my legs in and sat up. "You're a good friend to me."

"I meant the whiskey, but I guess you and I can be buds, too."

"Nice. Did Sara tell you what happened?"

"Sara's not talking to anybody. Everyone's sure you must have done something pretty terrible."

I swallowed hard. "Yeah... it was pretty bad."

"She'll get over it. She loves you and she's not about to change."

"I hope so."

"Well I still think she's lucky to have you."

"I wouldn't say that."

"Well, I would. I think you're pretty awesome."

"Uh, thanks." I was getting pretty uncomfortable.

"Do you think you two will get married someday?"

"I doubt it."

"Oh." She seemed disappointed.

"I still feel like I'm already married. I don't know if that will ever change."

"I understand. I still feel like I'm a kid, even after everything that's happened."

"You are a kid, silly. That's why I'm not sharing any of this delicious coffee."

"That's fine." She reached into her jacket and pulled out a silver flask with an eagle outlined upon it. "I don't drink coffee." She took a deep swig.

I laughed. She'd come full circle.

"You're awesome, Fiona," I said. I leaned in and kissed her on the lips; only after I'd done it did I realize that I hadn't gone for her cheek.

She smiled and let out a little giggle.

"Uh, sorry," I said.

"Don't worry about it. Now eat your pre-chicken sandwich and let's head back home."

I ate my breakfast and then we walked back together. From what I could tell, Sara was still hiding upstairs.

That suited me fine; I was still hiding from her.

Pretty much the entire morning and afternoon of the 31st was spent helping the Marchands to get set up in their new home. Graham, Matt and the skinny kid (whose name I still didn't know) had several more loads of supplies and equipment to do, but the rest of us — minus Sara — were on the job, cleaning and dusting and testing out the various appliances that were there.

The Marchands' new kitchen was completely electric, so that meant that it would be mostly useless until we could set up some power. There are still transmission lines connecting all of the cottages and beyond; we've never done any kind of inspection, but I'm pretty sure the lines are intact.

But even if we can hook up the new Marchand place to ours, we'd probably end up draining our battery banks faster than we could charge them, particularly now that the days are so short. So for the time being, the Marchands will have to get used to cooking dinner on top of the wood stove, unless they decide to use our place as some kind of restaurant; I don't know what we'll do if that starts happening.

Before I'd pissed her off, so obviously before I hit her, Sara had invited the Porters and Tremblays over for New Year's Eve. She'd felt it was an important gesture given that we'd both done our best over the past few days to make them hate us. She didn't seem to care that Justin Porter was no better than the Spirit Animals in my mind. Obviously the Marchands were invited by default, so by the time everyone had arrived, almost the entire first floor of our cottage was jammed with people.

I was feeling tired, so I was tempted not to say anything or even show up, but I knew that I still had a job to do.

"I need everyone's attention," I said as I walked into place in the middle of the living room.

It didn't take long for the talking to die down; I guess everyone was sober enough to listen, for the time being.

"I need to go over a few things," I said. "It won't take long. A lot of you might get a little inebriated this evening, and that's fine... but try to remember that you can get into trouble if you're not careful."

Everyone seemed to still be listening so far, but I knew my time was short.

"If you leave this cottage for any reason," I said, "make sure you leave with someone who is sober and has a way to defend you. Do not go outside alone, no matter what. Everything seems really peaceful out here, but you need to remember that there are plenty of places for someone to hide, not to mention the coyotes, or the fact that if you pass out in the snow you'll probably freeze to death. And keep an eye out for snowmobiles... just because we haven't seen any tracks so far this year doesn't mean they won't be coming around. We can't trust anyone. If you see any person who is not a part of this team, you need to assume that they will take any opportunity to do you harm."

"That's a little paranoid," Kayla said.

"There's no such thing as being too paranoid... we've learned that lesson before. Over and over again. There's no harm in assuming the worst."

"So shoot first," Matt said with a grin. "Understood."

"You know what I mean," I said. "Just be careful. If you're outside at all, there's no reason to veer off the gravel road. Don't take any romantic walks down moonlit paths... no risks, okay?"

There was a collective murmur, and I knew that there was no point in saying any more. I'd said the important part: trust no one.

Short and sweet.

I was even more tired now, so I tried to hide out in the kitchen with Fiona, while she finished prepping the finger food, but she kept shooing me out like she was doing me a favour.

"You should be out there having fun," she said on what I think was my third incursion. "Have a drink for me."

"You know I don't like to do that. Well, yes to the drinking part... but I'd rather just stay in here with you."

"It ain't breakfast time... we don't need any eggs folded in here, boss." She picked up a tray of what looked to be spring rolls to take to the oven.

I opened the oven door for her with a rather stupid bow. "Then I can wash dishes."

"Don't you dare... that's my excuse for staying in here after the appetizers are served."

I didn't like that she was walling herself off from the others. "Why don't you want to be in there?"

She stopped working and stared at me. "Why don't you?"

"Seriously, Fiona... it's New Year's Eve. Do you know how many normal sixteen-year-olds would dream of having all the liquor they could drink?"

"I guess I'm not normal, then."

"I don't get you, Fiona. There are all these people out there who would love to know you better, but you don't seem to want to let them."

She rolled her eyes. "They don't like me, remember?"

"That's all in your head."

"Oh, really? Exactly who else around here likes me?"

I knew she was fishing, that she just wanted me to make her feel wanted. I didn't have a problem with that. "Well, obviously Sara loves you like a little sister, but that's not a surprise. And Lisa thinks you're pretty cool..."

"I call bullshit on that," Fiona said.

"I'm not going to debate this with you." I counted on my fingers. "Lisa likes you, Graham likes you..."

"Kayla hates me..."

"I think Kayla's jealous of you."

"Come on."

"I'm not kidding. You're smart, you're pretty, you're funny in a way that doesn't bring anyone down... you're like the total package, Fiona. Plus you're younger than she is."

"She's only like twenty."

I laughed. "One thing you'll learn as you get older is that there's not much to look forward to after you turn eighteen. You might pay less for car insurance, but that's about it. One day soon, guys like Matt will stop looking at Kayla and they'll only be looking at you."

"Guys like Matt? What does that mean?"

I wondered if I would regret having mentioned the village idiot. "Think about it," I said.

"Did he say something about me?"

"The next time you walk into a room, keep an eye on Matt. You'll see it."

Fiona let out a faint giggle. "Bullcrap," she said. But I knew she believed me. "Keep an eye on those spring rolls... I'll be back in a few minutes."

She walked out of the kitchen into the chaos. I kind of wanted to go then, too, but I think I would have just gotten in the way.

Sara came downstairs fifteen minutes before midnight. Most of us were a little drunk by then, and I'm pretty sure she was drunk, too; I have a feeling Kayla's flask gets loaned out anytime someone wants a private nip, no matter the customer.

I didn't go up to her; I felt like she needed to decide what to do with me. She gave and got a few hugs from family and near-strangers alike, slowly circling the room for a good ten minutes before she came to me.

"Hey," I said.

"Hi."

"I'm sorry."

"You can kiss me at midnight." There was no smile on her face.

"You're still angry."

"We're not talking about it."

I reached out for her hand. She didn't pull away. "I love you, Sara."

"You'll say anything, won't you?"

"I just want to make this better."

She didn't answer me.

People started counting down, so I joined in. Sara's lips didn't move.

"Happy New Year," I said as I kissed her on the lips. I wrapped my arms around her and held on.

"Happy New Year, Baptiste."

I hugged her for a good twenty seconds before she pulled away and moved on to everyone else. I gave Kayla a kiss on the cheek and offered Lisa a hug, and shook hands with pretty much everyone, even an in-the-bag Alain Tremblay.

Fiona came last, as though we'd both planned it that way.

She walked up to me and grinned. "Time to practice your aim," she said, in a quiet voice.

I drew her in, with an arm around her shoulder, and kissed her gently on her forehead. I lingered for a moment, my lips just off her skin, enjoying the warmth of another body, of someone who still thought I could do no wrong.

"Happy New Year, beautiful," I said.

"I was going to say the same thing to you. Thanks for everything, Baptiste."

"You know I love you, Fiona. You're like..." I thought of Cassy and how much I missed her, and before I knew it, I had begun to cry. "You're like a daughter to me."

That's what I told her, and that's all I want to feel.

Sometimes I wonder if it's true.

Despite our collective hangover, we were all back to work before ten in the morning, Sara along with us. She wasn't really talking to me yet, so I mostly kept out of her way. She was in the background, mostly, helping out but not taking charge. For all intents and purposes, Lisa was leading the setup of the Marchand cottage, and she was doing an excellent job.

Lisa was smart enough to know that Sara was still angry with me, so she sent me and Graham up to the Porters to check out their extra cookstove. Justin Porter went with us, while Rihanna continued to work at the Marchands; he and I hadn't really talked that much since he'd made it clear just what he thinks of my leadership.

The three of us walked together up the road; I didn't want to hitch up the horses just yet, since I had no idea if we were even dragging the backup stove out of the Porters' place, or how much time it would take to get it ready to move.

"Thanks again for letting us check it out," Graham said to Justin as we walked.

"We're all in this together," Justin said. "But if our other stove conks out, you know we'll be showing up at your place wearing lobster bibs."

"Will you settle for coyote?" I asked. I didn't realize until after I said that I might be throwing out some kind of challenge.

"Look, Baptiste... I know we have our problems right now."

"You could say that..."

"But you could be worse. I mean... I'm okay working with you. You know how I feel about who's in charge, but until the group decides to make a change... well, you're it. I can deal with that."

"So which Justin Porter am I talking to right now?"

"I know things get heated sometimes..."

"Heated? Is that what you call it?"

"I'm sorry, Baptiste. I want you to trust me. I want us to be a team. This won't work unless we can get along."

I couldn't figure out his angle. I couldn't see what he was plotting.

"Look, Justin," I said, "I don't know what this is about."

"I made a mistake," he said. "More than one. I know that you've made some too... we all have. But that's no reason for us to turn on each other."

"What's this about?"

He hesitated. "Rihanna fucked up."

"What?"

"Some of our supplies are missing."

"Missing? Like you miscounted?"

"Like someone's been breaking in and taking shit."

"What? How long has this been happening?"

"She told me yesterday. Says it's been happening for a while. A week or two... maybe longer. I went out and checked, and found footprints."

"And you sat on it for a day and a half?"

"Did you follow the tracks?" Graham asked. "Any snowmobiles?"

"No snowmobiles, from what I've seen. We tried following them, yeah... but there are trails all over the damned place. And the footprints are pretty much everywhere."

"Hold on," I said. "Are you telling me that there could be any number of unknown people wandering around in the woods and taking our supplies?"

"Who could it be?" Graham asked.

"Fuck, Justin," I said. "Have you even mentioned any of this to Sara?"

"I was going to bring it up at the next meeting," Justin said. "Rihanna's still checking her counts to be sure. It looks like someone may have found a way into our basement, through the old cellar door."

"But there's a heavy chain on that door, isn't there?"

"Shit happens."

"Shit happens? What the hell does that even mean?"

"I think Rihanna left it unlocked."

"Rihanna... yeah, okay... so someone could be in your house right now and you wouldn't even know it."

"It's a problem," he said. "I should've kept a closer eye on everything. But you know... delegation..."

"We don't do excuses around here. You say you want to keep us safe, but you don't even notice strange footprints in your own backyard? You have some nerve challenging me... some real fucking nerve..."

"I messed up. I already said that."

"Let's just figure out the damage," Graham said. "We can make Justin feel like crap afterwards."

I knew he was right.

Once we reached the Porters' cottage, I walked over to the wood door the led down into the cellar. The chain was completely off, curled up in the snow over a meter away.

"Goddamn it, Justin," I said. "So what's missing?"

"We don't know for sure."

"Then what do you *think* is missing?"

"Food. Apparently it's a bag of sugar here or a box of salt there... if Rihanna's right on her counts."

"Come on," Graham said, "do you really not know your own counts?"

"I don't think we're wrong. It's just been hard to believe that someone would break in and steal one or two things every few days."

"No one broke in," I said, "since you don't even know how to keep this place secure. Do you realize how much effort we've put into setting you guys up with this place? You had nothing when you got here... it doesn't really look like you appreciate what we've given you."

"What you've given us? Because we haven't contributed at all, right? We didn't bring back how many truckloads of supplies from Silver Queen Lake? I guess I should just drive that stuff over to the dump."

"Don't bother... just keep that cellar door wide open and someone else will empty your basement for you."

"So we lock it up again," Graham said. "And maybe we track down some wireless cameras or something to keep an eye on the approaches."

"Someone's trying to steal my job," I said, giving my blessing to letting the tension drop. There was no point in yelling at Justin for being an idiot; that never makes people any smarter, or at least that's what all of my time spent on Matt has taught me. "We do need to figure out who's been doing this."

"I know who's doing it," Justin said.

"And?"

"Well... who else? Obviously it's people from New Post."

"Why is that obvious, exactly?" Graham asked. "You said they came from the north... not the south."

"Look," Justin said, "I don't want to be prejudiced..."

"Just say it," I said.

"They have a hundred and fifty people down there and we have no idea how they're feeding themselves."

"That's true."

He seemed surprised that I didn't attack him. "So who else could it be?"

"There could be dozens of people hiding out around here that we don't know about," Graham said. "You just don't know for sure."

"We've got boxes of electronics from Silver Queen," Justin said. "I'm sure there's a camera in there somewhere."

"If only we had inventory lists," Graham said.

"I guess we'll have those lists soon enough," I said. "Right Justin?"

"Right," Justin said. "I'll talk to Rihanna."

"Stop blaming someone else for your fuck up. You want to lead, don't you? Then learn to be a goddamn leader."

Justin didn't respond. For once I think he knew he had no leg to stand on. If only he'd realize that he was legless most days of the week.

But I didn't need to take shots at Justin Porter. I needed to do my job.

"Let's go take a look at this stove," I said. "Lisa's not the most patient woman on the planet."

No one argued with me on that.

TODAY IS WEDNESDAY, JANUARY 2ND.

SARA'S MOVED back into Lisa's room. I guess that's to be expected.

So instead of Sara, I've taken Sara's new inventory lists to bed with me two out of the past three nights (the middle night having been taken up babysitting new year's drunks), and I haven't figured out what to do.

Some of her scenarios seem less inevitable now; New Post won't be starting fights now that we have the Marchands on our side, and I don't think Justin's about to pack up and leave with half the supplies at McCartney Lake. But that leaves two scenarios, one that's all "rainbows and unicorns" as Sara had called it, and one that was more possible and pretty bleak. She'd titled that other scenario "no crops possible".

No crops. If we didn't find the right equipment. If we didn't get more fuel. If we just couldn't figure out how to do things properly. If we did everything else right and the weather sucked.

There were too many paths that ended in no crops.

And we've wasted so much time being shot at and almost blown up...

Usually, when there's a problem, Sara and I have a way to come up with a solution. We go for a walk together, or we sit on the porch together, or we lay in bed together until the wee hours of the morning.

But Sara and I are broken.

I told her at breakfast that we needed to come up with a plan for getting the farming on track. She told me I need to handle it myself.

I'm in no position to get mad at her for that.

So I took a walk up the road, but with Graham and Lisa instead. They held hands like high school sweethearts, and I held back the urge to vomit.

I wish I knew how to fix things with Sara.

"There's equipment all over the place," Lisa said. "Aren't there farms along 652?"

"Not really," Graham said. "There's very little on this side of the river, at least north of Twin Falls. And diesel or gas tractors won't help us; we're so low on fuel we'll need electric. Even on the other side of the river, electric farm equipment isn't that easy to find."

"We could go about this another way," I said.

"We could leave?" Lisa said with a smirk.

"We could accept that we need to use diesel for now. I'm sure there must be a place around here that hasn't been tapped for fuel yet."

"It's not like we're going to know where to look," Graham said. "And even if we find the fuel, we still need a pull type combine, a cultivator..."

"So let me ask you," I said. "If we took the risk and went across the river, how long would it take us to find everything we need?"

"It could take weeks."

"Weeks?"

"Getting a tractor is easy enough, but everything else is tougher. We need homesteader equipment, not huge fuel-guzzling machines meant for ten-thousand-acre agribusinesses; they don't have much of the little stuff around here."

"We'd be better off looking for a self-sustaining homestead," Lisa said.

"Or preppers," Graham said. "I guess that's Detour Lake."

"I don't think they'd be willing to share any equipment," I said.

"They wouldn't have much. It's not like you can grow crops up there."

"So we need to find some prepper nutjobs, but not *those* prepper nutjobs..."

"Good thing Kayla isn't here," Lisa said. "She'd kick you in the berries for that. She'd tell you, bub... preppers aren't crazy, it's everyone else who was crazy for not believing in creating a self-sustaining colony of blah, blah blah..."

"That's it," I said. "I need to talk to Fiona."

I starting jogging back toward the cottage.

I remembered the dream Fiona no longer held onto, that by the time she was sixteen she'd be living off-the-grid with other artists.

I remembered that she'd told me there were places like that right near us.

Everyone had gathered in the dining room before Lisa and I had even gotten our boots off.

"They call it Helena," Fiona said, "It's south of here, I think." She pointed her finger to a blank spot on the map we'd spread out across the table. "Somewhere around here."

"There's nothing around there," Kayla said.

"I don't recognize the name," Sara said. "Are you sure it's called Helena?"

"It's named for a Finnish painter," Fiona said. "She was the first female painter or something... apparently the area was settled by Finns. But they'd all moved away, and it was a ghost town up until a few years ago."

"Ahh... I think I know it," Sara said. "Arpin... south of Norembega. One of the old farming communities that didn't last."

"That's probably it," Fiona said. "I remember reading that the land was farmed once before. I think I still have it on my tablet. I'll go get it."

She ran upstairs.

"I'll bet no one's gone down that way," Graham said.

"New Post might have," Lisa said.

"Ant and I went down that way once," I said. "Norembega was hit pretty badly by The Fires; there wasn't much worth scavenging. I'll bet the road south of there hasn't been cleared."

"If they were really off the grid," Sara said, "is it possible that someone's still out there?"

"It's possible," Lisa said. "And it's also possible that Helena is just as burnt to a crisp as Norembega."

"Let's be lucky this time," I said. "I'd like a change of pace."

Fiona came running back down the stairs, holding her tablet up to her nose. I was surprised she didn't trip halfway down.

"This is the place," she said. "They had over two dozen people living there. I used to chat with one of the guys who lived there."

"You did?" Matt asked, roused from his drooling stupor. "Who was this guy?"

"I dunno... just some artsy guy. He'd have been cute if he'd washed and cut his hair."

"Good thing they're a bunch of artists," I said. "I'd be more intimidated if it was a colony of survivalists."

"I'm sure they could be both," Lisa said.

"They'd have to be if they're still out there," Sara said.

"So Graham and I should go," I said. "We'll take the cart up there to take a look. Once we know what that road looks like at Norembega, we can figure out if we can get a truck all the way down there."

"I want to go," Fiona said.

"I don't think that's a good idea."

"But if there are people there, I might be able to help talk to them."

"We can deal with them," I said.

"But if Rasheed is there... I can convince them to help us."

I could hear Sara chuckling. "You'd better go along, Fiona," she said. "We don't want Baptiste killing all your artist friends."

"Maybe I should go, too," Matt said.

"You've got work," I said. "You promised the Porters that you'd help them with their monitoring."

"That can wait."

"No, it can't. I need someone over there I can trust." I couldn't believe that I'd just said that.

Matt's face widened with a big grin. "Okay," he said. "I'll take care of it." He looked over to Fiona and smiled.

She smiled back.

I felt a tinge of jealousy... which was ridiculous. I took a deep breath.

"Let's get moving," I said. "We'll need to get that cart switched over to being a sled. And I'd like to be on the road before lunchtime."

"Then you'd better get your ass in the kitchen," Fiona said. "We have sandwiches to make."

It didn't take us long to switch the cart wheels for runners. We were on our way just about the same time we started getting hungry for the sandwiches.

The road to Arpin was blocked just south of Norembega, by a downed tamarack. Graham, Fiona and I couldn't move it on our own, so Graham figured out a way to get the mare involved, detaching the center shaft and jimmying up a contraption that looked like a cross between a net and a plow. The whole operation took him less than half an hour, and it's times like that when I realize just how much he brings to the team.

We ran into a few more downed trees and other debris on the untravelled road, but there was nothing we couldn't shove aside or pull around, and by late afternoon we reached a painted wood gate, a rather strange collection of red, gold, and white vertical planks with "Helena" slapped across it in blue.

The gate was closed but unlocked, and the trail behind it was just as untravelled as the road from Norembega. It looked like no one had come or gone since the snow had first fallen, back before Christmas.

"Looks pretty empty," I said to Fiona. "You may be wasting your time out here."

"I'm still glad I'm getting a chance to see it," she said. "Even if it's long forgotten."

We travelled for another few minutes up the driveway before we arrived at the homestead, a collection of rough-hewn log buildings next to a small array of solar panels. The snow had drifted across the yard with the wind, with no sign of anyone having shovelled. Even the panels had snow on them.

Graham was the first to notice the smoke coming from the chimney.

"Someone's in that building," he said, pointing to the largest cabin.

No one had to make a suggestion; the three of us put on our vests and helmets without a moment's pause. It reminded me of old times, when it was just the three of us, travelling from lake to lake looking for the right place to live.

"They must know we're here by now," I said quietly.

"Then I'll say hello," Fiona said.

"Just wait..."

Fiona hopped off of the cart, landing in the deep snow. She pulled off her helmet. "Hello there!" she called out. "We're looking for Rasheed."

She walked up to the front porch.

"Fiona," I said. "Just wait, okay?"

She went up the stairs and opened the screen door. "Hello? Rasheed?"

"Who are you?" a voice called out from inside the cabin.

"Oh, hello," Fiona said. "My name is Fiona Rees... from Cochrane."

"Fiona Rees?"

"Yup."

The door swung open. A young and thin Persian-looking man, probably mid twenties, with greasy and disheveled hair, stepped out and smiled.

"I'm Rasheed," he said. "It's so great to meet you, Fiona." He reached out and gave her a hug. "You're dressed like a cop. You're too young to be a cop." He looked over to us, and his smile disappeared.

"Are you the only one here?" Fiona asked.

"Who are those guys?"

"They're my friends, Rasheed."

I pulled off my helmet and tried out my best non-threatening smile. Graham did the same, to more success.

"We didn't think anyone still lived here," Fiona said.

"No one does," Rasheed said. "There's just the six of us sitting around and waiting to starve to death."

"That doesn't sound very optimistic."

He smiled. "Things were getting pretty dark. Until you showed up, at least."

I wasn't looking forward to more refugees. I just wanted equipment.

I left my shotgun on the cart and hopped down. I still had my belt and holster, and the vest, of course; I wasn't about to walk up to a stranger without a way to defend myself.

"Good to meet you, Rasheed," I said. "I'm Robert Jeanbaptiste. Call me Baptiste."

"You're not here to hurt us, are you, Mr. Baptiste?"

"We're the good guys... we don't hurt people."

Rasheed flashed me a nervous smile. "I guess we won't know if you're telling the truth until it's far too late for us to do anything about it."

"You're right."

"Be nice, Baptiste," Fiona said. "Rasheed is a friend of mine."

"Why are you here?" Rasheed asked.

"We're looking for farm equipment," I said. "We figured that you guys might have just what we need."

"We might. So you're just here to take our stuff?"

"You should come back with us," Fiona said.

Rasheed frowned. "I can't leave my friends."

"Your friends aren't bolted to the floor, are they? They can come, too."

"I don't think you understand. Maybe you should all come inside."

I nodded to Graham, and he climbed down to join us, bringing the shotgun with him.

"I'd rather you left all of your guns out here on the porch," Rasheed said.

"That's not possible," I said.

He just nodded, and opened the door for us.

We all went aside.

The living room looked more like a storeroom, with boxes and bags of food in piles along the walls, but on top of every surface was one or more scented candles, all lit and casting their signature stench into the muddle. The combined result was overpowering, but underneath it all I felt like I could smell rot.

In the center of the room were two single mattresses next to a wood stove. A young ginger-haired woman was lying on one, apparently asleep, with a sheet over all of her body, aside from her freckled face. She seemed thin and pale, much thinner than Rasheed, who himself was close to underweight.

"She doesn't look well," Fiona said. "I don't understand... you still have some food, don't you?"

"She hasn't eaten in a while," Rasheed said. "I think she's sad."

"Are you going to wake her up?"

"Just let her sleep... she's tired."

"Where's everyone else?" I asked. It didn't feel right.

"In the kitchen," Rasheed said.

I glanced over to Graham; he seemed to understand that something was off.

"You two wait here," I said.

Fiona looked like she was about to question me, but then she seemed to get the message.

Rasheed walked towards the kitchen door and I followed a few steps behind. He unlatched the door and pushed it open; I could feel the cool air pushing in towards us.

He'd closed off the kitchen; there was no heat in there.

But there was a smell that I recognized.

The smell of a corpse, that terrible odour of death that can't be covered up no matter how many scented candles you try to burn.

I followed him inside.

There was a fridge, a stove, and a large chest freezer. I didn't think any of them were running. I didn't think there was any electricity.

Just the cold. And the smell.

"Where are your friends, Rasheed?" I asked.

"In the freezer," he said.

"Did you kill them?"

"There wasn't enough food."

"Open the freezer for me, would you?"

He flipped up the lid and the rest of the smell came; it was far worse than the bodies in Cochrane, where the sunlight had done its job. In the freezer was a soup of turgid corpses, so rotten and putrefied that I couldn't be sure how many there were.

"The power went out last summer," he said. "I wasn't able to get it working again."

"Close the goddamned lid," I said.

He closed the lid and gave me another nervous smile.

"I don't know what to do, Rasheed," I said.

"Just leave me be, Mr. Baptiste. Take what you want and go."

I heard Fiona cry out from the next room. "Oh my god!" she screamed.

I ran out to the living room to see Fiona stooped down over the sleeping girl. She'd pulled off the sheet; the naked girl underneath had her wrists pinned to her side and her ankles bound, all with layer upon layer of fishing line.

"I think she's dead," Fiona said.

"She's sleeping," Rasheed said.

I dropped down beside Fiona. "She's still breathing," I said.

Graham pulled out his pocketknife and slowly began cutting the fishing line.

I stood back up and walked over to Rasheed.

"Take what you want and go," he said. His demeanor hadn't changed.

"Do you know what you did here?" I asked.

He nodded. "There wasn't enough food."

I punched him in the mouth. He fell to his knees.

"Baptiste, please," Fiona said. "He's obviously not well."

"We can't leave him here," I said. "He's dangerous."

"We're not taking him with us," Graham said as he kept cutting.

I knew what I had to do. "I'm sorry, Fiona."

"Please," she said.

I wanted to try to convince her, but we didn't have time. The starving girl needed help.

"We can't just stuff her full of food," Graham said. "We need to renourish her carefully. She needs milk, I think... Lisa will know."

I grabbed Rasheed by the neck and dragged him towards the front door.

"No," Fiona said. "Please don't..."

I pulled him onto the porch and down the steps. "Stay here, Fiona," I said.

She didn't follow me.

I dragged Rasheed to the side of the cabin, to where I was sure Fiona couldn't see. I pushed him down on his knees and pulled out my gun.

I fired a shot and he fell, and I fired again to make sure he was dead.

I left his body where it lay, and ran back in to help Graham wrap up the girl and carry her to the cart. Fiona held open the door and helped us lift the girl into place, and then she rode beside the girl all the way home, doing her best to give comfort.

I'm sure all she wanted to do on the trip back was cry, but she didn't. I'm proud of her for that.

I called Lisa with the handheld, to let her know what had happened, and by the time we'd arrived she was waiting at the door with Sara and Kayla in tow.

We laid the girl on the couch in the living room.

"Kayla," Lisa said, "pour some goat's milk into a cup, and warm it up by sticking it in a bowl of hot water. We want it close to room temperature. Sara, see if you can find some clothes for her." She turned to Graham and I. "You guys get back to work. We'll take it from here."

"What should I do?" Fiona asked.

"Just sit here with her," Lisa said. "You're her oldest friend right now."

I followed Graham back to the front door. "I don't understand," I said.

"You don't know Lisa as well as you think," Graham said.

"What does that mean?"

"She was a nurse up in Moose Factory."

"She's never mentioned that. And from the quality of the work she's done on me..."

"I know. And you shouldn't bring it up with her."

I nodded. "So we head back to Arpin?"

"I guess so. Rasheed did say they might have what we were looking for."

"They'd better. Or else we waded into a big pile of shit for nothing."

"Not for nothing, Baptiste. We may have saved that girl's life."

He was right.

I'd had to kill a young man to do it. But for whatever reason it didn't bother me as much as I thought it should.

The trip back was worth it.

We found exactly what we wanted at Arpin. They'd been trying to do what we hope to do, growing wheat and oilseed, and doing every bit of it with renewables.

We towed the tractor we'd found back to our place, to charge it with the battery bank. Once that's done it'll take at least another day to tow the rest of the equipment back with us, and then we'll want to take a look at all of the other supplies they have.

Rasheed may have bought us another few months of food by losing his mind and killing his friends.

I'm no Sara, but by cuddling up with her inventory doc, I can tell that even after adding the Marchands and that starving young girl, we should be able to last long enough to harvest our first crop.

At least something's going right around here.

8

TODAY IS THURSDAY, JANUARY 3RD.

FIONA HAS been with the red-haired girl since we got back. Last night, they moved the girl up to Fiona's bedroom, and Fiona slept on the floor, on an air mattress we'd had from happier times, when Marc Tremblay would show up drunk, or when Ant would kick Matt out of their shared room for his "Ant-on-Ant" time.

The girl hasn't spoken. We don't know her name.

She has smiled at Fiona a few times, as if to thank her, and each time I've seen it happen, Fiona's face brightens and she looks like she just won the lottery.

And I think it makes her a little less angry with me for killing Rasheed.

I tried to talk to Sara again today, about us, or about anything, really, and she shut me down right away.

I just needed her to be my best friend again. Just for a few minutes.

That wasn't going to happen.

So I checked my pockets to see how many tablets I had left. I'd hide in my room after dinner, and I'd find a way to cope.

But I didn't have the little plastic baggie.

I realized that I hadn't had it since before Christmas. Since Kayla had caught me.

I found her outside checking the water in the chicken coop.

"I need you to not lie to me, Kayla," I said.

"Okay... you're old and bald."

"Did you take my pills?"

"Your heart pills?"

"Come on... you know which pills."

She gave me a little shove on my shoulders. "Took you awhile. You obviously weren't using them very often."

"Why would you take them from me? You could have asked for

one."

"You have quite a few, don't you..."

"Why did you take them, Kayla?"

"You never did anything like that when you were in school, Baptiste? Taken the pretty girl's scarf so you'd have a reason for her to come and find you?"

"I'm not that pretty."

She chuckled. "I know you're not. Old and bald, remember?" She grabbed my left hand. "But I like you, Baptiste. You know that."

"This isn't a joke?"

"No joke."

"Well... okay then... but I'm still pissed at you for stealing my drugs."

"I'll give them back," she said. She stuck her right hand in her pocket.

"You don't need to do that. I have another bag."

"That's good. 'Cause I think I may have lost them."

"Please tell me you're joking."

"Still... no joke..."

"Fuck, Kayla... we can't just have that stuff lying around."

"Yeah... sorry... anything I can do to make it up to you?"

"Help me find the goddamn pills."

She pouted a little, as though she'd thought that would be the end of it. Then she gathered up a few eggs from the nesting boxes, and we went inside to search her room.

It felt a little weird, since it's Fiona's room, too. The best way to admire teenage girls is to do it from afar. If you spend too much time in their bedroom you'll realize just how ridiculous they are.

I searched Kayla's side, while she checked under Fiona's bed, and behind Fiona's desk.

"Should I search her drawers?" she asked.

"I don't see why," I said. "She'd tell someone if she found some pills."

"You don't know teenagers."

"I had a teenager."

"Oh, right..."

"They're not here. So you dropped them somewhere else in the house, or somewhere outside..."

"They could be anywhere."

"Shit."

I heard a knock on the door.

The door was already open, and I saw Matt peering inside with his stupid Matt smirk. "What are you guys doing?" he asked.

"Something private," I said.

"Sounds hot..."

"Shut up, Matt," Kayla said.

"Kinda looks like you're looking for something," he said.

"Don't you have work to do?" I asked.

"I'm done my work... I'm ready and willing to help you find those little pills with the maple leafs on them."

I had to groan. "Great... just great."

"They're your pills, Baptiste? You're a tabber?"

"What the fuck is a tabber?"

"Oh... sorry... I'll translate that into old man... a 'drug addict'."

"I'm going to kick your ass, Matt."

"No," Kayla said, "I'm going to handle this one." She walked over to the door. "Give me the pills, Matt."

"What'll you give me for them?"

She shoved him against the wall. "Give me the pills."

"Easy, Kayla... calm down already."

"Just give me the pills."

"I don't have them."

"You swallowed 'em without even knowing what they are?"

"As if I don't know... you think I've never seen Bronson and Zach's maple leaf soda before?"

"Well that was all I had," I said. "And you just used them. You piece of shit."

Matt laughed. "Nice try, Baptiste. I know you've got more of those hidden somewhere. You found their lab and some huge stash."

"You really are an idiot."

"Sometimes... but not this time. I know what I'm talking about. The Walker boys used to make unregulated E with maple leafs on them... they had a lab somewhere outside town... Bronson Walker heads off to Montreal for some kind of business and never makes it home... and meanwhile, no one seems to have found the lab..."

"But Zach Walker was still here," Kayla said. "What kept him from coming and cleaning out this giant stash?"

"Maybe Zach didn't know where the lab was... or maybe he was going to go but couldn't figure out a way to get past our gates..."

"Maybe you've swallowed too many pills," I said.

"Whatever Baptiste... I know what I know..."

"Not all that much," Kayla said.

"Whatever," Matt said again.

He gave another smirk and left down the hallway.

Kayla came back in and sat down on her bed. "Is this as big a mess as I think it is?"

"I'm not sure," I said. "The problem is that Matt's ass is directly attached to Justin's prick, so..."

"Come on, Baptiste... that homophobe shit again..."

"I'm old and out of touch, Kayla. You should have heard the things my grandma would say about black people..."

"*Your* grandma?"

"Yes... my Scottish grandma... she taught me all about Drambuie, black pudding and how to not trust the darkies. I was a confused teenager..."

Kayla grinned. "You always know how to make me feel better." She tapped on the bed beside her. "Come sit."

"I don't think that's a good idea," I said.

"Just close the door first... then come sit..."

"I don't think so."

"What is it? I don't understand."

"What, about Sara?" I said.

"I'm not interested in a threesome. Not today, anyway..."

"I'm serious. We're still together."

"You could have fooled me."

"Come on."

"Sorry," she said. "Just sit down and talk to me..."

"Maybe later, okay?"

"Yeah... sure..."

"No... really, Kayla. Later."

She nodded and stood up. "Later, Baptiste. And when you pull your next batch out of that secret drug stash of yours... save some for us to try out together."

She stuck her left hand on my scalp and squeezed.

Then she walked out of the room, glancing back once to make sure I knew what she wanted.

Kayla Fucking Burkholder. She wanted *me* for some ungodly

reason.

And Kayla isn't the type of girl who gives up.

I knew Matt would be a problem, that it was only a matter of time before he told Justin about his suspicions. I couldn't even guess what would happen when Justin found out about a hidden drug lab, but I had a feeling whatever it was wouldn't bring us all closer together.

He'd either use it to score points, telling anyone who'd listen about Baptiste, the unstable drug addict, or, more likely, he'd start searching, and not give up until he'd found the underground school bus and the treasure inside.

And then, knowing him, if he had drugs he'd sell them, especially the meth. He'd send it to Detour Lake, to The Souls in Timmins, to anywhere that had something to trade, and in the process he'd probably get us thrown right into the middle of a drug war. Assuming that one of his customers didn't simply decide to drop in and take his supply, and leave two dozen corpses floating in McCartney Lake.

The more I thought about it, the more plausible it seemed that Justin would find a way to get us all killed.

I had to make sure he didn't find the drugs.

And I'd need help.

Lisa and Graham still hadn't returned from their trip to Helena, to tow back the combine harvester, and I was tempted to just tell Sara and see if she'd help me for the greater good, but I heard her arguing with Fiona of all people, so I knew she wasn't in a charitable mood.

I thought of telling Kayla the whole story, what little she hadn't already put together, but I wasn't as confident as I needed to be that she wouldn't pass the information on to Matt. Truth is, I don't know her as well as Sara does, and there must be something to how much Sara hates her, even if I can't see it.

There must be something. Otherwise... if Kayla's as good as she seems lately... well, things won't end well with Sara and I.

So I waited, finding menial tasks to do, to keep myself busy, and to try and look less like a man trying to keep a secret.

Lisa and Graham didn't return until the sun had already set, and Fiona was already trying her hand at black bean enchiladas. She's never given much thought to the inevitable aftermath of a fifty year old man and too much goat cheese.

I wanted to pull Lisa and Graham over to the side, and talk to them, but one thing I've learned is that there's really no way to do that when everyone's downstairs waiting to eat.

So I waited, and we all waited, and then we ate, and as I stuffed my face full of black beans, goat cheese, and window-box cilantro, I thought about just how much colder it was getting outside, as evening headed into night.

I got my chance at Lisa when she quietly excused herself from the table, and headed toward the stairs. I made up a lame excuse about needing to check something on my tablet I'd left upstairs, and I followed her up.

"You after something?" she asked as we reached the top.

"I need your help," I said quietly. I nodded toward her room.

She laughed. "I don't help with that kind of thing."

She led me to her bedroom, but stood just inside the door.

"What's today's drama?" she asked.

"I have a drug problem."

"I know. Just stop taking those heart pills and life will improve for the rest of us."

"I found a school bus buried up Murphy Road. Some kind of lab, filled with MDMA and meth. Kayla told me it belonged to Dave Walker's boys."

"You told Kayla where to find a crapload of narcotics?"

"She doesn't know I found the lab. But she did find some of the ecstasy."

"So you brought it back here?"

"I took a bag of each... just to have it... in case of... uh..."

"In case of you're an idiot?"

I nodded. "And Kayla saw the ecstasy."

"And so you need me to kill her and dump her body in a snow-bank? I can do that..."

"We need to bring the rest of the drugs back here and hide them."

"Because you're an even bigger idiot than I could have imagined?"

"Because Matt found the ecstasy Kayla took. And somehow he's figured out where I got it."

"So Kayla told him you gave her drugs? Your reputation's taking a godawful shit-kicking."

"I know..."

"And if Justin Porter finds out about this..."

"Can you help me, Lisa?"

She tilted her head, thinking it over.

"I'll owe you one," I said.

"You owe me so much..." She smiled. "Are you wanting to do this right now?"

"Yeah."

"Does Sara know?"

"We're not really talking..."

"I've noticed. So how do you propose we move however many bags of drugs without anyone noticing?"

"I have no idea."

She shook her head. "Well obviously we'll use Helena as an excuse..."

"We've got more to bring back from there?"

"Supplies. Bags of flour, plastic tubs filled with sugar and coffee..."

"So we take a load from Helena, with some room to spare, and we mix in some extras from the magic school bus."

"We pile them in the basement," she said, "and while we're at it, we figure out a special storage area for your crap."

"Under the subfloor. There's a good half a meter under the plywood."

"Sounds pretty obvious to me."

"I'm open to ideas."

She shook her head at me. "You have a real talent for getting us to the worst case scenario, Baptiste."

"You think I should have just left it alone."

"Yeah... now you've stolen someone else's drug stash and brought it home with you. What part of that plan makes sense?"

"The previous owners are dead." And I'd needed the MDMA. But I didn't tell her that.

"Dead, eh? You sure about that?"

"Fifty percent sure..."

"I think the only question is whether or not we'll all live long enough to see this bite you in the ass."

At least I didn't need to guess how she felt about it.

By the time Lisa had pulled Graham aside and told him the story, it was almost seven at night, and we figured that it wouldn't make much sense to be out hauling supplies in the middle of the night. We'd have to wait until morning.

Of course, there's our weekly meeting in the morning... always at just the wrong time.

But I'd figure something out.

In the meantime, I could hear laughing from upstairs, in Fiona and Kayla's room. Not just the two of them, but another laugh that I hadn't heard before.

I went upstairs to see.

They were in the middle of a movie night, having brought the big screen upstairs and planted it on Fiona's desk. Fiona was sitting on the bed beside the red-haired girl, who was sitting up for a change.

Not only had no one invited me, but they'd decided to watch one of my old favourites.

Or maybe they'd picked it because they knew it would lure me in.

"*Anchorman?*" I said. "About time."

Fiona shushed me as Ron Burgundy explained the German roots of San *Diago*.

I sat down on Kayla's bed beside her.

She gave me a quick squeeze on the thigh and a warm smile.

I looked over to the red-haired girl and gave her a smile of my own.

She saw me and looked back at the screen. She didn't seem to want to acknowledge me.

"I've never heard of that expression either," Fiona said as she watched the movie. "When in Rome?"

I didn't know how to answer that.

"Yazz flute?" she asked a moment later. "What's that? I don't really get this movie."

"It's an acquired taste," I said. "Maybe you had to be there."

"I can't imagine you in one of those suits. Did you really dress like that?"

I laughed. "I'm not that old, Fiona. This is set in the 1970s. How old do you think I am?"

"Old enough to be born in the last millennium," Kayla said. "That's how old."

"Fuck," I said. "I *am* old."

I noticed that the red-haired girl was glaring at me.

I decided to shut up for a while.

And I listened to them laugh, often at the wrong parts, like they found the idea of the movie trying to be funny a lot funnier than the actual jokes.

But it was still nice to hear Kayla and Fiona laugh.

The other laugh didn't come back. The red-haired girl had withdrawn; she was still watching, but every few minutes she'd take a break from the movie long enough to give me an angry look.

She didn't want me there.

But Kayla did.

She was making sure her body was pressed against mine, nuzzling her head against my shoulder.

Every so often I'd pull away a little, so that Fiona didn't get the wrong impression.

Or maybe so Fiona wouldn't figure out exactly what I was starting to feel.

Once the movie ended, the red-haired girl laid back down in Fiona's bed.

Fiona seemed surprised by that, and stood up. "Aren't we going to watch number two?" she asked.

"I'm tired," the girl said.

"You can't be tired, Gwyneth," Kayla said. "Not when there's more Ron Burgundy on the way."

"Gwyneth..." I said. "So that's your name..."

"I'm tired," the girl said again.

"Maybe a drink?" Kayla asked.

"We can watch it tomorrow night," Fiona said. "It's okay."

"I can make my famous nachos," I said.

"I'm not interested," the girl said.

"You don't like nachos?"

"I'm tired... can everyone just let me get some sleep?"

"What's going on, Gwyneth?" Fiona asked. "You were fine a few minutes ago."

"No, I wasn't fine," she said. "I'm not fine. Can you get him out of here please?"

"I'm sorry," I said. "I'm not sure what I said..."

"Just get out of here!" she screamed.

"Calm down," Kayla said. "Don't yell at him."

I got up off the bed and started walking out of the room.

"You don't have to go," Kayla said.

"I think you should," Fiona said.

I left the room.

Kayla followed after me. All the way into my bedroom.

She closed the door behind us.

"I'm sorry, Baptiste," she said. "I don't know what that was about."

"She doesn't like me," I said. "That's okay. She isn't the first person to take an instant dislike to someone."

"It's not okay." She hung her arm over my shoulder. "I'll talk to her."

"Don't... she's been through a lot, Kayla. More than I think either of us could ever understand. If hating on me helps her... well, that's fine."

She nodded. "It's too bad, though, eh?"

"What do you mean?"

"She's pretty cute... you know, in spite of the whole vastly under-weight thing."

"I wouldn't know..."

"Come on... I'll bet you were delighted to add another girl to the mix. One more flavour for your collection." She wrapped her other arm around me and started pulling down on my neck. She gave me a quick kiss on the lips. "Don't try and tell me you're not interested in trying out a few new tastes."

I took a step back. "You can't do that, Kayla."

"What?"

"You can't just kiss me. You can't keep touching me. You can't do that."

"Why not? You seem to enjoy it."

"I'm still with Sara. That hasn't changed. And I'm pretty fucking old, remember?"

"I don't care... about any of that."

"What about Matt? Can't you molest him or something?"

"I don't want Matt," she said. "I want you."

"I can't."

"We're here, Baptiste. Just do what you want."

"I'm not sure what you're expecting."

She kissed me. "Like that."

"Oh."

"Well?"

I gave her a kiss.

Then another.

I wrapped my arms around her and lowered her onto the bed.

I grabbed her shirt and pulled it up over her head. I threw it on the floor.

I kissed her again.

She unclasped her strapless white bra.

I yanked it off of her.

I kissed her left breast and gently bit down on her nipple.

I'd thought about doing that since the day I'd watched her dance at Fleshy's.

I dragged my lips down her stomach, kissing as I went.

I undid the button on her pants. I pulled down the zipper.

There was a knock on the door.

"Baptiste?" Fiona said. "Can I come in?"

"Shoot," Kayla said in a whisper. "Tell her to go away."

"I'm in the middle of something," I said. "I'll be out in a little bit."

"Are you okay?" she asked.

"I'm fine." I said it a little too harshly.

The door opened.

And Fiona saw us.

"Oh, no," she said. "Oh, no..."

"Get out, Fiona," Kayla said, her breasts still exposed.

"Oh, no..."

"I'm sorry, Fiona," I said as I climbed off the bed

"Why the hell are you apologizing?" Kayla asked. "She's the one who barged in."

Fiona was still standing in the doorway, her lips mouthing the same two words over and over again.

"You can go now, Fiona," Kayla said.

Fiona didn't move.

"*Gawd*," Kayla said. She threw her shirt on and stormed out, leaving the bra on my bedroom floor.

"Fiona," I said.

She didn't answer.

"Fiona."

"How could you do this?" she asked.

"I don't know..."

"Do you even care about Sara at all? Do you even care about me?"

"What does this have to do with you?"

"I *hate* her. And Sara hates her. But you just couldn't stop yourself. I can't believe this."

"I didn't make a promise to anyone. Sara's not interested in me anymore. She won't even talk to me."

"For how many days? You couldn't even wait a week..."

"And you, Fiona... what am I supposed to do with this? You think you have any right to place some kind of veto on who I'm allowed to be with? Even if you were my daughter you wouldn't have that right."

"You're disgusting."

"It's none of your business."

"Fine." She walked out of the room, leaving the door open.

I closed the door and laid down on the bed.

I leaned over and picked Kayla's bra up off the floor. I held it in both hands for a minute.

I knew Kayla would let me try again if I wanted.

She wanted me.

A beautiful young woman, barely in her twenties... she wanted some old guy with a bald head and a dying heart.

When you get older, you realize how much life has gone by, how you won't get it back again.

How can I turn her down?

TODAY IS FRIDAY, JANUARY 4TH.

I GOT up to pee in the middle of the night. It happens more and more these days, but I'm just relieved that I still wake up before I let it rip. I won't need to start scavenging for adult diapers just yet.

I noticed a light from downstairs, as I walked toward the bathroom. It wasn't from an overhead fixture or a lamp; it was more like a glare from a tablet.

I took my piss and washed my hands, and then I found my way downstairs.

You're never too old to be nosy.

I expected it to be Fiona, actually, like she'd been struck with some kind of rage-induced insomnia, and I almost changed my mind and headed back to bed.

But it wasn't Fiona. In the living room, on the couch with no light but the shine of a small tablet screen, was Gwyneth.

I walked over to the couch and waited, but she didn't seem to notice me. Then I realized that she had earclips on.

I waited a little longer.

She saw me and gasped.

"Sorry," I said. "I didn't mean to scare you."

"Please go," she said. She sounded more frightened than angry.

"I don't understand this," I said. "But if you need to be mad at someone, I'm okay with it being me."

She was shaking.

"I'm not going to hurt you," I said.

"I... I don't believe you. Please go..."

"This is silly."

"I'll scream..."

"You know that Fiona is my friend, right? That we've known each other for almost two years?"

Gwyneth started shrieking.

Shrieking.

She was calling out for help, calling out for Fiona, and making more noise than I'd heard since Cassy was teething.

I didn't know what to do.

If I ran, I'd look... guilty?

Fiona and Sara came running down the stairs, one after the other.

Fiona sat down beside Gwyneth and gave her a hug.

Sara marched right up to me.

"What the hell are you doing, Baptiste?" she asked.

"I scared her," I said.

"Why are you down here? Why are you bothering her?"

"I was just checking on her."

"Who told you to do that?" Fiona asked.

"Just get him away from me," Gwyneth said. "Please..."

"Fuck this," I said.

I went back to my room, passing Graham and Lisa on my way. I just threw up my hands as I went by.

I laid back down in bed, but I couldn't sleep.

I was too busy wondering how many enemies I'd racked up this week.

Graham, Lisa and I skipped the meeting this morning, the first one with the Marchands, partly because we wanted to get the special "supply run" completed, but also because when I asked Sara if she'd be upset if we missed, she told me she'd prefer that I found somewhere else to be for a while.

I don't think Fiona's told her what happened with Kayla.

I think she just hates me for a few other good reasons.

I felt uneasy leaving the cottage in the hands of Matt and Kayla and one of the Mossbergs, but I dealt with the worry by telling Fiona to go with Sara; they'd be with Justin, which as of today means they *should* be safe.

We took the cart down toward Helena, our first stop, and on the way I couldn't help but ask them about Gwyneth.

"Have you guys talked to her at all?" I asked.

"I have," Lisa said. "She seems nice... a little shy."

"She wouldn't talk to me," Graham said. "I came into the room once with Lisa, and she went mute until I left."

"Did she ask you to leave?" I asked.

"Why? Do I smell that bad?"

"She's scared of me. She thought I was going to hurt her."

"I think she's terrified of both of you," Lisa said.

"Terrified?" Graham said. "That seems a little unwarranted."

"That's why she's been hiding from you, eating her meals upstairs. She doesn't have to stay up there all day if she's feeling strong enough to walk. And I think she feels strong enough... she was down on the couch last night."

"I remember..." I said.

"What did you say to her?" Graham asked

"Nothing much."

"Don't worry," Lisa said, "there's probably nothing you could have done to make her comfortable around you. She's traumatized."

"So what does that mean? How long is she going to avoid us?"

"I don't know. I'm not a psychiatrist. We just need to give her some time. She was held captive for months, maybe longer. I can't imagine what that would do to a person."

"Has she talked about it?"

"Not to me. Maybe to Fiona. She's the one Gwyneth trusts."

"Fiona's pretty awesome."

I wanted to tell Fiona I was sorry. I should have told her I was sorry.

"So tell me something, Baptiste," Graham said.

"Yeah?"

"Why do we want to keep these drugs? Why don't we just dump them?"

"They might come in handy," I said. "For barter... or in case someone's ever in need."

"In need of narcotics?" Lisa said. "Good luck."

"MDMA is legal when prescribed. Some people need it to function."

"Like who?" Graham asked.

"Like you, Baptiste?" Lisa said.

"You never know when we might need them," I said. "Maybe Gwyneth could use a little bit of medicating."

"Sure," Graham said. "I'll hold her down while you force it down her throat. That should fix her fear of men."

"That's not funny," Lisa said. "This isn't a joke."

"It's a little funny," I said.

"No. It's not funny at all, asshole. You guys have no idea what it's like. Goddamn male privilege."

"Easy, Lisa," Graham said.

"Fuck you, Graham. You have no clue. You don't live in a world where every second person thinks of you as an object to be used and abused, where you're expected to just accept that men will treat you like garbage day in and day out."

"That's a little harsh," I said. "Last time I checked people try to kill Graham and me all the freaking time."

"Oh, they want to kill us, too. After they beat us up a little, and rape the shit out of us, and make sure we're broken. Then they kill us. Believe me, that's worse."

"You're not exactly a damsel in distress, Lisa. You're the toughest woman I've ever met."

"Case in point, jackass. I'm a tough 'woman' to you... not a tough person. We're all women first to you. Women... as in pretty little pussies for you to take whenever you want."

"What the hell? I don't deserve this shit from you."

"No, you're right. You deserve this shit from Sara and you deserve this shit from Kayla, since you're playing them both against each other. And you deserve it from Fiona, for boxing her into that sick little daddy-daughter fantasy of yours. But none of them have the balls to give it to you."

"So you're giving it to me?"

"I'm doing you a favour, Baptiste."

"By ripping me a new one?"

"I'm helping you hide your drugs. So as payment you need to listen to me yell at you. I think that's fair."

She started to laugh.

Graham started laughing, too.

And for some reason I decided to join them.

We packed up supplies from Helena.

I went around the back to where I'd shot Rasheed; his body was lying in the snow like it had just happened.

I didn't regret it.

We had to go all the way around the string of lakes, skirting around New Post, and back past Nelson Road, up to 652, then through the gate to Murphy Road.

Nothing had changed in the buried school bus, the LED lights still running and no sign of any new visitors. We took the bags of meth and ecstasy and mixed them in with the tubs of supplies from Helena.

When we reached McCartney Lake, Fiona was walking back to the cottage from the barn. She wasn't wearing a jacket.

"Little cold out for that," Lisa said.

"Gwyneth is... she's missing," Fiona said.

"Missing?"

"It looks like she took some of Kayla's and my clothes and left."

"But where would she go?" I asked.

"I was hoping she was headed back to Helena. But then you guys would have run into her, right?"

That was if we weren't sneaking around picking up drugs.

"Not if she tried going through New Post," I said.

"New Post hasn't seen her."

"You went down there?"

"No," she said, "I messaged them."

"But we disabled their access."

"Matt turned it on for me."

"Did he turn it back off afterwards?"

"Does it matter right now?"

"There's no guarantee she stuck to the roads," Lisa said. "If she's trying to run away, she may have kept out of sight."

Fiona climbed up and started lifting a bag of flour.

"What are you doing?" I asked.

"What does it look like?," she said. "I'm getting this cart unloaded. We need to get out there and find her."

"You need to get your coat on," I said. "And a hat and some mitts. We'll unload the cart while you get ready."

Fiona went inside.

"Do you really think that girl just started walking back to Helena?" Graham asked. "That would take like four of five hours, at least."

"At least," Lisa said. "But she's obviously not thinking straight."

"She might be dead already," I said.

Fiona and I took the cart back toward Helena, while Lisa and Graham took the snowmobiles up to the Abitibi. Gwyneth had told Fiona she grew up in Timmins, so that meant she should know the area well enough to pick one way or the other. I doubted she was going to try and hoof it over a hundred klicks to Quebec.

We didn't see any obvious footprints in the snow, but that didn't mean much; we may have wiped them away with the horses and the cart, or Gwyneth may have walked in the woods and out of sight.

We wouldn't know until we found her.

"This is my fault," Fiona said. "I shouldn't have gone to the meeting."

"So Matt and Kayla didn't notice her leaving?"

"Matt and Kayla probably don't care either way."

"They both care," I said. "Kayla because she likes you a lot more than she lets on, and Matt because... well, same story."

"Whatever."

"We'll find her, Fiona."

I just hoped we'd find her alive.

We turned onto Birchill Road to avoid the gate at New Post, like she may have done, and by then we still hadn't found any sign of Gwyneth.

I had Fiona call on the handheld to see if Lisa and Graham had found anything.

Nothing.

"Do you think there are still coyotes out here?" Fiona asked me.

"Maybe. You remember what we read about them. They've got quite a range... they could be anywhere."

"They could be following her."

"I doubt it."

Since Gwyneth was maybe a hundred pounds on the outside, anything more than one coyote wouldn't have to stalk her long before deciding to make the kill. If they'd tracked her, she was already dead.

"We'll find her," I said.

That was all I could think to say.

We reached the green mailboxes that mark about halfway down Birchill Road. There was a little waiting-for-the-school-bus shack that looked like an outhouse with an aluminum door and windows.

I saw footprints.

I stopped the cart.

"I'll check," Fiona said.

I nodded.

She climbed down and walked toward the shack.

The door opened and Gwyneth stepped out.

"You can't make me go back," she said.

"We care about you, Gwyneth," Fiona said. "You need to come home."

"I'm not going home with you." She looked over and glared at me. "And I'm definitely not going home with him."

"We can't force you," I said. "If you don't want to come back with us, you can stay out here and freeze to death."

She looked back to Fiona. "I'll only freeze because they stole my supplies," she said. "You need to make them give me my stuff back."

Fiona looked up at me. "Baptiste," she said, "we need to bring her home. She's not thinking clearly."

"You can't force me."

"What do you expect me to do?" I asked. "Tie her up?"

"I don't know," Fiona said.

"I'm not forcing anyone to live with me."

Fiona looked back to Gwyneth. She held out her hand.

Gwyneth took it.

"Please, Gwyneth," Fiona said. "Please come back with me."

"I can't," she said. "I can't go back with him. You shouldn't go back with him, either."

"I trust him. I love him like a father."

"He'll hurt you. They all hurt you in the end."

"Let's go, Fiona," I said. "She's made up her mind."

"I'm not leaving her," Fiona said.

"I'm not forcing her."

"Then I'm going with her."

I almost laughed. "That's crazy, Fiona. You're not even halfway there. You won't make it."

"She's my friend. I can't just abandon her."

"I can't let you die out here," I told her. "I'm not above tying you up."

"That's it," Gwyneth said, "right there. He's going to tie you up and then he's going to rape you."

I didn't even know where to begin. What could I even say to something like that?

"He wouldn't do that," Fiona said. "Baptiste loves me like a daughter."

"Ask my father about that," Gwyneth said. "Ask him what that means. I came up here to get away from him. But I was too stupid to realize that I really needed to get away from all of them. He *will* hurt you, Fiona. He *will* rape you. He may even kill you one day."

Fiona looked back up to me. "We're going to keep walking," she said. "I'd really like you to stay with us. But even if you won't."

"I'll stay," I said. "I'll follow behind."

She smiled. "Thank you."

Then she and Gwyneth started walking down the icy gravel road.

I called Lisa on the handheld and told her the story, and I asked her and Graham to catch up with us as soon as they could. Lisa was a nurse and not a psychiatrist, and I wasn't supposed to know, but I knew that she'd have to have better luck with Gwyneth.

Or at least better luck convincing Fiona that there was no point in humouring that crazy-as-fuck girl for one more minute.

The two of them chatted with each other up ahead of me, sometimes even laughing together.

I kept a good fifty to a hundred paces behind, stopping the cart every few minutes just to keep from catching up.

Occasionally Fiona would look back and give me another smile. Like she wasn't even mad at me anymore.

Sometimes Gwyneth would look back and give me another glare. She was starting to wear on me.

Lisa and Graham arrived within twenty minutes. Lisa left her snowmobile in the ditch, and jogged to catch up with the girls.

Graham dumped his snowmobile as well, but climbed up on the cart to join me.

"Fiona's lost it, too?" he asked.

"She feels like she'd be leaving Gwyneth to die," I said. "And she's right."

"So what do we do?"

"We hope to hell that Lisa's more persuasive than I am."

"To be honest, I'm surprised you didn't try and force her to come home."

"I don't want her to come back with us," I said "She's almost as crazy as the fucker I had to shoot."

"Fiona cares about her."

"You are such a woman, Graham."

"Come on, Baptiste. Doesn't that matter to you?"

"Of course it matters, idiot. I love Fiona. I don't want her to be upset."

"She'll be more than upset..."

"Then go hogtie the crazy so we can get home before Matt decides to try and cook dinner. We don't need another forest fire."

"Lisa will figure it out," Graham said, sounding like a total fool.

"Yeah... maybe..."

Lisa jogged back to the cart.

"Nope," she said. "They're not interested."

"Neither of them?" I asked.

"Fiona seems like she just wants to keep Gwyneth happy."

"For how long? Are they going to set up at Helena and start some kind of Amazon collective?"

"They're both too short for that," Lisa said. "Let's just go with Feminazis for now. I think we should just let them walk for a while.

Eventually reality has to set in."

"I think Gwyneth left reality in her other pants."

"I can't believe this," Graham said. "How did I end up being the one who wants to brutalize these two girls and drag their butts home?"

"You have a dark side," Lisa said. "And I like it."

"I'm not going to put up with this," I said. "I'm not interested in holding this crazy bitch's hand."

Lisa nodded. "Then go. We can handle this. We're relieving you."

"I stand relieved."

"Is that a pee joke?" Graham asked.

"We'll keep the cart," Lisa said. "I don't want us to have to hump these girls back on the machines."

"Sounds good," I said.

Graham handed me his key.

I didn't wait around. I hopped down and started walking back toward the snowmobiles.

I went back home.

⸙

I didn't see Sara when I got back, but I didn't worry about it. If she wanted to hide out at the Porters or Marchands or wherever, I wasn't going to try and stop her.

Kayla and I made dinner in the kitchen, while Matt sat on the chair by the porch, holding the shotgun and looking exactly like the overzealous idiot he is.

Has he ever seen me on watch with the shotgun? Is that how he thinks this is done?

It was awkward at first with Kayla, neither of us talking about what I'm sure both of us were thinking. We hadn't seen each other since she'd been half-naked on my bed, about to let me pull down her pants. I wasn't sure what to say.

"I miss apples," Kayla said as she opened up a can of mandarin oranges for the salad. "More than bananas, even. Probably because we're just a little too far north to get them."

"We've got applesauce by the buttload," I said.

"It's not the same. That feeling of biting into an apple, that mixture of skin and the... er... apple guts..."

"Are we going to talk about it?" I asked.

"No."

"Why not?"

"Because there's no reason to. We'll just move on."

"Move on? Like try and be friends?"

She laughed. "Move on, like the next time we get a chance we'll fuck like bunnies and that'll be that."

"So that's still the plan?" I wasn't disappointed.

"That's the plan."

"I'll bet there are apples that can be grown here," I said. "I'm sure I've seen apple trees."

"You've seen them? But you don't remember where?"

"It didn't seem important at the time."

"I didn't start this because I want to hurt Sara," she said. "It just happened. Hurting Sara would just be a happy side effect."

"She wouldn't care. She's done with me."

"Yeah, right."

"I'll keep an eye out for apple trees. We ought to have an orchard."

"Yeah... our canned fruit won't last forever." She stopped making the salad and grabbed my hand. "What happened to those girls you rescued, Baptiste? What did they do to them?"

"They wanted to hurt them," I said. "To get back at me."

"No... before that. When you first found them, in that cabin on Silver Queen Lake."

"You don't want to know."

"I'm asking. Just tell me, okay?"

"They stripped them down and tied them to a bed."

"They tied them? To the bedposts?"

"With zip ties... why does it matter so much? It's not going to happen here, Kayla."

"Were their ankles tied? Were they blindfolded?"

"I don't want to talk about this..."

"I can't imagine what that would be like."

"Stop it, Kayla, okay? Just change the goddamn subject."

"Okay... sorry... I just wanted to know."

"Yeah," I said.

We finished making dinner without talking about much else, and I set the table and wondered why no one was back yet.

The three of us sat down and had dinner, Matt finally putting the shotgun down.

With the way Matt still looks at Kayla, I don't think he has any idea what she and I have been up to; I doubt he's been given a copy of that plan of hers.

The three of us sat in the living room after we'd eaten. We hadn't done the dishes, since we were expecting more diners to show up.

After a few minutes Matt went upstairs. He didn't tell us why, and we didn't ask for any details.

It was nice to be alone with Kayla.

I looked over at her.

She was looking at her tablet.

"Fiona just messaged me," Kayla said. "They're on their way home."

For a fleeting moment I was surprised she hadn't messaged me. Then I remembered how I'd left her behind, and what I'd done with Kayla, and it all started to make sense. I was now higher on her shit list than Kayla herself.

"Must not be far if she was able to send a message," I said.

"They're on New Post Road. Fiona sent me one earlier, not long after you guys found her, all the way from Birchill. I'm surprised she had a signal out there."

"I didn't even check."

"Yeah... apparently Sara's pissed about that."

"What?"

"She's pissed. Apparently you didn't tell her what was happening. She only found out when Fiona messaged her that you guys had found Gwyneth. Personally, I think she's lost the privilege of being the first person you tell."

"Yeah... it doesn't matter what she thinks."

"I don't disagree."

That time I was the one who leaned in for the kiss.

Then we went upstairs.

∽

I heard a snowmobile arrive a few minutes later. I went downstairs to check, leaving Kayla in my room. We hadn't done much.

But probably enough for Matt to figure out that something was going on.

Justin was the one who stepped into the house, which was odd, since I don't remember inviting him over.

"We got 'em," he said to me as he kicked off his boots by the door.

"Where are they, then? You just took off in front of them?"

"The cart's a little slow. And you know, I have a family to care for. It's hard being the support system for two of those now."

"So you're just here to taunt me? Like you're looking for a fist-fight?"

He smiled. "Come on, Baptiste... I was just messing with you. Don't be so mopey."

"Don't be such an ass, Justin. Let's start with that, shall we?"

"Sure," he said with a grin. "Sorry about Sara, eh?"

"What about Sara?"

"You know... that you two are on the outs. It was a good run, though."

"How is this your business?"

"Well, when Sara starts sniffing around me because you're not cutting it for her... that makes it my business. I mean, I'm a married man..."

I stepped up to him and gave him a shove. "Get out," I said.

"Easy, guy... the heart wants what it wants..."

"Get out of my face, Justin."

"Sure... I've got a place to be." He turned and headed toward the door. He stopped and gave me a smirk. "Don't worry... I'll make sure Sara isn't neglected..."

"Don't you have some supplies to give away?"

He walked out onto the porch. He gave me a wave as he left.

Kayla came downstairs.

"What an asshole," she said.

"You heard all that?"

"No... I just know he's an asshole."

I laughed. And then I followed her back upstairs.

367

We'd have a minute or two.

I heard the cart coming, and I started climbing off the bed.

"Don't," Kayla said. "They're fine. They don't need you right now."

She put her hand on my shoulder and started rubbing.

I laid back down.

"We can't do this now," I said.

"Why not?"

"What if someone comes up here?"

"Let them come. As long as I get to go first." She started kissing my neck.

I appreciated the sentiment, the initiative… but I wasn't really that type of guy.

I flipped her onto her back and pulled off her shirt.

"Oh," she said. "So that's how you want to do it, Big Daddy?"

I almost cringed at the nickname. But I held it in.

The last thing I wanted to do was turn her off.

I started kissing her neck, like she'd done mine. I listened to her moan… I loved the sound more than anything else.

Kayla Fucking Burkholder…

I felt like I was cheating now… on Sara… on Alanna… but I wanted to cheat… I wanted to just do what I wanted, to tell the world "to hell with it".

So I took Kayla on my squeaky double bed.

It was amazing.

She is amazing.

I am fucking amazing.

TODAY IS SATURDAY, JANUARY 5TH.

I WOKE up with Kayla beside me.

I guess there are no secrets anymore.

We dressed and then we went downstairs together, not clinging like newlyweds, but I'm sure it'd be obvious that we were a couple of sorts.

There was no one there.

I pulled out my tablet.

No messages.

"What the hell is going on?" I asked.

"I don't know," Kayla said. "We did sleep in."

"By a half hour, maybe..."

"Message Graham... he still... um... doesn't hate you..."

"Thanks." I pinged for Graham's whereabouts, rather than going out and writing a messaged. He was up the road, between the Tremblays and the Porters. "He's heading to see Justin," I said.

"That's... odd..."

"They're going to have a meeting about us," I said. "What to do with Kayla and Baptiste..."

She smiled. "Nah... probably just an orgy."

I went along. "But you love orgies."

She chuckled. "So I'm the one who should be worried."

We put on our jackets and boots. I unlocked the chest by the door and found all three sets of vests and helmets. I didn't put one on, but I can't say I wasn't tempted.

We walked up the road toward the Porters. As we passed the Marchands, I tried to see if I could see anyone through the windows. I couldn't.

We passed the Tremblays; I couldn't make out anyone there, either.

Then I saw someone, at the Williams place, the next cottage up the road. The skinny Marchand kid, splitting firewood just outside the boarded up front window.

"What's going on?" I asked him.

"Splitting wood," he said. "For the girls."

"The girls?"

He stopped splitting. "Uh... yeah..."

"Gwyneth's moving in here," Kayla said. "Am I right?"

"That red-haired girl..." the boy said. "And that pretty brunette... Fiona..."

"That pretty brunette is only sixteen," I said.

"So? I'm seventeen."

"They're moving out... fuck..."

The door to the Williams place opened.

I looked over to see Sara.

"I'm moving out, too," she said. "There's no way I'm going to be living with the two of you."

"We can't afford this," I said. "We're going to heat five cottages? This kid'll be splitting a lot of firewood."

"This kid?" the boy said. "Do you even know my name?"

I shook my head. "Sorry..."

"Same as you. Robert. Robert Émile Marchand."

"Nice to meet you," I said, really not caring. I turned back to Sara. "You can't do this, Sara."

"I can't do what, now?" she said. "I can't fuck Kayla behind your back... oh, wait..."

"You weren't even talking to me."

"So you start screwing the local slut?"

"Don't you call me that," Kayla said.

"Don't take this out on Kayla," I said. "This is between you and me."

"There's nothing between you and me," she said. "Nothing. You get that? Now go home and leave us alone. We have a shit-ton of work to do and the last thing I need is the two of you."

"We should help," Kayla said. "Fiona and Gwyneth deserve a nice place to stay."

"Don't bother," Sara said. "Just get out of my sight."

Kayla grabbed my elbow, like she was wanting me to back her up.

I wanted to...

So I did.

"Let's go, Kayla," I said. "If people want to put themselves at risk that's their deal. I'm not going to support this stupidity." I spun around and starting walking home. "Good luck, Robert," I said. "You're going to need it with that bunch."

Kayla seemed hesitant to leave, like there was something else that needed to be said.

I wasn't about to wait on her. I just kept walking.

"I'm sorry, Sara," I heard her say. "I didn't want things to go like this."

I did my best not to feel sorry, too.

Kayla and I stayed in my bedroom for most of the day.

I tried not to listen in to the sounds of the horde, coming in to pack up all the clothes, and food and dishes.

We were losing three and keeping five, assuming that Matt was sticking around and not planning to camp out in the bushes outside the old Williams cottage. I'm not sure how they were planning on divvying things up, but for whatever reason I didn't want to know.

Kayla and I watched *Anchorman: The Legend Continues* and we laughed more than we oughta, since we were both doing our best to show that we were happy and perfectly unaffected by outside events.

After the movie, I told Kayla about the first time I'd watched the second *Anchorman*, in a theatre in Pembroke, Ontario, with three buddies whose names I sometimes forget. I'd eaten the Perogy Pizza at Boston Pizza along with downing a few too many beers, and then we walked over to the East End Mall and saw it, and it was pretty good.

That movie is practically ancient now, and I was about the same age then as Kayla is now.

It's funny how a thought like that can be so impressive and so depressing at the same time.

TODAY IS SUNDAY, JANUARY 6TH.

THE TWO Porter children showed up just after midnight. They're pretty young, the boy around ten and the girl maybe thirteen, so in my mind they're nowhere near old enough to be wandering around on their own, at any time of the day.

The dogs had started barking before they'd even knocked on the door. As we'd practiced since Ryan Stems had shown up, Lisa and I went to the kids at the front door, while Graham watched the side porch with his pistol.

I could see who it was through the window, of course, but I opened the door with my gun in hand anyway, just in case.

"What's going on?" I asked them.

The girl was upset while the boy seemed almost giddy.

"My Dad's caught someone," the girl said. "In the basement."

"Shit," I said.

The boy started to giggle.

I turned to Lisa. "Who's staying here?" I asked. "You or Graham?"

"I can stay," she said.

I turned back to the kids on the porch. "Wait here," I told them.

I unlocked the chest near the door and pulled out a couple of vests and helmets.

Graham came up beside me. "Isn't that overkill?" he asked.

"Not these days it isn't," I said.

He didn't argue further as we both got dressed. Once we had our helmets on, we headed out the door.

"We'll take the truck," I said. It felt like the right kind of emergency.

When we arrived at the Porters, I noticed nothing unusual on the outside. Graham stayed back in the truck, with the kids, while I went in first, making sure that there wasn't anything amiss.

Justin and Rihanna Porter met me at the door. They looked shaken but okay.

"What happened?" I asked, lifting the visor on my helmet. "Where is he?"

"In the dining room," Rihanna said. "Matt's watching them."

I rushed into the dining room without another word. The two thieves were bound to chairs with zip ties, Matt standing over them holding a hunting rifle. They were younger than I expected, a boy and a girl, both around Fiona's age. The two of them were native, and they looked completely terrified.

"They're from New Post," Matt said. "Those bastards have been robbing us blind."

"What the hell are you doing here, Matt?" I asked.

"The Porters asked for my help."

"And you kept it all pretty quiet."

"That's my fault," Rihanna said. "I thought we were being a little overzealous, and I didn't want to alarm anyone... but I guess you can see that we weren't overreacting about New Post."

I took a closer look at the prisoners, at the scrapes and cuts on their faces. "They're bleeding," I said. "What happened here?"

"There was a scuffle," Matt said. "Not a big deal."

"They're kids, Matt... you do realize that?"

"They're thieves," Justin said. "We caught them with a bag filled with painkillers and first aid stuff." He pointed to a canvas bag lying on the floor and the spilled loot beside it.

"More than just a box of salt," I said. "So let's take them home so their parents can deal with them."

"I don't think so," Rihanna said.

"You have a better idea?"

"They stole some of our food before, and now they're after our medicine. That's a big deal."

"And?"

"And they need to make it up to us. They need to bring it all back and then some."

"Restitution," Justin said.

I wasn't sure I had reason to disagree.

I walked back out to the porch and waved Graham in.

"You're making some pretty big assumptions if you think everyone at New Post isn't in on it," Matt said to me on my return.

"Don't worry about me and my assumptions. Let's worry about the fact that somebody actually thought it was a good idea to let you hold their rifle."

"It all seems clear to us," Rihanna said. "New Post has been stealing supplies from us for months."

"You sure it's New Post? And not just a couple of kids?"

Justin held up a tablet. "Sugar, salt, baking soda, olive oil, yeast... not what you'd expect a couple of teenagers to steal."

I walked over and grabbed the tablet. "There's something odd about this list."

"Were you even listening to me?"

"No flour on the list. No rice, no beans, no potatoes..."

"Maybe those are next week's targets," Rihanna said.

"Maybe," I said. "But if I had over a hundred mouths to feed, I'd be focused on the staples. Sugar and salt are nice to have, but I doubt they're the most important things to be carrying back home."

"So they probably have enough flour," Graham said as he checked out the zip-tied kids. "Maybe they found some old grain... all they'd have to do is mill it."

"They don't have a mill," Matt said. He looked over to me. "Right?"

"Not that we know of," I said. "But they could be doing it by hand. But even then... everything else they'd need. I know they have some gardens at New Post, but they don't have enough to grow it all."

Justin walked over to the kids, almost shoving Graham aside. "So where do you get your flour?" he asked them.

Neither of the prisoners answered; I wasn't surprised.

"You'd better start answering me," Justin said. "I don't want anyone to get hurt."

As if on cue, Matt pulled the rifle up to the boy's head.

That was enough of that. "Give me the rifle, dipshit," I said, holding out my hands.

He looked over at me and hesitated.

"You're going to kill someone," I said.

He passed me the rifle.

I switched the rifle to safe and laid it on the floor. I looked over to the two terrified kids.

"I'm sorry," I said to them. "I'm sorry these guys have been acting like this. They're just scared. We're all a little scared."

The boy was motionless, but I could see the girl give me a slight nod.

"It would help if you'd tell us what's going on," I said. "Obviously you guys are stealing from us, but I don't really understand why."

"Don't bother," Justin said. "These piece-of-shit indians haven't said a word to us."

"Seriously?" Graham said. "You've got a pretty big mouth when Lisa's not here to kick your ass."

"Easy, Graham," I said. I turned back to give Justin a glare. "Strange... you'd think they'd want to tell all of their secrets to a bunch of thugs who want to beat the ever-living shit out of them."

Justin didn't answer.

I looked back towards the kids.

"Do you hit up a lot of other places?" I asked.

No answer.

"They're like those goddamned coyotes," Justin said. "They started off by circling us, nipping at our heels, just grabbing a few things here and there... not enough so we'd notice."

I sighed. "Well, you didn't notice... but I would have."

He ignored the dig. "Then they started getting desperate, less and less places to steal from... and they started coming back here more and more. And now, we've got 'em."

"Why wouldn't you just scavenge like the rest of us?" I asked them.

"We can't," the girl said.

The boy turned and stared at her.

She ignored him. "We don't have enough fuel to find everything we'd need out there."

"So you steal from us? Why wouldn't you just come and talk to us?"

"How should I know?"

She had a point. If we wanted answers, we'd need to get them from the people in charge.

"They send their children to us," Rihanna said. "They send kids because they know we won't kill them."

"They don't know anything for sure," Justin said.

"Either way," Graham said, "it's cowardly."

"We deserve some kind of compensation for this," Rihanna said. "We need to confront Gerald Archibald. No more pussy-footing around."

"I know," I said. "We'll talk to them. Obviously."

"We should hold these two here," Justin said. "New Post brings back our missing supplies, along with a little extra for pain and suffering, and these kids get to go home."

"That's insane," Graham said. "We're not going to hold people hostage."

"It's not your decision," Rihanna said.

"That's true," I said. "It's my decision." I did my best to make it a quick one. "We'll hold them up at our cottage until morning... and then we'll meet as a team and talk this out."

"Oh and so then we'll vote on it?" Graham asked. It sounded like he was mocking me.

"And then I'll decide what comes next. That's how it's going to be."

"That's fair," Rihanna said.

"What a surprise, Baptiste," Graham said, "it's all up to you again."

"I thought we'd discussed this," I told him. "All matters of security... or have you forgotten?"

"I haven't forgotten."

"Then don't get in the way, Graham. Trust me on this."

He left it there for the moment, but I don't think he trusts my judgement anymore.

Matt stayed on shift overnight, so ridiculously eager to play jailer that I didn't bother to argue; to be honest, I liked my chances of him sleeping right through the meeting.

He was still pacing around the living room couch when I went upstairs to sleep, watching over his prisoners as they huddled together with their jackets as pillows, their wrists now zip-tied in front on

Graham's insistence.

I wasn't sure what I could do for them. No matter what decision I made, someone was going to fight me on it. And I wasn't sure if these kids were going to make it home in one piece.

By the time everyone started to arrive, around seven the next morning, Matt was still going strong.

We met in the dining room, with Alain and Suzanne Tremblay, all of the Porters, and Eva and skinny Robert Marchand, who seemed an odd choice, until I realized how few Marchands are left alive. Kayla had taken it upon herself to make breakfast, with a little nervous help from me, but it didn't take long for the hot food to start running out.

Since it was a meeting about security, first and foremost, I chose to run it. Sara sat quietly at the table, pretending that she wasn't still wanting me dead, but doing it so poorly that I'm sure even those two kids from New Post knew I was on her shitlist.

"So I'm sure everyone knows what's happening," I said as I stood from my chair, "but I'll take a moment to explain it so we don't leave anything out. These two teenagers from New Post have been caught attempting to steal supplies from the Porters. There have been other thefts, most likely by these kids, too. And I'm afraid that, based on the types of items they're taking, it seems pretty clear that New Post's Chief and Council planned the whole thing. So the question is how we should react to these thefts. We may want to hold onto our prisoners until New Post provides us with adequate restitution."

"One minute," Eva Marchand said. "So they give us our food back or we kill their children?"

"No one said anything about killing," Rihanna said.

"But that would be the threat if they don't do what we want, would it not? Otherwise there is no reason for it."

"It's ridiculous," Graham said.

"It sounds like a great plan," Lisa said with a smirk. "Maybe we should cut off an ear to let them know we mean business."

"That's enough," I said. "There's no room for sarcasm here, okay? This isn't a joke."

"It seems like a joke," Graham said. "This isn't self defense here, Baptiste... just holding these kids hostage is a violent act. It's inexcusable."

"He's correct," Eva said. "You held these children here last night... you could try to argue that you did it to keep them safe and out of trouble. But now we need to take them home."

"This is life or death," Rihanna said. "Having our supplies stolen could cost us our own lives one day. This theft is an act of violence."

"That's a stretch," Lisa said.

"We just want our food back," Justin said. "Is that too much to ask? I mean, what the hell?"

"Then we should ask them," Graham said. "Let's go to New Post, bring these kids home, and ask for our food back. That's all we can do."

Justin pounded both hands on the table. "That's bullshit. So they've been double-crossing us, from day one, letting Stems tromp on through, stealing our hard-earned supplies... and you want to go down there and ask them for a favour? A favour... those fucking natives."

Lisa stood up from her chair, with so much force that it slammed backwards against the floor. "This fucking native would love you to keep shooting your mouth off," she said.

"Calm down," I said. "Everyone needs to take a breath here."

"Baptiste is right," Alain Tremblay said. "We won't all agree on what to do. So let's figure out what our choices are, and come up with some pros and cons."

"Just shut it, Tremblay," Justin said. "Just leave this to people who actually contribute something around here."

Alain rose from his chair, too.

"Easy," I said.

Justin rose to meet him, giving him a shove.

Lisa hovered around them, too... I knew she wouldn't hold back for much longer.

I looked over to Sara. She caught my glance and looked away. I stood up from my chair, trying to insert myself between the two men.

Justin pushed me and I pushed back.

He took a swing at me.

I dodged it and slapped him across the face.

He looked like he was about to start laughing.

"This is insane," I said. "Sit back down... everyone." I could hear in my voice that I was losing my temper; I'm sure I wasn't the only one to notice.

Justin came close to growling at me, but he didn't take another shot.

"This is ridiculous," Graham said. "These meetings have become a farce."

"That's because there's no point to them," Rihanna said. "If Baptiste is supposed to decide, then he should just decide." She looked up at me. "Well?"

"Just a minute, please," Eva said. "Why does Monsieur Baptiste get to decide? There is a vote, no?"

"It's my call," I said. "So I'll ask all of you to sit down and be quiet, so I can think for a minute."

That had the opposite result, and soon it seemed like every person in the room was trying to shout out their opinions at me. So I started yelling too, telling people to calm down and somehow managing to make everyone that much louder.

"Enough!" Sara screamed, as loud as I've ever heard her. "Just stop it!" She stood up and glared at me. "This is ridiculous... all of it."

"Things got a little heated," Rihanna said, as she rose from her chair.

"Just shut up, okay?" Sara looked around the room and then she shook her head. "This is so effing ridiculous. Why do I even bother?"

She turned and walked into the kitchen, coming back out with a pair of scissors. She walked over to the living room, to the two prisoners.

"Ridiculous," she said again as she began cutting the plasticuffs off the native boy's wrists.

"What are you doing?" I asked.

She cut the girl free as well.

The two prisoners grabbed their jackets and ran out onto the side porch. They kept going until they'd disappeared down the path that ran along the lake.

I wondered how many deer trails they'd memorized to find their way home through the woods.

Sara turned and went over to the front door. She grabbed her coat off its hook and walked out.

"Where is she going?" Rihanna asked.

"She's going," I said. I hadn't even thought of following her.

"It isn't safe," Fiona said. "She can't go out on her own."

"Well she just did," Justin said. "And she just gave New Post permission to keep stealing from us."

"I think things will be getting a lot worse than stealing," Lisa said.

"We'll need to hook up with New Post again," I said. "Matt... send them a message that we want to talk things through."

Matt looked over to Justin, who gave him a nod.

Like Justin was his goddamn boss.

"Okay," Matt said. "I'll set it up."

"Baptiste?" Fiona said. "What about Sara? Aren't you going to go after her?"

I nodded and sighed, and then I grabbed my coat and made my way outside. Sara was already on the road, walking along one of the ruts in the snow.

"Sara," I called out. "Come back here."

She didn't answer and she didn't look back.

"Sara... I'm sorry..."

I heard the clattering of footsteps on the porch as pretty much everyone came out to watch.

"Will you please talk to me?" I said. "Please... I need you to talk to me..."

"Leave me alone," she yelled back. "I don't want you anywhere near me."

"It's not safe out there by yourself."

"It's not safe with you, Baptiste. I'll take gun-toting marauders and those godforsaken coyotes over you."

There was no point in walking fifty feet behind her all the way to James Bay, so I turned back to grab my gear.

"I'm taking the truck," I said to Graham as I passed him on the front porch.

I took the shotgun, and then I drove up the road, watching the fuel gauge creep that much closer to the E. I caught up to Sara, at the junction with Nelson Road, pulling just in front of her and stopping. I rolled down my window.

She took a sharp left and headed towards the ditch.

"Are you going to tromp through ten inches of snow rather than talk to me?" I asked her.

She stopped walking, but still she wouldn't look at me. "Why can't you give me a little space?"

"You know why."

"I don't give a crap about being safe right now."

"I love you, Sara."

"You love me... and all that sex with Kayla was a mistake... and I'll bet you'll never hit me again... blah fucking blah, Baptiste."

"I'm not making any promises."

That got her to turn and face me. "What?" she said.

"I never thought I'd do anything to hurt you. And I don't want to hurt you, Sara. I don't. But it doesn't matter what I tell you, because it happened..."

"Yeah. It happened. And now we're done."

"I love you. I don't want to lose you."

"You cheated on me. With that skank. And you hit me. You fucking hit me. Did you really think that I'm the type of woman who lets guys beat on her? Did you really think I'd let you do that?"

"I lost control."

"You're goddamn right, you lost control. But that's not my problem anymore. I don't ever need to see you again."

"So you're going to leave? Like right now?"

"I'm going to leave. Right now."

"You're going to live in the woods."

"I'm going to live in the woods."

"You're going to eat nuts and berries."

"Nuts and berries." I could hear her voice starting to weaken.

"You're going to squat down to take shits in a little hole you've dug with your bare hands."

She sighed. She sounded defeated. "This is ridiculous. I'm stuck here. I can run off to a new cottage, but I can't get away from you."

"I don't want you to get away," I said.

"I'm not coming home. I haven't forgiven you."

"I know."

"Not by a long shot."

"I know."

"Here's what needs to happen," she said. "If you ever want the slimmest goddamn chance with me, ever again..."

"Yes?"

"No more Kayla. Ever. You don't touch her again."

I nodded, but I wasn't sure I was willing to do that.

"No more anyone else," she said. "You wait for me. You wait and you wait, or else you don't get me. Understand?"

"I understand."

She climbed into the passenger side of the truck. "It's a good thing you came after me," she said. "I forgot my gloves."

I leaned over to give her a kiss.

"No," she said. "Not now."

"Then when?"

She sighed. "Fuck. I don't know, Baptiste. *Mon dieu*. Just_. not now. You need to wait."

She turned and looked out the window. There were no tears in her eyes, no sign of worry on her face. It was like she'd made her peace with how things would be from now on, like she didn't mind at all that she and I would never be the same.

It was Sara not giving a shit about the two of us that hurt the most.

9

TODAY IS MONDAY, JANUARY 7TH.

I DON'T recall anyone from New Post ever coming up to see us. It's always been us visiting them, and that had always suited me fine, until we'd realized that they'd been coming up here the whole time, only they'd come up along the deer trails so they could steal our supplies.

So even though we'd heard back from them, and I'd been expecting them to show up today at noon, it was still a little bit of a shock to see two forest green pickup trucks making their way down the road, toward our gate on Nelson Road.

We brought out our two trucks, as well as a snowmobile. I'd been tempted to suit up all the way, but I knew that showing that level of distrust would destroy whatever positive feelings might be left. So Sara and I walked out to meet them, unarmed, while Lisa and Graham watched from the grain truck, vests on, with their guns and helmets kept out of sight, down on the seats.

The Marchands and the Porters were holding a second line halfway between the gate and the cottages, just in case.

Gerald Archibald came to talk to us, by himself. He seems to have become their spokesman when it comes to us; maybe they think he understands me.

"I want to apologize," he said. "What some of our young people have been doing is not okay."

"It's not just your young people," Sara said, beating me to it. "Just be honest with us."

"Why didn't you ask for our help?" I asked. "Maybe we could have worked out a trade."

"We're not allowed to trade with you," Gerald said.

"What?"

"We're not allowed. It's not something I can change."

"Then who can change it? Who made such an idiotic decision?"

"We have commitments in place," he said. "It allows us keep our people fed. Now those commitments mean we can't trade with you."

"So all that time, we'd drop by to help out... you were just leading us on? Or when you talked about trading for our crops?"

"The trade embargo is more recent."

"Embargo? That sounds pretty targeted. So you can trade with anyone who isn't us?"

Gerald shook his head. "Baptiste... there's barely anyone else out here now."

"Except the Walkers," I said. "But that's who you're working with. That's why we found them last month... driving back from the rail bridge."

"We did some work for the Walkers. They would bring us supplies in exchange. But that's changed now. We're part of the Nation. Walker works for us. He brings us supplies because that's a condition of keeping his land."

"But not enough supplies," Sara said. "Or else you wouldn't be stealing from us."

"They give us the basics... but we need more than that."

"So how long have you been stealing from us?" I asked.

"Not long. We scavenged quite a bit from the places between here and Iroquois Falls... but that couldn't last forever."

"None of that matters," Sara said. "What does matter is that you guys have been stealing from us."

"We can't give anything back," Gerald said.

"We don't need anything back. We just need a promise from you."

"I'm not sure I can make that promise."

"So wait," I said. "So you're actually telling us that you're going to send your kids back to steal some more?"

"We need those supplies," Gerald said.

"Then get 'em from the Walkers, Gerald. Or from your new best friend, Ryan Stems." I shook my head at him. "We're going to be adding even more security over the next few days. You should tell your people that it won't be safe to sneak up on us anymore."

"What's that supposed to mean?"

"It can only mean one thing," Sara said. "We are going to protect ourselves. Obviously no one wants things to get out of hand."

"I don't do well with threats," Gerald said. "And neither does Ryan Stems."

"Let's make this simple," I said. "If anyone approaches McCartney Lake from anywhere other than the main road, they are putting themselves in harm's way."

"It's not a threat," Sara said. "It's just the way it's going to have to be from now on."

"We are stronger than you," Gerald said. "The Mushkegowuk Nation is sovereign and it is powerful. We want peace, but we won't let our people starve while you hoard supplies."

"Hoard?" I said. "Are you kidding me? We need those supplies to live."

"So do we."

"No you don't... I'm sure Ryan Stems and your precious Nation have tons of supplies in some warehouse in Kapuskasing. If they aren't cutting you in on that... well, then you're a sucker."

Gerald sighed. "I guess there isn't anything more to talk about."

"I guess not."

Gerald turned and started to make his way back to his pickup truck.

Sara looked at me and frowned. "That didn't go well," she said.

"I don't see how it could have gone any better. At least we know where we stand."

"Yeah... around six feet underground."

I heard footsteps behind us. I swung around to see Justin. He was dressed in a riot suit, vest and helmet, and holding his hunting rifle.

"What the hell are you doing?" I asked him.

Justin ignored me, pushing right by. "Hey! Asshole!" he yelled out.

Gerald turned to look.

"Yeah... I'm talking to you," Justin said. He pointed the rifle and fired.

Gerald starting running towards his truck.

"Dammit, Justin!" I yelled. "Put the rifle down!"

He fired again.

Gerald fell into the snow.

I ran towards Justin, hoping to tackle him.

"Back off, Baptiste," he said. "I'm going to teach these shits a lesson."

"Then you'd better shoot me," I said.

He pointed the gun at me.

I didn't slow down. I went for his knees, bringing him down to the snow and gravel. The rifle flew out in front.

Sara walked over to it, but she didn't touch it.

"What the hell?" I said to him. "Are you a fucking lunatic?"

"Maybe," he said. "Did I get that fucker?"

I couldn't help myself. I punched him right in the mouth.

I heard the sound of boots; a number of people rushing towards us. Before I could look, my face was in the dirt.

They wrenched my arms behind me and I could feel the plasticuffs tightening around my wrists.

I watched from the mud as they did the same to Justin.

"Fuck, Baptiste," Justin said. "Who's side are you on?"

"Baptiste's the one who stopped him," Sara said. "This isn't right."

Two of the men from New Post grabbed Sara roughly and bound her wrists as well.

"Start shooting, dammit!" Justin screamed. "Shoot these assholes!"

"No one listens to you," I said. "Just shut up."

I looked over at Gerald; two of his men were helping him up. One was applying pressure to his shoulder. The other was scanning the trees as he lifted one of Gerald's arms.

Lisa didn't move from the cab of the grain truck.

I saw Sky walking up to me, his rifle drawn.

"I don't know what just happened," Sky said. "But it was a huge mistake." He reached down and picked up Justin's rifle.

"So that's it," I said. "You'll take us up the road and put bullets in our heads."

"We're not the ones who started shooting."

"It wasn't me, either." I nodded my head toward Justin. "That idiot doesn't speak for the rest of us."

"He's wearing your equipment, isn't he?" Sky said. "We're taking all three of you back with us. The council will conduct an investigation, and they'll decide what actions need to be taken. You'll have due process."

"You have no right to take us," Sara said. "This is kidnapping."

They shoved me into the first truck box, and Justin into the second. He and I both got two men by our side. Sky handed Justin's rifle to one of the men beside me, and the one on his shoulder to the men watching Justin. He then loaded Sara into the second truck, while Gerald was helped into the passenger seat of the first, by one of his other men.

And that's when Lisa climbed out with the Mossberg and started shooting.

She hadn't bothered with her helmet.

Two shots rang out, and then I heard Gerald's man start the engine. Two more shots and he reversed too quickly, slamming into the front of the truck behind him. Two final shots made him ditch the truck completely, running towards the other one and climbing into the box.

Lisa ducked alongside the truck and started reloading, as Graham stepped out, helmet on, pointing his SIG Sauer right at Sky.

Gerald opened the passenger door, but I could tell he wouldn't make it on his own.

Lisa popped back out with the shotgun.

I wondered if Lisa was going to take him out. I wasn't about to tell her not to.

The two guards who were with me jumped out, leaving me in the box. They grabbed Gerald and pulled him into the box of the second truck as Sky started it up and slammed into reverse.

Lisa came running by, with Graham not far behind.

"Don't shoot," I called out to her. "Sara's in there. It's too risky."

"*Takay,*" she said. "They're too far out. Let's go."

She and Graham helped me out of the box and into the cab of Gerald's truck. As Lisa drove, Graham cut my cuffs with his pocket knife.

I wondered if any of her shots had done enough damage to the engine block that we'd be left stranded halfway to New Post.

"I didn't see many weapons," I said.

Graham pointed behind us at a couple of rifles mounted on a gun rack at the back of the cab.

"So a gun each, maybe?" I said.

"More than we have," Lisa said. "But since we've got the body armour, we can take them. As long as we catch them before they get to their gate." With that, she sped up some more, even though I already couldn't believe how fast she was driving.

Sky didn't seem willing to go as quickly as Lisa; we were gaining on them quickly.

"We'll catch up to them," Lisa said. "I can run these assholes tight into a snowbank."

"Don't forget about Sara," I said.

I could see Sky slowing down as they reached New Post Road. As the truck turned the corner, I saw someone get thrown from the side of the box.

"Shit," I said.

"What?" Lisa asked.

"They just threw Justin out of the truck." I took a breath. "We'll have to come back for him."

"We've got to check him over."

"Sara's more important."

"Sara's okay right now... I'm not sure Justin is."

"I don't give a flying fuck about Justin Porter."

"Well, his kids do."

I knew she was right. "Dammit."

She stopped at the corner and Graham and I hopped out. Justin was lying in the snow. He was unconscious, but I could see his breath in the cold air.

I wanted him to stop breathing.

"We'll have to get him back home," I said. "God-fucking-dammit."

I turned to look at the truck that was speeding away. It was already past Brower Road, almost at the front gate of New Post. They had Sara now, and I didn't know how we were going to get her back.

Lisa took charge of Justin Porter, having us carry him up to her bedroom so she could treat him.

I told the Marchands to hold a line at the gate.

I wanted to find out who gave Justin access to my armour. But that would have to wait.

While Lisa and Fiona looked into making sure that Justin didn't die, I went back downstairs, to put on my riot suit, vest and helmet and tell Graham just what to expect.

"I don't plan on hurting anyone," I said. "They've got a fence along the river but they don't keep an eye on it. Hopefully I can find

Sara."

"There's no way you'll get her out without shooting people," Graham said. "Assuming they don't just take you out first. It's not that hard to aim for your exposed parts."

"Are you volunteering to come with me?"

He looked surprised. "No... sorry, Baptiste... I think this is a bad idea."

"So you'll just opt out, eh?"

"It's a stupid idea," Kayla said.

I hadn't even noticed her standing by the door. I wasn't paying enough attention to what was happening around me; that was a bad sign.

"You have a better idea?" I asked her, trying to not sound too harsh.

"We go and talk to them," she said. "You know... sissy stuff."

"That won't work."

"You don't know that."

"You're right, I don't know." But that didn't mean I could stand the idea of going to New Post and dropping to my knees.

"Think of it this way. They know you're coming either way. So you can sneak around just like they'd expect, or you can walk up to the gate and talk to them. And when that doesn't work, you can always go berserker on them afterwards."

I sighed. "At this point, Kayla, I think if I showed up at the gate they'd just shoot me."

"I know I would," she said. "I mean, if I were them. But they won't shoot me."

"No... not a fucking chance," I said. "You're not going."

"I'll go," Graham said.

"They won't trust either of you," Kayla said.

"You're right," I said. "Normally it would make sense to send Lisa, but since she's already shot at them once today... but I don't think I can allow this, Kayla."

"Do you think they've hurt Sara?" she asked.

"No." I just couldn't see it. They didn't want Sara dead.

"They won't hurt me, either."

"But what if they try to take you into custody?" Graham asked.

"For what?" Kayla asked.

"Conspiracy, maybe..."

"They're not going to touch me. No one wants a war."

Graham shook his head. "They threw Justin Porter out of a moving truck."

"They dumped him because they knew we were coming... they knew Lisa would catch up, and that people would get hurt... their people as well as ours."

"They could have stopped their truck."

"They could have shot Justin first."

"This has gotten so messed up," Graham said.

"It has," I said.

"Then let me try to fix it," Kayla said. "You have to let me try."

I drove the cart while Kayla sat beside me; she was in the spotter's seat, but she seemed too nervous to look at anything, aside from her feet.

I'd made sure everyone back at McCartney Lake was on high alert; New Post would be expecting a visit from me, so there was always the chance that they'd see it as an opportunity to hit us from the rear. They'd been up the deer trails before; what was stopping them from doing it again?

I'd never thought I'd have to consider the possibility that our neighbours might launch a sneak attack. But things were changing so quickly that I knew I couldn't make any assumptions.

Was I making a mistake? Would they actually shoot Kayla, even though she's almost the farthest thing possible from a threat?

I stopped the cart, just out of range of the gate at New Post. I was in full gear, while Kayla only had a vest under her robin's egg blue jacket, and her pink toque instead of a helmet.

"You should take off the toque," I said.

She pulled it off, and her blond hair tumbled out. "It's windy," she said.

"I know... but this way they'll know you're not Lisa, and they should be pretty damned sure you're not me."

"I know this was my idea, but I have to admit... I'm pretty fucking terrified."

"You'll do fine. Just remember that you're too pretty to shoot."

"Graham always says the same thing about you."

She climbed down from the cart and made her way towards the guards at the gate. There were four of them now, instead of two; I took out my binoculars to see all but one take cover behind a parked green pickup.

"Hold your arms out, Kayla," I said. "Let them see that you're unarmed."

She spread out her hands as she walked. She was moving a little quickly, but I worried that telling her to slow down would just add to her anxiety.

I kept my shotgun low; I knew that I'd have no hope of saving her if they decided to shoot. I'd be sure to kill every last one of them for it, but that wouldn't do much for Kayla after the fact.

I'd wanted to give her a handheld, set to broadcast every noise, but she'd made it clear that the last thing she needed was a strange bulge coming from the side of her coat.

The guard who hadn't taken cover behind the truck started toward her, his rifle pointed down at the ground. I could see through the binoculars that it was Sky; I felt like that was a good thing.

Kayla started talking, though I couldn't hear what she was saying.

Sky responded, but he did not smile.

Kayla kept going, gesturing with her hands as she started to argue with him.

Sky seemed calm enough, and after a couple of minutes he shook his head, and then he turned to return to the other men at the gate.

Kayla looked back at me; I could see that she was upset.

I wanted to head towards her, but I stayed where I was.

Slowly she started back toward the cart.

I watched as Sky went back through the gate and made a call on his handheld. The other guards came out from their hiding place behind the truck, but they still kept their eyes on me and the cart.

I waited for Kayla to reach me, wanting to hope for the best, but knowing full well that the news wasn't good.

"Is she okay?" I asked as Kayla came close.

"Apparently," she said. "But they won't let her go."

"What do you mean? They're just going to keep her?"

"They say they don't trust us... they think we're planning to attack."

"That's exactly what they're forcing us to do. Did you tell them that this is unacceptable?"

"I did."

"Did you tell them they have no right to keep her?"

"I did."

"Goddammit... what the fuck are we supposed to do now?" I knew that I was crying; I hoped that she couldn't tell.

She climbed onto the cart and wrapped her arms around me. "Don't worry, Baptiste... we'll figure this out."

She reached out and wrapped her arm around my neck.

"Don't cry," she said.

"Don't watch."

She started to laugh. "Sorry... I know I shouldn't be laughing. We'll get her back."

"I know we will," I said, not that I really knew anything. "I just worry about how she's doing."

"They won't hurt her."

I just nodded and hugged her back.

I confronted Matt about the armour. He'd just come back from flirting with Fiona, and he had that stupid grin on his face.

"I know you gave a key to Justin," I said.

"For the gate?"

"You know exactly what I'm talking about. You let him into the chest and he took my armour to use on New Post. I know it was you."

"Maybe it was Lisa."

"Don't even bother trying, Matt. This is your fault, you stupid piece of shit. Your fault that Sara's gone... your fault that we might end up going to war with those people."

"I didn't give him my key."

"It was never your key to give."

"I didn't give him anything."

"You gave him your key. Don't lie to me."

"I don't have to stand around here and be accused of something I didn't do."

I shoved him against the wall of the living room, almost knocking down that date sign I'd put up, from the bank. Today is... the day I finally put two bullets in Matt's tiny little brain.

I wished I could.

"You like Fiona," I said. "I know you do."

"Yes... I think she's great."

"Well you may have just killed her, Matt. Doing whatever you want without thinking, or asking anyone else if it even makes sense... you may have just killed the girl you were hoping to see naked. It's your fault, Matt. It's all you, buddy. All you."

"You can think whatever you want about me... I don't care. I'm doing my best to protect the people I care about."

"By starting a war?"

"By standing up for us. They're just waiting for a chance to get us, Baptiste. I know that. Justin knows that. You're the only one who doesn't."

"All I know, Matt, is that I don't want to see you again tonight. So find a place to be that isn't here."

"Whatever," he said. He shook his head and walked out to the porch.

I'm sure he was hoping he'd get to stay with Fiona.

I knew he'd end up at the Porters.

I hope he decides to stay there for a while.

TODAY IS THURSDAY, JANUARY 10TH.

IT'S BEEN three days of nothing.

We've sent five messages to New Post. Those messages have gone ignored.

Kayla wants to head back to the gate and talk to them.

I know that won't work.

Assuming Gerald Archibald didn't bleed to death, I'm sure he's convinced himself that Sara Vachon is his best leverage to keep me from taking him out.

There haven't been any attempts to steal our supplies... not yet. But I know they'll be back. And when we catch them, they'll try to wave Sara's life in my face.

They'll keep her for as long as I live. Maybe longer.

They won't give her back.

The only thing we can do is take her back.

One of the side effects of living in such a small world is that it's pretty hard to sneak around. This is why we don't have things like surprise birthday parties, and why everyone seems to know exactly who's sleeping with who; I learned that last one the hard way.

When I decided to start up an old fashioned conspiracy, I quickly realized that finding a place to meet might suck up most of my energy.

I could have gotten Lisa to distract Graham, but I wanted her opinion. So I had to get creative and ask Rihanna for help. She had no problem giving us a hand, and she came up with a way to keep Graham busy for a few hours; it's not a big secret that Graham can't say no when you ask him for a favour.

So Graham was over at the Porters, giving Rihanna some advice on setting up a miniature greenhouse, and we all met up in the barn to talk, all of us meaning anyone who wasn't Fiona or Gwyneth. And Graham, of course.

Justin Porter was there as well, his left ankle sprained and his face swollen, and Alain Tremblay came too, showing an aggressive side that reminded me more of his brother.

We didn't invite the Marchands; we still didn't know them well enough.

But I did let Matt be there. I needed help, and I could go back to hating him tomorrow.

"If we do this," I said, "there's really no way to smooth things over again. We'll basically be at war with New Post and possibly the Walkers. And Ryan Stems."

"Big loss," Justin said.

"This will go better if you don't talk," Lisa said.

That seemed to shut him up.

"The way I see things," I said, "there are two ways to do this. We can go in with just three or four of us, and keep some people back at home keeping watch with Graham and the Marchands. Or we can take a chance and go all in."

"If we all go," Lisa said, "will we all go in together?"

"I was thinking we'd have two groups. Three coming in from the front, while the other three sneak in off the river. They'll bring their people out to the gate, thinning things out for my team."

"Your team," Alain said. "And who leads the other?"

"Justin leads the other," I said.

"With a sprained ankle?"

"Me as a gimp is vastly superior to you at your best, Alain," Justin said. "So we just want to tie them down at the gate?"

"You got it," I said. "Make a lot of noise then back off a little. Don't lose sight of the fact that you're a decoy; don't try to take them out. But when you start backing off, don't let them think it's a rout... just keep it orderly so they think twice about chasing after you."

"And what if they do chase after us?"

"You'll have the pickup truck we got from New Post," I said. "That's assuming the thing is roadworthy, after Lisa put those nice holes in it. Take the truck and turn onto Birchill Road. Do *not* lead them back to McCartney Lake."

"And you're putting me in here somewhere?" Kayla asked.

"Have you ever even fired a gun?" Justin asked.

"I have."

From what I'd seen, the only time she'd ever done it was when I'd been trying to teach her. And I still hadn't started up those lessons again.

"You're extra padding," I said. "You, Justin and Matt make three. I'm really only expecting Justin to do the actual shooting. I'm not even sure we have enough guns."

"I can shoot," Matt said.

"I know... but Justin might actually hit the things he aims for."

"So I'm going with you and Lisa?" Alain asked.

"Are you okay with that?" I asked.

"Absolutely."

"Do we have any idea where Sara's being held?" Lisa asked.

"We don't know anything," I said. "But I'd guess she's at the band office."

"Or she could be in any other building on the reserve," Justin said.

"It's possible."

"So if she's not at the band office, we're going to wander from house to house looking for her?"

"If she's not at the band office, we'll take a hostage of our own. Maybe we'll be lucky and grab the chief."

"I like that," Matt said.

"I want to be clear," I said. "We don't want to kill anyone if we don't have to."

"And what if we have to?" Justin asked.

"This isn't for revenge... just remember that." Part of me knew I was lying.

"So we're really going to do this?" Kayla asked.

"We head out tonight at 6pm. I want everyone to meet back here at 5:15."

"What about Graham?" Justin asked.

"He'll need to stay here either way. I don't think he'll try to stop us."

I didn't want to consider how to deal with Graham if he did.

Fiona asked me to come over for lunch. I didn't really feel like it, since I had shit to do, and Gwyneth would probably be there to hate on me, but I was happy that Fiona was talking to me at all, after everything that has happened.

She started us off by barking out a list of ingredients for me to find.

"Now I'm mostly just an omelette guy, remember?" I said as I pulled down a bag of pinto beans. "I don't really know what any non-omelette ingredients look like."

"Nice try," she said. "I've seen you find your way around just fine when there are ice cream toppings involved."

"Okay... so that covers red peppers and chocolate chips."

I walked over to a small upright freezer to pull out some cheese.

"There's none left up here," Fiona said.

"So that's why I'm here," I said. "I'm just your basement delivery service."

"It's a crawlspace. But that's not it, actually... you're here because I need to talk to you."

"About the cheese?"

She wasn't smiling.

"What is it?" I asked.

"I'm not stupid, Baptiste. Just because I don't live with you guys anymore doesn't mean I don't notice when almost everyone at Mc-Cartney Lake runs down to your barn for secret meetings."

"Oh..."

"And yes, I know pretty much everything else you try and keep from me."

"Like what?"

"Like everything, Baptiste. What happened to Marc Tremblay, what happened to those girls at Silver Queen Lake, what happened to the Girards... what you did to Sara."

My heart started pounding. "What do you mean? What did she say to you?"

"She didn't say anything... but I can still tell. I always knew when my father hit my mom, too."

"Fuck."

"Don't you see what's happening to you? You're changing, Baptiste... all of this violence is... it's poisoning you."

"I don't think it works that way."

"It definitely does work that way. You've been around so much of it over the past few years. Being on the Protection Committee, and then The Fires and everything else... you can't go through that without some of it seeping in."

"You sound like Sara," I said, trying to make it a compliment.

"Oh, no... I'm not Sara. She was just letting it happen. But I'm not going to sit by and let you turn into a monster. You killed someone last week, remember? And not by accident, either... you took him outside and you shot him."

"I had to..."

"That's not what I mean. When you had the accident with Marc... you felt so guilty that you basically shut down for two days. And you guys weren't exactly close."

"And I haven't really thought about that kid at Helena."

"His name was Rasheed. Maybe you're telling yourself that you had no choice... maybe you didn't... but you should still feel something about it."

"I know."

"What do you think will happen when you guys try to get Sara back?"

"Hopefully we'll get her out of there."

"You're going to kill again," Fiona said. "You know you will."

I didn't want to lie to her.

"Please, Baptiste," she said. "Don't go to New Post."

"But what about Sara?"

"Sara will be safer if you don't come for her. I think you know that."

"I'm not sure about that."

"Please, Baptiste."

"We can handle this, Fiona. We can get Sara back and give New Post and the whole Mushkegowuk Nation a reason to steer clear of us."

"Even you don't believe that. If you attack New Post, Ryan Syms will come for you. But that isn't what this is about. I know you can rationalize this rescue mission no matter what. I want you to think about what you're turning into."

"I'm one of the good guys. You said you trusted me, Fiona. Don't you trust me anymore?"

"It's not about trust. You can't go to New Post."

"I'm going to go down and get the cheese."

I found the trapdoor and squeezed down into the crawlspace. I bent my head and made my way to the chest freezer they'd taken from our place.

It's funny the way you can ignore something for a good long while, until the very second that someone points it out. Then it's like it's out there for the world to see, and you start feeling embarrassed about something that wasn't troubling you at all before.

It was getting easier living with the tough decisions. At first you feel like that's a good thing, because if you always regretted every choice you'd stop doing anything. But with time you end up too far out, where you start making mistakes and you don't even care that you're making them, when you start losing control simply because you don't bother holding on to it.

That happened to me once before, on the other side of the world, when I started seeing the Afghans I was supposed to help as enemies I needed to brush aside.

That happened to a lot of soldiers I knew.

Fiona was right; it was happening again. I was losing perspective.

If I went down to New Post, I'd kill a lot of people. I'm not sure I'd even be able to bring Sara back with me. And I wasn't sure if I'd want to be the man who'd come home after something like that.

I grabbed the cheese from the freezer and made my way back to the kitchen. I dropped the cheese off on the counter and leaned over to give Fiona a kiss on the forehead.

I walked out without saying anything. I checked my tablet for Lisa's location and walked over to see her. She was out with Graham and Matt, strengthening the gate on Nelson Road.

"We're not going to go through with it," I said.

"Why the hell not?" she asked.

"Because I can't do it, Lisa... okay?"

She nodded. "I'll tell the others."

Graham was staring at me, but he seemed more concerned than upset. I have a feeling that Lisa hadn't really kept it a secret from him.

Something's changed with the two of them. They were different before Christmas, on-again, off-again. That's over now.

They'll be the ones to outlast the rest of us.

Of course, this year will probably outlast me.

I made my way back to Fiona and Gwyneth's cottage, hoping to make it in time for lunch.

I was relieved when Fiona told me that Gwyneth had sent her regrets.

Kayla was waiting for me when I got back after lunch. She was sitting on the couch, staring at her tablet, but the moment I stepped inside, she stood up and walked over to me.

"You just called it off," she said. "Just like that?"

She sounded angry.

"I thought you'd be happy with that," I said. "No one gets hurt."

"And I don't have to share you with her... is that what you think of me?"

"Uh... what?"

"You really think I want Sara gone."

"I didn't say that."

"I tried to get her back, Baptiste. I pleaded with Sky."

"I know you did."

"You say that... but you don't want anything to do with me now."

"What are you talking about?"

She started to cry. "You haven't even touched me... not since she was taken."

It had been longer than that. I hadn't touched her since we'd caught those kids, when Sara had let them go and then run away... not long after Kayla and I had finally talked about being together.

I'd been in a holding pattern. I hadn't decided what to do And with Sara being taken away from me...

"I'm sorry, Kayla," I said. "I love you."

"That's your stock answer, Baptiste. You love me... you love Sara... is there any woman you don't love?"

"I can't deal with this right now. I have shit to deal with."

"You can't blame me for this. It's not fair. I didn't do this to her."

She turned away.

I grabbed her shoulder and brought her back to me.

I kissed her gently on the lips.

"I love you, Kayla," I said. "It's just hard to focus on anything other than getting one of our people back."

"Do you blame me for what's happened?"

"What? No... it's not your fault. If anything, it's my fault. I should have dealt with Justin a long time ago. And I still haven't dealt with him. I should have let him die in that ditch."

"Do you still want me?"

"Yes. I still want you."

"Then prove it." She was still crying.

"Like right now?"

She nodded. "Upstairs."

She turned and walked over to the stairs.

I followed, even though it was the last thing on my mind.

We went into my bedroom.

We took off our clothes and we laid together under the sheets.

I rubbed her back, her shoulder, and her neck, occasionally pressing my lips against her skin.

That was all she seemed to need.

After a few minutes she fell asleep.

TODAY IS FRIDAY, JANUARY 11TH.

I RECEIVED a message this morning, before I'd even woken up.

It was sent from Gerald Archibald, but it wasn't Gerald Archibald. It was Ryan Stems. Evidently, Matt hadn't switched back to disabling their access.

We need to talk. This whole situation has gotten messed up. Let's meet, just the two of us. Hwy 652 over the Abitibi River at noon. Bring an appetite.

"It's a trap," Kayla said when I showed her my tablet. "He wants to take you into custody for the attack on Archibald."

"He doesn't need to trap me," I said. "If he wanted to, he could crash through our gates and shoot every last one of us."

"That's a happy thought."

"It's a happy day."

"You're not going to go..."

"I'm a curious person, Kayla. I have to find out what he wants."

"He wants you dead."

"I don't think so. Gerald Archibald might want me dead. Maybe. But not Ryan Stems."

"Stems said the opposite when he was here. Man... you are going to feel pretty stupid when he shoots you in the head. And you know what? I'll just laugh and say 'I told you so'."

"You'd laugh?"

"I'd laugh." She leaned in and gave me a kiss. "Seriously, though... don't go."

But she knew I was going.

✍

I told Lisa what was happening, and she and Graham went with me on the cart — in full gear — to 652, while Kayla and Matt headed over to the Marchands, to see about setting up another defensive line across the road.

"He's going to kill you," Graham said.

"He won't kill you," Lisa said. "But if he does... well, oops."

I laughed. I guess it was a nervous laugh.

"So if he tries to take you?" Lisa asked.

"Run up and shoot him," I said. "Or shoot me. Just shoot somebody."

"Will do, boss."

Graham stopped the cart at a driveway to one of the burnt-out houses, two back from the bridge.

I hopped down and started walking toward the river, with just my SIG and my vest. Graham and Lisa had an extra helmet for me, but it wouldn't do me any good back on the cart.

As I approached the bridge, I could see Stems through the metal gate, sitting at what appeared to be a folding wood table, like you'd see at a garden reception. He was sitting alone, but I could see a couple of trucks on the far side of the bridge.

He raised a hand straight into the air, some kind of wave.

I did the same.

I reached the gate and pulled out my key.

"It's a good gate," Stems said. "I'm not even sure we could bust through it without a tank or something."

"Then I guess you'd better get yourself a tank," I said.

"Working on it."

I disabled the alarm with my dongle, and stepped through the gate. I relocked and reactivated on the other side.

"We're thinking of getting our own gate for this bridge," Stems said. "Come and sit down, Baptiste. I think you'll like what we've got for lunch."

It was a little cold for dinner on a patio, but I sat down.

There was nothing on the table.

"Where's Sara Vachon?" I asked.

"We'll talk about her. Don't worry... we'll get there."

I saw a young woman walking toward us. It was Stems' young wife, Anna, carrying two plates.

She placed one down in front of me, and then the other in front of Stems. On my plate was a stack of four pancakes, with a square of butter on the top.

"Thank you," I said to her.

She nodded, and walked back toward the trucks.

"There's more," Stems said. "Hold on."

Another young native woman came to the table, with a porcelain pitcher of syrup and a matching bowl. In the bowl were fresh bananas, cut into pieces.

I thanked her.

She smiled and kept standing by the table.

"All the way from Georgia," Stems said.

"That's something."

He smiled. "I'm trying to impress you, Baptiste."

"I'm already seeing someone."

"These bananas came up the Mississippi on a barge. Then they put them on a truck and drove them across Michigan and dropped them off in Sudbury. That's where we got them."

"The Mississippi doesn't run through Georgia."

"That was the abbreviated version. Anyway, Anna's sister Genevieve went down to Sudbury and picked them up, just for us." He looked up at the young woman beside the table. "Thank you again, Genevieve."

"My pleasure," she said. She smiled at me again, and then she left the table.

I had a feeling that Stems was trying to keep me distracted with his cavalcade of pretty girls. Apparently my reputation has spread.

"You're supposed to ask how she got to Sudbury," Stems said. "Come on, Baptiste... you have to know a little bit about the local geography to get the full effect."

"I know the fastest way to get from Mississauga to Markham during rush hour. That's about it."

"Humour me."

"Okay... so how did she get to Sudbury?"

"Through Timmins. You see Baptiste, I can send my wife's little sister — with a light escort — through a town run by a motorcycle gang, without the slightest need to worry for her well-being. Because the Mushkegowuk Nation is strong enough to earn their respect."

"But not strong enough to scare off a few guys with painted

helmets and mounted machine guns."

That didn't seem to irk him as much as I'd hoped. "Do you see them anywhere?"

"I don't get out much these days."

"They're gone. Tucked their tails between their legs and run off home to Detour Lake."

"Detour Lake, eh? Not sure I buy that. One of those assholes reminded me a lot of you."

"Ruggedly handsome?"

"So fucking ugly he keeps his stupid helmet on. Thinks he's a coyote trapped in a pervert's body... likes to have fun with teenage girls... and seems to prefer it if those girls aren't having fun right back. Sound familiar?"

He chuckled. "Don't bother trying to make me hate you, Baptiste. I'm there already. Didn't stop me from saving your ass from those little boys and their technicals."

"You saved me, did you? And the proof is where, exactly?"

"The proof is in your other girls still being snug in their beds. No one's taken them yet, have they?"

"Is that a threat?"

He sighed. "I'm going to eat now."

He took off his gloves.

He took a spoonful of bananas and spread them over his pancakes. Then he drowned the plate in syrup and started eating.

I did the same, more or less, keeping my gloves on.

I hadn't eaten bananas in two years; they were gone from the shelves months before the comet struck.

"It's good," Stems said. "Right? I didn't even like bananas before."

"What kind of monster doesn't like bananas?"

"So Gerald's okay, by the way."

"Oh. Yeah... that's good."

"He doesn't blame you, Baptiste. He blames Justin Porter."

"Same here. So he'll trade Sara for Justin then?"

"I've told Gerald that this fight is over."

"What does that even mean?"

"You're not a threat to us, Baptiste."

"Thanks."

"We have three strategic rivals. And one rogue state."

"And which one are we?"

"You're not even on the list."

"Again... thanks..."

"I'm not worried about The Souls, or Aiguebelle, or Sudbury right now. We have an understanding with each of them. But I am worried about our little North Korea."

"Detour Lake."

"There could be up to three hundred people up there. And twice as many guns. And they're running out of food, with no way to replenish."

"No way short of coming over here and taking some."

"This way or Aiguebelle," Stems said. "And it's my job to make sure they head east instead of west. That's where you come in."

"So I do merit a mention?"

"You're our buffer state, Baptiste."

"I'm thrilled."

"You guys don't have near enough supplies to feed Detour Lake, and they know that if they attack you they're basically declaring war on us. So it buys us a little breathing room, some time to prepare if they make their move."

"I'm your canary?"

"Or guinea pig. Whatever you prefer."

"So you're asking me if I want to be your buffer?"

Stems chuckled. "No... I'm telling you how it is. Do you think anyone ever asked Afghanistan for permission?"

"And it's worked out so well for everyone."

"Look... this is win-win. You get to chart your own course, look after your own... and we get to continue bringing a better life to the people of the Mushkegowuk Nation."

"And you'll bring Sara home."

"Sara isn't coming home, Baptiste."

I kicked my chair back and stood. I pulled out my SIG and pointed it at his head.

He didn't flinch.

"Where is she?" I asked.

"Put the gun away so we can talk."

I put it away. I could always bring it out again.

I sat down.

"I had to give Gerald something," Stems said.

411

"What did he do to her?"

"Not like that, Baptiste. She's safe."

"Then where the hell is she?"

"Kapuskasing. She lives with Genevieve."

"No, she lives here with me. And it's time for her to come home."

"Gerald doesn't trust you. Can you blame him? So Sara will remain under the protection of the Mushkegowuk Nation until I can convince the Chief and Council of Taykwa Tagamou that you and Justin Porter no longer pose a threat."

"I have no problem handing Justin Porter over to you. You can make breakfast sausage out of him if you want. But Sara comes home."

"You didn't hear me, Baptiste. They see *you* as a threat, too. Now I told Gerald that his people are to stay out of your territory from here on in. He's promised to do that."

"Oh... he promised..."

"Unlike you, I have a way of making sure people don't lie to me. There won't be any more theft of supplies. There won't be any more trespassing of any sort."

"The only way to fix New Post is to move them to your side of the river," I said. "If the river is the border, the river is the border."

"I'm already working on that. There's no point in having them on your side of the Abitibi when there's plenty of room in the Nation."

"And if you really want peace, you need to bring Sara back here."

"She's not coming back. Get used to it. And don't bother shooting me. Neither of us are any good to her dead."

"Fuck you, Stems."

"Fuck me? This is good for all of us, Baptiste."

I stood up from the table. I had to get away from Ryan Stems. I wanted to kill him more than I wanted to continue living.

"We're calling you East Abitibi," Stems said as I walked back to the gate and pulled out my dongle and key. "Has a bit of an East German sound to it."

I didn't have anything to say.

I didn't know what to do.

"A buffer state?" Lisa said as we headed back home. "He's serious?"

"He's serious," I said.

"For how long?" Graham asked. "You know eventually he'll want our side of the river, too."

"Maybe someday... but not right now. For right now he wants to leave us alone. And move New Post across the river "

"What about Justin?" Lisa asked. "Is Stems wanting you to hand him over?"

"Stems isn't asking for anything," I said. "And he's not giving us anything in return. He refuses to let Sara come home."

"We can't accept that."

I didn't know how to respond.

"Baptiste..." she said. "We're not accepting that..."

"Stems told me he's sent her to Kapuskasing."

"We can find a way to get there. There are ways around any road-blocks Stems may have put up."

"Snowmobiles," Graham said. "We could travel almost anywhere on those."

"I appreciate this, guys," I said. "But it's not going to work. We can't risk everyone to save Sara."

"She's part of our family," Graham said.

"Sometimes families fall apart."

"What's happened to you, Baptiste?" Lisa asked "When did you become such a wimp?"

"That's not fair."

"You'd've never responded to me like that a month ago. You'd have told me to go fuck myself. Why can't I go fuck myself?"

"You can go fuck yourself all you want... but there's nothing we can do. Sara's gone."

"That's bullshit," Graham said.

"Really?" I said. "Now you start swearing?"

"We're not giving up on Sara. Some of us want her to come home."

"You want to try that again?"

"I'm not going to apologize for the truth, Baptiste. If you and Sara hadn't split up, there's no way you'd let this stand."

"Dammit, Graham. I haven't said I'm going to let this stand. I'm not going to let Ryan Stems get away with this. Or Gerald Archibald.

But that doesn't mean we should run off to Kapuskasing, against a hundred armed men."

"Then what does it mean?" Lisa asked.

"I don't know. But I would think that you guys would know me well enough to know that it wouldn't end like this. Do I think we can get Sara back? Fuck no. But if we can't, we'll make sure that these assholes regret the day they took her from us. That's how it is with us. That's how it is with me."

And I'll do the same to the men who killed Ant and his Natalie.

Kayla took me on a walk this afternoon. She told me that she had something to show me.

I had a feeling I knew what it was.

Kayla only had so many secrets.

She took me to the Williams cottage, to where Fiona and Gwyneth were now living, and where Sara had once hoped to get away from me.

We walked behind the cottage, toward the trees, to a large wood shed with a padlock on the door.

"Ant's shed," she said. "I guess it's my shed, now."

She took a keyring out of her jacket pocket and unlocked the door. She led me inside.

"No power?" she said. "No problem."

She knelt down and flicked a switch.

I heard the hum of a generator.

The shed lit up.

"You're using fuel for this?" I asked.

"Oh, hush."

She led me to the center of a workbench that ran along three of the walls.

"Ant's pet projects," she said. "You know what's great about men who are really short?"

"What?"

"They're always looking for ways to even the odds." She reached down and pulled up what seem to be a green fishing tackle box. "You'll like these... I hope."

She opened the box and pulled out a large bundle wrapped in butcher paper. She laid the bundle out on the table and unwrapped it.

"What the fuck?" I said.

"You recognize them?"

"Pipe grenades..."

Six of them.

I'd thought Ant's pyrotechnics went as far as cherry bombs and homemade firecrackers.

This was a much bigger deal.

"We've got three more boxes of 'em. But wait... there's more ."

She picked up another tackle box, only red instead of green. She opened it up and pulled out another bundle.

"A nail grenade," I said. "So this is what you guys were doing in here?"

"There's a lot more. That stuff to put out fires is in here. and even some stuff to start them... Ant wasn't sure if he should tell you. He was worried about what you'd say. This isn't exactly an honourable way to fight a war."

"Wars aren't honourable either way. Why are you showing me this? Why now? Why didn't you tell me about this before?"

"Ant didn't want you to know. He didn't want you to think less of him. I didn't want you to, either."

"I don't think less of him. I'm proud of him. This doesn't change that."

"Will it help?"

"What?"

"Will this stuff help to get Sara back?"

"I... I don't know. We can't get her back by blowing things up. But this could go a long way toward making us safer. That's important, too."

She nodded. "I know it is."

"We'll do what we can to get her back. You know that."

I gave her a hug.

I think both of us were crying.

"I've showed you mine," she said. "Now will you show me yours?"

"I don't have anything to show."

"That's such a big lie, Baptiste. Just let me in a little. That's how this works."

"What is it you want me to tell you about?"

"Anything," she said.

"I have something that Justin can't know about, that only Lisa and Graham have seen."

"The army machine gun?"

"Shit."

"Yeah... the whole world knows. That's what happens when you shoot the goddamn thing. What else you got?"

"I don't want to tell you where the drugs are."

"Why not? You don't trust me?"

"It's to keep you safe."

"Seriously? I'll tell you something, Baptiste. People are going to assume that I know. So if you think that me not knowing actually helps me..."

"It's off Murphy Road. By that pond that smells like gasoline."

"That doesn't sound so well hidden."

"It's underground. Looks like an old covered well." She didn't need to know that we'd moved them.

"There... was that so much to ask? Now we can be best friends."

And then she gave my ass a pinch.

10

TODAY IS MONDAY, JANUARY 14TH.

I DREAMT about Sara last night.

We'd met on the bridge, at a table like the one Stems had used. She asked me how I'd been, and I told her how I just wanted her to come home, and how I wanted to drown Stems in the Abitibi for trying to turn that home into some kind of buffer state.

She'd laughed, saying that being a buffer wasn't so bad. "Look at me," she said, "Vachon *Tampon*, remember? It's my job to stand in the middle and plug up the ick."

"Come home, Sara," I'd told her.

"One day, Baptiste... as soon as you deserve it."

I woke up and I felt like a piece of shit.

Things are getting easier, and it makes me feel guilty.

Sara's gone, Fiona's moved out, Matt spends most of his time out in the woods, trying to rekindle Ant's old firebreak project for some unknown reason. Lisa and Graham are handling the goats, and Kayla feeds the dogs and takes care of the chickens.

I don't do much of anything.

And I'm starting to like it.

I wake up with Kayla beside me.

We go downstairs and make some eggs and/or toast.

We don't worry about what anyone else is eating.

Then Kayla checks the chickens and spends some time playing fetch or tug with Carcassonne, and I may go out with her, if I feel like it; otherwise, I'll do the dishes or clean the guns or just sit on my ass in the living room screwing around with my tablet.

I'm not even writing much in this journal anymore.

We haven't heard a peep from New Post, and there hasn't been a single visit from snowmobiles, or unknown footsteps in the snow. Those Spirit Assholes from Detour Lake are gone, too, and I like to pretend that their absence is permanent, even if I know they'll be back eventually, once their supplies get low.

The thing is, I don't know how many supplies they have.

Or how many people they have. More than fifty, less than a thousand. I think.

I don't really know anything, really.

After the chickens and the eggs, and fun time with Carcass, Kayla and I might go and sit together in the living room and read, or we might watch a movie together.

Sometimes Lisa or Graham or even Matt will come in and glare at us, shaking their head or making a comment about the two lazy asses, but I really don't give a shit.

Well, aside from feeling guilty.

That usually hits me at night.

After a dinner of whatever's easy, Kayla and I will move upstairs to my room. We'll read or watch or just lay together, and eventually we'll either make love or she'll roll over and fall asleep.

And I'll lay in bed thinking about Sara.

On really bad nights I'll start thinking about Ant, too.

And that's when I start to wonder if I'll ever fix this family.

TODAY IS TUESDAY, JANUARY 15TH.

THE ALARM came from the gate on Nelson Road.

That likely meant New Post.

Lisa and I took the grain truck on what could be its last trip, since the arrow was now a long way past the E.

We threw on the gear, all of it, and Lisa held the Mossberg as I drove.

I stopped a good fifty meters from the gate, turning the truck to block the road as best I could, with my side toward the gate.

New Post knew we had an alarm.

It could be a setup.

Lisa climbed out and took position behind the engine block.

I followed behind.

She put the binoculars up to her eyes and looked up the road.

"It's Sky," she said. "Can't see anyone else. Can I shoot him?"

"Is he armed?"

"He's hiding it if he is."

"I guess Gerald isn't up to dropping by. I'll head up to the gate. You know the drill."

"Shoot anyone who shoots you," she said.

"Try to shoot them *before* they shoot me."

She nodded.

I walked up the road, my SIG in my belt.

"You couldn't just send a message?" I asked him as I reached the gate.

"This is a face-to-face thing," he said.

"I had one of those with your buddy Stems last week."

"He's not my buddy."

"So he's mine now?"

"Katie's here, too."

I looked around. "Where?"

"Back at the truck."

"So she's moved in with you at New Post? I would've thought it would be the other way around."

"I think that might be racist."

"I can't tell anymore."

"Are we safe here, Baptiste?"

"What?"

"Can I tell Katie to come up the road?"

I nodded. "I'm not going to shoot you, Sky."

Sky slowly reached into his pocket and took out a handheld radio. "We're good," he said into the transceiver. He put the radio away. "She'll be a minute."

"What are you here for, Sky?"

"To talk to you, Baptiste."

I sighed. "I don't really go in for mystery... I'm not really a guy who likes to guess. Just tell me what's going on."

"Katie and I are leaving the district. And we want you to come with us."

That I wouldn't have guessed on my own.

I decided to call a meeting of everyone at McCartney Lake, since with Fiona and Gwyneth starting their own "household" it would be pretty tough to invite them and not the Marchands.

And that meant that the Tremblays and Porters would need to come, too.

The dining room was standing room only, about as busy as it was for that fleeting moment on New Year's Eve when Fiona had brought out the homemade mozzarella sticks; you don't get much mozzarella these days.

Everyone other than Gwyneth was crammed around the table, some sitting, but most standing; she was out in the living room. She'd be able to hear us, and I doubt she'd have wanted to speak up anyway.

Since Sara's gone, Kayla took her place as chair; I know Graham wanted the job, since he was sitting in Sara's spot, but when it comes to meetings about leaving or staying put, he's not a man I can trust.

"We're going to Temiskaming," Katie said. "I refuse to be part of a system that treats some people as less than equal."

I didn't point out that the system didn't bother her before her family became subservient to the Nation.

"No one makes it to Temiskaming," Justin said. "I used to take people to practically everywhere else, but even I wouldn't risk a trip down there."

"What is so bad about down there?" Eva Marchand asked. "People tell me that, but they do not explain it."

"Ryan Stems wants us as a buffer between the Mushkegowuk Nation and Detour Lake," I said. "Any trip to Temiskaming runs through the buffer between Timmins and Aiguebelle. You don't want to go there."

"Why?"

"It's like *Mad Max*."

"What is 'Mad Max'?"

"*The Road Warrior*, then. Bikers with guns, pickup trucks with guns, souped-up Honda coupes with guns..."

"Souls of Flesh runs Timmins," Justin said.

"And who runs the buffer?" Graham asked.

"No one," I said. "And everyone... it varies."

"We think we've found a route that will get us through," Katie said. "Through Twin Falls, and backroads 'til Hwy 101."

"Your problems start at 101," I said. "And they continue all the way to Temiskaming. There's only one person who believes he's strong enough to get you past Souls of Flesh. And I'm sure if you thought Stems would help, you'd have already asked him."

"They have observers in Temiskaming," Sky said. "From the African Union. They're even sending aid now... but it's sporadic."

That sounded like an unsubstantiated rumour to me. But I didn't point that out, either.

"I'm not saying that Temiskaming isn't lovely this time of year," I said. "I'm saying that you won't make it."

"That's why we're asking for your help," Katie said. "If you guys come with us, we'll be strong enough to push through."

"No... we won't. Most of us would die."

Katie shook her head. "I can't believe that."

"It doesn't matter if you want to believe it. It's how life works."

"We're here to discuss this," Graham said. "So that's what we'll do. Hear all sides."

"Maybe let the chair decide how this will go," I said, looking over at Kayla and trying not to seem smug.

"Everyone should get a chance," Kayla said. "Isn't that how this goes? We can start with Graham."

"Thanks, Kayla," Graham said.

She grinned. "Just call me Madam Chair."

I wasn't sure what was so damned funny.

"We aren't safe here," Graham said. "Things are quiet at the moment, but we know that won't last. Detour Lake is running out of supplies, and the Mushkegowuk Nation is pushing up against us and not even letting us cross the river. It won't be long before things get bloody."

"So let's hurry up and get ourselves killed?" I asked.

"If we go together, we'll have the numbers on our side."

"We'll be the tastiest prize in six months."

"Baptiste," Kayla said, "just let him talk." I was starting to wonder if I should have asked one of the dogs to chair the meeting.

"We should go," Graham said. "They won't be expecting a large group coming through in winter. They won't be prepared."

"It doesn't take much preparation to shoot someone," Justin said.

"You'll get your turn, Justin. Just let me talk."

"Then say something that makes sense."

"Enough," Kayla said. "Do you have anything else to add, Graham?"

He straightened up in Sara's old chair, like he was about to make a speech. "I want to raise my future children somewhere that's safe. I'm willing to take some risks to get that chance."

Hands shot up across the room.

"How 'bout you, Eva?" Kayla said.

"Thank you, *ma chère*," Eva said. "I believe that Monsieur Baptiste is correct about the dangers of travel. But we know that it will not be safe here for much longer. I have lost half of my family in the last two years, most of them in one day because of a handful of men from Detour Lake. My family will not survive an attack from a hundred more. We should try the road."

Kayla nodded to Alain Tremblay.

I didn't know which way he'd go.

"My brother is dead," he said. "He died just across the river.

Maybe if he'd slipped and fell two years ago instead of last month, he'd have been picked up by an ambulance and taken to the hospital. Maybe he'd still be alive. And when it's my turn to have an accident, there won't be any ambulance for me up here, either. Then his kids, and mine, won't have a father or an uncle. Maybe in Temiskaming we won't have to worry about dying so easily."

"But you very well could die on the way," I said.

"It's not your turn," Kayla told me. She pointed at Rihanna.

"The road isn't safe," Rihanna said. "And even if we could somehow get through, there's no reason to believe Temiskaming has it any easier. Rumours... just rumours, of international observers, a trickle of foreign aid... what makes it any better than a refugee camp? Twenty people at McCartney Lake are easier to feed and shelter than twenty thousand somewhere else. We have farm equipment now, don't we? And a way to keep that equipment running? We can plant crops in a few months."

"We need more than crops," Graham said.

"We let you talk," Rihanna said. "Now it's my turn. The risk of staying is far less than the risk of leaving. No one can argue differently."

Kayla nodded to Lisa.

"I'm arguing differently," Lisa said. "There will be a war. Detour Lake will run out of food, and they will come. They will take everything we have and then they will push through, toward New Post and the Walkers. Even if Ryan Stems drives them back... even if he kills every last one of them, it'll be too late for us."

"They're preppers," Kayla said. "They probably have several years' worth of supplies."

"I'm still talking," Lisa said.

"Sorry."

"We don't know what they have up there. And they don't know what we have. No one knows anything."

"That's not exactly true," Justin said. "I know what they've got."

Lisa shook her head. "Yeah, right."

"It's no secret that Marc and I ran some people up to Detour Lake. We ran them up... all the way up."

"You've been to Detour Lake," I said. "You've seen their setup."

"You guys already know they've converted the plant into a refinery for biofuel... they're not hiding that. Back in September, we let the Walkers bring up how many loads of wheat flour and canola seed?"

"At least ten truckloads. Not sure of the breakdown..."

"They took some lye up there, too. And they trucked back who knows how many barrels of diesel from Detour Lake."

"So they have flour," Lisa said. "But how long can that last?"

"A long time," I said. "That plus what they have in storage, and what they can find in the forest and pull out of the lakes... sounds like it could be awhile before they start starving."

"They'll come sooner," Graham said. "They'll come the moment they feel they have the advantage."

"They don't have the advantage. Stems is stronger."

"Stems has an entire district to defend. He can't be everywhere at once."

I knew Graham was right. Stems wasn't enough of a deterrent. Neither were we.

"What about Sara?" Fiona asked. "Are we just supposed to pack up and leave without her?"

"We're no good to her dead," Graham said. "We'll get to Temiskaming and then we'll regroup. We'll come up with a way to get her back."

"We're not forgetting about her," Lisa said. "She matters to all of us."

"I don't believe you," Fiona said. "We won't see her again if we leave."

Lisa looked upset. "That's not fair, Fiona. Sara is my friend, too."

"You have friends?" Justin asked.

"More than you."

"We're getting off-topic," Kayla said.

I stood up from my chair. "It's my turn to speak," I said.

Kayla nodded.

"It's too dangerous," I said. "I'm not going. It's that simple."

"What the hell does that mean?" Lisa asked.

"It means that I'm not going."

"So you're going to stay here by yourself?"

"I'm not going, either," Fiona said. "Not without Sara."

"I guess you want to vote, then," Kayla said.

"Don't I get to speak?" Justin asked.

"Might be better for everyone if you don't," I said.

He spoke anyway. "Baptiste is right. It's a stupid idea to go."

"So we vote?" Kayla asked.

Some nodded; most of us didn't say or do anything.

"Okay..." Kayla said. "A vote. So... um, all in favour?"

"In favour of what?" Lisa asked.

"In favour of leaving."

"So all in favour of leaving, raise your hand?"

"Yeah."

Lisa's hand shot up.

So did Graham's... and Alain Tremblay's... and Suzanne Tremblay's... and Eva Marchand's...

I counted the votes.

The Tremblays and Marchands were four. The Porters were on my side.

"Five to six," I said. "The motion fails."

"Learn to count," Lisa said. "Six to three."

"Where are you getting these numbers?" Kayla asked. "Six hands up, but a very large number of hands down."

"Every cottage gets two votes," I said. "Except ours. We get three."

"That's right," Lisa said. "Graham and I say 'go'. That's two votes. That plus the Tremblays and Marchands equals six."

"You and Graham get one vote. And you're forgetting Fiona's cottage."

"Fiona doesn't get two votes."

"I know. Sara, Fiona and Gwyneth get two votes. And I know how Sara would vote."

"You can't split into two cottages and grow your vote," Alain said. "You had three before, you have three now. And Lisa and Graham voted with us."

"I'm the chair," Kayla said. "I'll count the votes."

"Sounds good," I said. I knew Kayla would see things my way.

Kayla took out her tablet and turned on the calculator pad. She started typing, on the keys lit against the pinewood table. "Five in favour," she said after almost a full minute. "Four against. Motion carried."

Those words kicked the shit right out of me.

"Bullshit," Justin said. "You have no authority anyway, Kayla. I don't remember agreeing to that particular ruling."

"Which ruling?"

"That the chair is automatically the last person Robert Jean-baptiste pounded in the ass."

"That's uncalled for," Kayla said. "You lost the vote, guys. Fair and square."

"You can't just make up the rules."

"No one's making up rules," Lisa said.

"It doesn't matter," I said. "We're not going."

"We voted."

"I'm exercising my veto."

"You don't get a veto," Lisa said. "Not this time."

"It's the will of the people, Baptiste," Graham said. "Just accept it, alright?"

"Half the people, maybe," I said. "Probably less than half."

"Five to four," Lisa said.

"I don't want to leave," Fiona said.

"I don't want to, either," Kayla said. "But we took a vote."

"And I vetoed it," I said. "Or did you not hear me?"

"Maybe there's a compromise," Matt said. "Maybe we can split up. Those who want to go can, well, go. And the rest of us will stay."

"No one's splitting up," I said. "We're staying put. All of us."

"I'm leaving," Lisa said.

"We're willing to take anyone who will come with us," Katie said. "The stronger we are, the better."

"It's suicide," I said. "You'd be better off just eating a gun right here. Then at least we'd have a place to bury you."

"You are disturbed," Alain said. "You need to accept the decision, Baptiste."

"I don't have to do anything. I'm in charge of security. That hasn't changed. It's not safe to go, so we stay. End of discussion."

"We're going," Lisa said. She turned to Katie. "If Baptiste won't come, that's his problem."

"Enough of this," Justin said. "We can't spare the manpower. No one is going."

"So what are you going to do, Justin?" Lisa asked. "Are you going to wave your little rifle around? Is that supposed to scare us into submission?"

"You're not going anywhere."

"He's right," I said. "We can't let you leave."

"You can't stop us," Lisa said.

She was right. I had nothing.

"We'll do a count of who's leaving and we'll split up the supplies accordingly," Graham said. "We can't take all that much, so I doubt it'll be an even split for most things."

"You won't get far without any vehicles," Justin said.

"We have several trucks," Eva Marchand said. "We'll make sure we have enough space for everyone."

"No, you won't."

"You don't have enough fuel," I said.

"We have fuel," Eva Marchand said.

"Fuel you haven't been sharing?"

"Emergency supplies. Your men know about it."

"My men?" I looked over to Graham.

He nodded. "They have enough."

"Not after we're done splitting up what they've been hiding from me."

"Fuel doesn't matter," Sky said. "We'll have enough fuel. We've got almost a full barrel of biodiesel in the back on our truck."

"We figured you'd need a few extra drops," Katie said.

"We're leaving," Lisa said. "So don't try and stop us. Don't try slashing tires or hiding supplies... we don't want this to get ugly."

"It's going to get ugly," Justin said. "You can bet on that."

"Cooler heads," I said. "Let's take a break."

"It's not a break," Lisa said. "The discussion is over. We'll get you our headcount, Baptiste. And we'll go over the inventory and figure out what we're taking. Seriously, guys... don't try to mess this up for us. It won't end well."

"Is that a threat?" Justin asked.

"Sorry I wasn't clear, Mr. Porter. Let me try again. If you get in our way, I will shoot you in the head."

"You're joking."

"I'm not."

I'm pretty sure everyone in the room knew she was serious.

Justin stayed around as everyone broke off. Only Kayla and I were left in the dining room with him.

"You need to leave, Kayla," Justin said. "I need to talk to Baptiste."

"She can stay," I said.

"I don't trust her."

"Because I'm trying to be fair?" Kayla asked.

"Kayla's staying," I said.

"Forget it," she said. She left the dining room and went upstairs.

"We need to stop them," he said.

"I know," I said.

"It's Lisa and Graham. They're the problem."

"I know."

"So we take them out of the picture."

"We're not killing them, Justin."

"Fuck, Baptiste. I know that. But we need to take them away from here."

"Take them where?"

"Anywhere. With those two gone, the rest will fall into line."

"I don't believe that. If we move against them, they'll just draw closer together."

"It won't matter. It'll blow over. Alain Tremblay is too weak to lead."

"Maybe... but Eva Marchand isn't weak. Neither is Katie Walker. If you want to eliminate every possible opposition... well, that'll be a lot of missing persons."

"There won't be any mystery here, Baptiste. We'll take Lisa and Graham away and we'll do it in front of everyone. We'll make it crystal clear that anyone who wants to risk our safety will be removed from the equation."

"You're insane," I said. "Certifiably insane. We're not going to start exiling people we don't agree with."

"Exile. That's what it is."

"I know. It's still a bad idea."

"It's the only idea we've got. Unless you've got something rattling around —"

"We lock down the supplies."

"With what?"

"We'll find something."

"There's no time. I'm sure they're already grabbing stuff they need. We can't police over a dozen people."

"We can't use violence to keep them in line."

"What violence?" he asked. He really did seem confused.

"Lisa and Graham aren't going to take a ride with us, just because we asked them nicely. We'd need to force them. Forced exile, remember?"

"So we find something we can drop into their drinks or whatever."

"Like roofies?"

"Yeah. Or sleeping pills. We've got those, don't we?"

The whole idea sounded ridiculous. I was tempted to lie, to say that we didn't have anything that would knock those two out on their asses. But our drugs were on the inventory list... if Justin wanted to find them, he would.

So I'd have to hide them from him.

If I wanted to stop him.

If we lost those people, we'd lose half of our strength. More than that. Rihanna can shoot, and Kayla still wants to claim that she knows how, too, but it would only be Justin and I who could do much to keep us safe.

And if something happened to me, there'd be no one left to protect the girls from Justin.

Everything we had would fall apart.

"I can get something," I said.

"Then go get it."

"I'll handle it, Justin. Not just Graham and Lisa, but Sky and Katie, too. They'll stay with us overnight, and I'll cook them a nice breakfast. Once they're out, we put them in a couple trucks. We'll make sure we've loaded up some of our supplies, too."

"How many trucks?"

"We'll give up our gravel truck to go with Katie and Sky's pickup. We'll take some of that biodiesel as compensation. When they come to in the middle of buttfuck nowhere, they'll keep heading south, if they know what's good for them."

"What if they come back?"

"We'll make it clear that they aren't welcome."

"We'll need three guys," Justin said. "Driving a third vehicle to take us home."

"I know. Between the two of us, we should be able to get Matt on board."

He nodded. "You'd better be sure about this, Baptiste. No half measures."

"It's worth it. As long as I can keep my people safe."

I realized after I said it, that Lisa and Graham would no longer be "my people". I'd be sending them off to be killed on the road.

It's what they want. To leave... but that doesn't get me off the hook.

TODAY IS WEDNESDAY, JANUARY 16TH.

MATT AND I met Justin by the junction last night, after we were sure that our guests were asleep; I made sure to sneak out of bed without waking Kayla.

I'd set the table; I'd used the frosted glasses, crushing up the pills so they'd be hard to notice before I filled them with Black Label. I'd offered a condolence toast, and things had gone according to plan.

Everything was working out.

Justin had already started loading up the gravel truck by the time Matt and I had arrived.

I wasn't sure I'd have time to check that he'd given them a fair share of supplies.

And I didn't have a way of knowing what fair actually was.

"You've got the keys?" Justin asked.

Matt handed him a keychain with a pink tag.

"Interesting colour for Sky," I said.

"I got them from Katie's pocket," Matt said. "Two sets, maybe? Her pants were closer to the door."

"I'll bring the truck in," Justin said. "You guys have some cans for the fuel?"

"We've got some in the barn," Matt said.

"Don't get your ass seen."

Matt jogged off back toward our cottage.

"You're sure about this?" Justin asked me.

"You're probing me for doubts?"

"I just want to make sure you don't change your mind."

"We're doing it. Either this, or we lose them all."

"We might still lose them all," he said.

"What's going on? Why are you so whingey about this?"

"I don't want any blowback, is all. People start hating on you, you can't just put it all on me. This is a joint decision, Baptiste. Both of us."

"I can handle it. I'm wearing my big boy pants today."

He laughed and took off jogging, toward the gate.

I started to check the load in the back. A bag of flour, a box of spices, one of Justin's hunting rifles...

If anything, Justin had been generous.

That was more suspicious than if he'd been stingy.

I felt a twinge in the back of my mind. I remembered what he'd done to that boy, Caleb, on the road to Aiguebelle.

I heard footsteps on the road.

I turned around.

It was Kayla.

"What the hell?" she said.

"Just splitting the supplies before they do," I said. "Making sure it's fair."

"Matt told me."

"What?"

"Yeah. Drugging people up and dumping them? Seriously... what the hell?"

"He told you that?"

"For some reason, Matt isn't comfortable with the idea of leaving Lisa and Graham to die."

"They've made their choice. If they want to kill themselves... whatever... but I can't let that ruin everything we've worked for."

"You're not doing this. This isn't something you would do."

"I'm doing it, Kayla. I have to. It's that or everything falls apart. And I need you to support me, Kayla... you know, like you should."

"Like I should? What would that make me?"

"A supportive partner?"

"I'm not a murderer, Baptiste. And neither are you."

"They're getting their supplies."

"And a helping of what, sleeping pills?"

"It's better this way. We need to keep our people together."

"But we won't be together. We'll lose Lisa and Graham."

"We're going to lose them anyway."

"Not if we go with them."

"No," I said. "We're not leaving."

"If that's the only way we can stay together —"

"It was their decision, Kayla. They're splitting us up."

"No, Baptiste. It was your decision. You lost the vote."

"That's on you," I said.

"Don't do this."

"It's already done."

"No, it's not."

I heard the sound of a vehicle coming up the road. Justin was on his way.

Kayla turned to leave.

I grabbed her arm.

"Let go of me," she said.

"You can't tell them."

"I'm going to them. I'm going to tell everyone, Baptiste. You may as well call this off."

Justin stopped the truck right beside us.

He hopped out of the cab.

"Matt got caught," he said.

"Matt gave us up," I said.

"Where the fuck is he?"

More footsteps. Hurrying.

"I'm here," Matt said as he hustled over to us with a gas can hanging from each hand. "Sorry, guys. She saw me."

"And you told her," I said. "What the hell is wrong with you?"

"She hasn't told anyone."

"She's planning to."

"She won't," Justin said.

"You know I will," Kayla said. "Even if I can't wake up the ones you drugged in time, everyone else will know you took them."

Justin reached into the cab. "Hold on," he said. "I've got something." He pulled out a length of yellow rope.

"We need to tie her up. Keep her out of the way. You need to cover her mouth, Baptiste."

"We're not tying her up," I said.

"You can't back out."

I turned back to her. "You need to support me, Kayla."

"I won't do it," she said. "I won't be responsible for this."

"Take her boots off," Justin said. "We need a sock for her mouth."

"You won't scream," I said to her.

"I will scream," she said. "You'd better do as Justin says. And then you should get used to doing whatever he says, since it won't be long before he'll start making all of the decisions."

"Come on, Kayla. Don't make me do this."

"I'm not making you do anything."

"This isn't going to work," Matt said. "Your whole plan is falling apart. It's not like Kayla's going to go along with the cover story."

"Shut up, Matt," Justin said.

"I won't," she said. "I'm going to make sure everyone knows what you did. So unless you're going to keep a sock shoved in my mouth for the rest of my life —"

Justin reached out and grabbed her shoulder. "The rest of your life is going to get awful short."

"Don't touch her," I said, shoving his hand away.

"And don't threaten her, either," Matt said.

"She'll come on side," Justin said. "She'll get there. Let's just tie her up and stuff her somewhere until this is done."

"You're going to have to kill me," she said.

"Why are you doing this?" I asked her.

"Sara would be ashamed of you, Baptiste."

"I don't care."

"That makes all of us," Justin said. "Now shut that bitch up."

I took a swing at Justin and missed, but only because Matt had thrown out both of his arms and given Justin a shove.

"Look, I'm sorry," Justin said. "That was out of line."

"I'm thirty seconds away from kicking your ass," I said.

"Just get her boots off..."

"I'm not going to do it."

"She'll come around... she just needs some time to think on it."

"I'm not tying her up,. That's final."

"Then this whole plan is dead in the water."

"It is."

"I won't accept that."

"You will."

He tried to stare me down. It felt like hours.

"Fuck this shit," he said.

He threw the pink keychain to the ground and then he walked away.

Lisa almost laughed at me. "It's a terrible deal," she said as she checked out the supplies in the back of the truck. "Not an even split by a long shot."

"And a breach of trust," Katie said.

Sky and Graham didn't add anything, but I could tell they agreed.

"I didn't know what else to try," I said. "We're out of options. You leave with less stuff, and maybe some people decide to stay instead."

I looked over to Kayla. She looked down at her feet.

She hadn't told them yet, what we'd tried to do, what we'd already done.

"Whoever wants to go should be allowed to go," Lisa said. "Honestly, Kayla, I'm surprised you got involved with this waste of effort. You know me better than to think I'd take this deal."

Kayla didn't answer.

"It wouldn't matter if you offered us both Mossbergs and all three sets of armour," Graham said. "We're not leaving anyone behind. Well, anyone who doesn't want to be left."

"Anyone who goes with you is signing their life away," I said. "I don't feel bad for trying to save lives."

"So self-righteous," Lisa said. "It's not attractive, Baptiste."

"Just be careful, guys."

I turned to leave.

"You're going?" Graham asked.

"You don't need me to supervise," I said. "You get one vest, one helmet, and one shotgun. Other than that... I don't care about the rest. Just take what you can carry."

"Wait, Baptiste," Katie said. She walked up to me and held out her hand. She was holding a small box. "Laneradine, right?"

"Yeah."

"It's not much... maybe a month's worth... but it's all I could find in our stores." She handed it to me.

"Thanks," I managed to say. "I hope I can keep me and my people alive long enough to use these."

"Thank you, Katie," Kayla said.

She gave Katie a hug.

And then Sky. And Graham. And finally Lisa.

"I love you," Kayla said.

"I love you, too," Lisa said. "That means something."

"I know it does."

Kayla walked over to me and reached for my hand.

I hoped it wasn't just for show.

∽

They left just before sunset. Nineteen people total, seventeen of them from McCartney Lake.

They took Tremblay's truck and the plow, one of the Mossbergs, and one set of body armour and riot gear. They took some supplies, of course, more than we'd had in that one truck, but on the whole we're left with more per person now that they've gone.

Kayla stayed with me as we'd waited for them to leave, and she's still with me now.

Every so often I run my fingers along her back and she gently moans. Like a litmus test for how much she hates me now.

I'm finding it hard to believe that she's moved on from what I tried to do.

Maybe she just doesn't know what to do with me.

TODAY IS THURSDAY, JANUARY 17TH.

JUSTIN SHOWED up before sunrise with his phone in his hand.

Kayla and I were in the living room.

"Alain left me a message with Marc's old phone," he said. "It's for you, I'd say."

"They need help," I said.

"They need help. The Souls have them trapped on 101, like we expected. Said by the time he saw the roadblock, they'd dropped another one in behind them."

"Let me see."

He handed me the phone.

"You tried calling him?"

"Signal's too weak right now. Too much snow."

"This came through ten minutes ago... now there's too much snow?"

"Try it yourself. Call him."

I pressed for Marc's phone.

"Won't even ring," Justin said.

"What will make it ring?"

"Higher ground, maybe."

"We don't have any of that."

"We might," Kayla said. "And it's further east... by Norembega... that helps, right?"

Justin shook his head. "So you two want us to waste fuel trying to get a signal from a guy who willingly split from us?"

"That sums it up," I said. "Isn't that what your electric shitbox is for?"

"They'll be dead before we get there."

"Then we won't have to feel like we didn't try."

441

≪◌

The three of us went together toward Norembega, driving in the ruts we'd carved on our cart trips to Helena, with Kayla crammed in the tiny back seat, even though she was the navigator. I appreciated her sacrifice, as I'm not sure Justin or I could have fit back there.

We reached the junction to Norembega and Helena.

"Turn left," Kayla said.

"We can't cut through that much snow," Justin said. "No one's driven there since the snow fell."

"We'll have to walk," I said. "How far, Kayla?"

"Not far," she said. "You can see it from here." She pointed to a rocky outcrop covered in snow.

"You won't get a signal," Justin said.

"Just give me the phone," I said.

"I'm coming with you," Kayla said.

Together we jogged up the road, toward the little mountain.

The road curved to the left. We moved off into the snow and made our way through the trees.

At some points the ground became so steep that we had to grip the pine trees like handrails.

We didn't stop until we'd climbed to the top.

And there I found a signal.

I pushed for Marc's phone.

And Alain answered.

"They're just waiting by the junction with 572," he said. "They know we're stuck. I guess they figure we'll just give ourselves up if they wait long enough. They're probably right."

"Are you sure it's The Souls?" I said.

"I'm sure. There's at least twenty of them at the roadblock now."

"At both roadblocks? Total?"

"No. In front of us. Twenty in front and I don't know how many behind."

"You need to find out."

"We need your help, Baptiste."

"I'm at least two hours away."

"We'll try to hold out."

"Do that."

I ended the call.

I looked over to Kayla.

"They're all going to die," I said.

"We've got to try to reach them."

"I know."

"Then let's go."

She started back down the little mountain.

I struggled to keep up.

"I'm coming with you," Kayla said, as Justin rushed us back to McCartney Lake.

"I can't let you do that," I said.

"Well, I'm not going," Justin said, "so there's a slot available."

"You'd turn their back on them?" Kayla asked.

"They turned first. I'm not risking my family's life on people who chose how they'd die."

"I think that's valid," I said. "I'm not sure I want to die for these people either."

"So we just leave them there?" Kayla asked.

"I'm not sure yet."

"Oh, really… and exactly when will you know?"

"Hopefully before we get down there."

When we got back to McCartney Lake, I started collecting the gear. Riot suits, vests, helmets… snowshoes to deliver our surprise to The Souls… I'd made sure to include my trusty guitar case; I still had rounds enough to cause some damage.

Kayla went to grab some food and water for the trip.

Once we were packed she asked me to drive over to the shed by Fiona and Gwyneth's cottage.

We went inside the shed and she started pulling out the tackle boxes.

"Might as well bring all of the explosives," she said. "If we don't make it back, it's not like Fiona's going to find a use for this crap."

"I had some of this earmarked for Detour Lake," I said.

"We'll worry about that later."

I nodded.

And I started loading the tackle boxes into the truck.

◆

Fiona came out to see what was happening.

"They need our help," I said.

"You're really going?" she asked.

"We are."

"Both of you?"

"I think I can be of use," Kayla said.

Fiona walked over to her. "Be careful, Kayla," she said. She gave her a hug. "I don't want to lose my arch nemesis."

"We'll be okay," Kayla said. "We won't do anything stupid."

"This whole trip is something stupid," I said.

Fiona walked over to me. "Don't let anything happen to her," she said. "Or to you." She reached up and kissed me on the cheek.

I wrapped my arms around her and pulled her close to me. "I love you, Fiona," I said. "Don't ever forget that."

"Then make sure you get your butt back here to remind me."

◆

We put on our riot suits and vests, and then we went up to Hwy 652, the fuel gauge getting so close to empty that I knew we might get the warning light before we even reached Hwy 101. If that happened, the only way we'd get home would be if we could take some of Katie and Sky's biodiesel.

If we didn't reach them in time, there was a chance we'd be stranded in Souls of Flesh territory, with just enough food for a picnic lunch.

That would be a long and hungry walk back to McCartney Lake.

From 652, we took the road that led to Iroquois Falls, following in the ruts that our former lakemates had made.

I'd seen from the map that we needed to turn just before the steel bridge over the upper Abitibi, but I decided that I needed to see if that bridge was still there.

And from the turnoff I couldn't tell.

I drove up a little further, through untracked snow that made me a little nervous of getting stuck. But we had weight on our side, as long as I didn't get sucked into the ditch.

The gray steel truss bridge started at the riverbank, but didn't make it across. It looked like whatever they'd used to blow it up had been planted at the base of a pier just off the far side of the water. The span had fallen there, landing on the bank.

In theory, you could climb across if you weren't afraid of heights or drowning, but there was no way to get a car across.

I guess that's all that mattered to the ones who blew it up.

We backtracked to Twin Falls road, heading southeast to the hydro dam, along the same ruts in the snow. No one had bothered to blow that crossing up, and I didn't even have to slow down as we drove across the long tail of Lake Abitibi.

We reached the concession roads outside of the town of Matheson, and we started counting.

We turned left onto the third road, heading due east, following the tracks.

As we passed the next road junction, I noticed more tracks heading south.

"There's other traffic here," I said. "Probably The Souls. Helmets."

Kayla passed me a helmet before she put hers on. "I hope you're just being paranoid."

"I'm not sure you can be paranoid when the whole world's out to get you."

We reached the end of the road. The tracks stopped.

I stopped the truck.

"Looks like they turned around," I said. "But there's supposed to be a turnoff."

"There isn't."

"Check the map."

"The map is wrong."

"What?"

She handed me the tablet.

"There's no road here," she said. "Maybe there was a road at one point, like a couple of ruts or something... but it's long gone."

"We'll have to get that much closer to Matheson."

"Do we know what's there?"

"Can't be anything good. It's too close to Timmins to be left alone. It's no wonder The Souls seemed to know they were coming."

"If that's true, they'll see us coming."

"We'll find another way."

I switched the aerial view, and zoomed in.

"Machinery road," I said. "Right there." I pointed to a small line of brown the led all the way to 101.

"We don't have a plow anymore. We'll get stuck."

"We might. Better than getting seen."

"This truck weighs like a ton."

"Well... it's a one ton truck, but it probably clocks in at almost five thousand kilos."

"If it gets stuck we can't just push it out."

"That's true."

If we got stuck, we'd be stuck. The only way to pull a one-ton truck out of trouble was with another truck. And we only had the one.

"We're going to have to risk it," I said.

"The machinery road?"

"Getting seen. For all we know, we've already been seen. Or no one was seen, and they keep that roadblock ready 24/7."

I carefully turned the truck around and we headed back.

We took the other road heading south, following the tracks which now seemed to have belonged to the Marchands and Tremblays *et. al.*

We reached 101.

I could see that The Fires had burned every tree and building along the well-plowed two-lane highway. I wasn't sure if I should be relieved, if scorched earth and skeletons of pine and birch were signs that there was no one there to spot us.

We turned left and headed toward the blockade.

It would be less than ten minutes before we met the first road-block.

"We'll need to surprise them," I said. "Do you see a way to get close to 572 without being seen?"

Kayla peered over the tablet. "Another machinery road. I doubt they're even guarding it."

"They might not have to, depending on if there are any trees left over there."

"No good?"

"I didn't say that. Where do I go?"

"Turn right on Birch Road."

"Where's Birch Road?" I asked. We couldn't rely on a legible sign still standing, not when everything else had burned away.

"Not this next one... the one after it."

I kept driving to the next junction.

"This one's plowed," I said.

"What does that mean?"

"I'm not sure."

I took the gravel road toward the south.

"Now turn left," she said at the next intersection.

The plow had turned left, too, leaving the other two directions to the snow.

I could see the green of living trees pushing through the black and gray stalks of dead pine.

Then I saw a yardsite.

"See any smoke coming from those buildings?" I asked.

"Yeah... I see some..."

"You sure?"

"Yes."

"Goddammit. That's why they've plowed."

The road curved up ahead, around what looked to be a lake.

"There's a couple houses on this lake," Kayla said with her gaze on the tablet. "Looks nice."

"Looks like the perfect place for murderers to kick back and relax."

"Oh... crap..."

I stopped the truck. "Your turn to drive."

As Kayla took the wheel, I checked the Mossberg; I was saving the C12 for the roadblock. Or I was hoping to save it for then.

"We'll drive right on by, like we belong here," I said. "Speed up a little so it looks like we're used to the road."

"What if they start shooting?"

"We keep going. It's not that easy to hit a moving truck from a good ways away."

"But they'll come after us."

"They might. We'll keep with the plan. We reach the machinery road, ditch the truck, and head toward the junction. Believe me, Kayla, there are enough Souls at the roadblocks that a couple more on our tail shouldn't make that much of a difference."

"You're just oozing with confidence right now..."

"I'm expecting the worst and hoping to be pleasantly surprised."

Kayla took us past the first yardsite. There was one pickup truck in the yard.

Nothing stirred.

We drove past the second yardsite. Smoke in the chimney, but no vehicles out front.

I had a feeling that the residents had rushed up to the roadblocks when they heard there was a big fish in the net.

The fact that they hadn't come back yet meant there was a chance the shooting hadn't started.

We rode the bend around the lake and the road started to straighten out.

And then I saw the pit.

We'd arrested a man for scavenging back in the days of the Protection Committee, back when we'd considered scavenging illegal and not the only way to stay alive.

He'd told me about the big pit; he hadn't been the first to mention it. He'd said that he and the rest of his work crew had been ambushed on Highway 11 that November, on their attempt to make it home to North Bay. He'd said that Souls of Flesh had taken them out to an open mine.

To a pit that was filled with the rotting remains of other men.

"This is where you'll die," the Sergeant-at-Arms had told the men. "The only question is how long it will take."

They were surveyors, the prisoner had told me, but that had been enough for them to be considered agents of a foreign government in the eyes of the Sergeant-at-Arms. One by one the men were interrogated, and one by one they had given nothing that had satisfied The Souls.

All three surveyors were chained up in the pit, he'd told me, chained by the ankle to eye screws that had been drilled and epoxied into the bedrock.

The Souls left them there to die.

It wasn't cold enough to die of exposure. They had to wait to die of thirst.

The prisoner told me that he waited for three days, and by that point he'd started to hallucinate.

And someone came to see him. An angel, he said, a beautiful woman with blond hair, so light that it was almost white. And she cut his chain and freed him, and she left a dead man in his place.

And she gave him a backpack full of supplies and she told him to run.

I'd never believed his story. Not all of it, at least.

He hadn't been the first to mention her, but everyone knows that the legendary Dalya Blue doesn't exist. There was no angel rescuing men from the pit. If anything, the men who'd been spared had given something to The Souls, something that made them unworthy of ever being allowed back into society.

We'd released him, but only because we'd made sure he'd kept on his way to the west.

I don't know if he ever made it someplace else.

"Are there people down there?" Kayla asked as we drove by.

There were. Dozens, if not hundreds, of bodies.

From up on the road, I couldn't see the chains.

But I knew... that was where they'd died.

"Keep going," I said. "We don't want anything to do with this place."

"They dump their bodies there. The Souls."

"No, Kayla. That's how they kill them."

We parked the truck at the intersection with a road called Tamarack. The only sign of a machinery road was a lack of trees across the road from us.

We were lucky; The Fires hadn't taken the forest between us and Highway 101.

We put on the snowshoes and loaded up with as much as we could carry. Kayla took the Mossberg and the backpack filled with grenades and shells, while I took out the C12 and stuffed the last four magazines into my small pack.

We started walking due east, past an abandoned yardsite, into the trees.

After a few minutes we reached a marshy stream, cattails poking above the snow.

"We should keep going to the next stream," Kayla said. "We can follow it up to the highway, look for our people."

"I'm guessing the fixed blockade is directly on the junction of 101 and 572," I said. "It's the first chance anyone coming from Quebec would have to turn off 101, so The Souls would try and stop that from happening."

"So the blockade is meant for people heading west?"

"They were probably surprised to see a caravan travelling the wrong way. But not too surprised to prevent them from throwing something together to box that caravan in."

"So the other roadblock is lighter."

"I'd guess so. So we hit the heavy one. We launch some of your grenades and we add some bullets to the mix. The guys at the other roadblock will think that there's an assault from Aiguebelle or something."

"And all of the sudden that caravan won't be so important anymore."

"Hopefully they'll just push right past. I'll let Alain and them know that once the roadblock behind them falls apart, they need to get moving back toward home."

"They won't want to head back," Kayla said.

"They don't have a choice. It's that or die, isn't it?"

Somehow I knew they wouldn't see it that way.

We followed the second creek north, to where the highway passed over it. We then took to the ditch, trudging through the tops of the snow-covered wigeongrass, trying to keep our heads low.

The three trucks from McCartney Lake weren't far away. I saw someone in matching armour... maybe Lisa, maybe Sky.

I wondered if whoever it was would start shooting.

"It's me," I said. "Baptiste."

"Thank Trudeau," Lisa said.

"And Kayla," Kayla said.

"Where's Justin?"

"Not here," I said. "I can't believe you guys are still in one piece."

"I can't believe you guys are on foot," Lisa said.

"Have they tried to get in contact?"

"They have a megaphone. They don't have that much to say. Just 'lay down your weapons and you won't be harmed'. As if we didn't notice their goddamn pit of corpses. So what's your plan, exactly?"

"You and I are going to hit the east roadblock from the other side," I said. "We've brought enough firepower to keep them busy, and to hopefully draw the guys on the other side of you into the fight."

"We don't want to draw people up here."

"Everyone needs to get into the trees. If they come through, they'll see you've all run off into the bush. You guys don't matter as much as the supplies you're leaving behind. And we'll make enough noise that they'll come straight to the two of us."

"And once they've joined in on trying to kill us?"

"Then everyone else gets the fuck out of here, heads back home."

"We're not going home."

"Well you can't stay here."

"We need a new plan."

"That's the plan," I said. "Take it or... well, you gotta take it."

"We're going to Temiskaming."

"You can take the last concession road south to 572," Kayla said. "Tamarack Road. That'll get you to Hwy 11, and you can try your luck on there."

"There's no way that junction's unguarded," I said. "It'll be just as locked down as the one up the road here."

"We need to destroy the roadblock," Lisa said. "It's our only option."

"No... the smart option is to come back home with us."

"This isn't up for debate."

"Well, here's what we'll do, then. You and I will try to kill every last man on that roadblock. And then we'll try to kill the guys rushing to reinforce from the second one. Once we manage to murder two dozen hardened and well-armed bikers, we'll go our separate ways."

"You don't think we can do it."

"I don't think we can. Because we're not John Rambo."

"What?"

"Fuck, Lisa. You're going to get me killed."

"I'm coming, too," Kayla said. "We have three sets of armour. We should use all three."

"Then we'll get Alain to suit up," I said. "You're of no use to us, Kayla. We need someone who can shoot."

"Alain needs to stay with his family... and all I need to do is lob some grenades at anything that moves."

"And you think you can do that why?"

"Because I know how to throw a ball, Baptiste. Haven't you ever heard of a strip club softball league?"

"I thought you were a free agent. Touring the north or whatever."

"You know a lot about it for someone who claims he never came to see me dance."

"Maybe I managed to sneak in a show." I know she'd seen me there, the only black guy at Fleshy's that night, sitting with Ant. "We're going to need another set of snowshoes."

"I don't need snowshoes," Lisa said. "You've got Justin's phone?"

"I do." I pulled it out of my jacket pocket and checked. "We've got a signal. Works better down this way."

"So we'll call Alain once it's done."

"Yeah."

"And we'll tell him to keep on down 101."

"Shit, Lisa," I said. "If we actually pull this off, you can tell Alain whatever the hell you want."

After Lisa passed the plan on to the caravan, the three of us followed the creek back into the forest. I could tell that Lisa was having trouble keeping up, with her boots sinking into the snow, but I wasn't about to mention it.

Once we were at least a klick in, we turned east.

We crossed and followed another stream. It led us to a plowed gravel road.

"572," I said, not that there was much doubt.

We kept as low as we could as we crossed the highway.

I could see a large truck at the intersection with 101. It looked like an old military cargo truck, the kind of deuce-and-a-half you'd pick up from army surplus.

I couldn't tell if they could see us.

We headed into the forest on the far side of the road, just deep enough that we couldn't see the highway from the trees.

Then we turned north.

We slowed down once we started to hear voices.

The voices were in French. It's nice that The Souls are functionally bilingual.

We crept toward the edge of the trees. Within throwing distance.

There were two men in kuttes standing by the truck. Both were armed with shotguns, like ours.

The rest of the men were spread along 101, facing east by their bikes, but they were more involved in drinking and talking than keeping an eye on the caravan.

I couldn't see well enough what weapons they had.

"Grenades," I whispered to Kayla. "We'll each take a couple to start things off."

Kayla opened her pack and pulled out a wrapped bundle. She held up a grenade for us to see.

"There's no fuse," she said. "Hard contact does it. So throw it hard and hope it doesn't land gently in a snowdrift."

I took two pipes and Lisa took two.

I nodded and then I threw the first grenade.

It landed just to the left of the two men by the truck.

And it exploded.

The blast threw them both to the ground; it didn't look like they were about to get up.

The other men took a moment to stir, but then they were up and moving around the far side of the truck.

A few took their first shots, but I doubt they could tell where to aim.

Lisa lobbed her first grenade at the truck.

Hard contact.

I saw two men fly out onto the pavement, their bodies mangled.

The other men started moving back toward their bikes.

Kayla threw hers next.

I don't think she caught any of them.

I passed my second grenade to Lisa and picked up my C12. I started shooting.

The Souls went into full retreat, heading west on their motor-cycles.

I hung the C12 on my shoulder and pulled out my SIG.

I found four men lying on the road. I gave each one a head shot.

"That was too easy," Lisa said as she joined me on the highway.

"I know. They aren't done with us."

I took out the phone and called Alain.

"They drove right by," he told me.

"Then get your people together and get over here," I said.

Sky and Katie drove Kayla and I back toward our truck, while everyone else kept moving east down 101. The four of us squished into the cab, with Kayla sitting mostly on my lap.

"We weren't expecting a roadblock there," Katie said. "I would have thought they'd be blocking the road closer to Quebec."

"It's easier to control a roadblock close to home," I said. "Smaller perimeter... just like our own little Green Zone, back in Cochrane."

"But what's stopping Aiguebelle from taking over everything between that roadblock and the provincial boundary?"

"There's nothing there. It's pretty hard to hold a big block of empty shield. Have you ever tried winter camping?"

"So we should be clear for awhile, at least," Sky said.

I shook my head. "I didn't say that."

"I think you did," Katie said.

"Just because they don't have roadblocks doesn't mean they don't have patrols. You keep a defensible perimeter and patrol the imme-diate area."

"We don't do that," Kayla said.

"Maybe that's why we keep getting our asses kicked."

"So Souls of Flesh patrols toward Quebec and Aiguebelle patrols toward Matheson," Sky said. "So they'd keep running into each other?"

"There's probably some kind of no man's land between their lines," I said. "Obviously we don't know where, but we might be there already."

"So that's why there's no one out here?" Katie asked.

"We just haven't seen anyone yet. I would expect someone to be out here somewhere. If you allow the enemy freedom of action in no man's land, you're basically letting them show up at your doorstep unannounced."

"Are they really enemies?" Kayla asked.

"Aiguebelle is a provisionally autonomous region within the Province of Quebec. Sons of Flesh is a criminal organization that has subverted the legal government of the city of Timmins. I doubt they're best friends."

"So we keep going," Katie said. "One more gauntlet to run."

"Don't you get what's happening? We just attacked a roadblock and killed four men. They're not done with us."

"Do they know it was us? And not an attack from Aiguebelle?"

"Doesn't matter. You guys aren't safe. They'll regroup further west on 101, and either hold there, or start on their way back."

"Well, we're not going to try and head back that way, then," Katie said. "So what else can we do?"

"The same thing Kayla and I are going to do," I said.

"Am I supposed to know what that is?" Kayla asked.

"We're going to Aiguebelle."

⁊

We said goodbye to everyone at the junction with Highway 672.

They wouldn't listen to reason, and I knew that Kayla and I wouldn't make it home if we kept on with them.

Graham and Lisa — and everyone else — would no longer exist for us, whether or not they somehow made it through. Like Cassy and the rest of the world, I wouldn't know what became of them.

The only thing I could do was hand Lisa a bundle of six pipe grenades.

"You'll run into them again," I told her.

"I know," she said.

"If these can't get you through... you might want to use them to —"

"To control my destiny. Thanks, Baptiste."

She wrapped her arms around me and squeezed.

I hadn't expected that.

Obviously she hadn't found out about those sleeping pills…

❧

I drove the truck, with Kayla, toward Quebec, expecting to run into Aiguebelle at any moment.

We drove by the "Bonjour, Quebec" sign without seeing anyone.

The highway was still just as clean and plowed as it had been in Ontario. Someone was keeping it open.

We drove past a clearing in the woods that was likely meant for plows to turn around. The clearing wasn't plowed.

"They have a gate well into our side back home," Kayla said. "But not here."

"We're not a threat to them, so they don't worry much about any attacks up there, I guess. Well, maybe from Detour Lake… but nothing like The Souls."

"So where are they?"

We passed a driveway. No signs that anyone had used it.

And another.

"I don't like the looks of this," Kayla said.

"Don't worry…"

"What if The Souls have pushed into Quebec? What if the next roadblock is a pile of angry bikers who know exactly what we just did?"

I decided to ignore her for a while. I didn't have an argument to make.

I had no reason to believe she wasn't dead on.

Then we came to the first real intersection.

"Roads are plowed," I said.

"I don't see why…"

"To draw us in."

"What?"

"They want people to go deep inside their territory."

"Why?"

"Because then they have the advantage. They know we're here. I'm sure they've been watching us. Cameras, maybe drones…"

"We'll be coming up on some cottages soon. Lac Hébécourt. Do you think they'll stop us there?"

"We need to ditch the truck."

"But we don't even know what they'll say."

"We won't get a second shot, Kayla. Once they stop us, that's it. They might just tell us to turn around, or they might take everything we've got and send us back on foot. It's not like we can ask for a do-over."

"So we dump the truck and then what? We go live in the woods?"

"We'll find another truck," I said. "We just need to get off the road and past their defensive lines."

"Which we haven't even found yet."

I stopped the truck.

"Dammit, Baptiste... this is seriously our worst date yet."

"I'm sure it can get worse."

We packed up for the trip, shoving what little food we'd brought into our packs. That was when I realized that we hadn't even eaten since we'd left McCartney Lake.

The sun was maybe a half hour from setting. I was surprised the day had held out that long. It felt like it had gone on forever.

We headed southeast, still wearing our vests and helmets, and with our snowshoes strapped to our boots, toward what we hoped were still just cottages.

For all we knew, the entire lakefront had been converted into a military base.

We came to a section of marsh at the edge of a good-sized lake. I could see a house on a spit of land where the marsh met the open water.

I took out my binoculars.

"I see smoke," I said. "Someone lives there. Wish I knew who..."

"I should go."

"What?"

"I'll go take a look. No one feels threatened by me. If they catch me, they aren't going to shoot me."

"You can't be sure of that."

"No... I *am* sure of that. People do like me, Baptiste. Well... people who aren't Sara." She clasped her hand against her helmet, where her mouth should be. "Sorry..."

I nodded.

She took off her helmet and her vest, then slowly peeled off her riot suit. She pulled her jacket out of her bag, followed by her pink toque and scarf, and her light blue mittens.

"See?" she said as she dressed. "I'm all sweet and innocent."

"You're beautiful," I said. I took of my helmet and gave her a kiss. "Be careful, Kayla."

She smiled and started walking. She kept her head up and her pace was casual, and she looked exactly like someone who should have been there.

She peered into the window of the cottage, then looked back at me. She held up two fingers and then pointed back to the cottage.

Two people.

She held up her index finger, then ran her hand through her hair.

I was pretty sure she meant "one woman".

A married couple, maybe? Or two off-duty border guards?

Kayla crawled in the snow beneath the window frame. Once she was past, she stood back up and looked perfectly normal, like she hadn't just been sneaking around like some dangerous fugitive.

I was impressed.

She walked toward the garage. She went around a corner.

I couldn't see her.

I had to get closer.

I grabbed her pack along with mine and followed the treeline toward the garage. I kept going until I could see her.

She'd opened the garage door.

No locks.

She went in for a moment, and then she came back out.

I started off toward her.

She stuck a finger up to the tip of her nose — to keep me quiet — and slowed her pace.

"A snowmobile," she said in a whisper. "We could take it on the lake. People would just assume we're cottagers."

"Not bad."

We opened the overhead door by hand, doing our best to make sure we didn't make much noise. Then we pushed the snowmobile across the yard and around the back of a gray and white boatshed.

We had trouble getting it through a clump of bush, but we eventually got it down to the lake.

"I can drive," Kayla said in a whisper. "You're in charge of shooting people."

I nodded.

We climbed on and she started the engine.

I hoped the couple in the cottage would think it was the neighbours going for a ride.

Assuming they had neighbours.

We drove along the lake, heading to a collection of lights that had just started to turn on at the far side.

I was hoping we'd find a cottage that was dark, but not forgotten; if they were still used as cottages, there'd hopefully be some owners who weren't home.

It didn't take us long to find just that, a small A-frame that seemed out of place among the newer builds. We found a shed filled with firewood, and so I gingerly broke into the back porch and we found a place to stay.

I could tell they had electricity; everyone on that lake seemed to have it, even though I hadn't noticed an overabundance of solar or wind installs. It looked like Aiguebelle still had their grid.

Probably ran all the way to the lines from the James Bay Project, from the middle of Quebec.

We left the lights off, but we started a fire after we ate, just big enough to keep us above freezing as we laid together, on a couch by the fireplace, under a heavy enough blanket that we could take off our damp clothes.

"Worst date ever?" I asked her as I ran my fingers along her shoulders.

She laughed.

And then we did what two people tend to do when their lying naked together by a half-roaring fire.

I'm not going to bother writing about it.

TODAY IS FRIDAY, JANUARY 18TH.

I WAS woken up this morning by the slamming of a car door.

I poked Kayla's shoulder.

"I heard it," she said.

I put on my shirt and grabbed my SIG. I walked over to the nearest window.

There was a car right outside, a green electric two-seater. A young woman was holding open the passenger-side door. She was probably twenty or so, blond hair. And petite. And wearing the kind of tight black t-shirt that you'd expect to see on a girl out on the town.

"*Vas-y,*" the woman said.

She started tugging on someone inside the car.

A young man, about the same age, but significantly taller and wider, stumbled out of the car.

"*J'ai besoin de mon camion,*" he said. He needed his truck.

They argued a little, too quickly for me to understand the words. He finally started trudging toward the door of the cabin, weaving as he walked.

He was drunk.

"*Tu seras okay?*" she asked him.

"Okay," he said.

And then I think he said thank you. That or shit. He was mumbling.

She turned around and went back to her car.

"We need that car," I said.

I heard the car door close.

I rushed toward the door.

The door opened and the drunk man stepped inside. I slammed him against the wall. It wasn't hard to put him down and out.

"What did you do?" Kayla said. Too loudly.

"Theo?" the woman called out. "*Que se passe-t-il?*"

461

I heard the car door open. She was coming to check on him.

She probably thought he'd passed out. She obviously cared if he choked on his own tongue.

"No," Kayla said. "Don't hurt her."

"I won't," I said.

As she walked inside I wrapped my arm around her throat.

"I have a gun," I said. "Do you understand?"

"Yes," she said.

"We're not going to hurt you," Kayla said. "We just need your car."

I let go of her neck. She stepped back from me.

"You're from Timmins?" she asked.

"Matheson," I said. "What's your name?"

"Elodie."

"You live around here?"

"This is our cottage," she said. "My brother stays here when he's too... *soûlard* for my parents to see."

"Your parents live where?"

"*À* Rouyn," she said.

"Please sit down, Elodie."

She shook her head.

"It's okay," I said. "*S'il vous plaît.*"

She sat down on the couch.

I didn't bother telling her what Kayla and I had been doing on it the night before.

"Get our gear," I said to Kayla. "Pile it up next to the car... uh, please."

Kayla started carrying things outside.

"You're going to need to come with us," I said to Elodie.

"Please," she said. "Let me stay with my brother. I won't tell what happened."

"Sorry... if you tell anyone they'll track your car."

"I won't tell."

"We can't risk it."

Kayla came back inside for a second load. She went into the kitchen and started opening cupboards.

"There's some food in here," she said.

"Bring it," I said.

I motioned for Elodie to stand up.

"*Je ne suis pas stupide,*" she said. "I know you will kill me. That is why you want to take me with you. *Non...* I won't go."

I didn't know what to say. I didn't have time for an argument.

I grabbed her by her hair and pulled her up from the couch.

I pushed her in front of me, out the door.

"What are you doing to her?" Kayla asked.

"We don't have time for this," I said.

"There's no room in the back. Not for her."

"There's room." I turned to Elodie. "Climb in," I told her.

She shook her head. She was crying.

I swept my arm under her legs and lifted her up. I lowered her into the back of the little car, her face to the floor.

I pulled her hands behind her back, holding her wrists together.

"Get some rope," I said to Kayla.

She ran back to the cottage.

"Please," Elodie said. "Please..." She wasn't fighting me. I lightened my grip on her wrists.

"You'll be okay," I said.

Kayla returned with a spool of blue and white nylon cord.

I bound Elodie's wrists, and then I pulled her feet together and brought them up toward her hands, tying her ankles to her wrists.

"I don't like this," Kayla said. "She's terrified."

"She'll be okay," I said. "You know that."

"I wonder if that's what they said to Tabitha and Natalie."

"What the fuck?"

"Just... go easy on her."

"We need to gag her," I said.

"Yeah, that's just what we need. She'll end up choking to death."

"Your scarf."

She frowned, but handed it to me anyway.

I tied a double knot in the middle. "Open your mouth, Elodie."

She didn't.

I shoved the knotted scarf against her mouth.

She wouldn't take it.

I pushed harder.

Kayla reached in and pinched the girl's nostrils. "Hold it over her mouth," she said.

I kept holding it.

After a few seconds Elodie gasped.

I shoved the knot into her mouth and tied the scarf around her head. "That was a waste of everyone's time," I told her.

We piled the packs and snowshoes on top of Elodie's bound body, along with my tattered guitar case. She wouldn't be able to see what was in it anyway.

I stuffed the Mossberg in the passenger seat and climbed in. "You're driving," I said to Kayla. "Remember... if anyone asks, your name's Elodie and I'm your step-dad or something."

"Okay," Kayla said as she got in. Once she was sitting, she craned her neck toward the back. "I'm sorry, Elodie. Everything's going to be okay."

Elodie tried to say something in reply. Whatever it was, it didn't sound too friendly.

Kayla drove us deeper into Quebec before we turned to head north. I'd figured that we'd have less chance of running into any kind of security checks if we were a long way from any borders.

We hit a few farms, not long after the cottages, and I was amazed at how normal everything looked. There'd been fires here, I could see, but wherever the flames hadn't reached looked just like the farms around Cochrane used to look.

We'd pass by pickup trucks and electric cars and even the occasional minivan, and everyone looked happy and healthy and a million miles away from the end of the world.

I would have been tempted to stay, if we didn't have people depending on us back across the line. And if we hadn't already kidnapped a young woman and stuffed her in the back.

We dipped into forests again, the edge of the clay belt, I guess, and then we turned north and soon were in farmland again, more farms and houses and life than I think they'd ever had on the Ontario side.

We drove through a beautiful little village, with a church with a silver steeple, and they even had a gas station with an open sign in the window.

"Wish we had money," Kayla said. "It'd feel nice to buy something again. I don't even care what."

"I doubt they use money," I said. "If they do, it probably some kind of weird French money."

"They probably use something as currency... poutine, maybe?"

"That or a smug sense of superiority."

I heard another muffled curse from the back.

"We're just joking, Elodie," I said. "I used to date a French woman. She was Catholic and everything."

I heard Kayla sigh.

I was trying to sound friendly and non-threatening, for Elodie's sake, but I had a feeling that she was probably chalking it up to some kind of serial-killer psychopathy.

I decided to stop trying. Efficient was better. Brusque was better.

We kept going, through the towns of Macamic, La Sarre, and Beaucanton, all with official signs sitting beside cute wooden hand-painted ones.

We'd keep heading north, so far north that no one would be expecting us, north enough that they didn't think they had neighbours to the west.

After two and a half hours, we arrived in the town of Val-Paradis, the last piece of civilization on our way home. It was not much more than a few houses and a church.

"We should find a place to take a break," I said. "Figure out our plan."

"Okay," Kayla said.

She turned north.

"Wrong way," I said.

"Taking a break."

She drove up the road until the we reached a point where it was no longer plowed.

"Guess no one's living up this way anymore," she said. She slowly turned the car around and stopped. "This okay?"

"Looks good."

I opened the back and took our gear out.

I untied the pink scarf and pulled it out of Elodie's mouth.

"Are you hungry?" I asked her.

"Yes," she said.

I rummaged through the packs until I found a box of crackers.

I held one up to her mouth.

"Can you untie me, please?" she asked.

"You'll try to run," I said. "Sorry."

She took a bite of the cracker. She didn't seem to enjoy it. "*C'est fétide.*"

"I think they're a little stale. Blame your brother."

She took another bite. "Do you have water?"

I found my canteen and gave her a drink.

"*Merci,*" she said, thanking me.

"*Pa de kwa,*" I said, automatically uttering the Haitian my father had taught me.

"You two having a moment?" Kayla asked.

I smiled. "We're bonding."

Elodie started to cry.

"What's wrong?" I asked her.

"I don't want to die," she said.

"We're not going to hurt you," Kayla said. "We're the good guys."

"My parents will be worried about me."

"You'll see them soon," I said.

I could tell she didn't believe us.

It didn't matter.

"We can't take this car much further," I said.

"What wrong with it?" Kayla said.

"We can't take any car. They'll be blocking the roads. They'd be guarding them anyway, but I'm sure they're looking for us."

"Too bad you don't look like anyone around here," Kayla said. "I could maybe pass for Elodie, but you're a tougher sell."

"They wouldn't let Elodie pass through, either. I'm sure it's locked down to any traffic."

"So we need another snowmobile."

"You got it. Assuming we can get all the way home on a single tank."

"And assuming we can find a snowmobile. Or a full tank."

"So you understand the challenge," I said.

"I do... and I know that I'll have to be the one to find it."

"What do you mean?"

"You stand out..."

"I know... but it's too risky."

"It's not risky at all," Kayla said. "*Je débrouiller assez bien en français.*"

"I can help," Elodie said. "I can go with you. No one would be suspicious of two girls driving around."

"We'll all go," I said. "Elodie and I will trade places. That way, if things go bad... well, I'll be there."

"Okay," Kayla said. "But please... oh pretty please... let's stick that moist wad of scarf in *your* mouth."

I chuckled and started untying Elodie's ankles.

We found two snowmobiles on a trailer hitched to a running truck. The truck was parked outside a house, not far south of Val-Paradis. Kayla dropped me off on the road, a few metres away, and after she'd driven back north for a minute or so I made my way to the truck.

The door was locked.

Unusual for being out in the country, but still too perfect a find to pass up.

I smashed the window with the butt of my SIG.

I climbed in and followed after the little two-seater.

I don't think the owner heard a thing.

We went back to our resting place north of Val-Paradis.

We repacked the best we could, using the saddlebags that came with our new snowmobiles. I had no choice but to strap the C12 over my shoulder and leave the guitar case behind.

When Elodie saw the big gun she started to panic.

"Please," she said. "I helped you..."

"It's okay," I told her. "I'm not going to hurt you."

"Can I have my car keys?"

I shook my head. "Sorry, Elodie... you need to come with us."

Kayla grabbed my elbow. "What are you doing?" she asked me.

"We can't leave her here. She'll drive into town and tell them about us. They'll find us."

"We'll be off the roads."

"Not really... just until we get clear of civilization. Then we'll need to follow the road so we don't get turned around out there."

"Then tie me up again," Elodie said. "Leave me in the car. It will be some time before someone finds me."

"That could work," Kayla said. "As long as you don't freeze to death first."

"It won't work," I said.

"Why not?"

"Why would we risk getting caught? We'll take her with us and let her go just past the gate at Eades. By the time she makes it there we'll be home free. That's the best plan. For all of us."

"So just another couple hours or so?" Kayla asked. "Then we can let her go?"

"A couple more hours. That's it. Then they'll take her back to her car and she can go home." I turned to Elodie. "Then you can go home."

I went over to the trailer and tilted it, before pulling the first snowmobile down to the road.

I checked the fuel gauge. Pretty close to full.

"You'll ride with me, Elodie," I said. "No more rope."

But I did pack it in one of my saddlebags.

The sun set while we were riding; it set just before we crossed what the map told us was the Pattern River. By the time we reached Abbotsford Lake, I was half-frozen. Snowmobiling isn't much fun when you aren't dressed for it. To be honest, I'm not sure when snowmobiling *is* fun.

We reached the intersection of the two logging roads, and we turned left, heading south toward the gate at Eades. We skirted around an unexpected steel and concrete barrier that would have been pretty effective against anything wider than a snowmobile, and then we came to the next junction, a little triangle of roads that probably hadn't seen a visitor in two years.

I stopped my snowmobile.

Kayla pulled up beside and cut her engine.

"Problem?" she asked.

"What's your gauge at?" I asked her.

"Shoot... less than half."

"Me, too."

"We're not going to make it."

"I'm not sure," I said. "You know these gauges seem to jump a little. But we should adjust the route to make sure."

"Skip Eades?"

"Yeah."

"But what about her?" Kayla asked, nodding toward our captive.

"How far is it?" Elodie asked. "Can I walk there?"

"Not safe," I said. "It's at least a couple of hours."

"Well it's not your decision," she said.

"We should risk it," Kayla said. "Take her down there, or closer at least... if we have to add an hour of walking to our trip... I think that's fair."

"I'm not getting stranded outside our gates," I said.

"We can siphon fuel out of one of the machines... We don't need two of them once we drop Elodie off."

"We don't have a hose... look, Kayla... it's not going to work."

"You just said my name."

"Yeah. It doesn't matter. I'm easy enough to describe as it is."

"You're going to kill me," Elodie said.

"Baptiste," Kayla said. "Come on... she doesn't deserve to die..."

"No one's gonna die," I said. "Can we all just shut up about dying already?"

"We can't take her with us. That's not much better."

"What's wrong with that?"

"Have you forgotten what we just saw?" Kayla said. "I'd give my left nut to live in Aiguebelle. We live like a bunch of cockroaches compared to them."

"She'll adjust."

"No. There's no way."

"What?"

"I said no, Baptiste. We are not taking her home with us. You don't get to keep her. She goes home."

"Aiguebelle will know what we did," I said.

"That was your plan all along, was it? To take her with us. Another girl for the harem."

"No," Elodie said. "I won't..."

"I just want to get home, Kayla," I said. "I didn't really think about what we'd do with her once we were clear."

"Well I'm thinking about it now," Kayla said. "And we're not taking her back with us."

"Is this some kind of jealousy thing?"

"Screw you, Baptiste. We're not ruining this girl's life."

"So living with us would be ruining her life?"

"Yes. Yes it is. If you can't see that... well, then I don't know..."

"So what did you want me to do?" I asked her.

"We'll give her one of the snowmobiles. She'll take it to Eades. If we run out of fuel before we reach our gate, we can rest assured that we still have body armour and a goddamn machine gun."

"And if she tells them about us... they'll come for us."

"They might. If they want to risk starting something with Ryan Stems."

"I don't think Stems could give a shit what happens to us."

"He cares. It's that buffer thing."

"She's going to tell them," I said. "And then they'll come after us. We won't have a strong enough lead."

Kayla pulled the key out of the ignition. "You want a head start?" She threw the key into the forest, dropping a little hole into the snow. "There. By the time she digs that out we'll be long gone."

Even when I want to scream at her, I admire just how clever Kayla can be.

The world's shittiest snowmobile ran out of fuel not that far past the junction at Wade Lake. It took two hours of walking before we made it to the gate at Murphy Road.

Once we were inside, I raised Matt on the handheld to tell him we were home. Then Kayla and I sat down in the middle of the road, exhausted.

Justin pulled up fifteen minutes later, in his electric car. He acted surprised to see the C12 hanging from my shoulder, but he didn't ask about it.

I guess Kayla was probably right; it hadn't been much of a secret for quite a while now.

TODAY IS SATURDAY, JANUARY 19TH.

I NOTICED I was getting a signal on the phone this morning. I tried calling Alain but the phone didn't ring.

That could mean so many different things.

Justin didn't have anything to report on the day and a half that we were away. I half-jokingly said that I was surprised he didn't crown himself king, and he replied that he'd been giving me until Sunday night before he'd assume I wasn't coming back.

There was no joke on his end.

Kayla spent most of the day in a rage, since Matt didn't bother to do a single thing for the goats or chickens while we were away. I think she should have been happy; Matt touching your livestock is a great way to lose your livestock. Even an old hen can fend for itself for a day or two.

That night Matt called on the handheld to let us know that he was just going to stay at the Porters; I didn't want to ask if he'd left our cottage empty last night, too.

He had no problem wasting twenty hours a week on that stupid firebreak, but actually taking responsibility for something that mattered?

Not his style.

So it was just Kayla and I in that big house; I didn't mind.

I made us some raspberry tea and took it upstairs to her.

She was sitting on the bed. She'd changed, but not into her pajamas. Or even into something more... inviting... she was dressed in a tight black t-shirt. And just her panties.

"Thank you for the tea," she said as she cupped one of the mugs in her hands. "I've had a chill all day."

"Today you've had a chill? Not yesterday when we spent half the day outside, in minus twenty-five?"

"Today I'm allowed to feel it." She smiled. "I'm so glad to be

471

home, Baptiste."

"I wish we'd brought Lisa and Graham back with us."

"I know... but let's leave that alone for now. I... I want to try something different with you."

"Okay..."

"It's a little... different..."

"You said that part."

She reached down beside the bed. I couldn't see what she was reaching for.

"I have a fantasy," she said.

She put her pink scarf on the bed.

She reached back down and brought up a length of blue and white rope.

I think it was the same rope we'd used on Elodie.

"I want you to tie me up just like you did her," she said.

"What?"

"Pretend I'm her... pretend you need to restrain me... that you need to gag me with that scarf so I don't scream for help."

"I don't think I'm comfortable with this."

"*S'il vous plaite*... please don't tie me up..."

There was something about the way she was looking at me. That fake pleading in her eyes, that was so close to making me laugh.

It was pretty damn sexy.

I guess knowing that I could make it happen for her... knowing that she wanted something that only I could give her...

I pushed her down on her stomach.

I tied her wrists.

I brought up her ankles.

I tied her arms and legs together.

"The scarf," she said, almost breathless.

I picked up her pink scarf. The same one that I'd stuffed so violently in Elodie's mouth.

The knot was still tied. Kayla hadn't done anything to clean it.

I forced it into her mouth and tied it around her head.

I heard her moan.

I sat back and watched her struggle.

She tried to say something; I couldn't quite understand.

She tried again.

"Touch you?"

She nodded.

I slowly lifted her tight black t-shirt.

I ran a couple of my fingers along her side, giving her a light tickle right down her hips.

Her body jerked. She moaned again.

I moved my fingers between her legs, gently nudging her onto her side.

I brought my head down and kissed her just above the place where I had my fingers.

I kissed her some more.

Kayla had never climaxed that quickly before.

Her entire body buckled, like a series of jolts were rushing through her.

She tried to say something else.

I took a guess.

I untied her ankles and spread her legs apart.

And then I took her.

It was the best sex we'd ever had.

It was the best sex I'd ever had.

So far.

Afterward I was about to take out the scarf, but she shock her head.

"Leave it in?" I asked.

She nodded.

I wrapped my arms around her.

And I told her that I loved her.

﹏﹏﹏

12

﹏﹏﹏

TODAY IS SUNDAY, JANUARY 20TH.

I TOLD Matt that it was time to come home, that he was starting to get creepy with his new life as Justin's shadow.

He didn't argue; I think maybe he had a feeling that if he kept at it, Justin might tell him the same thing. I'm not sure Matt could survive that shame.

It was warm today, warm enough that I had no qualms about helping Kayla with the outside chores, and I even split a little firewood with Matt, as a sign that I was glad to have him back.

I didn't mean it, but I did it anyway.

Fiona dropped by in the afternoon to invite herself over for dinner. Sometimes I wonder if she's as frightened of Gwyneth as Gwyneth is of me. I don't think Fiona can even imagine living in fear that way, no matter what she's seen over the years; there's just too much sunlight in Fiona. That's why I miss her so much these days.

The four of us sat down for dinner around the pinewood table, bunched on one side and leaving the other half to four empty chairs.

We did that thing people do when they're trying too hard to not be sad, laughing at jokes that aren't funny and being freakishly kind to one another.

I know we all miss them. We don't just miss Ant and Sara, but Lisa and Graham, no matter how they left.

Tonight is the first night in over twenty years that I've come close to praying.

I came close, but I couldn't make it all the way.

I just hope they made it through.

I can't imagine how they could have.

TODAY IS MONDAY, JANUARY 21ST.

WE COULDN'T smell the smoke from our end of the lake. We didn't hear a sound as the farthest cottage along Nelson Road burnt to the ground.

We didn't know what happened until Justin Porter came to our door and woke us up, yelling my name.

"I can't reach them," he said. "I need help."

"What's going on?" I asked.

"I can't reach them... help me, Baptiste."

"Okay."

I followed him as he ran through the snow. He was only wearing one shoe. He tripped more than once.

It wasn't long before I saw the smoke.

"Oh... fuck..." I said.

"They're inside... I need help..."

I sped up and overtook him. Why had he come all that way? He should have stayed with them...

When I reached the house, there wasn't a part of it that wasn't on fire. The flames had started to leap onto a nearby stand of tamarack.

I didn't have anything to stop it.

I grabbed my tablet from my pocket and called Kayla. "Porters... their cottage is on fire," I said.

"We're coming." That's all I'd needed her to say.

I saw Rihanna lying in the snow. I wasn't sure she was still alive.

I couldn't see the kids.

Justin came up beside me.

"Help her," he said. "I need to find my kids."

I wanted to hold him back, but I knew he'd probably just punch me in the nose.

I stood by and let him try.

He started at the front door. The heat was too much.

He ran around to the back.

Then he came back to the front.

"I need to get in there," he said.

"You can't," I said.

He climbed on top of the small stack of wood by the kitchen window. He reached for the window frame.

He jumped back down.

"The cellar," he said.

He ran to the cellar door.

I took out my SIG and joined him.

It took two shots to get the lock open.

We grabbed a handle each and pulled.

The heat was bad, but not as bad as the rest of the cottage.

"Maybe they're down here," he said. "Keeping down, below the smoke."

"Maybe..."

He started down the stairs.

I followed him. It was possible that they were okay; at thirteen or so, the girl was old enough to try.

Justin called for them, his voice uneven.

I called for them, too.

We each took a side and circled around the entire basement. I peered around the stacks of supplies, even opened an old armoire that was probably too small anyway.

"They're not here," he said. "We need to get upstairs."

I heard the sound of an ATV headed up the road.

I didn't think there was much they could do to help us.

"I don't see a way upstairs," I said. "Is there anything? A hatch or something?"

"God... I don't know..."

"The axe. Find me the best spot and something to lift me up."

I ran back up the cellar stairs.

I pulled the axe off of the splitting stump.

I came back down.

Justin snatched the axe from me.

He climbed onto a plastic crate and started hacking at a joist in the ceiling.

I stood back and held my hands over my eyes, to keep the splinters of wood from blinding me.

"Try knocking the boards upward," I said. "Prying them..."

He used the handle to push through the floor.

I climbed up onto the crate beside him, trying to balance on one foot. I cupped my hands together to make a step.

He dropped his leg into my hands and I brought my rear foot forward to steady myself. I threw my arms up, boosting him through the floor.

He didn't wait to help me up.

I took my best jump. I wasn't getting far.

I hopped down and grabbed a second crate.

I piled it on top and climbed up. I had just enough reach to boost myself.

I couldn't stand the heat. It felt like putting my entire face on a stove element. But what the hell else was I supposed to do?

I couldn't find the fire; the heat was there, but the flames weren't. I tried to remember how backdrafts work.

"They're not here," Justin called out from somewhere behind me. "They must be upstairs."

"Or they got out," I said.

"I'm going up."

"Shit, Justin... be careful."

I found my way to where the stairs ought to be.

They were there, but each step was charred and probably not far from full-on charcoal. I wasn't sure they'd support Justin's weight.

But he didn't waste any time, and he bounded up the stairs, his feet crumbling the wood like he was pushing through heavy snow.

He made it to the top, and he disappeared down the hall.

I wasn't sure the stairs would hold me. I didn't want to damage them more; Justin needed to get back down.

It's times like that when you forget all of the shit. When the guy who's caused you more trouble than genital warts is back to being just a guy you've gotten to know, a guy who might be on the verge of losing everything...

I heard a scream. At first I thought it was one of the kids, high-pitched and hysteric.

But it was Justin.

I knew what that meant.

I don't think those kids ever woke up.

᪥

I helped Justin carry the children's bodies outside and place them gently in the snow.

I saw that Fiona and Matt were carrying Rihanna over to the next cottage over. The one with the busted padlock.

Kayla was standing between the house and the stand of tamaracks. She was wearing a large plastic tank strapped over her shoulders. She was spraying suppressant foam on the remaining flames.

I'm glad Ant had taken the time to find that gear. We'd lost one cottage, and most of one family... but we could have lost a whole lot more.

᪥

Fiona and Matt did their best with Rihanna, but without Lisa it was mostly two frightened amateurs digging through first aid articles on a tablet, and in an old dog-eared book we still had on a bookshelf in the living room.

Rihanna was burned... almost everywhere.

Her skin went from pink, all the way to a charred white.

We didn't dare attempt to pull off her clothes; we knew we might pull off her skin along with them.

"I don't think she's going to make it," Fiona told me. "Even if we can figure out how to bandage her... the risk of infection..."

"She needs a tetanus shot," Matt said. He held up the first aid book. "Do we have that?"

"We have syringes somewhere," I said.

"I've got them," Fiona said, nodding to an open kit. "I'm nervous to do it."

"You can do it, Fiona. Just... just do it."

"So inspiring," she said.

"Where's Justin?" Matt asked.

"Kayla's with him," I said.

"You should be there," Fiona said. "You're his best friend."

Matt seemed a little offended.

"He needs you," she said.

I didn't argue.

I found Kayla and Justin sitting on a couple of wicker chairs in the front porch of what was once the Tremblays' cottage. Justin was staring out at the charred house just up the road. Kayla was sitting silently on his right, holding his hand.

"She's gone, too," Justin said.

"She's still fighting," I said.

"I should have gone for the kids... I should have left Rihanna."

"You did your best, Justin."

He started to weep.

I knelt down to his left. I held the other hand.

There wasn't much else to do.

TODAY IS TUESDAY, JANUARY 22ND.

RIHANNA GAVE up the fight not long after midnight.

Justin had fallen asleep in the wicker chair.

I told Kayla to let him sleep.

I didn't know where to put Justin's children. I didn't want to leave them out in the snow, but I couldn't bring them over to the Tremblays' old place.

And I didn't have the right to bury them.

I wandered a little along Nelson Road. We'd never planned for burials; we didn't have any caskets.

We did have a lake.

I went back home and dug out my snowshoes. I walked along the frozen lake until I found what I needed. I dragged a small fiberglass canoe up from behind the cottage next to the Porters, right up to where we'd laid the children down.

I placed them inside and covered them with extra blankets Fiona had taken when she'd moved out.

Justin could decide if he wanted to bury them instead with the smoke-logged sheets they'd slept with.

Then I went back to the porch and waited with Kayla for Justin to wake up.

Justin made a choice when he awoke. Between two lives he could live, one of grief and one of anger, he picked what came natural to him. He let the rage fill his head until it frightened everyone but me away.

"I will kill every last one of them," he said as he slammed his cold shovel against the frozen ground. "Those fucking indians are going to pay."

I was still setting up the portable stove. I'd decided against lighting a fire to warm the shovels.

"You'll help me, right?" he asked me.

"I'm just getting the stove ready. We'll heat the shovels —"

"You're going to help me fuck them up."

"We'll figure it out..."

He stopped trying to break the soil. "No, that's not what I'm asking, Baptiste. Those pieces of shit set my goddamn house on fire. We need to deal with that."

I didn't want a fight. I couldn't expect him to be reasonable.

But I couldn't make a promise he'd force me to keep.

"Let's put your family to rest," I said.

"To rest? Are you fucking kidding me?"

"We need to get them buried, Justin. We need to get it done, right?"

He just nodded.

Then he stood and seethed, as I finished setting up the stove.

TODAY IS WEDNESDAY, JANUARY 23RD.

JUSTIN DIDN'T want any kind of funeral for them. Yesterday, once the bodies were buried, we went to where the Marchands had lived. Somewhere that was closer to us, and farther from where he'd lost his family. I set up two rooms, and then we had a drink.

And then Justin had five or six more.

He was asleep before ten pm.

Kayla dropped by a little while later.

"He's asleep?" she asked me as she gave me a hug.

"Pretty much."

"How are you doing?"

"I'm fine. Not sure what the hell we're going to do with him."

"What do you mean?"

"He was hard enough to deal with when he had a family. Now he's alone and angry, and looking to hurt people."

"He wants to hurt us?"

"He thinks New Post set the fire. To get back at him."

"That's... there's no way."

"There's not much chance of it. But enough of a chance to drive him crazy."

"You don't think that's actually possible, do you? That they'd want to murder Justin's family?"

"No... you're right. It's not possible. But try telling him that."

"I don't even know where to start," she said.

"Neither do I."

"We just need to wait... wait and see..."

"This isn't going to end well. I don't think he'll let this go. It would have been better for him to die, too."

"Yeah," Kayla said. "Better for all of us."

I nodded. "I'm not coming home tonight."

"I know. That's why I'm here."

"We have plenty of booze."

"Yeah... but I think you need some of me. I just want to hold you, Baptiste. That's all I want to do."

I led her to the bedroom and we laid together on the bed.

And then I fell asleep.

Justin wasn't there when we woke up.

Kayla went to check the grove where we'd buried his family.

I checked for his car.

He'd left McCartney Lake.

And I didn't have a way of finding him.

If he'd gone to New Post, I wouldn't get there in time to stop him.

If he'd gone off to kill himself... I wouldn't want to stop him.

Kayla had gone to take care of the goats and chickens; I'd stayed behind at the Marchands in case Justin came back.

He came back just before sunset, right as I was starting to get hungry for dinner.

"You pick up a pizza?" I asked as he came in.

"Two walleyes," he said. "I guess I can share."

"You went ice fishing?"

"There are huts at the old ranger camp on Wade Lake. Just dragged one out and got it done."

"Okay..."

"I'm feeling okay, Baptiste. Really."

"That's good, man."

"Yeah... thanks. I think I'll be alright here. You can head home."

"What about the fish?"

He smiled. "I don't actually want to share."

Something about his smile didn't seem real to me.

But I might just be passing how I feel onto him.

I can't tell him how to get better.

TODAY IS THURSDAY, JANUARY 24TH.

I'D GIVEN Justin back his phone, back when Kayla and I had gotten back from our trip through Aiguebelle.

He came by after we'd finished breakfast today, to tell me he'd received a call.

It wasn't from Alain, or Lisa or Graham.

He showed me a message from Fisher Livingston.

Funny story. What was Sara's nickname in high school?

"I have no idea what it means," Justin said.

"He's fucking with me."

"He calls me because he wants to fuck with you? By asking some obscure question about Sara?"

"Vachon *Tampon*," I said.

"Tampon? What?"

"It can mean a lot of things in French. But yeah... tampon."

"Fuck... French kids are messed up."

"Send it back to him," I said.

"Why?"

"Please, Justin. Just send it. I want to know what the hell he's doing."

Justin typed out the response.

"Signal's weak," he said.

"Signal's always weak."

Justin sat down on the couch in the living room.

I took the recliner.

We sat silently.

I wanted to ask: "Hey, Justin... so... you still plotting revenge?"

But I didn't. I knew at least some part of him was.

Maybe that's healthy or something. Externalizing some of the anger...

Justin's phone chirped. He took a look.

"He wrote back already," he said.

He handed the phone to me.

Still at McCartney Lake?

"Small talk?" Justin asked.

"I don't know... do you think he actually has Sara with him? I'm not sure I can believe that."

"Why wouldn't he just come out and say it?"

"Maybe he doesn't trust you."

"Trust *me*? You're the one who threatens him as a hobby."

"I do that to everybody. Just tell him yes."

"You tell him. I'm sick of being the go-between. I think you two will make a lovely couple."

"I'm just going to come out and ask him."

I typed out a reply:

At McCartney. Do you have Sara?

"You guys have anything to eat?" Justin asked.

"Oh yeah... I guess you don't have much food at the Marchands."

"They left a jar of wheat germ and a bag of raisins."

"I wouldn't have left raisins behind. Just check the kitchen. Take whatever, as long as you keep track so I can update our numbers."

Justin nodded and took to the kitchen.

Another chirp.

LOL.

"What the fuck?" I said.

"What?" Justin asked from the next room.

"He typed 'LOL'."

"He *is* fucking with you."

I heard footsteps on the porch.

Kayla stepped inside.

"Take a look at this," I said to her.

She came over and took the phone.

"He's with her," she said. "I think he's trying to find a way to bring her home."

"Then why doesn't he just say it?"

"I don't know... he's nervous... he's worried that someone's tracking him somehow?"

"I do think he's with her," I said. "He's found his way to Kapuskasing or wherever Stems is really keeping her, and he's decided to taunt me."

"That's not like him... you know that."

"Then what do I do with this?"

"Nothing. Just trust him."

"I don't trust him."

"Well you don't have to trust him, then. But maybe if we're lucky, Fisher Livingston's about to help us out."

"Yeah... maybe."

I really did want to believe that.

IT WAS FRIDAY, JANUARY 25ᵀᴴ.

EVERY DAY starts off pretty much the same. Maybe you wake up with a different girl in your bed, or with no one, but from most mornings you get about the same feeling.

You don't see what's coming.

That day I woke up and everything was the same. Same as it's been since Sara was taken, anyway.

But I found out before breakfast that everything was changing.

Matt's been handling the horses lately, which has worked out better than I'd expected. That morning he ran back in after just a couple of minutes outside.

"The horses are gone," he said.

"You didn't close the stall doors?" I asked.

"The cart's gone, too. Someone took it."

"Who could have done that?" Kayla said.

I already knew.

"He's taken the cart," I said. "So either he doesn't think his car can handle where he's headed, or he doesn't want people to know it's him."

"He's going to New Post," Kayla said.

"That's suicide," Matt said.

I walked over to the chest by the door.

It was unlocked. And empty.

"He took both sets," I said.

"So you couldn't follow him," Kayla said.

I nodded. "Won't stop me."

"I'll come, too," Matt said.

"No one else is coming. People are going to be dying today. But none of my people. You two get over to Fiona's. Take the Mossberg. Stay there until I get back."

"There's no way he can get through," Kayla said. "They'll stop him at the gate." It sounded like she was trying to convince herself more than anyone else.

"He won't get through on his own," I said.

"You're not planning on helping him."

"No... but Justin isn't stupid. I'm not sure he's doing this on his own."

"Detour Lake?"

"That's the most likely possibility. I doubt he'd be able to convince Aiguebelle to come with him to shoot at old people and children."

"I don't know, Baptiste," Kayla said. "I think you should stay. You can't go up against them. Not on your own."

"Don't you see, Kayla? I have to try. If I don't at least try... then Stems has no reason to believe that this wasn't us. He'll take it out on you... and Fiona... and I'm not willing to give him an excuse."

"But what if you don't come back?" Matt asked. "What the hell are we supposed to do?"

"Find a way into Aiguebelle," I said. "Keep looking until you find someone's who willing to help you. That's the best I can do."

Kayla wrapped her arms around me. "I love you, Baptiste."

"I love you, Kayla. All the way."

I felt another set of arms clamping my waist. "What the hell, Matt?"

"Thought it was a group hug," he said.

"I think you just made it one," Kayla said.

For my part, I didn't push him away.

That took some work.

⤸

I had no riot suit, no vest, no helmet. And it didn't take long for me to find out that Justin had known exactly where in the basement I kept the C12. Of course, it was more obvious now without the guitar case.

He had me outgunned. I was leaving the Mossberg with Kayla and Matt. All I had was my SIG.

I took one of the electric ATVs down toward New Post.

I found the horses and the cart, just outside the open gate.

The horses were fine.

Three men were dead on the ground.

None of them were Justin.

I saw two pickups just up the road, stopped right in the middle, facing the gate. Both windshields were shattered.

I climbed off the ATV. With my SIG in my hands, I walked over to the trucks.

I saw the blood in the snow before I saw the bodies.

Four more.

No Justin.

I started walking along the treeline, down Archibald Road. I passed behind a couple of modular homes, looking for any sign of life and listening for any sounds of dead or dying.

It was all very quiet.

It felt like spring was coming early, but I didn't see any children outside. I couldn't even find any dogs.

Maybe they'd heard the gunfire at the gate, and they'd known to run. Maybe the people of New Post were safely across the river

I saw a dead dog. More blood in the snow. It looked like it had been running away from the shooting.

Then I saw another man in the snow. Wearing a set of riot gear and armour, with yellow lettering: "OPP".

I approached slowly, in case he was still alive. But his helmet was a good two metres away, and his head was soaked in blood. They'd hit him in the delts to bring him down. Then they'd pulled off the helmet and made sure he was dead.

It wasn't Justin.

He'd given a set of our gear to someone else.

I grabbed the dead man by his feet and pulled him into the ditch. I pulled off the vest and the riot suit. I put them on. Then I climbed out and grabbed the helmet.

And then I kept walking.

I heard what was likely my C12. Multiple rounds. No pause, no discrimination, like he wasn't even bothering to stop and take aim.

It was coming from the west; I ran across a treeless yard toward the noise. I had no cover. But now I had my armour.

I dropped down into the ditch along the main road, trying to keep my head lower than the drifts.

From the ditch I could see it all.

Seven men in armour, all but one with painted combat helmets. The Spirit Animals. I recognized our gear on the other, but he was holding a shotgun instead of my C12.

Probably Justin.

The man who had the C12 wore a helmet I recognized. The coyote. Justin had given him my gun.

There were a couple of deuce-and-a-half military cargo trucks parked right behind them, with canvas tops. They'd come from the northwest, over the old rail bridge and up the stretch of Takwata Road that New Post had built to meet it. Justin's attack from the northeast had drawn the bulk of the defenders to the other gate.

That wasn't much different than the plan I'd made to get Sara back. But they weren't there to rescue anyone.

I saw a large group of children sitting terrified in the snow.

At least twenty women on their knees.

A line of a dozen men against the wall of a house, their hands on their heads.

And at least a dozen men in front of them, lying dead in the snow.

Coyote opened fire again.

The line of men fell.

I couldn't take them out. Not all of them. At least not all at once.

I had to wait.

With the men of New Post shot and bleeding, the women were next.

Twelve of them were pulled up by their hair and forced against the wall of the building, standing right over the bodies of their men.

Coyote didn't point my C12 at them.

Instead, he walked forward and pulled one of the women off the line. One of the prettiest. He dragged her by her hair, away from the building, and pushed her down on her knees.

A second man walked over to the line and took his pick. A little young and a little chubby, but he seemed happy.

Four of the other men picked out their trophy.

One man did not. He shook his head, his helmet painted with orange and black tiger stripes.

Coyote took off his helmet.

It was Justin.

"We're waiting," Justin said to the man in the tiger striped helmet.

"I don't want one," the man said.

Justin laughed. "Whatever. We take shifts. You, you, and you... stay here and watch for the rest of 'em. Don't touch anything yet."

They were taking orders from him; there was no denying that.

Justin had always been the Coyote.

He was the one who'd been so worried that Natalie and Tabitha would recognize him as he raped them. He might have thought one of them would eventually figure out who he was, and tell me the truth about him; that might be the real reason he'd made sure those girls were tortured and killed.

He might have snuck off to meet his crew at the Girards, so he'd get a chance to brutalize those young girls himself.

And he'd wanted me to know that I was to blame for what he'd had to do.

But that wasn't all of it.

Justin Porter was the one who'd shot Ant. He'd killed Ant and then he'd tried to tell me it was Ryan Stems.

He'd done his best to start a war.

This was his last kick at the can.

He and three of the men walked off, to two of the houses to the left, pushing their chosen women in front of them. Justin took my C12 with him.

The men who stayed behind were still in full gear, two armed with assault rifles, the other with the shotgun. Tiger stripe was one of them.

I couldn't take them out.

Not like that.

I crawled through the ditch, moving away from the gunmen and their captives.

I reached a culvert at a driveway and I quickly darted up and over.

Most good soldiers would have spotted me.

Those guys didn't.

I kept moving back, until I reached the end of the ditch, right next to the hockey arena.

I ran along the south side of the building, covered from their view. I'd have to cross a field to get to the next bit of cover, a stand of trees behind the houses that Justin and his fellow Spirit Animals had commandeered.

I took the risk.

They didn't see me.

I reached the first house, where two men had gone with their prisoners. The back door was unlocked; I opened it and stepped inside.

I followed the sound of a man laughing. He hadn't bothered to close the door.

He was naked aside from his socks. He had the woman on the twin bed, still clothed, lying on top of an afghan with squares of playful moose and deer.

He was trying to pull down her pants, and he seemed to be enjoying the fight.

I reached for a stuffed bear sitting on a forest-green dresser.

I stuffed the barrel of my SIG into the belly of the little brown bear. I shoved it against the back of the man's head and fired.

The woman screamed.

"Stay here," I told her.

I heard footsteps in the next room. He'd heard something... but I doubt he knew what.

I heard the door open. He was coming over to check.

I started moaning. "Yeah," I said. "Yeah..."

I heard the door to the other room close.

Footsteps again. The bed started to squeak.

I ran out to the hall and over to the next room. I had the bear and barrel to his scalp before he could turn around.

The second woman didn't scream when I pulled the trigger; she covered herself with a blanket and just waited for something.

I tossed the bloodied teddy bear on the floor. Then I nodded and left the room. I checked out the front window.

No one had noticed.

I went out the back door.

I reached the second house.

The back door was locked.

As bad as those gunmen were at their job... they'd see me if I tried to get around to the front.

I'd have to be quick.

I shot out the lock. It took two rounds to get the door open. I had six left.

And I'd just made a crapload of noise.

In the first bedroom I found a man who wasn't Justin, still wearing a bullet resistant vest, but not his helmet. He was pointing his

AR-15 rifle at the woman in the room, trying to get her to take her clothes off.

He hadn't give a second thought to the gunshots at the door.

I guess he'd assumed it was just another dumb indian getting his or her head blown off.

He was completely focused on getting his victim to strip.

The woman was shaking, but she was defiant.

"Just shoot me," she said.

"I'll do worse than that," he said.

I shot him just below his left ear.

I heard footsteps from the next room.

I swung around to meet them, pointing my SIG at the open door-way to the hall.

But Justin didn't come for me. I heard him run right out the front door.

I ran behind to see.

He'd taken off his armour. And he didn't have my gun.

He hopped off the front porch and kept running.

"Shoot the goddamn house!" he screamed.

The gunmen started firing.

I fell to the floor.

"Get under the bed," I said to the woman. "Stay down until the shooting stops."

I crawled to the second bedroom, just as the burst of firing stopped.

I found the fourth woman. And the C12.

She'd dropped low, but now she was getting back up.

And she did her best to point the C12 right at me.

I was still on my hands and knees.

"I'm a friend," I said. "Robert Jeanbaptiste, from McCartney Lake. I'm here to kill these men."

"You're dressed just like them," she said.

"I just shot three of them. That should count for something."

"Just go."

"I can't. I need that weapon."

"You have one," she said, nodding to the SIG in my right hand.

"Only five bullets left. Not enough."

"I don't trust you. I can't."

"Do you see what I'm wearing? It's body armour. Bulletproof.

You can't hurt me."

"I don't believe you."

"Please..."

"You're here to help us? Swear to God?"

I took off my helmet. "I swear on my daughter's life."

She looked into my eyes. "Okay."

I stood up slowly.

I took the C12 away from her.

"Now please get low," I said. "Under the bed if you can."

She did as I asked.

I went out the back door.

I walked around the side. I looked around the corner.

The three gunmen were there, still aiming their guns at the bullet-riddled house.

But I couldn't see Justin. And one of the trucks was gone.

I saw movement from the south, the opposite direction.

Five men. With rifles.

Men from New Post. One was Gerald Archibald.

I lowered my C12. To show I wasn't a threat.

They ran up to the building, taking cover beside me.

"Three gunmen with helmets and body armour," I said. "Aim for their kidneys."

"They have hostages," Gerald said.

"Those aren't hostages, Gerald... anyone who's still alive just hasn't been killed yet. We need to get this done before they finish the job."

He was hesitating.

I had no time for that.

I swung around the corner. I looked down the sights and took aim.

The first target went down.

I pulled back behind the house as they fired back.

I swung around again.

The second target fell.

The third took off running toward the cargo truck. The man with the tiger stripes.

I took shots at his legs, trying to cut him down.

I couldn't pin him. He reached the truck.

I fired on it. But those trucks are built to take some heat.

He drove right past; I was lucky he didn't try to run me down.

He turned the corner onto Archibald Road and disappeared

I ran to the two wounded gunmen.

"Hands on your heads," I said.

They complied.

Gerald Archibald came up beside me.

"Stay back," I said. "This area may not be clear."

Gerald ignored me. He walked right up to the men on the ground.

"Take off your helmets," he said.

They did as they were told.

He turned to his men. "Do it out of sight," he said.

The other four men from New Post took the two prisoners away.

"You're going to kill them," I said.

"Put your guns on the ground, Baptiste."

"Not until we've secured the area."

"Put them down. I'm placing you under arrest."

I looked around. Gerald had one rifle slung over his shoulder. The only four men he could count on had just dragged two prisoners off for execution.

I could take that rifle from him.

I wouldn't even have to fire a shot.

"Justin Porter got away," I said. "And one other. I need to find them."

"You're responsible for this. You let this happen."

"I put a stop to it. I saved dozens of your people."

"I count thirty-two of my people dead. Someone needs to pay."

I heard two shots in the distance.

"Put your guns on the ground, Baptiste," Gerald said.

I could take that rifle...

The four men were on their way back. I could see them.

I stepped toward Gerald.

"Baptiste..."

I grabbed his rifle from him.

And then I ran.

I ran to the gate on New Post Road. The horses were still there and still hitched.

I didn't want to ask those horses to drive, not after how many hours with the yoke on, but my snowmobile was nowhere in sight.

The gelding seemed shaken, but the mare calmed him down.

We made our way back toward Nelson Road.

Not that I could take them all the way home. If Justin was there, he'd hear them coming.

I'd taken the horses down Blackwell Road until we reached the abandoned houses by Sheen Lake. I unhitched them there and left them. I'd come back for them if I was still around.

I headed as close to due north as I could get, along the edge of the marsh, following the creek up to Couple Lake. From there I knew the path that could take me up to the trail, the one that led around the south end of McCartney Lake. I'd be able to come up from behind, to see what had happened.

I heard a truck engine before I reached McCartney Lake. Diesel and heavy, like the trucks we used to have. We didn't have those anymore.

It was possible that it was New Post, or even Stems, but that didn't feel right.

I knew it was Justin.

I had the feeling it would be smarter to head east, toward the burnt-out cottage where the Porters once lived; he wouldn't be expecting me to come from that side.

I pulled out my tablet. Still no access. It wasn't a problem with a hop; he'd made Matt cut me off.

I turned right and headed toward the Porters.

There was no sign of life at the Tremblays or the Marchands.

If Kayla and Matt had listened, they'd gone to the Williams to hold up with Fiona and Gwyneth.

Justin would know where to look.

502

I reached the Williams. There was no truck out front.

I went inside.

I started downstairs and swept upstairs, and then I even checked the crawlspace.

No one was there.

But nothing was taken. The kitchen was still stocked and the lights were still on.

That made me hopeful that he hadn't searched the shed.

I grabbed a backpack hanging from a hook by the door.

I went outside and grabbed the axe from the splitting stump.

I walked over to the shed and smashed the padlock.

I found the tackle boxes. Kayla had rewrapped the pipe grenades and put them back inside.

She hadn't come back to get them.

I took six grenades and put them in my pack. I tried not to envision what would happen if I jostled them a little too hard.

I walked down to the lake and started heading toward our cottage.

I could hear a truck, on the move, but I couldn't see it.

It was leaving.

I'd missed him.

If I couldn't find anyone... he'd either taken them, or...

I reached our dock and turned toward the cottage, trying to stay concealed behind the trees that stood between the lake and the porch.

The lights were on. But I couldn't see anything else.

I reached the porch and I waited, trying to listen for any sounds.

There was nothing. Just the howl of the wind.

I opened the door to the porch and crept along it, hoping to miss the familiar squeaks of the wood panels. I opened the inner door and stepped inside.

I didn't see or hear anyone.

I walked into the dining room and saw seven half-eaten bowls of oatmeal, along with glasses of orange juice and cups of coffee.

Someone had stopped in for breakfast.

Justin wouldn't have had time for that.

I went upstairs, checking each bedroom.

There was no trace of Kayla or Matt, no sign that Fiona or Gwyneth had come here to hide.

Someone had taken them, then tried to eat a leisurely breakfast.

And then they'd been called away.

It wasn't the seven gunmen who'd attacked with Justin. That didn't seem right to me; they'd reached New Post before I did.

In all likelihood... there were seven more.

Maybe they'd come to stop me from heading to New Post; but if that had been the plan, they would have followed me out there.

Justin had known I would go to New Post; he'd sent the other men to McCartney Lake, for the girls.

And I'd left those girls there to be taken.

There'd been no signs of struggle, no tipped over furniture of blood on the wood floor; to me, that meant that the men from Detour Lake had convinced Matt not to fight. Kayla might have tried to resist, but in the end she'd have known there was no point, and she'd have done what she could to keep Fiona and Gwyneth safe, as they were loaded into the back of a truck, like cattle.

They'd take them back to Detour Lake, the girls, at least.

I'd never see them again.

I had promised to keep Fiona safe.

I'd failed.

But there was still one chance.

Kayla's not stupid.

She knows I wouldn't give up on them. And she'd have just the right offer to stall their captors.

I grabbed my snowshoes and headed north, past Ant's sugar maples and our makeshift graveyard. I walked across the firebreak, which still seemed too narrow to me.

I kept in the trees and followed the highway east, until I reached Murphy Road. There I crossed the highway, into a stretch of burnt forest. There wasn't much cover to be had, but that was the only way to reach the little pond, the one that smells like gasoline.

I saw three deuce-and-a-half cargo trucks, with canvas tops, parked on Murphy Road by the water.

And five men in armour, standing watch.

Three were looking down the road; they hadn't seen me yet.

The other two were watching the cargo area of one the trucks.

I saw who they were watching.

Gwyneth was sitting in the truck with her head in her hands. Just her. No Kayla, no Matt... and no Fiona.

I could throw one of my grenades, but with Gwyneth so close...

I heard a branch snap behind me.

I turned to see Matt.

Matt and a hunting rifle.

He was pointing it right at my vest.

"Hands up, Baptiste."

"Give me the goddamn rifle," I said.

"They won't hurt us. That's the deal."

"You think there's a deal in place? You really are the dumbest man on Earth."

"Hey... Justin trusted me enough to give me a rifle."

"Yeah... an empty rifle."

"What?" He lowered the rifle to check.

I grabbed it from him.

"Dumbest," I said. "On Earth."

"It really is empty," one of the men said. His helmet was a bald eagle.

I pointed the rifle at his left kidney and pulled the trigger.

Nothing happened.

The man chuckled. "Take off the helmet and the vest."

I was out of ideas.

I needed Kayla for Plan A to work.

I took off the helmet first, then the vest.

"Now both of you... get in the truck."

I climbed into the truck and sat across from Gwyneth.

"You tried," she said. That was as friendly as I'd ever gotten from her.

Matt sat down beside me.

"They're going to kill us," I told him. "Because of you."

"Whatever."

"Where's my shotgun?"

"Justin took it."

"And gave you a rifle as a replacement," I said. "Does that make any sense?"

"It's over and done with... just drop it, okay?"

"Fuck."

It was less than a minute before I heard footsteps crunching in the snow.

Kayla was in front, her hands on her head.

Justin was behind, holding the Mossberg.

Three more men with armour and AR-15s were following behind.

I couldn't see Fiona.

"Excellent work, Matt," he said, as he reached the truck.

"You tricked me."

"Yeah... it was super hard to pull off, too." He turned to me. "What did you do with my drugs, Baptiste?"

"So now they're your drugs?" I asked.

"You moved them. And you didn't even tell your girlfriend." He gave Kayla a shove.

Her head slammed against the side of the truck. She fell onto her knees.

"You be careful with her," the man with the eagle helmet said.

Kayla glared at him.

"I'm going to kill you, Justin," I said.

"Yeah, okay. Later, though... right now I need my goddamn drugs."

"I dumped them."

"Bullshit. You're a fucking tabber, Baptiste. Matt told me about you and Kayla and your little mini raves. You've got them hidden somewhere."

"And you want them, do you?"

"Tell me where they are."

"Or what? You'll have Matt pretend to shoot me?"

"I'll kill them, Baptiste. All of them." He grabbed Kayla by her hair and pulled her to her feet. "Starting with her."

"She's as good as dead anyway. She told me she'd rather die than be taken to Detour Lake as some prepper's fucktoy."

"You think this is an empty threat? You think I won't torture her to death while you watch?"

"You don't have the balls for that, Justin. You're too soft. That's kind of your big secret, isn't it?"

"We all know," Kayla said. "You're a fucking pussy, Justin."

"I'm not an idiot," Justin said. "You can't goad me into doing something stupid. And you know what I did to those girls, Baptiste. To little Natalie Girard..."

"You're not going to hurt her," the man with the eagle helmet said.

Justin turned to face him. "Just shut up, Eagle... okay?"

"Just kill me," Kayla said. "Slowly if you'd like."

"Come on, Kayla," Eagle said.

"Fuck you, Bren."

"They have a history," Justin said. "They'll work it out. Now... the drugs..."

"You can't get information out of me unless I want to give it to you," I said. "So let's make a deal. A real deal, not one for a moron like Matt."

"Like what?"

"I'll get you the drugs. And you give me the girls. You can keep Matt."

"What the hell?" Matt said.

"Shut up, Matt," Justin said. "Sorry, Baptiste... those girls are worth more than a little ecstasy."

"One of those girls is spoken for," Eagle said.

"I've got more than little ecstasy," I said. "I have a shit-ton of meth as well. I'll bet they'd love a piece of that down in Timmins. You'd be ass-deep in biker handjobs."

"How much is a shit-ton?"

"At least twenty bags... maybe a couple kilos each..."

"Okay... so carry the Y and that gets you Kayla. I keep the red-head and I'll put a bullet in Matt for everyone's sake."

"I want Gwyneth, too."

"I want Kayla," Eagle said.

Justin didn't seem to hear him. "I need at least one, Baptiste. So unless you want to bring Fiona over here to trade, I'm keeping the redhead."

He didn't have Fiona.

"Okay," I said. "You can have the redhead."

"Screw you, Baptiste," Matt said.

"I'll need your truck," I said. "And Matt to help me load the drugs."

"You can take Tiger," Justin said.

"Who the fuck is Tiger?"

"The guy with the motherfucking tiger stripe."

"I'm not revealing the location. I bring a small sample up front.

Then I trade you Matt for Kayla and we take our leave."

"I want all the drugs," Justin said. "Not just a sample."

"I'll give you the location when I have Kayla."

"How will I know you're telling me the truth?"

"Why would I lie?"

"To fuck me, Baptiste."

"Well, this is a pickle, then. Someone has to have a little faith here."

"You bring all the drugs. Or I hurt Kayla."

"I bring a sample. You take me at my word. If I'm lying, you can chase on after us. We won't be hard to catch."

"I don't want to waste my time on this."

"You won't be wasting your time," I said. "You see, I won't just be taking Kayla with me. I'll also have Fiona. So if I renege, you get to take both of them. Three girls instead of two."

It felt weird to talk about them like they were commodities; but that's all they are to guys like Justin Porter.

Justin nodded. "I think we've got a deal," he said. "Don't fuck this up, Baptiste."

"I wouldn't dare." I tapped Matt on the shoulder. "Time to go, buddy."

"This isn't the plan," Eagle said.

"Just shut up," Justin told him. "We'll buy you someone better."

"I want Kayla."

"Shut up, goddamnit. Or I'll shoot your goddamn nuts off."

That shut him up.

Matt and I climbed down from the truck.

I looked over at Gwyneth.

She gave me a nod.

It looked like she knew.

I figured that Justin knew, too.

That I wasn't about to let him walk away with anything.

We took one of the cargo deuces back to McCartney Lake; I had Matt drive as I sat in the back, to make sure we weren't being followed.

The gate on Nelson Road was wide open, as though someone from McCartney Lake had opened it up for the Spirit Animals. after I'd left for New Post. Part of Matt's deal, I assumed.

Matt pulled in front of our cottage.

I waited until he got out of the truck before I climbed out of the back.

"Tell me you've got a plan," Matt said.

"Other than letting Justin kill you?"

"Come on, Baptiste..."

"I've got a plan... well... I'm working on it."

"That's something, I guess."

"Give me the truck keys."

"Why?"

"Because I don't trust you. Now wait here."

I went down to the basement. I pulled up the plywood subfloor with no real thought to the mess I was making.

I grabbed a bag of MDMA and a bag of meth.

I loaded them into the front of the truck.

"Get in," I said as I climbed into the driver's seat.

"Still not getting this plan..."

I drove the truck up the road, to the Williams cottage.

"Fiona isn't there," Matt said. "I looked."

I climbed out of the truck. "I know. Maybe if you hadn't booted me off the network, I'd be able to find her."

Matt got out, too.

We walked over to the shed.

"She didn't take her tablet," Matt said. "She didn't want to be found... guess she didn't want to waste time figuring out how to disable the locator."

Fiona would have known I'd come looking...

"Get back in the truck," I said.

"What?"

I got back in.

Matt hopped in just as we started moving.

I took the keys with me again, having Matt wait at the truck. I ran down the path that followed the lake, around the bend, to the maple tree.

I stepped off the path. And that's where I found her.

Well, the dogs found me first. Des and Juju ran up and started jumping.

Fiona was sitting in the snow, keeping her head low with the thicket.

"You're okay," I said. "I'm glad you took the dogs this time."

"I'm okay."

She stood up.

I gave her a hug and a kiss on the cheek.

"Have you found Kayla and Gwyneth?" she asked.

"I know where they are. We're going to get them back."

We jogged back to the cottage.

"What's he doing here?" Fiona asked, pointing her finger at Matt. "He's working with them."

"He's an idiot," I said. "Not a traitor."

"He let them in. He opened the gates. He pointed the shotgun at Kayla."

"Yeah... he tends to do that kind of thing. He pointed an unloaded rifle at me. But we need his help to pull this off."

"What is it we're going to do?" Matt asked.

"Simple," I said. "We're going to burn the forest down."

～⌘～

Fiona drove the deuce, which I think was the first time she'd ever driven anything other than an ATV; luckily the truck wasn't old enough to have a manual transmission.

Des and Juju were on the bench beside her, happy to be going for a ride.

Matt and I were in the back.

He had my C12 hanging from his shoulder, and a pack containing four of Ant and Kayla's pipe grenades.

I had a shoulder-mounted foam launcher strapped to my back, along with four grenades of my own. And a few other odds and ends: a spool of fishing line and a steak knife, a box of matches, scotch tape, a ball of yarn, Des' food dish, and a big bottle of lighter fluid.

It was one of those ideas that had sounded a little stupid even when I'd first thought of it. I'd made a MacGyver joke about it, and Fiona had thought I'd meant to say "MacGruber"; the whole exchange had been a little depressing.

The first piece of the plan didn't have to work; it was the second step that counted. Ant had brought back a half dozen fire suppressors from the test site on Wade Lake, so he'd felt free to make a few creative alterations to one of them.

I hoped it would do the job.

Fiona took us to Murphy Road, stopping just north of the junction with Highway 652.

Matt and I hopped out. I had all my gear, while he was wearing nothing more than mechanic's coveralls.

But in my defense, my job was harder.

"Remember," I told him, "what you care about is making sure the girls are clear. Don't start until they're in the cab with Fiona."

"I know," he said.

"And if you try and fuck me over..."

"I know."

I walked over to the driver's side door.

Fiona opened it.

I handed her my SIG. "They've got armour," I said. "So hide this until they let their guard down. If things go bad... if I'm gone and Matt's down, they'll probably take off their helmets and relax. That's when you start shooting."

"I've never done it," she said.

"I know. Your goal isn't to kill them; it's to slow them down enough that you can back this truck out of here. If they're on your tail, you take this truck to New Post and you cross the bridge. Keep driving 'til you get to the Walkers."

"What if we haven't found Kayla and Gwyneth by then?"

"You leave them, Fiona. I need you to be safe. That's what matters the most." I stepped up and gave her a kiss on the cheek. "I love you, Fiona. You know that."

She nodded.

I hopped down and closed the door.

"Now remember guys," I said, "as long as I can hold them back, and you get away, you head to Helena with the girls and wait for me. And if I'm not there by tomorrow morning, you take the old rail bed to Aiguebelle."

I made my way into the forest of blackened trees and young gray birch. I wouldn't have much cover.

But I had my armour, and a couple of pipe grenades, and the box of fire on my back. There wasn't much stealth required for this plan.

There were nine men total.

And two prisoners.

I had to put something between them.

With my binoculars I was able to count off five. Justin and three others were out of my view. Maybe one or two were taking a dump in the woods, or maybe they were all packing up the remaining lab equipment in the underground school bus.

I didn't know where they were.

I snuck around to the north side of the trucks... northwest, really. As far from Kayla and Gwyneth as an attacker could get.

I took out the fishing line and tied a loop around one of the charred pine trees that stood lifeless in the burned forest. I pulled the line back slowly, moving the trunk along with the warm south wind.

Justin should have told his men to keep an eye on all approaches. The boys from Detour Lake had no clue how to set up a defensive perimeter; you'd think that would be mentioned on the first day of prepper school.

I cut the fishing line with the knife, and tied the end to the base of a foot-tall birch,

I poured some of the lighter fluid into Desmond's metal food dish, and then I cut a two meter length of yarn. I soaked it into the bowl of lighter fluid for a few seconds, then I laid it out from the base of the birch, making sure to wrap it around the fishing line for good measure.

And I did the same thing at another pine tree a few metres to the west, with a slightly longer stretch of yarn.

With both pine trees pulled back, and both little birches wrapped in fluid-soaked yarn, I used the scotch tape to cradle two grenades in each of the bent-back trunks; the tape would hold, right up until those trees really started to move. That or I was just wasting my time.

I pulled out the box of matches.

I set the farthest line of yarn on fire, and ran back to the other. Once both were lit, I kept on moving east, hoping to circle around before the fun started.

The closer line went first, snapping the tree forward and tossing the two pipe grenades.

I saw them launch but I didn't stop moving.

Both grenades struck about three meters away from the first truck. That didn't do much to blast it; I'm not sure that truck felt more than a little vibration.

But that was never the point.

The five men behind the trucks rushed northward, keeping on my side of the vehicles in the hope of staying covered from whoever was coming in from the northwest.

They were maybe ten meters away from me.

The second tree went. Two more grenades, but only one made hard contact. It landed even farther away from the trucks, but it was convincing.

They weren't looking in my direction.

I started running toward the third truck.

I heard someone yell out as I reached the back. I'd been seen.

Then they opened fire.

"Hold your fire!" someone yelled. I think it was Justin.

They didn't hold it.

"Stop shooting, dammit!" Justin yelled again. "Don't hit my girls!"

The shooting stopped.

I saw Justin running up from the entrance to the lab. He'd dropped a box of glass equipment in the snow.

I waved Kayla and Gwyneth down from the back of the cargo truck. "Head into the trees," I said. "Towards the highway."

I opened the fuel line of my foam pack. I pointed the hose toward the trucks and pulled the trigger.

The canvas caught fire.

I released the trigger. I didn't have much fuel.

I pulled one of the last two grenades from my pack.

I threw it at the far truck. It hit.

They wouldn't be able to chase Fiona.

I started walking backward, behind the girls, making sure that I kept enough of a buffer that the girls would be out of firing range.

Once I reached the trees, I aimed for a stand of birch and pressed the trigger again.

I tore the cap off of the half-empty bottle of lighter fluid. I tossed the bottle at the burgeoning fire.

I heard the gunfire again.

I guess Justin had given up much hope of holding on to any of the girls.

"They're clear!" Matt yelled from behind me.

I was almost at the truck.

I dropped down to the ground.

Matt opened up with the C12. Not much accuracy, but enough to slow them down.

I crawled over to Matt.

He handed me the gun and his pack with the extra magazines.

I was a little overloaded; I could feel my breath shortening.

I put down the suppressant pack.

"Get the SIG from Fiona," I told him. "Then climb in the back and go."

I couldn't leave with them; I couldn't leave until Justin was no longer a threat to us.

I changed magazines in the C12 and fired a burst. I fired again until the chamber was empty.

I checked back.

Fiona had put the truck in reverse. They were almost at the highway.

I heard another volley from the north.

I picked up the foam pack and started moving again.

I felt my left leg give out on me.

I looked down and saw the blood.

Not far from the last hole they'd put in that thigh.

There was no way I could carry the C12 and the foam pack across the highway.

I wasn't going to be able to lead them on a chase, to pick them off in pieces.

Whoever was left would come for me, and they'd find me.

So I had to make it count.

The flames from the stand of birch had spread, but not by much, since the ground was cold and wet with snow. I limped over to the edge of the fire, dragging the suppressant pack behind me and hoping that it wasn't particularly susceptible to exploding from the jostling.

I put the C12 down, and threw the suppressant pack over my shoulders.

I pulled the trigger and drew an arc around me with the flames, leaving only two small gaps, one between me and Justin's men, and the other to my rear.

That was all the fuel I had in that suppressor.

I dropped the pack and picked up my light machine gun.

I waited.

Two men approached, Leopard Spots and what looked like Bee Stripes. Or maybe a wasp.

They walked into the gap.

I opened fire.

I got one in his side.

Leopard Spots fell into the snow.

The other took cover before I could hit him.

I felt a sharp pain in my left shoulder.

I pushed back through the narrowing gap behind me.

I heard one of the men coming after me.

I saw Bee Stripes.

I fired at his right kidney.

He dropped his gun.

I rushed him. I knelt down and pulled off his helmet.

I took out my steak knife and slit his throat.

I fell back farther, as the flames started to follow me. The fire was heating up, to the point where I wasn't sure they'd be able to reach me.

One gunman was dead, one was wounded. Those were the numbers I had so far.

I headed west. I'd sweep that way and then I'd head south to meet anyone taking the highway.

Some might choose to cut through the woods to McCartney Lake.

It wouldn't matter.

My people were halfway to Helena.

As I moved west I saw another, the man with the Tiger Stripes.

I got low; he hadn't sighted me.

"Did you see him?" I called out.

No answer.

I tried again. "Porter says he was heading west."

"Nothing here," Tiger said. "I bet he caught up to that truck."

"He's laid out traps," I said. "I'm caught on some type of snare."

"Don't you have something to cut it?"

"Dropped my knife."

"Jesus..."

I'd irritated him enough to lower his weapon.

I stood up and started firing.

Tiger Stripes dropped.

I couldn't tell if I'd hit him.

I heard a radio call.

"Pull back. I repeat... pull back to the rally point."

Justin was ordering a withdrawal.

I wouldn't get my shot at him.

I heard more gunfire. I dropped to the ground.

It was probably Tiger Stripe. Covering his exit.

He hadn't hit me.

But I'd already been shot twice. The leg wasn't bad; I could find some way to tourniquet it... but the shoulder... the shoulder was going to be a problem.

I was feeling the blood loss. I was weak... I wasn't sure I could get up.

The flames had caught up to me. It had reached a point where the snow and damp weren't stopping it anymore. I wasn't sure if it had enough heat to jump the highway in the middle of winter... but I realized that I wasn't going to make it to the highway.

I wasn't going to make it back to being upright.

I heard the handheld.

It was Matt.

"Baptiste... come in."

I reached into the pack that Matt had given me. I found a hand-held tucked inside.

"I won't be coming in," I said. "Hopefully I'll bleed out before I'm burned alive."

"What's your twenty?"

"You mean where am I, jackass?"

"I'm coming to get you. Where are you?"

"I'm gone, Matt. And you don't owe me anything."

"I'm coming —"

"You need to get those girls to Aiguebelle. Do whatever it takes to get them across the border. Do not come for me."

I turned off the handheld.

I didn't want to give him more of a reason to think he'd find me.

I knew Matt was an idiot... but I hoped for once he'd use his head.

I was slipping... I could feel it...

I closed my eyes.

And wondered if I'd see Cassy.

I woke up in the backseat of a car.

The car wasn't moving.

The fabric seats smelled like canned ham.

"Your car stinks," I said to whoever.

I tried to get up, but it hurt.

So I decided against it.

I saw that my shoulder was bandaged up; not professionally, but better than I could have done at the time. My thigh was bandaged, too.

"Is your place safe?" someone asked me.

I thought I knew the voice. "What?"

"Your place... McCartney Lake. I need to know if it's safe, Baptiste."

I realized who it was. Fisher Livingston apparently drove a car that smelled like canned ham.

"Did you spill something on the seat?" I asked.

"Your place..."

"I don't know... it might not be safe. Are we there?"

"We're on Nelson Road," Fisher said. "At your gate. Do you have the key?"

"Should be open... Matt opened them."

"I already checked, Baptiste... it's locked."

"You check my pack?"

"I didn't find your pack. You're lucky I found you."

"Then I don't have the key."

"Shoot... someone's coming," he said. "Some kind of military truck."

"Then get us out of here, Livingston. It's Detour Lake."

I heard him switch gears and slam on the gas.

The car jerked backward quickly enough to throw me to the floor. I hit my head on a metal kit.

First aid.

"Fucking ouch," I said.

"Sorry."

"I knew it... you saved my ass so you could make me suffer."

"Shoot..."

"What?"

"Another truck coming up the road."

"Another deuce-and-a-half?"

"What? Like a military truck?"

"Yeah."

"Looks like a pickup. Green. What do I do?"

"Hell if I know," I said.

"I knew I should have waited on giving you the morphine."

He slammed on the brakes.

Luckily I had nowhere else to go. But my head did get knocked against the back of his chair.

"Better get out of the car," I said. "Before they start shooting."

"Why would getting out help?"

"Makes you easier to shoot... you're going to want it to go quick."

"That's not funny."

"You're better off trying to laugh about it, Livingston."

"Screw you, Baptiste."

He got out of the car.

I couldn't see anything.

"Please don't shoot!" Livingston yelled. It wasn't quite a whimper.

"Down on the ground! Hands on your head!"

It wasn't Justin. Just some other angry guy with a gun.

"My name is Fisher Livingston. I am an indenture from the Mush-kegowuk Nation. Shooting me would be considered an act of war by the Mushke —"

"Shut up, Livingston," a woman's voice said.

It was Kayla.

"I don't think he's a threat," she said.

"If he's an indenture, we need to take him back."

"With all due respect, sir —"

"Sergeant."

"He's on our side of the Abitibi, so I'd need a written request from the Mushkegowuk Council before releasing him to you."

"That's a good plan, Kayla," I said from my smelly resting place. "That'll take a day or two."

I heard her gasp. And then footsteps. The gate being unlocked.

She ran to the car and opened the door.

"Baptiste... oh my god, you found him... are you okay?"

"I'm alive... but Livingston drugged me... the bastard."

"Morphine," Livingston said. "And he's lost a lot of blood."

"You sent him to find me?" I asked.

"Matt said you told him not to come," Kayla said.

"Can you send these men away?" Livingston asked.

"We're ordered to check each cottage on McCartney Lake," the sergeant said.

"Please," Kayla said, "go ahead. Our people are in the first cottage, right at the junction. And one man's walking the line."

"Why are you here?" I asked her. "You're supposed to be on your way to Quebec."

She smiled and gave me a kiss. "No one listens to you, Baptiste. Haven't you figured that out?"

Kayla helped me out of Livingston's ham-mobile once we reached the cottage. It wasn't too bad as long as I didn't try to use my left leg that much.

"I have something else," Livingston said.

"Tell me it's more morphine," I said.

"You can't be angry with me, okay? I had to do it like this."

"What the hell are you talking about?"

He walked over the trunk and opened it.

"Ugh," he said. "I'm not sure if she's sleeping, or..."

Kayla helped me over to the back of the car.

It was Sara.

She was lying in the trunk, her eyes closed. She had a large rag stuffed into her mouth and wrapped with duct tape. Her wrists were bound behind her with tape. Her ankles were bound as well.

The only thing she was wearing was a ripped and dirty white t-shirt with a faded Canadian flag dead center. She had nothing on below her waist.

Her skin was close to blue.

I pulled away from Kayla and leaned against the car.

"Get her out of there," I said.

Kayla and Livingston lifted her from the trunk.

I wanted to take her, to carry her inside.

But I knew I couldn't do it.

Kayla and Livingston brought her up onto the porch.

I hobbled behind, glad for the morphine, but well aware that I was probably fucking my leg up that much more.

They brought her to the living room and laid her down on the couch. Kayla covered her half-naked body with a blanket.

I stumbled over and fell to my knees, leaning against the couch.

I put my hand on her cheek.

She was cold, but not that cold.

And I could feel the warmth of her breathing.

"What did you do to her?" I asked.

"I had to drug her. Didn't know how much I needed. She had to look like she was close to death."

"Fuck, Livingston... why?"

"There are five Mushkegowuk roadblocks between here and Kapuskasing. There's only one between Kapuskasing and Timmins."

"You took her to Timmins?"

"I forged two letters from the Council. One that told The Souls I was taking a runaway indenture back to Sudbury... that was for the first couple of checks. The other said I was bringing your beaten and violated stepsister from Sudbury up to you, so you could watch her die. After what your friends did to that roadblock on Highway 101... let's just say they really liked that letter."

"What if it hadn't worked?" Kayla asked.

"She wanted to come home... she took the risk."

"But why did you strip her naked?" I asked. "Why did you tie her up?"

"Because I'm an indenture. One indenture shows up with another indenture... it looks suspicious, like maybe we're trying to run away together. But not if she looks like this."

"Did she tell you to do this?" Kayla asked.

"She did," he said. "She did."

"If I find out you're lying," I said, "I'll kill you."

"I just saved your life. And probably hers."

"And I'm grateful for that. But I'll still kill you."

He nodded.

"Where's Matt?" I asked. "And Fiona?"

"Matt's out on the line," Kayla said. "Fiona and Gwyneth are out in the barn with the horses."

"What line?"

"Ant's stupid firebreak, remember? The one you told Matt to stop wasting his time on? He's out looking for any sign that the fire crossed the highway and is heading towards us."

"It's still a stupid idea," I said.

"I'm sure it is..." She bent down and gave me a kiss. "I'll take care of Sara, Baptiste. You need to take care of yourself."

There was an unevenness in her voice.

And tears in her eyes.

I struggled to get up.

I stood with most of my weight against the arm of the couch.

I took her hand.

I looked into her eyes. I wanted her to know that I still wanted her, that I still choose her. I wanted her to know that we hadn't changed.

"Livingston can help you up to your room," she said.

TODAY IS MONDAY, JANUARY 28TH.

FIONA FOUND me a walking stick. That's what I'm calling it, even if it looks a little too much like an old man's cane.

When you're over fifty, you tend to limp for a long while after getting your leg shot up. There are two holes in it, now; I may be a gimp for the rest of my life.

Or maybe just a few weeks.

Who knows?

Livingston is sticking around for awhile; Stems sent his written request and Kayla wrote back with a denial, and we haven't heard anything about it since. So he's in Graham's room for now.

The sergeant from Mushkegowuk, Sergeant Mullen, came by again on Sunday with a couple of soldiers from the Nation, and said that they'd be regular visitors to our side of the river. They didn't trust us to keep Detour Lake out of our backyard, and I saw no reason for them to change their opinion any time soon. No one is scared of me anymore. I don't know if it's because I've got an old man's walking stick, or because the people who were so worried about me before have already been shot up, by the other guy they didn't trust.

A guy they haven't caught.

Both Kayla and Fiona were expecting me to rail against the occupation, but I've made it my goal to not even think about that shit until sometime in February. Maybe after Valentine's Day, assuming that Valentine's Day is even a thing.

I'm tired and I've got a limp. I deserve a goddamn vacation.

Everyone's back in one cottage now; Gwyneth put up a fuss, but when she realized that Fiona couldn't be swayed, she sucked it up and moved in. She still disappears more than a regular human being, but she's trying to treat me decent.

It doesn't come regularly, but it's better.

⊷

Kayla dropped in on Fiona and I, as we worked on dinner. Somehow, the moment she came in I saw it as a disturbance; obviously I'd missed my kitchen time with Fiona Rees.

"I wanted to ask you about Justin," she said.

"No small talk, eh?" I said.

"Sergeant Mullen said that Detour Lake says they don't have him."

"When were you talking to Sergeant Mullen?"

"Some people like talking to me."

I ignored that. "Detour Lake says a lot of things. They say that they had nothing to do with the attack on New Post, that it was 'individual actors'. That's the fun of calling yourself an objectivist collective... you don't have to take responsibility for anything."

"I think Ryan Stems killed him," Fiona said. "That's why he was so quick to head back to Kapuskasing. He isn't worried anymore."

"He was more worried about Detour Lake," I said.

"You took out like a dozen of those guys single-handedly," Kayla said. "They don't look so scary these days."

"Don't ever start thinking like that. We won't be safe as long as they're out there and running out of food. Stems was right; they'll either strike out to the West or to the East. They've tried the West..."

Kayla nodded. "So now they try the rest. Aiguebelle?"

"I hope so. Because we're in no shape to fight them off right now."

"I'm working on it. I've been out shooting a few times with Matt."

"Learning to shoot from Matt? That's like having me teach you how to tap dance."

"And that would be..."

"Hilarious," Fiona said.

"Well... I'm improving," Kayla said. "Soon I'll be able to hit the side of the barn."

"Remind me to start wearing body armour around the house," I said.

Fiona laughed.

Kayla didn't. "I'd recommend that to you for a lot of reasons," she said.

I'm not sure she was trying to be funny.

Kayla never came back to my bedroom.

She took over Lisa's room, not bothering to ask Sara if she wanted her old bed; Fiona moved back into the room she'd shared with Kayla, while Gwyneth took Kayla's spot.

Sara slept on the couch for a couple days, partly because she was barely conscious for most of it, but also because I don't think she knew where she belonged.

She'd been away for almost three weeks and everything had changed. I know she had no doubt in her mind as to who had been sharing my bed.

But last night, she knocked on my door, just after ten; I was on my tablet, looking at my personal reserve of "adult info-tainment", my hand down the front of my boxers.

Luckily I remembered to pull my hand out before I answered.

"Can I come in?" she asked.

"Of course. You're always welcome here."

I sat back down on my bed.

I'm sure she could see the bulge.

She walked inside but didn't sit. She was fidgeting with her hands, gently wringing them together.

"She's not staying with you?" she asked.

"No."

"Are you two...?"

"I don't know. Honestly, I don't." What was I supposed to say? It's not like you only ever love one person.

"I can't do this if you're going to hurt me. I need to know that you're here... with me..."

"I'm here. With you, Sara. And that's where I want to be."

That was true. I wanted to be with her.

And I wanted to be with Kayla, too.

"Okay," she said.

I'd expected her to sit down beside me.

She didn't.

"So... goodnight," she said.

"You're leaving?"

"For now... yeah..."
"Okay. Goodnight, Sara... I love you."
"Okay."
And that was it.

TODAY IS TUESDAY, JANUARY 29TH.

MATT AND I went down to New Post today.

We'd heard from Sergeant Mullen that the people had been relocated, and that they didn't have any intention of going back there; that for all intents and purposes, the place was our problem to deal with.

To me that sounded like a prime scavenging opportunity. Say what you will about the patrols from the Mushkegowuk Nation, they certainly make it less likely that we'll have any unwanted visitors at McCartney Lake. Well, aside from Stems' black tracksuit soldiers themselves, but they're usually too busy chatting up Kayla and Fiona to start being all menacing.

That left me willing to risk leaving Kayla with the Mossberg. I'd filled it with buckshot, in case she needs to hit something smaller than the wall of our barn. Livingston's got a little mousegun, too, but there's nothing intimidating about that.

We took the cart, since all the diesel we have for that deuce-and-a-half is what little's left in the tank, and I doubt we'll be making any trades with Detour Lake for some of their fuel.

I let Matt drive; I've started running out of options.

Since we only have one set of gear left, I told Matt to wear it. If shit goes down, he'll be the one who has to take my SIG and run toward the problem. I can't run toward anything at the moment.

We found the gate wide open.

The houses were there, but there were no vehicles. We checked a few buildings and found a couple nice items in each   three-quarters-empty boxes of cereal here, or the last few drops of peanut oil there. Good enough for us, at least.

We checked the band office, even though I didn't expect there to be anything worth taking.

In Gerald Archibald's cube, I found a laminate desk with a locked filing cabinet sitting underneath. I looked around for the key, but there was nothing.

It was possible that someone was messing with us, just locking things up after they'd cleaned them out.

"Shake it," Matt said.

"You shake it."

We did it together.

It made a happy little rattling noise.

"You can pick the lock?" Matt asked.

I didn't feel like it. "Just bring me the crowbar."

Once he had, I pulled the drawers open.

I pulled out three boxes of drugs.

All three were Laneradine.

"Gerald had a heart problem like yours?" Matt asked.

"These aren't even open. He was hoarding them... waiting for me to die."

"Joke's on him. You're still alive."

"Yes, Matt. I know."

I tossed the boxes into my canvas goody bag.

I'd be alive for a good while longer.

∽

Once we'd finished gathering what supplies were left, we headed back toward the gate.

"Now Stems controls both bridges," Matt said.

"He doesn't need two," I said.

And I knew Stems wasn't stupid.

"Head up the rail bed," I said.

Matt took us up the gravel trail, curving around to the Abitibi River.

The bridge had been destroyed. The piers demolished with charges.

"Better job than got done at Iroquois Falls," I said.

"One less bridge to watch."

"Yes, Matt... I know."

He just laughed. I think he's starting to like the way I treat him.

❦

We were back to McCartney Lake before sunset, so a little too early for dinner.

"Let me off here," I said as we reached the cottage.

"What about the horses?"

"You drove 'em... you can stow them."

He stopped the cart and I climbed out.

He continued on toward the barn.

I walked in, hoping to get a chance to help Fiona with dinner. It's definitely become a thing with me.

I saw Livingston on the floor.

There was blood.

Then I saw Justin Porter, sitting on the couch with his boots on the wicker coffee table, with Livingston's little .380 lying next to his socked feet.

Sitting on the floor were all four girls, in a semicircle around the coffee table. They looked terrified, but they were okay.

I reached for my SIG.

"Put it on the floor," Justin said.

"How 'bout I just kill you?" I said. I pulled out the gun and pointed it at his head.

He didn't reach for the .380. "Look under the coffee table."

I saw one of Ant's nail grenades. At least a hundred nails, bundled together and ready to shred anything within its reach. And the fuse cord ran up to a plastic tip in Justin's hand.

"It reminds me of that shit the rebels used in Burma," he said. "I pull the ring wrapped around my finger and your girls won't be looking so hot."

"That coffee table won't do much to shield you."

"I have nowhere to go, Baptiste. Detour Lake wouldn't take me without some way of paying my way in."

"And now that you got so many of their guys killed..."

"Yeah... they'd probably just shoot me if I showed up there. Thanks in large part to Kayla's fucking ex-boyfriend, Bren the Wonder-Shit."

"So you've been hiding around here?"

"That new army of Stems isn't very good at what they do. They didn't even bother checking the crawlspaces. But that's not important right now, Baptiste. What's important is that I'm going to ignite this blasting cap, and then there's gonna be a whole lot of nails fucking up your living room."

"So there's no point in not shooting you?"

"My wife is dead. So are my children."

"Yeah... I know that feel, bro."

"You get to come home every night and you get to take your pick. You can fuck the curvy brunette, or the slutty blonde... now you even have one in redhead... and once you come up with the right occasion, you've even got little Fiona's cherry to pop..."

"I'm not feeling less inclined to shoot you in the head."

"So take your pick, Baptiste. Choose which one of your girls you're going to cover from the blast. I know you won't pick the redhead..."

"Take the redhead," I said. "Take her and go."

"You can't let him do that," Fiona said.

"Don't worry, Fiona," Justin said. "He won't let me take her. And I don't want her anyway. All I want to do is restore a little bit of balance in the universe. I swear, Baptiste... if there's a god in this fucking reality, he'll take this all away from you. Because you don't deserve them. Yeah... I don't, either... I get that now. But this isn't about me."

I could shoot him. One shot and he'd be dead. But his finger was on the pull-ring; that bullet was just as likely to start the fuse than not.

That would kill all four of them.

If I made the choice... I could shield one of my girls. If I was lucky enough...

I heard the door open.

Matt stepped inside. He was still in full gear, even his helmet.

"Sit down, Matt," Justin said.

"Let's just kill Baptiste," Matt said. "We can take the girls. Two each... that'll get us into Detour Lake..."

"Not gonna work, Matt."

"Just pass me your gun and I'll kill him myself."

Matt stepped toward the coffee table.

"Back off, Matt," I said.

He dived at the coffee table.

Justin pulled the ring and lit the fuse.

I took my shot. I sent a bullet into Justin's forehead.

I started to move toward the coffee table. If I could reach her in time...

The nail grenade exploded under Matt's chest; it sounded more like a pop than a boom.

I couldn't see any nails.

"It didn't go," Kayla said.

I stopped to look.

"It didn't ignite the explosives," she said.

Matt rolled over onto his back. "What the heck just happened?" he asked.

"You didn't get blown up," I said.

"You could have died," Fiona said.

"It would have been worth it," Matt said.

I realized I was too proud of him to vomit.

I walked over to Justin.

He was dead. At long fucking last.

Sara had gone to check Livingston.

"He's breathing," she said.

"Then let's get him to the couch," Kayla said.

I grabbed Justin Porter by the feet and dragged him out through the front porch, and left him lying next to the driveway.

I knew Stems would want his men to confirm it.

Sara came to my room tonight.

She didn't say a word.

She climbed onto my bed and burrowed into my arms.

She kissed my left wrist.

I kissed her, gently, on her shoulder.

She craned her neck and kissed me on the lips.

"I love you," I said.

She kissed me again.

I laid her down.

And I made love to her.

TODAY IS WEDNESDAY, JANUARY 30TH.

SARA ALWAYS knows when I'm homesick.

She knows a lot about me.

"You're thinking about your family," she'd said gently as we'd laid together, the day after Ant had died.

She turned over to face me, wrapping her arm around my side.

I kissed her lightly on the mouth and turned my head into my pillow. I was sure she could still see the tears on my cheek.

"I don't think it's gotten any better," I said. "I thought it would slowly get better."

Sara started drawing her fingers up and down my back. I could feel her breasts pressing against me. Lying beside her and feeling her softness and feeling her warmth, I knew that I shouldn't have felt so numb.

It always comes and go, but that night the numbness clawed at my throat and made it hard for me to breathe.

"I know it's not the same," Sara said, "but it is starting to get better for me."

I turned my head to look at her. "It isn't the same." I ran my hand along the side of her face, trying to show her that I wasn't angry, that I was used to feeling that way. "Losing Cassy was like losing a limb. No... that's not enough. It's more like I lost everything else, and all that's left is a couple of dismembered toes."

I reached up and kissed her on her lips.

"I can't drink a glass of water without remembering when Cassy used to fish out the ice cubes with her fingers, long after she was old enough to know better. I miss her all the fucking time, and it's torn most of me away."

"But there's enough of you left to love me." She didn't sound unsure.

"I guess so. I do love you."

535

"And I love you. I don't know what's going to happen, but maybe someday you'll decide that you want to be with me all the way."

"All the way? You're lying naked in my bed. That's pretty far along."

She smiled. "You know what I mean. I'd like to start a family with you... if that's what you want."

"I'd like that," I said. I didn't know what else I could say.

"You're just telling me what you think I want to hear. I like that you care so much about me. But you're not ready to talk about this."

"I don't think I'll ever be ready to talk about this."

"That's fine." She kissed me a couple of times, finding her way down my left cheek. "I'll be here."

Back then I hadn't really considered the possibility.

But now I think I might be ready someday. I'd love to try it all again.

My whole family died from cholera. I'm not a doctor, but I think that means they literally shat themselves to death.

Cholera makes me think of Sherlock Holmes for some reason, though I guess Sherlock should probably make me think of syphilis or something.

When things got bad my mother asked me to come home to Iroquois Falls. But I had two months left of practicum, and they'd said they'd keep me on for the duration if I wanted. So I stayed.

If I'd gone, I wouldn't have been able to save them. I would have gotten to know firsthand what it's like to die on the toilet.

I don't feel guilty... there's no survivor's guilt on me. I'm sure if Eduard had been the one to escape the shitpocalypse, he'd be doing his best to eat pussy and take names. In honour of me, of course.

"I claim this tasty pink taco in memory of Antoine Lagace."

Baptiste wears his guilt like a chastity belt. He's afraid that if he starts living again, like really living, that he's doing his wife and daughter some kind of disservice.

It doesn't matter what you could have done or should have done... you can't let it ruin your life.

Because ruining your life doesn't do anything for anybody.

It just makes you less fun to be around.

❧

We were pretty sure that Livingston had a concussion, but he seemed otherwise okay. If anyone could stand to lose some brain cells and somehow become more likeable, he'd be the guy.

It seemed a good two weeks too early to me, but today Fiona decided that she wanted to prep the spiles and the drill and the ATVs, and try her hand at sugaring off one of the maple trees. She invited Fisher Livingston first, and he said yes; I guess he likes the idea of someone wanting him around.

Sara and Gwyneth decided to go with them, and naturally Matt chose to tag along, too; it was a good idea for him to be there, and he took the Mossberg to keep them safe.

They also took along a serious amount of liquor to stay warm; I had a feeling that they weren't actually too concerned about whether or not the sap had started to run.

With all of them gone, Kayla and I were alone in the cottage, and for the first time since Sara had come home.

And she didn't waste any time.

"I want you to come upstairs with me," she said.

I was confused. "You do still hate me, right?"

"I don't hate you, Baptiste. Come upstairs. Actually... give me five minutes, then come upstairs."

It's not like I didn't know the right choice. No matter what you want to do, you know what you ought to be doing.

I watched the clock for the longest five minutes of my life.

Then I went upstairs.

I checked my room first, out of habit, but she wasn't there.

Then I heard the shower.

I went back to my room and sat on the bed.

I stuck my right hand below the waist of my boxers.

I didn't really want the wait, the anticipation... she didn't need to get all spic and span for me.

The water stopped, and after a minute or so the door opened, and she started walking down the hallway.

She continued down the hallway, past my open door.

She was on her way to her room.

I got up and followed.

"One more minute," she said.

"Come on..."

"Count it down, Baptiste."

I managed to wait a full twenty seconds.

I found her lying on her bed with the covers thrown off onto the floor. She'd even pulled the bottom sheet off the mattress.

She was wearing a white t-shirt and nothing else. Then I recognized the shirt, ripped and dirty with the faded maple leaf. It was the shirt that Sara had been wearing in Livingston's trunk.

The roll of silver duct tape was there, beside Kayla's vibrating egg, and so was a dirty bunch of cloth, lying on the bare mattress.

"You're wearing her shirt," I said.

"I know."

"That's a little fucked up."

"Don't ruin it. Just tape me up. Tape me up and have your way with me."

"Have my way with you?"

"Shut... the fuck... up."

I grabbed the rag. It was the same one from Livingston's trunk. I stuffed it into Kayla's mouth.

I wrapped the tape around her head, trying to match how Livingston had done it to Sara.

It felt wrong.

But Kayla wanted it so badly.

I rolled her onto her back. Her skin was freezing.

I pinned her wrists.

I thought I heard footsteps.

I stopped.

"Someone's here," I said.

Kayla just moaned.

I got up to close the bedroom door.

And then I saw Sara, standing in the hallway, with a handheld in her hand and her mouth wide open.

She was looking at me, but then she looked at Kayla.

She dropped the handheld.

It hit the floor and broke into several pieces.

There was no longer a reason to close the door.

At first she'd just seemed angry, but not all that surprised, like she'd known it would just be a matter of time before I ended up with Kayla again.

Then she saw the duct tape wrapped around Kayla's mouth.

And then she saw the t-shirt.

Her face changed. It wasn't anger.

She began to sob.

"This is what you wanted?" she said. "You wanted to force me?"

"It's not like that."

"You already had me..."

"Sara... I'm sorry..."

She turned and ran toward the stairs.

Kayla was muttering through her gag.

I pulled off the tape.

"Fucking fuck that hurts," she said.

"Do you not get what just happened?"

"Relax. It's fine."

"What?"

"I'm willing to share, Baptiste. This is news to you?"

"I just broke her heart."

"She'll get over it. She loves you. And you love her."

"I need to go after her."

"No... you need to finish what you've started."

"This isn't funny, Kayla."

"Neither is taping a girl up and not fucking her."

I stuffed the wad of cloth back into her mouth. I rewrapped the tape around her head. Then I rolled her back onto her front and taped her wrists.

"Is that nice and tight? All done?"

She nodded.

"Good. Now I'm going after her."

I stood up to leave.

She moaned.

I took another look at her.

She moaned again.

I climbed back onto the bed.

I picked up the vibrating egg and I finished what I'd started.

The maple syrup crew came home a little later.

Sara wasn't with them.

"She didn't come find you?" I asked Matt.

"We haven't seen her," he said. "Kayla called her on the handheld and told her to head back."

"Kayla called her?"

"Yeah. Said the two of you'd arranged a bit of a surprise for her. What was it, anyway?"

"Oh, shit..."

I threw on my boots and grabbed my SIG.

I had no idea which way Sara had gone.

I went up to the junction with Nelson Road, to check for fresh footprints in the snow; she'd gone that way before.

But there weren't any footprints there.

I saw some tracks heading up the trail to Ant's sugar maples, so I followed them. All footprints, no ATVs... but as it hadn't snowed in three days, it could have been from some other time.

As I neared the graves, I saw sharp paw prints in the snow. Two sets of them. Two coyotes.

They were headed up the trail, following the various bootprints.

I passed by the burial plots and the sugar maples; one set of boot-prints had kept on across the frozen stream, and the coyotes had crossed it, too.

The trail moved north, out of the clearing and back into the trees, the last batch of trees before the highway and the burnt forest beyond.

I reached the firebreak.

And then I found her.

She was lying in the snow, on her back.

The coyotes were hovering over her.

I pulled my SIG and shot them both.

They'd torn her open... her neck, her hands, her chest.

They'd begun to strip her body like it was nothing more than a chunk of meat.

I took my SIG and shot both coyotes again.

And I shot them again.

But I knew I had to save one round.

She'd loved me. She'd given me all of herself.

And I'd hurt her. Over and over again.

And now I'd done this.

There was no way to fix it. There was no way to bring her back.

I took the barrel of my SIG and slowly pushed it into my mouth, past my teeth, pointing it up toward my brain.

I thought of Sara, of how beautiful she'd been. How she'd known me so fully and loved me anyway.

I thought of Kayla, of how much I'd wanted her, so much that I'd never realized that she'd been pushing for this to happen. She'd have to live with what we'd done.

I thought of Alanna; I'd never appreciated her as much as I should have, as much as she deserved.

And Cassy... I'd never had a chance to make my way home to look for her. Or really... I'd never taken the chance.

Then I thought of Fiona.

When Justin had told me to choose, I'd already known. It hadn't taken me any time to decide.

I would choose Fiona. Always.

Fiona was back at the house, laughing about a wasted day of trying to tap the frozen sap.

Soon she'd start dinner without my help, cooking enough to fill seven supper plates.

She had no idea that Sara was gone.

And she had no idea that I was about to go, too.

She'd never understand how I could make that choice.

So I pulled the SIG out of my mouth.

And I emptied the clip on those goddamn coyotes.

BOOK TWO

AFTER THE FIRES WENT OUT:
SHARDS

NOW AVAILABLE

AN EXCERPT:

ᥲ

TODAY IS THURSDAY, APRIL 11TH.

Over two months since the last entry.

THREE YEARS ago today the comet was sighted and the world started to fall apart.

Today I marked the occasion by staying in bed until noon. I assumed that Fiona had gotten up to do the chores; I didn't ask her, and she didn't bring it up.

April 11th is the one day when I let myself go, when I give up for the day and just let myself be miserable. I think one day off a year is perfectly reasonable.

When I came downstairs, I saw that Fiona had made pancakes. She'd added some chocolate chips to make them special. They were cold so I heated them up in the microwave. Thinking myself clever, I added some lemon juice and whisky to the maple syrup and made a nice hot toddy to pour on my pancakes. This brilliant idea allowed me to stay good and surly even though the view out onto the lake was looking beautiful and Fiona even more so.

Fiona spent most of the afternoon alternating between giggles and sighs, before she disappeared into the kitchen to make a dinner I planned to drown with yet more whisky.

She brought my meal out to the back porch, carrying it on a wooden tray I didn't even know we had, and luckily I chose to say thanks rather than give her an appreciative pat on the ass.

"Just one day, right?" she said.

"One day."

She leaned in and kissed me on the cheek. "You're funny when you're drunk. But you're also pretty useless."

"I know, lady... you might have to wait until tomorrow to try and seduce me."

I shouldn't have said that.

"That's sure to happen," she said. "Now I'm going to go upstairs and lock myself in my bedroom."

I watched her as she walked back into the kitchen, but with my whisky in hand, I lost track of her soon after that. I finished my dinner and then I rested a while on the couch, staring up at the hanging stained glass loon and thinking of Fiona.

I wanted to stay drunk forever. I couldn't even remember what was so important about the eleventh of April.

I woke up after the sun had set. I found my way to the grandfather clock and saw it was almost eleven. I didn't feel drunk anymore, and I decided to go outside, to listen to the sounds of the lake.

I'd never have chosen to live up here, where the winter is colder than fuck and the summer is short and filled with hurricane clouds of black flies and mosquitoes.

But this place has grown on me.

As small as this world can feel sometimes, just me and Fiona now, it's also a place that can be so big that you could go out and get lost forever.

I would have lost my nerve after The Fires went out... I would have lost the will to live the moment I'd climbed out of that lake and seen the charred forest.

I would have... if not for Fiona.

There's something special about her; she's everything I'm not, and everything I thought the world had lost. And it sounds pretty strange, but I still know that the worst can't get me as long as Fiona is here, as long as I can keep her safe.

That's enough to keep me going. It's enough for me to get out of bed on every day that isn't April 11th.

And it was enough again tonight, to get me to write a new entry in this journal after two months of nothing, instead of finishing off that bottle of whisky and throwing myself back under the water.

ABOUT THE AUTHOR

Regan lives in Winnipeg, Canada with his wife, two children, and enough animals to bleed through six layers of carpet.

You can find out more about Regan at his website:
www.reganwolfrom.com

www.ingramcontent.com/pod-product-compliance
Lightning Source LLC
Chambersburg PA
CBHW020455020726
47493CB00001B/50

* 9 7 8 0 9 9 1 6 8 0 4 5 0 *